Prologue

For as long as anyone could remember, they had called him the Egyptian.

Not that he looked like one. He was thin and small, with a flat grey face and flat grey eyes. He had a face like those above the door of the church, grey chalk weathered into slippery contours.

But then, the Egyptian was not like other men.

He came down the long white stone stretch of road that skirted the coast. He came in a red barrel-topped waggon, holding the horse slack-reined, while the mare staggered down the gradient towards the sea.

He had not been to the village for eight years. When he had left them, they had been safe, because he had secured earth's Gate, as his father had done before him. And they would be safe still, if they had not broken into Poor Heart Hill.

He stopped the mare where they had sunk the first shaft just below the summit of a hill. He looked long and hard at the workings. There was no breeze, only the distant murmuring of the tide below them.

He closed his eyes.

There was such danger here.

They had taken away the tomb and sunk the pit shaft where it had been. An apprehension for the ignorance of the people here squeezed his heart. They had opened the field, Great Ox Leys, to a road for the coal. Taken away the trees. Ripped a hole in its body.

And when he had looked in the face of the priest – when he had seen him a month ago in the city – the Egyptian had seen this desperate parish. He had smelled the green-washed pages of the prayerbooks. He had run his hand over the ochre velvet on the cushion where the priest had knelt.

And he could see down the long dark shaft of Poor Heart Hill, a long way down into the sulphur-smelling seams. Nine hundred feet under the ground, down a pit shaft only five feet wide.

His eyes clouded over.

With slow and infinite care, the Egyptian got down from the waggon, and, still holding the long loose reins in one hand, he touched the soil, and prayed.

One

She stopped, and listened. At first, all she could hear was the wind against the windows. Then, like a faint voice beyond the sound of the rain, she heard the car again.

It seemed as if the house, too, were holding its breath in the darkness, waiting. Anna edged out of the bedroom and looked over the banister, into the gloom of the rooms below. It was one o'clock in the morning. She could see nothing except the phone on the hall table, the red light winking in the darkness. *Message waiting.*

She watched the light for a few seconds before turning away, knowing that there would be no more silent messages now; no more subdued click on the phone as it was put down – for, above the rain, the sound was unmistakable. Somewhere up the valley, up the thin uphill track to the road, a car was blowing its horn. He had given up his long strategy of silence at last and was bearing down, through another sleepless night, to find her. Only this time it was not a nightmare. It was real. The waiting was over.

She took several deep breaths, trying to force a clear thought.

She could get downstairs in thirty seconds. Out the back door . . . and where? There was nothing but treeless downland behind the house. A long sweep of open field dropping down to the beach, with no other shelter, no other houses, not even a hedgerow. She could hear the sea a quarter of a mile away, sucking on the shelves of pebbles, grinding the beach to gravel. It was a filthy spring night. A high tide.

She ran to the window, and raised the blind.

For a moment, the night divided itself neatly into two: the pitch black of the hill, the lesser tone of the sky. She looked to the right, up the track. It was then that she saw the car's headlights.

He must have opened the gate up beside the road and come down a mile, slowly dropping through the long valley. At night, the drive down to the cottage was a disorientating journey, like driving through fog – featureless, mesmerizing – the road a white line disappearing into the middle distance, like dropping off the end of the world. But that was not deterring him. Nothing deterred him.

Don't just stand here! Run.

Nowhere to run to. *Too late,* her heart screwed to a point of pain.

At the same moment, she heard the car come into the yard outside, heard the axle scrape the uneven surface. Heard the brakes. *Too late, too damned late.* She froze, listening for the sound of a door opening. For his fist slamming on the door. For his voice shouting her name. But all she could hear was the car's engine: a battered, rumbling choke under the wind from the sea.

You should have run before now, she thought desperately. *Last week. Last month, when the calls began again. Trusted your instinct then. You should have run . . .*

In a sudden flurry of movement, she pulled the Victorian chest of drawers across the bedroom door. The loose carpet wrinkled under the heavy wooden feet. She hauled on the large mahogany cabinet, the muscles in her arms and shoulders straining with effort. With this obstruction in place, she stood in the centre of the room, eyes closed, waiting for the sound of her name called above the rain.

One minute – the car engine below drumming.

Two minutes.

She opened her eyes and inched back to the window, far to one side of it. Holding her breath, she looked for him, for his shadow, or his face. The headlights below her sliced the yard. She moved further around until she could see the front of the car. It was an old-fashioned shape, a little grumbling tub of a car with a snub-nosed bonnet. Not the car he used to have. Some other car. Suddenly, the driver's door opened.

Anna was surprised to find herself still at the window. Even the instinct to shift backwards was paralysed.

A girl got out of the car.

Just a girl.

Her breath snagged in surprise. The girl was tall, with long fair hair. A complete stranger. She wore an old-fashioned paisley frock that reached her ankles. Anna gripped the window sill, confused now, frowning, silently shaking her head. The girl was young . . . seventeen, perhaps? Eighteen? Someone's tidy daughter, looking neat and careful as she stood motionless in the drenching rain, her hair tied in a single straight plait that clung to her back. She had a round, white face, bland and moonlike, and she was not even looking at the house.

Anna peered back at the car. She could see a shadow in the other seat, a passenger, the outline of a head and shoulders. They, too, seemed to be looking at something, just as the girl was looking, not at the house but ahead of the car.

'Get out, then,' Anna whispered. 'Why don't you get out? What are you waiting for?'

She glanced around fearfully at the barrier by her door; when she looked back, the girl was nowhere to be seen. The driver's door remained open, and the downpour was streaming in. The door hung crookedly on its hinge, showing a turquoise lining that could have been leather. The passenger had not stirred.

No knock.

No fist, no voice.

She leaned forward. Pain in her throat. Constriction. Tension. She could see part of the passenger's shoulder now, the upper curve of the arm. And a coat . . . a pink coat.

Slowly, with difficulty, she edged out of the bedroom door. With the lights still off, she almost crawled downstairs, hand over hand along each tread. She went down the hall, out into the kitchen. She pressed her ear to the outer door that led through to the old scullery.

Nothing . . . no sound except the rain dripping from the leaky guttering on to the concrete path outside.

Anna went back through the kitchen, trying to discern shapes in the dark, feeling her way through to the sitting room. Here, the curtains were open a little. She pulled the nearest one back.

There was a sudden movement in the corner of her eye. The gate to the field was open, swinging. The girl was standing at the field gate, saturated by the storm, her dress clinging to her body, her arms hanging loosely at her sides.

Anna stared at her a moment, then back to the car. She leaned closer to the window.

It *was* a woman in the passenger seat.

She went to the front door, wrenched it open, gasped at the force of the rain.

'You!' she shouted.

The girl didn't look at her, only towards the hill and the sea.

'What do you want?' Anna yelled.

She looked back to the car.

Grabbing a coat from the hall rack, Anna ran out into the rain, through the beam of the headlights, towards the girl. She drew level with her, and caught her by the arm. Both of them were blasted by the wind's force, out here beyond the shelter of the house. The girl turned to her with an astonishing expression, one of perfect calm.

'This is my house,' Anna said. 'You're soaked, for God's sake. What do you want?'

The girl shook her head.

Anna raised her voice. 'What is it? Who are you?'

The girl glanced at the car.

'You've come the wrong way,' Anna said. The rain dripped from the hood of the coat and into her eyes. She wiped it away. 'Have you had an accident, or something?' she persisted. 'Do you know that you're at the wrong house?'

She recognized relief flowing through her, and a thought forming itself into two words. *Not him.* The thundering relief. *Oh God. It's not him.*

'Come inside,' she said. 'What do you want? A phone?'

The girl followed her. They reached the door. 'Do you want to close your car door? Does your passenger want to come in?'

The girl stepped past her, into the hall. Anna switched on the light and, to her amazement, the girl sat down on the hall chair, while the water ran off her clothes and pooled on the stone-flagged floor.

'Do you want the phone? Is it an emergency?' Anna repeated.

The girl shook her head again.

'Well, look . . .' Anna began. She hesitated. The girl's utter lack of response was unnerving. 'You should at least turn off your car engine, and shut the door. Your car seats will be soaked.'

Nothing. The girl stared down at her hands, curved one upon the other in her lap.

'Hellfire,' Anna muttered.

She ran back out to the car, through the rain and the twin piercing beams of the headlights. She ran around to the driver's side, turned off the engine, pulled the keys from the ignition, turned off the lights.

'Are you all right?' she asked the passenger. 'Come into the house.'

It was an old woman, seventy-five. Maybe eighty.

In the shadows, Anna could make out a shock of uncombed, unruly white hair. The woman wore a thick pink tweed jacket, and there was a pair of spectacles hanging on a chain around her neck, the metal and glass glistening in the dark. Her eyes were open, and her posture rigid.

Anna put out her hand. She extended her fingers, so that only her fingertips brushed the face before her.

The woman was unbelievably cold.

Two

Matthew Aubrete walked out of the hospital and into the dark.

It was two o'clock, and in the soft darkness, the rose gardens along the entrance still smelled alluringly sweet, a warm memory of the day. He stopped, drinking in their shadowy presence, the yielding thumbprint of scent.

The car was parked only a few feet away; he walked to it and got in, more tired than he had ever been. When he had closed the door he sat staring ahead at the lit windows of the block, trying to discern which window was the one close to his father's bed.

'Get the hell out of my life,' his father had said yesterday. Then fallen back to his pillows, rasping laughter, exhausted by his own joke. 'You see?' he had asked Matthew, hand grasping at the edge of the sheet. 'You can't. You never could. I'll get out of yours, then.'

It would be that window, almost hidden by the beech tree, he decided. When you stood at the bed, the branches almost touched the glass.

'Why don't you bring Anna?' his father had demanded.

'I can't,' Matthew had told him. 'She won't come.'

'She would if you told her.'

'I've told her, Father.'

The old man had grimaced. Fury, not pain.

'You can't do anything.' Spat into the air between them. Nightlight on the bedside. Mouthwash. Wet wipes and balled tissues in a brown paper bag on the side of the locker. His father's mouth, stained brown, the lips cracked. Sudden descents into snoring sleep. Sudden flurries of words. 'You don't bring Laura either. She brings herself, the bitch.'

It was taking the old man weeks to die. Everyone was weary of it, even the nurses. They bore his curses with indifference, just as they bore, or ignored, his groping shows of affection.

Matthew had been called at eight last night. 'Would you like to come, Mr Aubrete? You might prefer it.'

Or he might not.

Still, he went, to watch his father. Watch the numbers on the faces of the machines slowly creep higher. Blood pressure, pulse.

'He knows you're here,' the nurse had said tonight. 'He rallies.'

Does he, he thought.

The last few days had been reduced to this empty landscape. Walks down the long corridors with a drink. Daily pacing along the same routes. So much of it at night now. Black coffee. Empty rooms, waiting for the day shift.

Beyond his father's window, beyond the beech and the sibilant hushing sound of its leaves, beyond the hospital itself, stretched the yellow-on-black panorama of the town. Matthew would press his face to the cold glass. Small country town. Haphazard grid of light. Small landscape of fields stretching away behind the yellow string of illumination.

Matthew picked up the mobile phone from the seat now, and dialled Anna's number. He heard the machine answer. Her terse voice. Yet, just as he hung up, he thought he heard the handset picked up. He hesitated, then decided against re-dialling. After all, what time was it? Two in the morning. No need to wake her. Not yet.

He switched on the ignition, put the Shogun into gear, and swung out.

He drove home on the lower road, and so never saw the police standing guard at Anna's gate.

'You can't even tell us her name?' the Chief Inspector asked.

Anna turned and looked at him.

It was five a.m., and just beginning to get light. Anna was standing at the fence, overlooking the field, down the long slope of the hill. The inlet of water just before the beach showed as a thin strip of white, the sea itself an iron blue. The rain had gone, the late spring storm blown out as quickly as it had come. The morning was surprisingly still, the blackthorn blossom blown about the field like wet confetti.

She looked at him. 'I've told you everything,' she said.

'Not everything. Perhaps there's something you missed.'

She was so exhausted that she could hardly stand up. 'I don't know her. I really don't. I've never seen either of them before.'

The Chief Inspector was forty-something, wiry and tall. He, too, looked tired. The uniformed constables came first, then he and another man, in rumpled suits, a little while later. He had shown his warrant: *Detective Chief Inspector Robert Wilde.*

'And you touched nothing,' he said.

'The ignition, the door, the keys. And her.'

'Nothing else.'

'Perhaps the seat, the dashboard . . . I don't know.'

'And they came here at one o'clock,' he said.

'Past one. Ten past? Something like that.'

'And woke you up.'

'I was already awake.' She looked away from him.

He seemed to decide to change the subject. 'Nice spot,' he said. 'Nice little valley. Lived here long?'

'A year.'

'Not local, then.'

'No.'

'Come far?'

She put her head in her hands, resting her elbows on the top slat of the fence. 'Does it matter?'

'It might,' he said.

'How can it?'

'If they came from where you came from. If they know you.'

'Look, they don't know me,' she repeated irritatedly. 'I don't know them. I've never seen either of them before. Never. I don't even know their names.'

He leaned on the fence next to her. He seemed to consider the coastline, the distant grey line of the horizon, the dark blue foreground of the sea, before he replied. 'Alisha Graham.'

'The girl is Alisha Graham?' she asked.

'No. The woman in the car. She's from Manningham.'

Manningham? Anna's heart gave a small, painful thump of surprise. 'I don't know her,' she repeated.

'Don't you?' he asked. 'She was coming here, to the gardens.'

'The Manor Gardens?'

Aubrete Manor was a mile up the coast, a semi-tropical miracle carved out of the downs, its lawns and lakes, redwoods and flametrees, magnolias and lilies stretching to the very edge of the beach.

'You work there, don't you?' Wilde asked.

'I work in the café,' she replied. 'Three days a week.'

'Do you know Matthew Aubrete, the owner?'

'No,' she lied.

'He had invited Miss Graham here,' he said.

She waited a while before she spoke. 'They came to the wrong house, then,' she said.

'Do you think so?'

She shook her head, smiling, sighing in exasperation. This deliberate dimness was obviously designed to provoke her. 'The road to the Manor is the next turning, a mile further on.'

'But it looks nothing like yours.'

That was true. Hers was a crude gate, awkward to open, on the brow of an exposed hill. The Manor was entirely different, shaded by chestnut trees, now in full candle-heavy flower. Or perhaps not, after last night; perhaps all the candles were spattered on the road. Like the blackthorn. She, too, gazed at the landscape ahead of her. 'No, it looks nothing like mine,' she agreed. 'But if she'd never been here before, and was looking for a left-hand turn . . .'

'Very late to be travelling,' he said.

Anna knotted her fist at her forehead. In other circumstances, any other circumstances, she might have thought that Robert Wilde was a nice man, perfectly polite, perhaps a little slow, a well-lined and amiable face, a wedding ring on the left hand – a family man. He had patience. Numbing, persistent patience. Of which she had none.

'She wasn't travelling, though, was she?' Anna said.

'How so?' he asked.

'It wasn't her travelling, was it? I mean, it wasn't Alisha Graham driving.'

'That's true,' he said.

She turned, leaned her back on the fence, looked at the house.

The girl was inside. Anna hadn't seen her in an hour or more. In fact, she had gone nowhere near her, even after seeing the woman dead in the car. Instead, she had grabbed the cordless handset from the hall table and run with it into the kitchen. Dialled the police. She must have sounded insane. Garbled, insane.

'What has she said?' she asked Wilde now.

'The girl? Nothing.'

'She said nothing to me either,' Anna murmured. 'I ran inside, I don't know what I said, I think perhaps I said, your friend has died . . .'

'She has been dead more than a day,' Wilde said. 'I should think.'

'My God,' Anna whispered. She turned now to stare at the car, where a team were working in white protective overalls. Inside, Alisha Graham still sat in the passenger seat. As the light grew brighter, it was possible to see her face. The mouth was a little open, the eyes fixed.

'Do you know where Mr Aubrete is?' Wilde asked.

She forced herself to look away from the car. 'At the Manor,' she said.

'There's no one there. Just an answerphone.'

'Well, how would I know? I've hardly met him.' More lies.

'Did anyone at the café mention that he was away this week?'

'No. But . . . I heard someone say that his father was ill, in hospital. Perhaps he was there. You could ask Richard Forbes. The estate manager.'

'We will.'

'More than a day,' Anna murmured. 'That's . . . grotesque, isn't it?'

'Yes.'

'That girl must have driven, with her dead . . .' Anna's voice trailed away. 'What's her name? Who is she?'

THE WRONG HOUSE

Elizabeth McGregor

THE WRONG HOUSE

MACMILLAN

First published 2000 by Macmillan
an imprint of Macmillan Publishers Ltd
25 Eccleston Place, London SW1W 9NF
Basingstoke and Oxford
Associated companies throughout the world
www.macmillan.co.uk

ISBN 0 333 74525 6

1 3 5 7 9 8 6 4 2

A CIP catalogue record for this book is available from
the British Library.

Typeset by SetSystems Ltd, Saffron Walden, Essex
Printed and bound in Great Britain by
Mackays of Chatham plc, Chatham, Kent

'We don't know.'

'She must have a handbag, a suitcase . . .'

'Did you see one?' he asked.

'No, but . . .'

'There's nothing in the car except Miss Graham's holdall. Nothing in the boot, nothing in the glove compartment but Miss Graham's licence, personal papers, and service history of the car.'

'A coat, then?'

'No coat.'

She stared at him. 'But it was pouring with rain. It had been pouring all day. And not just here.'

'Yes.'

Anna stared at the ground. 'When she got out of the car she looked dry. Neat. Dry.'

'Which means . . .?' Wilde asked.

She paused, bit the inside of her lip against her impatience. Same game. A shame he never got bored of it. 'She doesn't look like a person who had been travelling for hours, let alone days. She's so neat and tidy.'

He stayed quiet for some time.

Light, the light of a May morning, began to flood the valley, turning the house rosy, then white. The climbing rose that grew up the side and across one of the top windows was a vibrant pink. When Anna had moved here last year, in this same month, she had looked out at the sea through those beautiful apricot-pink roses and thought, *This is an omen. Roses framing the view. I'm going to be happy here.*

Oh, God, you could be wrong. You could be very wrong.

'It's the wrong house,' she murmured.

Wilde seemed not to hear her.

'Why was she coming to the Manor?' Anna asked. 'Alisha Graham.'

'There was a letter in her holdall from Matthew Aubrete, arranging for her to come to check the groundwater. She's a researcher at the Ashworth Trust.' She said nothing. Wilde was watching her. 'Why does he need her, I wonder?' he asked.

She shrugged. 'There's some problem with the water. Something in it killing the lily beds, the fish. So they tell me.'

Robert Wilde knew Aubrete Manor well. He remembered the lilies as a perfect Monet picture, light reflecting light under the trees, floating as if mid-air in the high Victorian ponds. Once built as a necessity, in which to keep fish alive for the table, they were now a piece of magic, a study in green and white. Lilies in full flower, drifting in water that mirrored the sky. Looking down into the water was like watching the sky plastered with flowers.

'I haven't been up to the gardens in ages,' Wilde was saying, his tone conversational. Over by the car, they were taking photographs of Alisha Graham. 'How long have you worked there?'

'Six months. Since just before Christmas.'

'I thought they were closed until June.'

'They are, to the public. But there are school visits, gardening clubs in the winter.'

'And the parties.'

She glanced at him. Wilde smiled – a bland, conversational smile. 'I hear that Dominic Aubrete, the old man, throws parties.'

'I don't know,' she said.

'You don't know anything about the parties?'

'No.'

He laughed. 'You must be the only one in the village who doesn't.'

'I don't live in the village,' she said.

He paused. 'Miss Miles,' he said. 'Are you all right?'

She smiled, the best she could summon up. 'A strange girl dumps a dead woman in my drive,' she murmured.

'A girl you don't know.'

'Yes, that's right.'

'Did you live in Manningham, Miss Miles?'

'No,' she said.

'You don't have a local accent. Not even a south-west accent.'

'No,' she admitted.

'Are you Irish?' he asked. 'I can hear a lilt.'

'I'm not Irish.'

He paused. 'The Lakes, perhaps,' he said. 'I know the Lakes. Which part?'

'It's not the Lakes.'

'A little rural community like this one?'

'Yes.' *No. Not like this one at all.* She pushed herself away from the fence. Another car had pulled up in the drive.

'Excuse me a minute,' Wilde said.

She touched his arm briefly. 'Can I go back in the house?' she asked. 'Have you finished looking in it?'

'I'll let you know,' he said.

Three

Matthew Aubrete walked up the long drive to the Manor's visitor centre at eight o'clock that morning.

He saw Margot Latham at once behind the plate-glass windows, taking the chairs down off the tables and laying cloths. She looked up as he tapped on the door, came over, unlocked it, and stood on the step for all the world as if it were she who owned the place, and not him.

'I haven't made any coffee yet,' she said.

'That's OK. I don't want any.' He looked past her. 'Is Anna here?'

'She just rang. She's not coming in.'

'Why not?'

'She didn't say.'

He smiled, the embarrassed smile of a man who is a spare part in his own kingdom. Margot was one of his wife's employees, one of the many formidable women who ran the Manor like a battleship. Just for a moment, Margot seemed to pity him. 'Do come in,' she said.

'No, no. That's all right. I can see you're busy,' he said.

He turned back towards the woods, feeling her eyes on his back. He gave a little twisted smile of self-reproach. Ever the gentleman.

He stopped at the edge of the formal gardens. He thought of his father's face and the brown paper bag taped to the locker. Of the other roses by the hospital entrance. Of the tube on the back of his father's hand that had caused such a violent and enormous bruise. He took a deep breath. He needed fresh air in his lungs.

He took the path through the woods. The trees here in the deep shade still dripped on to the carefully laid gravel. He took the steps down to the stream, and saw how red it was, redder than ever, not even hinting at orange any more. Iron. Iron in the water that made the clay so impenetrable higher up the estate, that made the cliffs fifteen miles down the coast mottled and ashy, mixed with slate. In the evening sun they could look exactly like the embers of a fire. He slid down the bank a little way and pinched soil between thumb and forefinger. There were black granules in it. He looked critically at it, then made his way back to the path, slipping in the mud.

Coming out from the wood two hundred yards further on, he saw the sea, and, to his right, the house.

Aubrete Manor sat on a shelf of higher ground, facing the Channel, with trees curving around behind it like a protective arm, and the formal gardens laid out in front like an immense and multi-coloured rug. It was a beautiful house, over a hundred and fifty years old, white and red when built, now rubbed and weathered to sand and pink.

It was surrounded by a moated lake, a broad blue ring now reflecting the morning sky, fringed with soft turf walks and beeches of enormous age. The borders had been planted magenta, rose and blue. The herb garden, behind its walls, murmured with the ever-present whispering of water through the little weirs. Matthew passed through the gate of the garden, and onto the terrace.

His wife Laura was standing there, with her back to him, dressed in a pair of muddied trousers and one of his own flannel shirts. She was dead-heading the roses.

She didn't turn, but talked to the wall.

'I've only just got in myself,' she said.

He bit the inside of his cheek. He didn't want to lose his temper with her. She paused, looking at a handful of petals.

'How is he?' she asked.

'There isn't any change.'

At last, she glanced up. 'How long is it going to go on?'

'I don't know.'

'Well, won't they say? Days? Weeks?'

'They don't know either.'

'They must. Do you want me to talk to Donald Bouvier again?'

'No, don't,' he said. 'It's not his patient.'

He sat down on one of the benches.

'Everything's awfully wet,' she said. 'You ought to have seen this bed. Covered in petals.'

He looked at the ground. A few shreds of colour clung to the stones. He tried to fight down the feeling that things were coming apart. A woven world, with the threads unravelling. He sat looking at the sea. He had always relished this hour when the garden was still his, and still fresh-seeming. In the evening they cleared litter, raked the gravels. But the morning had always been sweet, and this one was particularly so, belying the subdued horror of the hospital, and bright with sunlight. He tried to erase the picture in his head of the old man on the bed, and the blossom crushed underfoot.

Laura threw the last rose into the plastic bucket at her side.

'I must change,' she said airily. 'All mother's little helpers will be here in ten minutes.'

Laura had a small army of willing and voluntary stewards who helped her oversee the visitors. All like Margot Latham – women of a certain age, rather well-dressed, invariably well-spoken, who knew more about the house than he did, more about the gardens.

'Sit down a minute,' he said.

Compromising, she perched on the arm of the bench, brushing down his trousers, picking at the dried mud with a delicate finger.

But, before he could speak, Richard Forbes, the estate manager, appeared. With him was a man that Matthew did not know, a tall man with a thin face. He ambled around the side of the house with a curious air, hands in both pockets. As Richard glanced back at him, he stopped, peered at a display in one of the borders, and then followed. As he got nearer he smiled, took the hands from the pockets, and held one out to Matthew.

Forbes appeared agitated. 'Mr Aubrete, this is Detective Inspector Wilde.'

'Oh,' said Laura, amused, her curiosity piqued.

Matthew shook Wilde's hand.

'What a beautiful place,' Wilde said.

'This is my wife, Laura,' Matthew said. Laura smiled, and offered her

18

own hand, palm down, as if she half expected Wilde to raise it to his lips.

'We've been trying to get hold of you, Mr Aubrete,' Wilde said.

'Neither of us has been at home,' Matthew told him. 'My father is very ill.'

Out of the corner of his eye, he saw Forbes look purposefully at his feet, disguising his reaction to the implication that Laura might have been with him at his father's bedside.

'I'm sorry to hear that,' Wilde said. 'This won't take a moment.'

'What is it?' Matthew asked.

'You have a property up the coast a little way. End House?'

'Yes.'

'With a tenant.'

'Yes. Anna Miles.' A curious silence seemed to settle. Neither Laura or Richard moved a muscle; Matthew, by contrast, felt a tiny reflex tic, perhaps of fatigue, perhaps of apprehension, flicker on his eyelid.

'Excuse me,' said Richard Forbes. 'If I'm not needed . . .'

'Thank you, Richard,' Laura said. She smiled at him. The man turned, and walked away.

The policeman glanced over the front of the house, across the gardens, towards the sea. 'Is it Miss Miles?' he asked. 'Or Mrs?'

'Miss,' Matthew replied.

'How long has she been your tenant?'

'A year. Why? What's happened?'

'Did you have any references?' Wilde asked.

'I'm sorry . . . for what?'

'For Miss Miles as a tenant.'

'No . . .'

Laura leaned forward on the arm of the bench, with a mesmerized and amused expression.

'A bank manager,' Wilde persisted. 'That sort of thing?'

'No,' Matthew answered.

There was another pause. Laura Aubrete gave her husband a look, rather askew, rather perverse, as if she had caught the punchline to an unpleasant joke. She raised her eyebrows at him. 'I'll get some coffee,' she said. She put a light hand on Wilde's arm. 'Is that all right?' she asked him. 'You don't need me just now? If I just pop inside?'

Wilde had seen the crooked smile, its lingering traces. 'That's fine,' he said.

He and Matthew sat down on the bench.

'What has happened?' Matthew repeated.

'Do you know an Alisha Graham?'

'Alisha? Yes.'

'You invited her to come here?'

'Yes. Last week.'

'To do what, precisely?' Wilde asked.

'She's a historian.'

'Oh?'

'Specializing in industrial history. Look . . .'

'And you invited her here because . . .?'

'It was to do with the house. The grounds,' Matthew told him. 'She said she wouldn't come at first. Then she rang a few days ago and suddenly agreed. What is this to do with Anna Miles?'

'Did they know each other?'

'Anna? No. Of course not.'

'You're sure? Did you mention Miss Miles in conversation with Miss Graham?'

'Well . . . no, I'm not sure,' Matthew said. He put his hand to his forehead. A headache was beginning, a small patch of pain between his eyes. 'I can't be sure,' he continued. 'But I think it very unlikely.'

'Why?'

Matthew laughed in exasperation. 'Well, why would I? And how could they have met before? When?'

'Before Miss Miles came here?'

'I'm sorry?' Matthew was genuinely confused.

'Didn't Anna Miles come from somewhere near Miss Graham?'

'Manningham? No,' Matthew said. 'I don't think so.'

'Oh,' said Wilde. 'My mistake.' He smiled. 'Where did she come from, then?'

'I don't know. I confess I'm guessing.'

Wilde looked at him. Nothing showed in his face: neither puzzlement nor surprise. Hardly even interest. His tone was that of a man mildly discussing the weather. 'She just appeared,' he said.

'Yes, she . . . in a manner of speaking.'

'A manner of speaking,' Wilde repeated.

'She was given a job in the café,' Matthew said.

'And you asked for no references.'

'It's just a café. She was very well-spoken, pleasant. Mature person. Not a kid.'

'And you interviewed her, and . . .'

Matthew felt something, a cold hand, a ripple of unease, pass down his spine. 'No, not exactly.'

'Oh?' Wilde said.

'Look . . .'

Laura came out with the coffee.

'You didn't interview her, but you gave her the job,' Wilde repeated.

Laura looked at Matthew, tray poised mid-air.

'Her car had broken down,' Matthew said.

'Is this still Anna Miles?' Laura asked.

'Yes,' Matthew said.

Laura set the tray between them on the bench, took her own cup, and perched on the low stone wall opposite them. 'Matthew found her on the top road one day, fixed her flat tyre, and gave her a job,' she said. 'All on one day.' She sipped her coffee. 'Wasn't that nice of him?'

Matthew looked at Wilde. 'My wife usually does the hiring and firing,' he said.

'She's been awfully good,' Laura said. 'Terribly good. Very willing.' She gave a slight smile. 'Has she done something criminal?'

'No,' Wilde said.

'Then . . .?'

'A car arrived at End House this morning, at about one o'clock,' Wilde said. 'Alisha Graham's car.' He paused. 'By the way, when were you expecting her, Mr Aubrete?'

'Sometime this week.'

'Any specific day?'

'No. She said she was busy. She said she would ring before she set out.'

'And did she ring?'

'No,' Matthew said.

'And how did you know her?'

'I didn't know her,' he replied. 'She was recommended to me. I've only spoken to her once or twice on the phone, to arrange the visit. To confirm that she would come down.'

Wilde leaned forward. He reached to take something out of his jacket pocket, then stopped. 'First she said she wasn't coming,' he repeated, slowly. 'And then she said she was.'

'That's right.'

'Why was that?'

'She didn't explain.'

'Did you ask her why she'd had the change of heart?'

'No,' said Matthew. He blushed slightly. 'She was quite a forceful sort of woman. When she rang to say she'd come, I was just grateful she'd changed her mind. She didn't give me time to ask. She just said she would come soon, would ring on the day she left . . . that was it. She was brusque. Very short. Businesslike, I suppose.'

Wilde held Matthew's gaze for a second, then took a photograph out of his pocket, a Polaroid, and gave it to Matthew. 'Do you know this girl?'

Matthew looked. It was a girl of about eighteen, with blonde hair in a plait over her shoulder. 'No.'

Wilde passed it to Laura. 'Mrs Aubrete?'

'No,' Laura said, looking critically at the picture. 'Who is she?'

'She was in the car with Miss Graham.'

'A niece? A granddaughter?' Laura asked.

'Miss Graham has only one unmarried sister.'

Matthew leaned forward. 'What is this all about?' he asked. 'Why didn't Alisha Graham come here? Why did she go to Anna?'

'This *girl* went to Anna,' Wilde said. 'Miss Graham was in the car. But Miss Graham was dead.'

Four

The storm that had swept up the country had left the city streets greasy, and Beryl Graham slithered a little coming up the steps to her sister's house. She stopped, steadying herself on the iron handrail.

Beryl Graham was a small woman, with iron-grey hair. Eight years younger than her sister, she nevertheless bore a strong resemblance to Alisha, in the set of the shoulders, and in a kind of rigid smile, a smile of determination, that both habitually wore.

Beryl looked up now at Alisha's window, trying to determine if her sister were in. A wind chime hung behind a looped blind, a slatted wood blind that Alisha could never fathom, or bother, to drop straight. Stacks of books stood on the deep window sill. Two spider plants lay drooping, dying, next to the books, their leaves heavy with dust.

Still breathing heavily from the climb, Beryl put her key in the door.

The first thing she saw as she stepped into the hall was a blue light from the back room, the thready light of the computer screen.

'Alisha!' she called.

She walked down to the sitting room, glancing at her watch. It was just past nine o'clock. Pushing back the closed curtains, Beryl glanced around herself, frowning. Papers were all over the floor; inadvertently, she had stepped on some. She picked them up and looked about the desk, not knowing where to put them. Alisha habitually spread projects, notes and books about her – the whole of the top of the desk was covered with them, with other sticky notes attached to the edge of the computer screen itself. Beryl peered down and looked at the screen. A message, the screensaver, was scrolling across it. She caught the last few words – *in a vain shadow and disquieteth himself in vain . . .*

The machine itself radiated heat, the fan whirring. It had obviously been switched on for hours.

'Alisha!' she called. 'I'm here!'

She knew that sentence on the screen; it struck a familiar chord. She had heard it recently, at church. She stood for some seconds, trying to locate the verse. She frowned. Then she turned away from it, and walked back out into the hall.

'Alisha!'

There was no reply. Beryl went into the kitchen, and noticed that the light was still on. She stopped, looking up at the flickering fluorescent tube, then turned it off. It was then that she saw the cups – two, each with a teaspoon of coffee, each with a spoon. But no water. Beryl put her hand against the kettle, and found it cold. In the sink were two dirty plates, crumbs, a pan with the remains of poached eggs. On the draining board stood an opened packet of biscuits. She stood for some moments, frowning at the two plates and two cups, and the unfinished preparation of the drinks.

In a vain shadow. . .

She knew that, she knew it.

She went back to the kitchen door.

'Alisha?'

Standing at the bottom of the stairs, her hand resting on the wooden banister, Beryl tried to remember what Alisha had told her last week, the date that she was leaving.

'I'm going away next week,' her sister had said.

'When next week?' Beryl had asked.

'I don't know.'

'Before I come on Thursday?'

'Perhaps. Use your key to get in. I'll leave your money on the fridge.'

Recalling the conversation now, Alisha went back to the kitchen and looked on the fridge. Nothing. The little brown saucer where Alisha always left the five-pound note was empty.

She took the cleaning box from under the sink, and went upstairs, preoccupied with every step.

Lights were on upstairs, too. Alisha's bedroom curtains, at the back of the house, were drawn. A suitcase lay on the bed, half-packed. Alisha's clothes – her heavy sweaters, walking socks – were piled both inside the case and on the bed. An unmade bed.

Beryl walked up to the case, looking at the pulled-back bedspread, the rumpled sheets and pillows, the case dumped on top, the walking shoes on top of the sweaters, dried mud from the boots all over the other clothes. The wardrobe doors stood open, and the drawers to the chest. And, on the floor, a book.

Beryl picked it up. It was a biography, something that Alisha had been reading, fitfully, for weeks. Several of the pages were torn: not quite torn through, but crumpled. Underneath it, she saw on the carpet, was a photograph, turned so that the picture faced the floor.

She put the book on the bed, and picked the photo up, and turned it over.

'Alisha!' she called. 'Where are you?'

She looked down at the image. She didn't know, quite, what she had been expecting. Sometimes, Alisha had photographs of the sites she visited. And Beryl knew that she also had, somewhere – though she hadn't seen them for years – family albums that had belonged to their mother. Green-bound volumes with carefully preserved, tissue-separated sepia prints of nameless aunts and cousins. Holidays, with themselves as children, buttoned against gales, each holding an adult hand . . . but this was nothing like that.

It was a photograph of a woman, a young woman.

The focus was slightly blurred. Beryl went to the window, parted the curtains, and peered closely at the picture. Whoever it was had their back to the camera, and was bent over slightly. Caught in the act of dressing, the girl was naked. Her hand was reaching to the floor, and an item of clothing – something white – was in her fingertips. The face was hidden – the camera had centred on her body. All that could be seen was the neck, and the edge of the chin. Rounded white shoulders, the back, the line of the spine curved gracefully to one side, the broad buttocks, all with the smooth incandescent quality of youth, unlined, unscarred, unmarked.

Beryl stared at it. It was not an old picture. Sunlight lay in the room around the girl, touching the furniture in the background. The chest by the end of the bed, the carved footboard of the bed itself, the pattern of the carpet at the girl's feet . . . Beryl's eyes wandered momentarily to the floor under her own shoes. The same carpet, the same bed.

She dropped the image as if it were hot, then stood staring at it where it lay next to Alisha's clothes.

Downstairs, there was a sudden knock at the door.

Three heavy knocks, repeated.

Beryl went back to the landing, bent down and looked at the glass panel in the door. She breathed heavily, alarmed and ashamed by the discovery of the photograph, feeling as if she had intruded on something nameless and faintly unclean. Unconsciously, she wiped the fingers that had held the photograph against her skirt.

Downstairs, she could see two figures through the door. The imprint of a fist, knuckles, on the glass, where a hand was resting. It knocked again.

'All right,' she called. 'All right.' She went downstairs with difficulty, wincing at the steps and the little arthritic needles of complaint in both knees. Two men were on the doorstep. One showed an identification wallet.

'Miss Graham?'

'Yes.'

They looked at each other.

'Not Alisha Graham?'

'No, no,' she said. 'That's my sister. This is her house. I'm Beryl Graham.'

'I see,' said the first. 'May we come in?'

They sat in the living room, among Alisha's dusty books and plants, on the hard chairs upholstered in red moquette that Beryl had never wanted, that Alisha had taken from their father's house.

Beryl knotted her hands in her lap. She felt disorientated – not by the mess in the house, for that was perfectly Alisha – but by the persistent puzzle still rattling in her head: the lights, the drawn curtains, the lines of smooth flesh on a stranger's back. The words on the screen. She closed her eyes for a second against the two bland faces opposite her, one man standing, the other sitting. She tried to push the day back into its ordinary groove: cleaning Alisha's bathroom, wiping dust from sills, hoovering her carpets, trying not to touch Alisha's papers or books. Or the plants on the sill in this room. She opened her eyes, and stared towards the window. She never touched those plants. She hated spider plants. They were so sharp to the eye.

'Miss Graham,' one of the men said.

Unforgiving chairs, these. A memory of their father, cold in his last house, cold to the last, clung to the very fabric.

She tried to bring herself back to the room, the point at issue. Alisha's car, they had said. And two women in it . . .

'She can't have gone,' Beryl heard herself say. 'Her clothes are upstairs. Her suitcase. How can she be in Dorset? She's only out somewhere. For a while. She left her computer on, dishes in the sink, everything.'

They handed her a piece of paper, a slippery paper with a colour photograph imprinted on it.

Just for a moment, Beryl's mind sprang back to the other photograph upstairs, and the unmade bed. She forced herself to concentrate on the picture in her palm.

'This was faxed to us this morning,' the man said.

It was Alisha, her eyes only half open. Her head was resting on a car seat, the faint outline of a house behind her, out of the car's window. Two or three strands of hair were blurred, as if the wind had lifted them.

'Is this your sister?' one of the men asked.

'Yes,' Beryl said.

There was a silence, a silence in which she could hear, very faintly, the sibilant murmur of the computer.

'Would you like a cup of tea?' the standing man asked.

'She has left all her dinner things in the sink,' Beryl said.

He went out. She heard him filling the kettle.

'What happened to her?' she asked.

He took the photograph back. 'She was found this morning, in a car.'

'But what happened to her?'

'I'm afraid she has died.'

Beryl drew herself up. 'I can see she has died,' she told him. 'That's not what I meant.'

He looked surprised. 'There's an examination being carried out,' he said.

'On her?'

'Yes.'

'I see,' she said. She smoothed her skirt, her hair. 'I cannot bear people beating around the bush,' she said.

The tea was brought in. They sat drinking for a moment.

'Two women?' Beryl asked, finally.

'Yes.'

'Who was the other one?' she asked.

'We don't know.'

'Is she alive?'

'Yes.'

'But you don't know who she is?'

'No,' they replied.

'Was it an accident, in the car?'

'No.'

'She was just . . . found?'

'The car pulled up at a house during the night,' they told her.

'Whose house?' she asked.

They paused, exchanged a glance. 'Do you know a woman called Anna Miles?'

'No.'

'Did your sister?'

'I don't know. She had a lot of friends she didn't introduce me to. People at her work. And she wrote to a lot of people.'

'Why was that?'

'Work,' Beryl said. 'They wrote about her books, or because they had a problem and wanted her advice. You can see letters on her desk. Always that kind of thing. And she was on this computer, this internet.'

'E-mail.'

'I have no idea,' Beryl retorted.

'She was an expert in her field?'

'Industrial history.'

'So she might have known Anna Miles through that?'

'She knew dozens of people, hundreds of people. Go to her desk. There are folders underneath it, folders in the drawers, on the couch, on the floor.'

The man opposite her put down his cup. 'Did she have a particular friend? A younger woman, eighteen, nineteen?'

Beryl paused. The feeling of intimate intrusion returned. She knotted her hands in her lap. 'She was a lecturer,' she replied. 'Ask at the university. She knew a lot of girls of that age.'

'A blonde girl, long hair.'

Beryl sat regarding them for some seconds, torn between providing some kind of privacy for her sister, and a long-harboured resentment at her exclusion from Alisha's world. From the parties at the university, and the summer courses. From Alisha's aura of significance, reputation, respect.

At last, with great deliberation and at tortuously slow speed, Beryl climbed the stairs again and took the two policemen to the bedroom. The photograph was still lying on the floor, where she had let it drop.

'You can't see her face,' she said. 'But she's young, I should think.'

They made no move to pick it up.

'When did you last see your sister?'

'Last week,' she told them. 'A week today.'

'Was there a girl here then?'

'No.'

'Have you spoken to her since then?'

'No.'

'But girls have been here before,' they said.

'Students,' she admitted.

'Girls would stay here?'

'I don't know.' They looked steadily at her. She returned the gaze. 'It's her business,' she said.

They were looking at the room.

'She was interrupted,' one said. 'Packing.'

Beryl started to move forward. Her arm was gently caught.

'I think we ought to call someone in to see this,' he said.

Beryl looked him in the eye. 'You never told me what happened to her,' she said.

'I don't know what happened,' he said.

'She was as fit as a flea.'

'We shan't know until tomorrow. Or perhaps later today.'

'She was a walker, a hill walker,' Beryl insisted. 'She could walk twenty miles a day. She was examined only last month for her health insurance. Fit as a flea.' Beryl looked down at her own hands, which ached fiercely. She thought of the inhaler she sometimes had to use. She thought of mortality, of the dangerous, threatening ripples of ill health that dogged old age. But not Alisha's old age. Beryl had thought all her life that her sister would live to a hundred – infallible, intransigent, inflexible. Always the fitter child, the stronger child. Never the one to catch a cold, or any of the miserable baby illnesses that had kept her, Beryl, sick in bed for weeks at a time. Alisha had always been the unfazed teenager, the careless one, the unhindered one. The faster one, the cleverer one. Untouched by weakness. Yet now she was dead, and her weaker sister was alive, standing in her bedroom, discussing her, a photograph of her dead face folded in this stranger's pocket.

Beryl felt curious. A touch of tasteless triumph, a breath of vengeful freedom.

Then, a thought suddenly struck her, a realization.

'Do you know your Bible?' she asked.

'I'm sorry?'

Beryl almost stumbled going down the stairs again, leading the way. The three of them went into the back room. The computer sat humming, the screen blue, the white message slowly scrolling across it.

. . . *himself in vain . . . Lord let me know mine end and the number of my days, for man walketh in a vain shadow and disquieteth himself in vain . . .*

Feeling faint, Beryl sat down heavily on the nearest chair. 'Alisha wouldn't say that at all,' she told them. 'I've heard that twice in the last year, but Alisha wouldn't know it. I couldn't think where it was from.

Now I know. Now I remember. She hated the church. She didn't believe.'

'*Walketh in a vain shadow*,' the man repeated. 'What is that?'

Beryl gave him a tepid smile. 'Alisha liked facts,' she said. 'Not stories. And everything said in a church was fiction. She told me that. A hundred times.'

'But what is it?' asked the second man.

'Don't you see? She wouldn't have put it on.'

'On the computer?'

'On there, on anywhere. She wouldn't have put it on,' Beryl insisted. 'She couldn't bear religion in any shape or form.'

'And this is a quotation, from the Bible?'

'Yes,' Beryl said, sighing. 'It's Psalm 39.'

The message flickered, the screen blanked. Then the screensaver reappeared, smoothly rolling from left to right. 'Psalm 39,' Beryl repeated quietly, almost to herself. 'They read it sometimes at funerals.'

Five

Anna sat on the beach below End House. It was a stony triangle, inaccessible except from the cottage, and she was deeply glad of its privacy. Occasionally, after storms – like today – the sand would vanish under seaweed and stones. Yet it was still an idyllic spot – paradise, in the summer.

It was eleven o'clock. A handful of men were still at the house; she had gone for a walk when the transport truck came to collect Alisha Graham's car. In the daylight, it seemed a pathetic little thing, an old Austin A35 that had been customized, resprayed turquoise. Lovingly kept, it looked desperately abandoned there on the windswept yard. Its sadness had struck Anna suddenly, even more than witnessing the mortuary car drawing up earlier for Alisha herself.

The beach was Anna's sanctuary. But now, as she gazed out to sea, she heard her name called.

She turned around and saw Matthew Aubrete. He had come along the narrow path that led on to the Manor estate, along the cliff top. As she watched, he descended rapidly to the beach via the stony path, slipping and sliding as he did so, reverting to hands and knees, clutching at the scrubby hawthorn to steady himself.

She let him run up to her. He stopped, out of breath, then leaned forward, his arms open. She got up, and immediately side-stepped him. He looked at her with an almost childlike expression, rebuffed.

'Don't,' she said.

'Don't what?'

'Don't start all that . . . I just can't.' She started to walk, angry with him, at herself. Angry, tired.

'It's not my fault,' he called after her.

She increased her pace; behind her, she heard him running. He got in front of her, obstructing her path. She stopped and looked up at him.

'Let me come up to the house and talk to you,' he said.

'No. How can you? The police are still here. Go home.'

He glanced up at the field. 'Come and sit down on the rocks, then.' The rocks were at the very edge of the beach, out of sight of almost anyone until you were nearly upon them. It was their place, a place resonant with memories.

'I can't,' she told him. 'I said I was only going for a five-minute walk.'

'Tell me what's happened,' he said.

She did. It took a full minute. He listened intently.

'They want me to go in again this afternoon, into town,' she said.

'What for?'

'I don't know,' she said. 'I don't understand any of it.'

They sat down together on the flat piece of granite at the water's edge.

'Did you go to the hospital?' she asked.

'All night.'

'How is he?'

'The same.' Matthew stopped, bit his lip. Changed the subject. 'The police came up to the house this morning – about this girl, and Alisha Graham,' he said.

'I don't even know who she is. You never said.'

'I sent for her,' Matthew said.

'I know. They found a letter in the car.'

'For the soil analysis, the old workings.'

'I've never heard you mention her.'

'The Royal Society suggested her.' Matthew suddenly grasped her hand. 'Oh, Anna,' he sighed. 'Everything else. Now this.'

'The girl didn't speak,' Anna murmured. 'And she didn't run inside, or knock on the door. The car came down the track. But when she got here, she just stood by the field. In the rain.'

'What do you mean, she didn't speak?' he asked.

'Exactly that. Not a word. Nothing.'

'Perhaps she was in shock.'

Anna withdrew her hand from his. 'She looked almost happy.' Then she corrected herself. 'No, that's not right. She wasn't happy. But she wasn't concerned. She looked . . . as if it were none of her business.'

Matthew took some moments to register the sentence. 'Not concerned?' he repeated, finally. 'With a dead person in the car?'

He saw that she was hardly listening: saw the familiar, removed, remote look.

'Anna,' he prompted.

'Look, Matthew . . .'

'I know what it is. It's Laura.'

'No.'

'I'll ask her for a divorce,' he said.

'No, no . . .'

'I promise.'

'I don't want you to,' she insisted.

'I'll ask her today. I'll ask her when I get back.'

She fisted her hand. 'I don't *want* you to,' she repeated. 'It would ruin you, the house, all your work. It's exactly what she wants, to have the upper hand, to strip you of the house. She'll turn you out.'

'She can't turn me out of my own family's house,' he said.

She shook her head. 'She'll take it all. It's what she's been waiting for.'

'It's not as easy as that.'

'And what do you suppose she wants as a divorce settlement?'

'She won't get a penny.'

Anna started to laugh. 'This is what I mean,' she said. 'The two of you live in a fantasy world. Do you think she'd go without a murmur, with a few thousand pounds?'

'I want to marry you,' he said. 'Let me tell her today.'

She glanced at him. 'I don't want you to tell anyone.'

'Do you really think that no one knows?'

A silence fell.

Anna put her head in her hands.

'Anna . . .'

'It's absurd,' she said.

'I wish you wouldn't keep saying that.'

She turned round. 'Why not? It *is* absurd. The two of you have a series of affairs, you're constantly at war, and have been for years, like a game. I think you actually enjoy it.'

'How can you say that!' he objected.

'You do. You enjoy being martyred by her,' Anna murmured. 'She puts you on a spit and roasts you, and you endure it. It's medieval. And you want me to join in this bloody dance.'

'I don't want you to be any part of it,' he countered. 'I'll divorce her, I'll settle an income on her. She has this man in Blandford . . .'

'It's a dance,' Anna repeated.

'We'll get married.'

'No – no!' She put her hand to her head, then let it drop as she got some sort of fix on her temper. 'Look, this is just a deflection from what really matters,' she said. 'Which is that I don't want to marry you, Matthew. If Laura were on the scene or not. If you were free. I don't want to, I can't.'

'Can't?' he said.

'Won't.'

He stood up. 'But why not?'

She shook her head.

'Give me a reason,' he said. 'Anything that makes sense.'

She was silent, staring at the sea. He tried to hold her hand again, but she resisted, and shifted her body so that she didn't have to look at him.

'It's not fair, Anna,' he said. 'What can I do without a reason?'

'I just gave you a reason.'

'What, Laura?'

'Yes.'

He put his hand on her shoulder. 'I've loved you since the first day I met you.' She made a slight sound, an exhalation of breath, a sound of disbelief. 'All right, I know how that sounds,' he said. 'I know it sounds like a cliché.'

'Go home,' she said, at last. 'Please, Matthew. Just go home.'

Six

Detective Chief Inspector Robert Wilde sat with his back to the door, watching the street outside his office. He had opened the windows, and the sound of the traffic streamed in along with the midday sun.

The day had become unusually hot, and humidity was high. He had peeled off his jacket after coming back from Aubrete Manor, but still his shirt was sticky, and the scent of some plant clung to him, as insidious as prying fingers. He thought of Laura Aubrete, standing over her husband with that faintly supercilious expression belied by her smile, a pair of secateurs in one hand, the dead rose heads in the other.

As he had driven away, he had stopped before he got out of the grounds, and looked back down the long drive. Paths swept away to left and right, dipping below the trees; the parasol-shaped roof of the café hung like another exotic petal above the greenery.

He sat thinking of Anna Miles' drive, the difference between the two houses – the cottage track with its potholed and rutted surface, the grass beginning to grow in the centre, two deep wheel ridges on either side, and bordered by a barbed wire fence until the pasture stopped at a scrubby and windswept garden. There was no comparison at all between the two. Even in the dark, even in rain, even to a stranger, it was impossible that anyone would think that Anna Miles' drive was the drive to the Manor. No signposts, for a start. No glossy gold-on-green boards by the gates. No chestnut trees. No lake. It was the wrong house . . .

It made no sense. But then, nothing at all made sense about this case.

He considered Anna Miles, a woman he had never met until that morning: the slight and defensive stance as she leaned on the fence. A face of absolute weariness. A pair of piercing and very pale eyes. Long-fingered hands, the hands of an artist.

He thought of her room upstairs in the cottage, of the chest of drawers that they had found pulled almost across the door, as if for defence. And Matthew Aubrete's phrase. *She just appeared . . . in a manner of speaking.*

She just appeared. Like the girl in their custody room downstairs now. The girl in the car with Alisha Graham.

She just appeared . . .

He put his hand on the intercom to the main office.

'Is Sandys there?'

'No sir ... he's gone down to Comms to get the stuff from Manningham.'

'Tell him to come in to me when he arrives.'

Wilde stood up, easing the fabric of his shirt away from his back. From this window, he could see the whole length of the town's main street. It was packed with shoppers, a moving stream of bodies. Suddenly, he saw what he had been waiting for – Alice, coming up Cornhill, running, her blue holdall slung across one shoulder.

He hoped that his daughter would glance up to the second-floor window, and see him. He raised his hand to indicate that she should stop at the kerb, watch the traffic, be careful. Then, almost as soon as he had raised his palm, he dropped it. It would only earn him another lecture, he realized, with a slight smile. A lecture about her being fourteen and perfectly able to cross the road alone.

Able to do almost everything alone, he thought.

Or so his daughter was absolutely convinced.

Alice came to the edge of the pavement, saw a break in the cars, and jogged across. He watched her at the oblique angle afforded by his elevated view: her very square shoulder under a blue sweat top, the shoulder of a tennis player. A narrow waist, narrow hips, long legs with no shape at all, straight as dyes. Hair pulled back in a severe ponytail. She had grown out the fringe only last year, much to his disappointment.

'Dad, *no one* has a fringe. Only babies.'

That was it, he supposed. The last little fragment of her dependent childhood, the thick, straight-cut blonde fringe, going the way of all other things. The sticky grasp of a small hand in his own. The My Little Ponies. The pink plastic lunchboxes. Alice was stranded now somewhere in the strange landscape of adolescence, sometimes wanting him, sometimes strenuously not wanting him. He tried to keep up.

She disappeared under the frontage of the Victorian building that was the police station. He glanced at his watch. She was on time, as always. Not his trait, but her mother's.

There was a knock on the door.

'Come in,' he said.

Sandys entered, with a sheaf of papers in his hand.

'What have we got?' Wilde asked. 'Anything?'

'Not much.'

Wilde walked round his desk. 'Show me.'

Sandys handed him the first sheet. 'Anna Miles. Nothing. No criminal record. Driving licence. No credit cards. No mortgage records.'

Wilde looked at the sheet critically. Sandys gave him the next. 'Alisha Graham. Address in Manningham, checks out. Sister living. Car is hers. Got a record.'

Wilde looked up at him, not the sheet. 'Alisha Graham has a criminal record? For what?'

'Obstruction and possession.'

'*Possession?*' Wilde echoed, astounded.

Sandys grinned. '1978. Two counts. Speed. Got six months.'

'You're joking. Drugs? A woman like that?'

'It's all here in the sheet.'

'How old was she?'

'Let's see,' Sandys said, referring back to the papers. 'Fifty.'

'And doing what? What job?' Wilde asked.

'Down on the list as a lecturer at Knettleworth.'

Wilde shook his head in disbelief. 'And the obstruction?'

'Same time. It was some sort of student strike.'

Light dawned a little in Wilde's mind. 'Student strikes at the university. I remember.' He remembered the occupation of the Vice

Chancellor's office; if he recalled right, over the dismissal of a Marxist on the staff. 'Was she a Communist? An activist?'

Sandys shrugged. 'No record.' The man laughed. 'Quite a joke.'

Wilde considered. 'Speed is not a whim,' he said. 'Or a joke.'

'She claimed it was someone else's,' Sandys said.

'OK. Let it pass,' Wilde said. 'What else?'

'Ran the girl's fingerprints through,' Sandys said. 'Nothing.'

'Get on to the Missing Persons Bureau at the Yard,' Wilde said. 'See if they know her.'

Sandys raised an eyebrow.

'I know,' Wilde said. 'So they'll come up with a hundred missing teenage girls. Or a thousand . . . we'll just have to sort through them.'

'OK,' Sandys said.

There was another hasty knock at Wilde's door: Alice came in, breathless from running up the stairs. She rushed over to her father, and flung one arm about his neck, and kissed him unselfconsciously on the cheek. 'Hi, Dave,' she said to Sandys.

Wilde looked at her. There was a grass stain on her jawline. He wet his thumb and tried to rub it off: laughing, she caught his hand, and took over herself.

'You missed it,' he said.

'There?'

'There. What've you been doing?'

'Cricket.'

He shook his head.

'Why not?' she demanded.

'Because the boys don't do netball.'

She laughed. 'They're not up to it. No co-ordination, no patience.'

He smiled. 'Can you give us a minute?'

She pulled a face. 'Only a minute.' She went out into the corridor, leaving the door open. They could hear her whistling.

Wilde sifted through the papers, considered, and put them on his desk. 'Is the girl still downstairs?'

'With the doctor,' Sandys confirmed.

'Has she said anything?'

'Not a word.'

'Did you give her a drink – a cup of tea? Offer her breakfast?'

'Yes. She just smiled. I gave her some tea.'

'Forensic seen her?'

'First thing.'

Wilde fretted, pacing. 'She's in a car with a dead woman . . . and she smiles.'

'It's a proper smile, too,' Sandy observed. 'I mean, it isn't crazy, it's not vacant. She doesn't look traumatized. It's a just a little, everyday, polite smile.'

'Is she deaf?' Wilde wondered aloud. 'Deaf mute?'

Alice came back to the door. 'Dad, *please*.'

'I'll be back in half an hour,' he told Sandys. 'I want to talk to the doctor – and the girl.'

He put out his hand for Alice to take.

Smiling, she hooked her hand under his arm, and pulled him away down the corridor.

She thought of motion.

Not a movement of her own. After all, there was no need for that.

Instead, the girl thought of the motion of water. A little water running through strands of grass, over stone, down the long, long gradient through forest. Thought of the stream just below the summit. Thought of it dropping three thousand feet through the forest to the lake. Thought of water running out of the lake, through fells, through farmland. Little water. Little murmuring moving water. Little drops of water. Drops of water scouring grains of earth, taking mountains to the sea through green fields, dark slopes. Water pouring, unseen, under streets. Thought of water in the sea, the motion of waves, the movement of currents.

She imagined herself in one of those currents, carried tirelessly down. There was no need at all to move, even to scoop her hand through the wave. It bore her down the long liquid avenues, effortlessly, silently. She had only one task – to lie back and look at the stars. And to find the Gate.

Little drops of water, little grains of sand . . .

'Open your eyes for me,' said a voice.

She did as she was told – opened her eyes, and looked at the doctor.

'Look at the chart.'

She looked.

'Can you read the chart for me?'

He came around the side of her chair, and looked intently into her face. 'No?'

She smiled.

'Can you read letters?'

She smiled.

'Are you English? Do you understand English?'

She smiled.

He pushed a piece of paper, and a pen, across the top of the table next to them. 'Would you like to write anything down? Would that be easier?'

She looked at the paper, but didn't move her hands.

He picked up her right hand, and looked at it, looked closely at the fingertips, the colour of the nails, the palm. Gently, he pushed back the edge of her sleeve, that came just below the elbow. He looked at the skin on the inside of the elbow, checking both arms.

'Do you take any medicine?' he asked.

She smiled, not at him, but at her innocent hands now curled in her lap.

She thought of hands plunged into water, into the wave. Thought of the same hands on the sharp, fine strings, the taste of dust, the smell of the violin cases, the sensation of the crowds, more oceans and seas, a sea of faces and hands and instruments. Carried with the strong sweet wave of music. She thought of Anna Miles, face turned intently over the black-and-white bars of sound, long hair falling over the bow, obscuring her face so that she became all hands, strings, instrument. The sun falling into the fine high colour of her hair, across the dusty practice-room floor. The plastic-seated chairs, warm in the heat. Dozens of other intently bent heads and fumbling fingers, trying to get the melody right. Thought of herself, another face in the back row. Anna Miles suddenly looking up.

And across the rows, the violins, the other faces and hands, she recognized the same look in Anna Miles' face that she had in her own heart, that frozen empty fear.

Anna Miles looked different now. Much older. Older than she must be. Thirty? Thirty-one? Her hair was still the same length though. Still the same colour.

She had been carried for miles on the same strange currents.

Swept on the tide.

The doctor straightened up, frowning. 'Come and stand on these scales for me,' he said.

She did as she was told, watching as he checked the reading.

'Eleven stone two,' he said. 'And you're . . .' He looked at his sheet. 'Five foot eight. That's what we call well nourished.'

She inclined her head.

He sat down and wrote on the file in front of him. Afterwards, he looked up and continued to stare at her for some time, his fingers steepled in front of him. 'Is there anything you would like to tell me?' he asked.

She watched him, but said nothing.

'Do you have your own doctor, someone that you would prefer to talk to?'

She studied his face, listened to the sound of his voice, heard its strained tone. He was tall, sandy-haired, with a freckled complexion. She concentrated on the drifts of faint colour on his skin, and connected them to no one, just as she connected his questions to nothing, least of all herself. She heard the shape of the words, their hard and soft edges.

Once you had practised this for some time, it became easy, an art of a kind. The desire to respond, ingrained since birth, the necessity to make contact, was easily lost, given up like a worthless gift, an unwanted talent. Other people talked. They talked at great length, if you allowed them to. And once they had exhausted the topic of your own silence, they began talking about themselves. The doctor did not disappoint her now.

'I once knew someone else like you,' he said. 'A child. A boy.' He paused. She waited.

'He had had a very tough time,' the doctor said. 'With his father.'

She watched, waited, listened. Hearing the tidal rhythms far away, a distant and reassuring beat. Carrying her forward to the place where she wanted to be.

'Perhaps something like that happened to you,' the doctor said, kindly. 'Something you would like to talk about, but can't.'

She remained still.

'Perhaps you would like to talk to a woman,' he offered.

She gave him a smile, and closed her eyes.

'Is that what you'd like?' he persisted.

Sooner or later, she told herself, he would go away.

Seven

They wanted nothing to do with him.

They were going to be rich, now, the villagers told him. Even when he had come eight years ago with his father, and there had been a Red Fair on Poor Heart Hill – even when they had laid a ring of offerings on the tomb, and brought a good summer to the village and cured the filthy cholera here – even that counted for nothing now.

They had the new mine.

They were turning away from the crops. Not many were set to weed the wheat, so that poppies grew tightly in it, turning the lee side of the hill red. It pained the Egyptian to see it. It was blood in the crop, he thought. And there were rats where there had been no rats before.

He had met the man in the lane one spring morning, three days after he had arrived.

'You again,' the man had said. 'Go back to your own country.'

'I have no country except the one I'm in,' the Egyptian had replied, stepping to the side to let the man pass.

The man raised his hand to him. He looked deeply into his face. 'We don't want your curses here,' he had said.

'I don't curse,' the Egyptian replied.

'You buried the dead in your own land and laid curses on them.'

'I've buried no man.'

'You came to that pagan tomb.'

The Egyptian's eyes had strayed to Poor Heart, where the pit-head building housed the horse gin, whose wheel could be heard slowly grinding. The man had leaned towards him with a sly grin on his face.

'We took that pagan grave away,' he said. 'We take coal out of that hill,

44

and the money it makes feeds our children. We're colliers now. You see that pit? 'Tis the 1800, for the century. You fear that name, Egyptian. That 1800 pit is money.' He grinned. 'We even got pennant stone a'tween the seams that be taken up to Bath for the paving of streets. We got coal and stone out of that hill. We don't want no gypsies here no more.'

'Who took the mine?' the Egyptian asked.

'Why?' the man asked. 'You cursing they, too?'

'No . . .'

'Overseers and Aubrete and parish clerk and Reverend Blake. You curse they family?'

'No,' the Egyptian objected. But the blow came. The man struck him across the shoulder, as if to force his way past, although the way was clear.

'You go away from Christian folk.' He spat on the ground. 'We don't need you no more.'

The Egyptian watched him go down the lane, the leather of the man's shoe cracking at the misshapen heel, the shirt torn at the collar, the tin of cold tea in his other hand. He looked down at the soil by his feet.

'God have mercy on you,' he whispered.

Eight

The heat in the hospital ward was oppressive.

They had drawn the blinds at eleven o'clock, and even pulled the yellow-sprigged curtains across the blinds, but the light pierced through in thin lines, a laser-like grid crossing the bed, the floor, the walls.

Dominic Aubrete lay now in a cot with raised bars. He was asleep, drugged into submission, but his mouth continually worked, as if laboriously forming letters, pulled first into one shape and then another. Occasionally his eyes flickered open, then closed with a screwing of expression. He was naked to the waist, wearing only a pair of pyjama bottoms whose cord had worn loose and the fabric of which was pulled tight across his hips. He looked uncomfortable, like a boy condemned to bed on a summer afternoon, and only fitfully sleeping, miserable in his solitude.

A tube led from his arm to a saline drip. His face, crossed by one of the pencil-thin lines of sunlight, seemed sectioned, as if for analysis or demonstration. It was red, fleshy, bruised. Other bruises showed on his body, on his stomach, elbows, hands, shoulders.

Laura Aubrete arrived at midday. She came to the side of the bed and bent down, so that her face was only inches from his. She smelled his breath, then, with a single fingertip, touched the largest bruise, the blood under the skin on his stomach. She straightened up, crossed her arms, and considered him. The contrast could not have been more acute: the woman in the acid green suit. The man on the bed.

A nurse put her head around the door.

'Is Mr Aubrete with you?'

'No,' Laura said.

'Is he coming in?'

'No.'

'Could doctor speak with you, then? . . . In a couple of minutes, when he's finished the round?'

'Yes,' Laura said. 'I'll wait here.'

She walked to the other side of the room, and sat down on the only chair.

Dominic Aubrete turned his head.

'What are you doing?' he called.

Laura arranged herself, put her handbag on the floor next to her.

'Come down,' he whispered. 'Or I'll break your bloody neck.'

She could see that one eye was open, and the pupil rolled back in the socket. His mouth hung loose, and then he started to mumble incoherently, and his hand strayed to his face, where it picked at the flesh on his forehead.

'Come down . . . off it . . . off the wall . . .'

Laura sat composedly, legs crossed, hands clasped over one knee.

She had first met Dominic ten years ago. There was not much comparison, now, to the man he had been then: the kind of man who had completely dominated a room. And that was something he was well used to doing, commanding the centre of the stage, expecting a silence to fall when he began to speak. It was incredible, even now, to think that Matthew was his son. Poor polite Matthew, who never quite knew which direction he ought to follow. Matthew who had grown up in Dominic's shadow, where Dominic's wife had lived until she had given up the unequal struggle and succumbed to pneumonia.

Laura looked down, now, at her nails. Pneumonia at forty-seven. Not so much an illness as a signal of defeat, of absolute withdrawal. Alison Aubrete had lain down, exhausted, humiliated, and she had never got up again.

The whole scenario always inevitably reminded Laura of one of those Victorian melodramas where, as the heroine falls dying in the snow, a child creeps from her skirts. Matthew was such a child, a sallow and eager-to-please little boy who had been no good at games, no good in the army, and whose only interest seemed to be the kind of fawning, dependent woman who reminded him of his mother.

Ten years since the Christmas party at the Manor.

Laura had been working as a secretary to the estate manager for just three months. Alison Aubrete had been dead for six. The house, as soon as you entered it, gave off an aura of swiftly escalating decay. Dust had clung to every corner. The curtains, an appalling moth-eaten red brocade, hung faded in pleats at the windows. The Christmas decorations were perfunctory, the food abysmal. It was only the drink that seemed to be in any abundance. Defeat and negativity clung to every piece of furniture, every inch of faded carpet. The guests hung about in awkward groups, afraid that Dominic might come into the room and begin talking at them. In the dining room, the table had been pushed back and a four-piece band was playing *Knock Three Times*. Stepping back from the sight, Laura had forced herself not to laugh. The whole house, and all its grounds, and tenant farms, were like ripe fruit hanging from the tree, waiting for a hand to reach out and pick them.

She had not met Dominic until that night. He had a flat in London, and spent most of his time there. So, when he at last appeared, she had positioned herself at the foot of the stairs to watch his descent, rightly calculating that what the lord of the manor wanted most of all was an audience. She stood, not to one side so that he would easily be able to pass her, but dead in the centre below the last step.

It was the Eighties, and she had bought herself what was then the height of fashion: a purple taffeta dress, an enormous Scarlett O'Hara balloon of a dress, with a full and flounced skirt, and a neckline that barely clung to the last inch of cleavage. Her hair was neatly taken up to the top of her head. She probably looked like a bridesmaid, and the effect could not have been more to Dominic Aubrete's liking. If she were Scarlett O'Hara, he was not above believing himself to be Rhett Butler, and he had descended with a raddled gleam in his eye.

She had held his eye with a straight face, and had even given her hand up to be kissed.

'It's wonderful to meet you,' she said.

'The pleasure is all mine,' he had responded.

He really believed himself to be attractive, and perhaps had once been. Now, he was nothing more than a great square block of a body with a wet handshake. His hair was thinning, and there were a few threadlike red veins over his face, and his clothes sagged over a large stomach. His hands were large and flat, the fingers long, the knuckles pronounced. She looked at his hands and thought of a prize-fighter coming out into a fairground ring for another bout, another parade in front of the ladies. He started to speak in that booming, overstated upper-class voice, that strangulated tone.

She had felt deeply, and very abruptly, sorry for him.

The door to the hospital room opened now.

Jolted out of her memories, Laura looked up.

'Mrs Aubrete.'

The doctor and she shook hands: then they walked to the corridor, and to the seats arranged at the far end.

'I see there's no change,' Laura said.

The doctor hesitated. 'Actually, there is a change. We'd like him to go to ICU at the General.'

'Oh?' Laura said, raising her eyebrows.

'Yes. The retention of fluid, the liver failure . . . his blood pressure needs monitoring more closely.'

'I see,' she said. She glanced out at the trees in the grounds. 'Has he been conscious at all?'

'No.'

'Not any more than we've seen over the last few days?'

'No.'

She wondered if she could push it any further. 'Has anyone else been in to see him?'

The doctor looked at her, puzzled. 'I'm afraid I wouldn't know for sure. You might ask the nurses. Were you thinking of anyone in particular?'

Laura stood up, smiling. 'No,' she said. 'Simply curious.'

'Your husband was here last night . . .'

'Yes. Yes, I know.' She smoothed her hair. 'When will you transfer him?'

'Today.'

She nodded. They stood awkwardly together for a few seconds

longer. 'This is terrible to watch,' she murmured. 'After the stroke last year he seemed to rally . . .'

'There's only so much repair a system can manage,' the doctor said.

They talked for a few moments longer, in hushed voices, discussing the man lying in the private ward behind them.

Alone in the airless room, Dominic Aubrete thrashed in the heat. For a few agonized seconds, his feet paddled the sheet in a parody of shuffling steps. His hand began to pull at the needle in his arm.

'Anna,' he whispered.

The name floated unheard, unanswered.

'Anna . . .'

Nine

It was nearly two o'clock by the time that Detective Chief Inspector Wilde saw the girl from the car again.

They had kept her in a cell, where, the duty sergeant had told him, she had eaten the lunch that they had given her. 'Cleaned the plate,' the sergeant had said, with a sardonic smile. 'Obviously racked with trauma.'

The girl was put in an interview room, one of the better ones, with two high windows that let in the sunlight. As he came in the door, she looked up at him, and he was struck again with her calm. He held out his hand; she took it. Her grip was light, but not featherweight. There was a little pressure in the fingers. The touch was warm and dry.

He sat down opposite her.

'How are you feeling?' he asked.

She held his gaze. He saw that her eyes were brown. Her hair looked smooth, as if she had been brushing it – although, as far as he knew, there had been nothing in the car that belonged to her. Perhaps one of the WPCs had given her a comb. She was really quite pretty: smooth-skinned, wide-shouldered, a full mouth. A round, wholesome-seeming girl. She looked like a Thomas Hardy milkmaid: Tess, whose skin would have smelled of milk. Even the dress she wore was a milkmaid dress, blue cotton with little cream flowers all over it. A tight bodice and a full skirt. Laura Ashley, he thought.

'I don't know what to call you,' he continued. 'I'm not very good at guessing.'

Her eyes were ranging over his clothes and hands. She looked as if she were cataloguing what he was wearing, remembering it.

'My daughter's called Alice,' he said. 'She tells me that there's no one else in the country called Alice. She thinks I ought to be reported to someone, for cruelty, choosing a name like that. But I thought it would suit her. Her mother liked it, too.' He grinned. 'But what she *really* wants is to be called Frankie. After a girl in her class. Francesca.'

The girl gave a little smile.

'Irritating, isn't it?' he said. 'You give your child a nice name and all they want is to use something else. A name's a kind of sign, I suppose. A kind of category. Terrible to get that wrong.' He leaned forward, smiling. 'So I don't want to call you Edith if it's Elizabeth, do I?'

She said nothing. 'You look like an Elizabeth,' he said. 'Or Anne. Or Judith. Nice names. Names for girls.' He paused. 'Like Alice.'

She shifted a little in her seat, dropping her gaze into her lap.

'Mum and Dad,' he said. 'Brothers and sisters? What would they call you?'

The bait was not taken. Yet he thought he saw something, some slight, passing, momentary change at the mention of her parents.

'What day is it?' he said. 'Tuesday. What about that? Miss Tuesday. Makes you sound like a calendar.'

There was no response.

Wilde glanced at the WPC standing by the door. She widened her eyes by way of exasperation.

He changed his tack. 'How old are you?' he asked.

Nothing.

'Eighteen, nineteen?'

Nothing.

'Was Alisha Graham your friend?'

Nothing.

'This is an awful thing to be involved in,' he commented, still keeping his voice low. 'A dead person. Perhaps someone you didn't even know. Any kind of death is a shock. Sometimes, so much of a shock that we don't want to think about it. Sometimes even a road accident we might pass . . . it strikes you, makes your blood run cold. Much worse if you're actually involved.'

Now, the girl showed all the signs of her attention wandering. She was looking around at the floor, moving some microscopic piece of dust with the tip of her shoe.

'Tell me about Alisha Graham,' he said.

Blankness. He leaned forward and tapped the table lightly with his knuckles, wondering if the doctor could have been wrong, and she did have a hearing problem. If that were so, the movement of his hand ought to have made her look up. But she only glanced very briefly at his hand, then looked away, back to the floor.

He thought back to the contents of Alisha Graham's car. They had been laid out, bagged.

There had been a single holdall, brand new. Still with the price ticket inside. A bright blue and green holdall. He had stood for some time staring at it, thinking that it was not the kind of thing you might expect a seventy-year-old woman to be carrying. Yet it was full of her possessions. A picture frame with a photograph of another elderly woman who bore her a slight resemblance. Her sister, he guessed. Two paperback books. A notepad and pen. A wallet containing forty pounds, stamps, change, a scrap of material, a card place name from a conference or a meeting. A pair of tights, underwear. A sweater, a skirt. Thick and unforgiving material in the clothes, even the underwear. Support tights still in their packet. A Lycra girdle, the same, in a chainstore packet. Two pairs of walking socks . . . but no shoes.

He had wondered for some minutes what was odd about it, besides the shoes. Besides the price tickets, the unworn clothes. Then he had realized that the unticketed, old clothes were unwashed. They were badly creased, and smelled stale. Two sets of clothes. New, still carefully kept in their wrapping, as if taken from a drawer. And used. Crumpled. Taken from a pile of laundry. Or the floor.

He had opened the notebook and the books.

The notebook was well-thumbed, thick, a spiral-bound pad of five hundred pages. He had flicked briefly through it, seeing sheet after sheet of notes and sketches, and a dozen different location headings. Then, halfway through, he came to a page marked *The Aubrete Estate*.

On the top of the page was Matthew Aubrete's name and number.

Underneath it, the Manor's postal address.

Then, something he failed to understand at all.

A vein of aborescent marcasites at nine hundred feet . . .

He had flipped the page, turned it on its edge. There was a drawing of four sets of parallel lines. The same handwriting had made notes around the edges of the drawing.

The horse walked the pulley.

The head lay on Poor Heart Hill.

The blue vein was interlaid with Bath pavers.

Wilde had turned the page round and round.

What was she, an industrial historian? That's what Aubrete had said. A kind of chemist. A vein of arborescent marcasites . . .

Where was Poor Heart Hill?

He considered the girl now, the neat parting on the top of her head, the hair combed flat on either side, drawn back to the plait at the nape of her neck. She didn't look like girls of eighteen looked these days, he thought. She had no make-up, no jewellery. Some of the girls at Alice's school, not much older than Alice, wore all kinds of rubbish: nose studs, belly rings, ankle chains. Alice was always telling him that he was not much of an authority on anything, least of all women, and yet he knew enough to realize that very few girls of eighteen still wore plaits. The shy ones, perhaps. The over-protected ones. The innocent ones, of which, God knew, there were precious few left.

He wondered if the girl in front of him were innocent.

'What is an arborescent marcasite?' he said.

She looked up. Seemed surprised.

'Do you know what it is?' he asked.

No reply. She lifted one hand, and scratched her neck.

As she did so, he noticed the marks that the doctor had remarked upon.

On both forearms were several straight lines. Not deep. Not scratches, but grazes about an inch wide. They were not inflamed, and they had formed a slight scar, which had led the doctor to believe that they were perhaps a week old.

'What are they?' Wilde had asked him.

'Defence marks,' the doctor said.

And the man had raised both arms across his own face, fists turned inwards and elbows pointed forwards as the hands were brought up towards the face.

'The outside of the forearm takes the blow from an attacker,' he explained.

'And she's got these marks?'

'Yes.'

'What caused them? A knife?'

'No,' the doctor replied. 'Nothing as sharp as that. It's as if she's been hit with something blunt and abrasive. Glancing blows. A piece of wood, perhaps, a roughened edge.' He thought for a moment. 'Probably not by anyone trying to really harm her. More like a flurry. In a temper.'

'They couldn't have been caused by falling?'

'Not really. If she had fallen on anything gritty or coarse, like concrete, she would have similar marks on the heels of her hands or her elbows or knees, or all three. No . . . this is as if she pulled her arms up and put her hands by her ears. Perhaps she was even trying to put her hands over her ears.'

'And someone hit her in that posture.'

'Exactly.'

Now, as the girl dropped her hand, he held out his own.

'May I?' he said.

She froze, her hand mid-air, not extending her fingers to his. He got up from his chair and walked around the side of the table. He sat on the edge of the desk, not too close to her, and held out his hand again, palm uppermost. Very slowly, she lowered her hand to his.

He turned the palm over, and looked at her wrist. Just as the doctor had said, there were no signs of abuse: no marks on the wrists themselves, either of having been tied, or of her having tried to cut the flesh. There were no track marks for needles inside the elbows. This, he thought to himself, was not a disturbed girl. Not in any immediately recognizable way, at least.

He gently turned the arm and looked at the marks.

'Did someone hit you?' he asked.

She looked, too.

'This looks as if someone hit you,' he said. 'Did you have an argument with someone?'

She gave a little tug, to be released from his hold. He held onto her, running a finger down the arm and back to the hand. He held it quietly between both of his.

'Now, if I were a fortune-teller, I might be able to know a bit more about you,' he observed. 'And that wouldn't be difficult, would it? To find out more than you're telling us.'

He looked at her hand closely, as if he really could tell her life from the lines there. The skin was smooth and soft. No sign of any manual work. The nails were manicured, though without varnish. Most of them were flecked with white.

'You know, when I was a little boy,' he said, 'my mum used to tell me that white bits on the nails were because I didn't get enough calcium. But there's another theory now.' He looked into her face, tried once again to read its impervious expression. 'They say it's because of pressure on the nail bed.'

She looked at her hand in his.

He turned her hand over, and it was then that he saw the flattened tips to the first three fingers. He stopped, raised the fingers closer. Turned them over, and looked at them from the other side. They were definitely rounder and flatter than the other hand. Just for a second, he thought of the grid in Alisha Graham's notebook. Then, a distant bell rang far back in his mind. He knew that he had seen such fingertips before; reddened tips to the first three digits of one hand. But he couldn't think where.

The girl abruptly withdrew her hand. She wiped it, with methodical care, on the fabric of her dress.

'What is it?' he asked.

She closed her eyes.

'Why did you go to Anna Miles' house?' he said. 'Alisha Graham was due at the Manor. You were only two miles from the Aubrete estate. From the right house. Why didn't you go there? Why did you drive down to Anna Miles?'

She might have been carved from stone. For the first time, Robert Wilde felt his temper rising.

'What is Anna Miles to do with you?' he demanded. 'What are you to do with Alisha Graham? Why were you in that car?'

Staring at her face, he saw her squeeze her eyes tighter shut.

And then, more eloquent than any words, a tear formed on her eyelashes, and ran slowly down her face.

Ten

Beryl Graham was trying very hard not to think of her sister.

It ought not to have been difficult: after all, even after Alisha came to work at the university fifteen years ago, their meetings had been irregular.

When she had first known that Alisha had bought a house nearby, Beryl had entertained a romantic notion that they could be reconciled: she had imagined them perhaps even sharing a house, helping each other along what Beryl perceived to be the ever more intractable and unnegotiable path of old age. She had fondly imagined keeping Alisha's house while her sister pottered with some dusty thesis or other in which the world was no longer interested. Alisha's work was, to her, a foible, a kind of weakness that had to be tolerated and occasionally indulged, rather like discussing her health or the failings of the Labour Party, an animated discussion for a limited period on a subject that neither of them could have any possible effect upon.

It had come as quite a shock to discover that, after her twenty years of working abroad, Alisha's attitudes had not been mellowed by her age. At a time long after she ought to have retired, Alisha had become, if anything, more astonishing. In Beryl's mind, her sister had forsaken anything even mildly approaching decency. She smoked, for one thing. And not just cigarettes. The house would sometimes reek of what Alisha called grass, a disgusting habit in anyone, least of all a woman of Alisha's upbringing. And then there were the friends: young people, thirty and forty years Alisha's juniors. She had them up at the house, she went to faculty parties, and she stayed for weekends in God knew what circumstances, at addresses that had remained a mystery to Beryl.

58

Alisha had looked so wrong, too. She dressed herself in jeans, or Indian skirts, or even, sometimes, in overalls. 'It's for my work,' she told Beryl once, as she was packing a document case. 'For heaven's sake try and understand. I go into pits, Beryl. Underground, Beryl. I look at machinery. I go into derelict warehouses. It's my *work*.'

But Beryl did not understand.

She refused to understand. She came to clean every week as a kind of martyrdom, a paid cross to carry, a symbol both of her selfless willingness and Alisha's selfish egotism.

Beryl Graham wanted a *real* sister. Someone to come with her to the WI. Someone to read the paper with. Someone to pick up in her car on a Sunday morning, and go to church with, and to sit with in the lonely, overpolished pews. Someone dressed nicely in a suit, who knew the right page numbers for the service, and could turn her own page for her when her hands were fixed in their occasional rigid arthritic clutch. She wanted to able to introduce Alisha to those women who had pitied her for having no family, no children, no grandchildren. She wanted to be able to say, 'This is my sister Alisha. She lived in America for a while, and now she's come home.' Alisha who had done perhaps something rather interesting in teaching, but whose life in that was now over. A person who was as redundant and respectable as herself, a nice pleasant person, useful for fêtes and the sewing circle.

It wasn't much to ask, was it? To have a proper sister who kept her company.

But it *was* too much for Alisha. Going down the path to the church now, Beryl's mouth turned down in a grimace of despair.

And now Alisha was dead.

And she couldn't even die in a respectable fashion.

Beryl pushed open the church door. From inside came the reassuring flavour of godliness: strong tea, damp, and flowers just past their best. She looked up at the stained-glass window closest to the font, at a Christ surrounded by saints, a portrait in blood red and gold and green. Under Christ's feet lay the wretched sinners, their tautly clothed Victorian bodies descending into the ground, their hands reaching up to beg for divine intervention before they were consumed in hell. They had vacant, colourless eyes and pinched little faces. Crying for forgiveness. Begging for mercy. Christ's face was averted from them as if He couldn't bear to see their degradation. Others clung to Him, to the hem of his cloak – the righteous ones, secure in the prospect of heavenly bliss. As Beryl gazed upwards, she saw Alisha's expression – that of surprised superiority – in the faces of the sinners swiftly disappearing through a hole in the ground. She couldn't see Alisha in the blessed, who lined up so regimentally behind their Saviour on the grassy slopes of Elysium. She shuddered slightly, with something like sensual gratification. Poor Alisha was to burn in eternal fire for all she had done.

For she had certainly sinned.

I mustn't think of it, Beryl told herself. But she did. With some satisfaction.

Walking up the aisle, nodding to the two or three other worshippers gathered for midweek prayer, Beryl's mind reverted to the photograph. She settled in a pew, took the hassock down, and knelt on its slippery leather surface, her knees clenched tightly together, the hands clenched even tighter on the shelf before her. She closed her eyes.

Immediately the girl in the picture sprang to her mind. The naked back, the rounded shoulder. The angle of her posture, like a dancer reaching to the floor. Alisha had had a naked girl in her bedroom. She had taken a photograph of a naked girl. And she had kept the photograph in her room.

Beryl pressed her hands tighter, until her painful knuckles showed white.

She could still see the computer screen, still see the colour reflected on the faces of the policemen, the blue wash in the shadows. Someone who knew their Bible had put that message on the screen. Beryl had racked her brains all day yesterday, trying to decode, to decipher in her own mind, if the words were a joke, or a serious message. The kind of people that Alisha knew were not above taking God's word in vain. Alisha herself had done so many times. And yet . . . there was something coldly penetrating in the words. No punctuation, no exclamation marks, no cryptic little aside at the end. No quotation marks either, as the police had pointed out. This phrase was close to someone's heart, held a meaning. They didn't hold it apart from themselves by showing a reference. It wasn't a footnote like the ones in Alisha's books, with a chapter and verse. It was personal, breathed out. A message, a fluttering line of letters.

Even trying to sleep last night, Beryl had been preoccupied with it. It wouldn't leave her head. It was as if she had caught a virus, a virus composed entirely of words. Words forever linked to Alisha's face. And a girl in a picture.

When the service was over, Beryl did not move from her seat. The other half-dozen members of the congregation filed out, and the vicar extinguished the single candle on the altar, went into the vestry and came out dressed in jeans, a white shirt and blue linen jacket. When he saw Beryl still sitting there, he gave a little start of surprise.

'Miss Graham,' he said. 'Are you all right?'

She opened her mouth to assure him that she was and, to her horror, a little mewling cry came out. She fumbled for her handkerchief and stuffed it against her mouth, but the sobs seemed to have taken her over. Tears splashed down on her hymn book.

'Whatever is it?' he asked.

'It's my sister,' she said. 'She died.'

Reverend York took her into the vicarage.

There, ten minutes later, while she sat on a minimalist sofa in his immaculate study, he brought her a cup of sweet tea.

'I'm so sorry,' she told him. 'I can't think what came over me.'

'No doubt it's shock,' he said.

'I didn't cry at all yesterday,' she whispered. 'Not even when the police showed me her picture, and it had been taken when she was dead, and . . .'

'The police?' York echoed.

She glanced up at him. 'She was found in her car, miles away from here.'

'Whereabouts?'

'Somewhere on the south coast.' He took her cup from her. She blew her nose. 'We were apart for so much of our lives,' Beryl murmured piteously. 'And now we shan't be together at all.'

The vicar nodded sympathetically. 'She taught at the university,' he said.

'Yes.'

'I've seen her there once or twice,' he told her, conversationally. 'She was always very busy.'

'Yes,' Beryl said. Then she registered what he had said. 'You go up there?' she asked.

'That's right. Once or twice a month,' he told her. 'There's a kind of revivalist group there. The students.'

Beryl fixed him with a suspicious gaze. She had thought that he was a sound traditionalist. Not one of these happy clappers. 'Revivalist?' she asked.

'A kind of praise service and a talk, and a chat afterwards.'

Beryl's face fell. She could just imagine it. A lot of noise. No dignity, no control. All crossed-legged on the floor, swaying about. Some sort of music going on that was not a proper hymn. Bare feet and holding hands. She shrank back from York as if he had admitted being the carrier of some contagious disease.

'A chat,' she said.

'Yes. Alisha came to one or two.'

He could not have said anything that astounded Beryl more. To be told that he was some kind of closet evangelist was bad enough, but to hear that Alisha – godless, heartless from the day she had been born – had come to such a meeting . . . it was too preposterous.

'*Alisha?*' she said. 'Not Alisha.'

'Oh yes,' he told her. 'Not often, you know. But sometimes.'

'But . . .' Beryl's mind raced. In a few short seconds, she travelled from a state of complete astonishment to one of total betrayal. Alisha had believed. In however misguided a fashion, she had believed. She had gone to church. A kind of church, anyway. She had gone to church with the students, sat on a floor somewhere, talked about . . .

She looked away, shuddering involuntarily.

It was an invasion. That's what it was. It was invasion of her own territory. For God belonged rather nicely, rather exclusively, to Beryl herself. She knew Him, she understood His rules. She could recite the services word for word. Beryl had a relationship with God, the only kind of truly intimate relationship that she had ever had. Beryl gave herself up to Him secretly behind the prayerbook pages, in the draughty silences, in the wet Sunday evenings, in the solitary Lent Wednesdays, in the small strict corrections to her spirit, in the empty wastes of her heart. He was a remote and critical ruler, one to whom she took gifts, a tax on life, a levy on joy: she took Him her time and loneliness, she knitted them into clammy-fingered offerings. Her soul was made up of Christian Aid packets and brass-cleaning rotas and in having a good hat to wear at Easter and Christmas. She was not excitable, or rash, or talented, or optimistic, and the sweetness in her nature had long since matured into sanctimony, but she *belonged* in church, was a little humble cog in God's mysterious plan, and Alisha – Alisha most emphatically did *not* belong. Alisha could not be saved.

'Alisha won't get to heaven,' she said.

The vicar leaned forward, to catch her words. 'I'm sorry?'

'It doesn't matter,' she retorted.

'God's mercy is infinite,' York said. 'You can rest assured of that.'

'I don't want to be assured of it,' she told him.

He paused. 'We all have our ways of coming to Christ,' he said, quietly. 'I think perhaps Alisha was finding a way.'

Beryl spluttered with indignation. 'With all those students,' she said. 'With all those drug addicts and the like.' She was suddenly finding it difficult to breathe.

He smiled. 'I don't know very many addicts,' he said. 'But those I do know are addicted to alcohol and live in this parish.' He sat back in his chair. 'Most of the boys and girls are very nice. You would like them. Girls like Alisha's friend.'

Beryl managed to get to her feet, where she drew herself up to her full height. 'I don't want to know them,' she said. 'I don't want to know anyone like that.'

And she went out of the vicarage, stumbling over the cat lying in the doorway, and finding a curse in her mouth. She hurried down the path, in a frame of mind she could not put a name to, rubbing her hands against her coat before she put on her gloves, as if to wipe away anything that might have touched her in the last hour.

Eleven

He lived another life in dreams.

And he was, in the last hour before dawn, dreaming now.

Robert Wilde travelled backwards, dropping the years as always, like redundant clothes, running faster to a point of light. He would feel the days, the weeks, brush past him with their ghost-like voices, with their tenuous hands, their prickling fingertips brushing his body. And, as he swept past them, released from the present night, he would become less heavy, as if his flesh were falling away from him with the backward-falling passage of time. He would have a sensation of dropping, of faces flickering, of rooms, streets, and hills, flexing and fading as the light became brighter.

Then, it would stop.

There would be a moment of absolute tension, while he hung stranded between two worlds. And then, abruptly, and with intense gratitude, he would find himself standing in the old place, in the old silence.

The lake was thousands of feet below him, the grass was cropped short under his feet, and there was a faint veil of dew on his face. It was always first light. Six a.m. Far down the valley, Crummock Water was an unreflective curve of grey.

It was thirty years before, the summer of his eighteenth birthday, the year that he met and married Christine. He was on Fleetwith Pike, waiting for his father, whose progress up the mountain was slower than his. He sat down on his haunches, hugging his knees, looking at the track, at the mist dissolving on further peaks, at the pattern of grey and green and slate blue below, at the thin white line of water, a near-vertical fall of water from Sheepbone Buttress to the black surface of Buttermere.

Three thousand feet below, the village was two or three small white rectangles – the walls of the hotel, and the houses on each side. Somewhere down there was their own house, and his mother.

Then, he would hear a movement on the track, and turn his head. But, instead of his father, it was always Christine. Christine when they were first married. She wore, improbably, a pair of pedal pushers and a white shirt. Her feet were bare on the bright green lichen stretched over the rocks of the summit. She would come to a stop. He would stand up. They would face each other over the few yards of empty air, at what might have been the top of the world, the sides of the mountain disintegrating on each side, the first light touching their heads and shoulders.

He would always know, in the familiar repeated phases of the dream, that Christine had never really climbed Fleetwith or The Stacks with him. But even though it was an experience that they hadn't shared, his brain perpetually reran it, trying to make the regretful fantasy fit. It was a picture of Christine walking up his parents' lawn in her bare feet that his sleeping self tried to superimpose on the mountain. Eerie softnesses would touch his face as he stared at her. Strangely textural caresses.

And then he would realize, with utter certainty, that the moment was real. That he had been truly transported back to this place, that he actually stood on the mountain in the delicate hour of dawn. That far under his hand, birds circled the lake, shapes in an unseen current. That he was no longer forty-five, but eighteen. That he had stepped through some kind of unmarked door, into a country where she was still alive.

He watched her face, waiting for the old words.

'Hello, Robert,' she said.

And then, as always, he woke up.

For a few seconds Robert Wilde lay on his back, staring up at the ceiling. It was already light, here in the alternative world. He turned his head and looked at the clock. Six a.m. The same time as the dream. But six o'clock three hundred miles and almost thirty years away. Six o'clock on a . . . what was it? He forced himself back into the present day. It was

Wednesday. Wednesday in June. He sighed deeply, and levered himself up on to one elbow.

The coming day filtered through in disconnected details. Alice had a French test today. They had spent last night going through French vocabulary, then discussing her school trip in three days' time. He put his hand over his eyes momentarily. He saw past Alice's face, frowning over the book yesterday evening. Saw past into today, to work. To his office. To the incident room they had rigged up, the thirty desks, the computer screens, the faces lined up before him. He took his hand away, opened his eyes again. Christine standing on a mountain. The smile, like Alice.

He swung his legs out of bed, pulled on a pair of shorts, and opened the curtains to look at the street. It was sunny already. A quiet suburban picture met his gaze. Cars lined up in neat driveways in neater gardens. One straight road leading down to the school. Carefully tended colours. Not a leaf out of place.

He went downstairs, plugged in the kettle, telling himself to let go of the dream.

Alice had been five years old, and had just started at primary school, when her mother, Christine, had died. Alice was a most organized child, insistent that her lunchbox should be sitting on the kitchen worktop, in sight the moment she came downstairs in the morning. Always aware what she needed the next day. It had made Christine laugh, because Christine was possibly the least organized person on the planet. Robert would bring her a cup of coffee every morning, early. Christine would make the effort to sit up, complaining. Yet, after her shower, another person would emerge – Christine the whirlwind, the working mother, gathering up Alice and bundling her into the car along with her own folders and bags. Christine had had a research job that year, in a laboratory connected with the Constabulary. She had an eye, an ear, for the specialized mystery of forensics.

He poured the hot water into the cup.

And Christine would have had an idea about this girl – this girl that had been in the car with Alisha Graham. The girl who wouldn't speak. Christine would find the fact that slipped just beyond the conscious list;

she had had a talent for pinning down fragments. In the kind of work that took facts and only facts – facts as cold and hard as they came – Christine had been able to let her mind take leaps. It had come naturally to her. And in those leaps would occasionally be a nugget of truth. Robert had tried to emulate that talent ever since, and sometimes he got it right, but more often than not, like everyone else, he got it wrong, or he was unable to make even the slightest leap into the unknown, reluctant to move past the security of figures on a sheet, names in a file.

'You have to let go of what you know,' Christine had always said. 'Look away from it, pretend you don't care about it. Think of it like a game. A game of hide-and-seek. Turn your attention away, and it'll come hurtling up from behind. Like answers come in dreams.'

In dreams . . . in dreams.

He had taken the coffee up, as usual, that terrible morning.

It had been the same as always: her gradually sitting up in bed, uncurling herself. He had put the coffee down on her bedside cabinet, and pulled the curtains. Then, behind his back, he had heard her breathe in sharply. When he had turned around, he had seen his wife sitting quite upright, her eyes widened a little in an expression of surprise, and her right hand at the back of her head.

'What is it?' he had asked.

'I don't know,' she had told him. 'My head . . .'

He made the coffee now, grimacing, telling himself to shut the image away. Christine had suffered a cerebral haemorrhage at the age of twenty-nine.

One other memory remained of that black hole of a week.

Alice being picked up by another mother and taken into school, the day before the funeral. Her grey school skirt had needed to be ironed. He remembered standing in the hallway, having ham-fistedly rigged up the ironing board. Remembered trying to get the pleats into the skirt, his fingers feeling like lead. He hadn't known the right way to do it, and the task, simple though it might have been, had defeated him. Alice had stood watching him.

'Mummy doesn't do it like that,' she had said.

He had bent over the ironing board, tears springing to his eyes, fear and grief knotted in his throat. Defeated by this one small task for his little daughter.

Alice had taken the skirt from him and solemnly put it on.

'It's all right . . . look,' she had said, trying to reassure him, thinking that he had started to cry because of the awkwardness of ironing the pleats. And the studied intensity of her reassurance, and his anxiety to protect her from the dreadfulness of Christine's loss, and the fumbling over the fabric of the skirt, had swept over him, dragged him down. When Alice had gone to school, he had lain on the living room couch and wept for a prolonged hour, wretched at his ineptness, afraid of the future.

A long time ago. Nearly ten years. He looked down at his left hand, where he still wore the wedding ring.

He opened the back door of the house now, and walked up the path into the garden.

'Let go of what you know.'

All right.

He sat down on the bench under the apple tree.

Letting go of what they knew in this particular case wasn't difficult, for they knew next to nothing about the girl. They knew that she had been in the car, they knew that Alisha Graham was dead, they knew – or, rather more accurately, they guessed, until the post-mortem came in today – that Alisha Graham had been strangled. Knew that by the marks on her neck and around her eyes. Knew that the girl seemed unperturbed . . . at least, he had thought so until she had cried yesterday. No words, just tears. So he knew . . . what? He knew she had feelings, at least. Perhaps that she felt afraid. Perhaps grief. Did that mean that she knew Miss Graham, cared for her? Was she weeping for the dead woman, or herself?

The police surgeon's report had come in late in the afternoon. The mouth swabs, the hair and nail samples. All facts recorded. They may – or may not – mean something once the reports also came in from Alisha Graham and the girl's clothing, and from the interior of the car.

What else did he know about the girl?

He let his mind drift, and it came to rest on her fingers.

On her fingers, and the marks on her arm.

He frowned as he looked down into his coffee cup. Flat, rounded fingertips, slightly reddened . . . he ought to know what that was. He had seen it before, on someone else, someone . . .

He tried to meet the knowledge that skimmed at the edge of his consciousness. Tried to grasp it. But it evaded him. He drained the coffee cup, stood up, and stretched. Damn it, he was still no good at Christine's game of hide-and-seek.

But it *would* come to him.

In time.

In the police station, they were just changing shifts.

The sergeant was going through the book, running through those kept in the cells. There were only two: an elderly drunk, known to them all, who was a regular visitor. And the girl.

'Seemed to sleep during the night,' the sergeant said. 'No sound, no fuss. Nothing at all.'

His successor gave him a questioning glance. 'Hasn't she said anything yet?' he asked.

'Not a word.'

'Funny business,' the younger man said. 'Funny peculiar.'

Together, they went to the cell doors.

The drunk was lying on his back, snoring loudly. Even through the grating in the door, the smell in the small room was overpowering. They closed the aperture, grimaced at each other.

'She's in cell three,' said the sergeant. As he reached her door, he paused for a second. 'Feel a bit sorry for her,' he said quietly.

They opened the slat in the door.

At first they couldn't see her: she was not on the bunk.

The sergeant did a reflex double-take, and leaned forward, expelling his breath in a grateful sigh when he glimpsed her sitting on the floor. Just for a second, an image of finding her stretched out, as dead as Alisha Graham, had illogically sprung into his head.

But his relief from perplexity was short-lived.

The girl was facing the door. She was kneeling on the floor in a

69

little patch of early sunlight. Her arms were raised to the light in an attitude of prayer. She was utterly still, carved from rock.

And down each forearm, blood from the scratches of her own fingernails was already dry.

Twelve

The doctor saw her again at nine.

By that time Robert Wilde was in the station. While the doctor examined the girl again, Wilde spoke to the custody sergeant.

'Her knees were cut too,' the man said. 'From kneeling on the floor.'

Wilde ran a hand through his hair in exasperation. 'And still nothing – no word, no kind of explanation?'

The sergeant shook his head. 'We went in, we helped her up. She didn't resist. She sat on the edge of the bed.'

'What was she doing when you checked at six?'

'Sleeping.'

'And at seven?'

'She looked as if she was praying.' The sergeant demonstrated the hands raised in the air.

Robert Wilde looked at him closely. 'But no words, not even a whisper, like a prayer?

'No, sir.'

'Anything else?' he asked. 'Anything else at all?'

The man gave a slight shrug. 'When I went in, when we picked her up . . . she let herself be touched. And she looked up at me.' He pursed his mouth as if embarrassed. 'She gave me this look . . .'

'What kind of look?'

'Grateful. Pathetic.' The sergeant pulled a face, as if he knew that what he was about to say might well be misinterpreted. 'It was a sweet look,' he said. 'Kindness in it. Kindness, sadness.'

'But nothing actually said.'

71

'She opened her mouth as if she was about to say something. Then she just squeezed my arm. We brought her a cup of tea.'

'Did she drink it?'

'Yes.' The man sighed. 'If she's guilty of murder, I don't know . . .'

Wilde considered him. 'What do you make of her?' he asked.

'I don't know what to make of her,' the other man replied honestly. 'She looks like a decent girl. But . . .'

'But what?'

The sergeant gave a rueful smile. 'Something strange. When I touched her.'

'What?'

The other man turned his face away and dropped his voice, so self-conscious was he of what he was about to say. 'Gave me an electric shock,' he said. 'A real ripple of shock.'

'Static?'

'On a concrete floor?'

Wilde went up to the incident room, a part of the station that had been the old cells, and was now a shell. Two days ago, builders had been in here converting the place to a new suite of offices. Behind thick plastic tarpaulin held together with miles of masking tape, junction boxes hung on cables. The cleared space, still with the distinct odour of brick and plaster dust, was now full of desks, phones, and VDUs.

At a large table in the corner, two officers sat side by side reviewing video tapes. Every closed circuit TV tape from every petrol station on the likeliest route between Alisha Graham's house and Anna Miles' cottage had been brought in. Now the painstaking job of watching every tape through a thirty-six-hour cycle had fallen to the two men sitting in front of the TVs.

Wilde went over to them. 'How's it going?'

He looked at the nearest screen. Grainy night light filled the picture. 'Where is this?'

The detective picked up the box and read from the side. 'Place called High Park Ash. Just outside Bristol.'

It was a little garage. Empty wire racks showed where newspapers and flowers were displayed during the day. An ice cream sign, no doubt inadvertently left out overnight, spun lazily in a slight breeze. The clock on the bottom of the screen read two-forty a.m. They watched it through another five minutes on fast-forward, the scene never altering.

'How many have you done?' Wilde asked.

'Eighteen.'

He put his hand on the detective's shoulder. 'Keep at it.'

By the time that he went back upstairs, the girl had finished with the doctor. She was shown into another interview room, and Wilde sat down opposite her with Sandys. The doctor had put a dressing on both knees and on one arm. She wore a shift dress and a sweatshirt that had been provided for her. Her clothes were evidence.

If I have a case, Wilde thought wryly.

He made no attempt, this time, at prevarication.

'We want to help you,' he said. 'And you must help us.'

She looked down at her hands.

'How did Alisha Graham die?'

Sandys sighed heavily.

'You were found this morning,' Wilde said. 'Kneeling on the floor. You were praying . . .'

A flicker went over her face, like a shadow.

'You were praying,' he repeated.

The faintest, the slightest inclination of her head. It might have been a nod.

'You were praying for help, perhaps?'

Nothing.

'We pray to ask God for something, to tell him something.'

Nothing.

'Do you believe in God?' he asked.

She stiffened a little in her seat.

'Do you believe in God?' he repeated.

The effect was extraordinary. Wilde had been through a lot of interviews in his time, seen what he had in more cynical moments thought of as a constant and unvarying pattern of petty criminals, heard the same story a hundred times with only minor variations – the deprived childhood, the lack of a job, the addiction to drugs or drink, the temptation unresisted. Seen guilt and perversity. Shame. Wry embarrassment. Frantic anxiety. Blithe good humour. All the ranges of human reaction.

But he had not seen this.

The angel-faced girl put a hand to her neck as if she were being choked. She scrambled from the chair, and went back to her knees on the floor, her hands now covering her head. She kneeled down so that her forehead touched the floor. And her whole body shook.

Wilde resisted his gut response, which was to rush around the side of the desk and lift her up. Sandys stood up immediately, apparently with this same intention, but Wilde put a restraining hand on his arm. He strode quickly around the desk himself, kneeled down at the girl's side, and put his face close to her ear.

'What is it?' he said.

The breath came from her in ragged gasps.

'Tell me,' he urged. 'I can help you find a way through this. Find an answer. Tell me.'

She looked up at him, stricken. Then her gaze trailed past him, to the window, to the light. She stared up so intently that he, too, turned his head. He saw only cloudless sky, the sky of a spring morning, another warm day.

'What is it?' he asked.

She trembled.

'Is it God?' he asked, a realization suddenly dawning on him. 'Is God looking at you?'

To his intense relief, because it meant some kind of communication, something more, if only a little more than yesterday, the girl began to nod distractedly.

'God is looking at you, watching you?'

She tore her eyes from the bland blue sky and stared into his face.

'And you're afraid . . . of what? That he's angry with you?'

There was no confirmation. Her expression told him that he had missed the point. He felt like a useless player in a game of charades.

'God is up there . . .' he murmured. 'Watching, waiting?'

She put her arms around his neck.

He felt her sweet breath, warm against his skin.

Thirteen

Slowly, carefully, Alisha Graham's house was taken to pieces.

It was midday by the time that the upper team reached the bedroom, having examined the hall and upstairs landing. There had been nothing much to remark on. The skirting boards were dirty, but the sills reasonably clean; the curtains had not been washed for some time, and bore an odour of dust, mothy sunlight, stale air. It was noted that the fastenings to the metal windows were rusted, as if they had never been opened – the catch was impossible to shift. Here and there on the walls, by two of the upper doors, were brown drips, the kind left by the careless carrying of a teacup. The effect was one of occasional and hurried housekeeping, by someone who had more important things to interest her.

As the team reached the first bedroom door, one of the officers turned to his colleague. 'You know what it is?' he said, looking about him. 'What's different?'

'Surprise me,' the other man said.

'It's not an old woman's house.'

'What d'you mean?'

The first man shrugged. 'What was she, seventy?' He smiled. 'My gran's seventy-three. There's this smell in Gran's house . . . polish, mothballs . . . ornaments everywhere. It's not a bad smell, don't get me wrong. Sort of reassuring. I mean, you know where you are, even with your eyes closed. Polish and cake. The smell of the gas fire that she's had on all day and turned off just before you got there.'

The other man was laughing.

'No, but that's what old age smells like, you know?' the first man insisted. 'Tea and boiled sweets and carpets and cake. Liniment in the bathroom. Starch on tablecloths. Fridges with tomatoes and half loaves in them, opened tins of peach halves.' He smiled at last. 'People who live alone, you know? Old people with no appetite. Medicine next to the bread bin.'

'There's nothing like that here.'

'That's what I mean,' the first man continued. 'No ornaments. Every bloody woman I know collects the sodding things. Framed photos. Plants. Pot pourri.' He paused. 'I mean, this isn't even a woman's house. Not one bloody cushion. Nothing on the walls. It's like a bloke's house.' He gestured towards the front door, below them. 'The stuff on the table by the door. My Linda's got this picture of a dog and she's got like a basket with flowers round it, pottery one, and she's got this telephone index in a brass holder with a bird on the front . . . but what's down here? Couple of motoring catalogues, house insurance for renewal. That's it.'

They both looked down. In the office at the back, they could hear the other team sifting through Alisha Graham's papers.

The idiosyncrasies turned up here were of a more definite and obvious kind.

Spread out on the carpet by the door were several books, still with their markers in place where they had been left by Alisha. Piled next to them were the photographs. On first seeing them, the Inspector had taken a sharp intake of breath; but as time went on, he ceased to be surprised. The pile was growing bigger.

The picture in the first open book seemed innocuous enough. Through a giant stone gateway in some foreign landscape, the sun was setting. On either side, sand stretched away. *The Gateway of the Sun, Tihuanaco*, read the inscription under the photograph. *Five towns, built one on top of the other, abandoned in the thirteenth century.* On the opposite page, five stone heads, set into a wall, stared out, two square and ritualized, two decayed, and the fifth of disturbing vacancy, with a wide and open mouth and a deep crease in the forehead and the top of the skull. There was something deeply unpleasant in the last face, which had the look of a madman. The eye was continually drawn to the indentation in the bone above the eyes. Little round eyes too close to the top of the head. Mouth opened in a cry.

The second book was also open on a page of faces. *Teotihuacán's gods*, ran the footnote. Old men's faces with protruding teeth. The square and machine-like masks of rain gods. Animal faces with feathered head-dresses. White eyes with black pupils and rims.

The third book was now almost engulfed with paper. The book, and the papers, had one curious and everyday theme: gateways. Gates of cities and temples. Deserted church doorways; megalithic altars flanking the doors in Tarxien; ruined earth benches in L'Anse aux Meadows in Newfoundland. The sacred enclosure of Marduk in Babylon; the open jaws of the jaguar god of the Olmecs. Pathways to secrets guarded for centuries. Uppermost on the pile was the face of a weeping child, a pre-Columbian statuette made of jade. Foreshortened limbs and paw-like hands only added to the helplessness of the gargantuan head. The child, alongside the masks of the Incas, looked up at the men clearing the room with mute distress.

It was almost exactly one o'clock when the Inspector got up from his knees, surfacing from Alisha's endless files with a sigh. At that moment, his mobile, still sitting on the floor next to the books, rang. He reached down and picked it up.

'Wallis.'

'Inspector Wallis, this is Detective Chief Inspector Wilde from Melkham.'

'Afternoon, sir.'

'How's it going?'

'Slow.'

'Anything obvious?' Wilde asked.

'Nothing that leaps out. No sign of struggle, blood . . . it's untidy in places. Unusual bits and pieces. Early days.'

There was a slight pause on the other end of the line. Wallis could hear several voices in the background, the ringing of more than one telephone. 'Unusual?' Wilde repeated. 'Unusual how?'

Wallis tried to put a name to it. 'Considerable amounts of paper, academic stuff. Essays by students – must be forty of those. Back issues of magazines. Three or four hundred, all seem to be history, mechanical, industry. Lot of mining stuff – coal, tin. Got a room here full of books. Some odd subjects.'

'Odd?'

'Lot of literature on . . .' He searched for the word. 'Ritual places. Temples. Archaeological sites. Death masks . . .'

Another considered pause on the other end of the line.

Wallis looked out of the window, to a steady drizzle of rain that he hadn't noticed until now. 'Do we have a time of death, sir?' he asked.

'Yes,' Wilde told him. 'Alisha Graham died sometime late on Monday.'

'But we don't know where. Yet.'

'Precisely right,' Wilde said. 'Yet.'

They finished the call. Wallis put the phone down, smiling to himself. Wilde was obviously one impatient man, too impatient to ring his opposite number in their own incident room. Or maybe he had already rung, and wanted whatever was extra, whatever was current, from the men in Alisha Graham's house. Wallis gave a little nod of appreciation. He recognized that feeling, the feeling of frustration, of trying to fit pieces of a puzzle together that consistently refused to fit. He wondered what they had got from the girl who had been with Miss Graham, wondered if he ought to have asked. Wondered how long it would be before he saw Wilde, who, he estimated, would not long be able to resist coming up to talk to them.

'Funny business,' he murmured to himself. 'Funny business, old woman, young girl.'

The younger man in the room looked up. 'Sorry, sir?'

'Nothing,' he said. 'Nothing.'

The afternoon wore on. The rain grew heavier outside as the team upstairs worked once more over the territory covered yesterday. They opened Alisha Graham's wardrobes and drawers, taking out every item, examining every pocket, every collar, cuff and hem. They, too, noticed the same strange mixture of clothing that had been found in Alisha's suitcase: old and new mixed together, the new often still with the price tag in place. There was no rhyme or reason to the distinction. It was not as if, for instance, Alisha had simply decided to buy new underwear, or shoes, and throw away the old sets. Here old and new sat uncomfortably side by side: shoes that had seen years of wear sitting next to boxed ones, wrapped in tissue, in the bottom of the wardrobe. New sweaters lay along-side old in the drawers of the wooden chest and in the storage spaces under the divan bed. Crumpled blouses with frayed collars were folded in piles with new shirts still with their pins and wrapping. Looking over the stacks of clothing, the team estimated that Alisha Graham had spent several hundred pounds recently on clothes and shoes. Clothes and shoes she had not yet worn. Clothes and shoes sitting in their boxes and bags, almost as if they were never intended to be used, as if they had some other purpose than to be worn.

'You know what this is like,' the officer muttered. 'It's like that place in Stow we went to. The shoplifter's place, with all that gear stacked on the floor. All those jackets. Remember?'

The other man did remember. This was the same, and yet not the same. Chronic thieves like the sad middle-aged woman in Stow never mixed their thefts with their ordinary clothes. They lay like trophies, inanimate and lifeless spokesmen for a disease. Persistent professional thieves did not often mix their thefts with their personal stuff. Theft wasn't personal. More often than not, as with the shoplifter, everything went into a spare room or a loft, a room packed floor-to-ceiling with stolen goods. He hadn't seen anything like this before, where the new items were carefully put away with well-worn clothes. It was like two lives being pushed together, two sets of desires, two images of a person. It was hard to define, hard to get a handle on. It just didn't sit right.

The first man went to the stairs, and shouted down.

'Inspector . . .'

'What is it?'

'Sir . . . did you find any credit slips, receipts?'

'Just got to her finances now.'

It was the thinnest, neatest wallet in the whole house. No back issues, no old documents had been kept here; everything related either to the current year or to the previous one. Alisha Graham's insurance and credit cards were up to date, paid off monthly. Electricity, gas and phone were paid by direct debit.

'I don't get it,' Wallis murmured.

'Get what?' his colleague asked.

'This.' He indicated her finances wallet with a wave of his hand. 'This woman doesn't spend much. Look at that electricity bill. Low, even for a spring quarter. Gas is low, too. Not much food in the kitchen. No new furniture in the house.' He tapped the wallet with one finger, thoughtfully. 'This woman doesn't spend except on books and her car. She isn't one for home comforts. Doesn't turn the heating on. Doesn't cook much, by the look of it. Spends most of her time out, or on this computer. Doesn't care much about the house except to give it a rough clean over every now and again. Doesn't like fuss. Doesn't have anything that isn't purely practical.'

'And nothing for clothes . . . with all those clothes upstairs.'

Wallis shook his head. 'Exactly. A person who doesn't spend has a room full of new clothes. Either she stole them, or they were given to her. She certainly didn't buy them recently.'

'Maybe she's had them a long time.'

'Could be. Have to look into it. Take the stuff back to stores, find out when the items were last on sale. This year? Last year? When?'

'If she didn't buy them herself . . .'

Both of them looked at the laser print of the photograph that had been found in the house the day before, tacked now to the mantelpiece above the empty grate. Looked at the naked girl stretching down to the floor in Alisha Graham's bedroom. Another print like this one had already been sent to the investigating team in Melkham, but there was no word yet as to whether it bore any resemblance to the girl that they were holding in custody.

Wallis sighed. 'Presents from an admirer?' he wondered exasperatedly. 'To a woman of seventy? All kinds of clothes she didn't want to wear?'

He looked down again at the papers in piles on the floor. 'So much doesn't add up,' he said, voicing out loud a thought he had had fifty times already that day. 'A message on the computer screen that doesn't tie in with the tone of all this academic stuff. A picture of a girl like that . . .'

'A girlfriend,' the other man said. 'Special friend.'

'Sexual. Intimate, anyway. Intimate enough with her to take a photo like that . . . it would mean that the girl was often here. But there's nothing here that belongs to a young girl. Not an earring, a bar of soap . . . I mean, look in the bathroom. Ever seen a teenager's bathroom? Full of body sprays, Tampax, three different kinds of shampoo . . .'

'She didn't live here, then.'

'Not only didn't she live here, she didn't leave a trace of ever having been here.' Wallis looked hard at the photo. 'Yet she was undressed in Alisha Graham's bedroom. What was it, then? A joke with one of her students? Strange kind of joke.'

'Maybe . . .'

Wallis glanced round at him. 'What?'

'Maybe Alisha Graham paid her. For . . . services.'

'Sex, you mean.'

The younger man blushed. 'Yes.'

Wallis smiled at him. 'You're too sensitive by half,' he said. His fingers drummed on the desk top. 'There's nothing else here of a sexual nature. Nothing in the books and mags.' He frowned. 'This wasn't a sensual woman,' he said. 'Look around you. This is a practical person. She wouldn't pay to get warm, let alone for someone in her bed. And she's not a touchy-feely woman at all. This is what you'd call a spartan existence.'

He went back to the finances wallet. 'The only thing she appeared to care about at all was the car. The most expensive thing in this wallet is a repair bill for a new car radiator, just before Christmas. Servicing two months before that. The credit cards . . .' He looked at the two statements again. 'Petrol. Internet provider bill. Magazine subscription. Print cartridges. Food bill from a supermarket – wouldn't feed my cat.'

There was a footstep on the stairs. They glanced out to the hallway. One of the team was coming down from the bedroom, with a small box held out in front of him.

'Inspector Wallis . . .'

'What is it?'

The man got to the doorway. His expression was unreadable. He held the box out in front of him as if it might explode.

Wallis got up. 'Another pair of shoes?'

'No,' said the younger man. He glanced into the box. His mouth turned down, suddenly, with distaste. 'Not shoes,' he said. 'Not shoes . . .'

Fourteen

He made half a living catching rats that spring.

They were all over the hill, right through the thirsty crops and into the mine buildings. Aubrete himself had come to him, to his waggon hidden among the copse of trees, covered with a green cotton sheet so that the colour could not be seen from the lane. He didn't want to be in their eyes, held in their sight.

The Egyptian never went down to their houses, not even in search of women. Sometimes they looked at him with their small half-smiles, looked at his arms, looked at his body. But he never went to find women. Not here, not now.

Aubrete found him in the evening.

The mine owner came striding through the trees as the Egyptian tended his fire, gutting the rabbit he had taken from Aubrete's own land. It was a killing offence, the rabbit. But Aubrete hardly looked at the carcass, though it lay in the Egyptian's grasp. And that was when he first knew, for sure, how wrong things were.

'I want you to come to the pit and set traps,' he said.

The Egyptian looked at the landowner, at the soft dark coat, at the white face. 'I can't come there,' he said. 'I go anywhere else you want, sir. But not there.'

'I will pay you.'

'No matter,' he said. 'Begging pardon, I can't come.'

'Why not?' Aubrete had demanded.

He couldn't tell him. He couldn't come near. Even within half a mile of it, the screaming of the entrance made his skin crawl. The door was broken, the Gate lay naked. It was a terrible thing, terrible in his throat and head, like fever. It woke him with its keening in the darkness.

83

He saw Aubrete hesitate. He knew that there was something else. He read it in the man's face.

Water.

Too much water.

'Will you come and look, at least?' Aubrete asked.

The question was so soft that it astonished him. It caught him so off-guard that he heard himself say, across the smoke of the fire that drifted between them, 'I shall come and look, if it pleases you.'

And that was all, a few little words.

The end began that way.

Fifteen

It was early afternoon when Anna Miles came back to the police station in Melkham. Robert Wilde was waiting for her.

'I'm sorry to bring you out again,' he said, as she stepped over the threshold.

'It's all right,' she replied. She was surprised to see him waiting for her in the foyer.

'I wanted to check something in your statement,' he said.

He led her through the station. She walked behind him, her handbag held close to her chest, her arms crossed over the bag. They reached the bottom of the stairs, and he paused to let her pass, indicating that she should go on up ahead of him. As she did so, he noticed how tired she looked. She gave him a tentative half-smile. He took her to his office, and, once inside, brought forward a chair for her. 'Tea?' he asked.

She shook her head. 'No thanks.'

The door opened. Sandys came in, and sat down in a chair in the corner of the room, next to a tape deck.

'You don't mind if Inspector Sandys is here?' Wilde asked.

She looked from one to the other.

'You don't mind if we record the conversation?' he reiterated.

She stared at the tape now poised above the deck. 'I thought this was just a chat . . .'

'That's right. We have to record things, though.'

'Just a minute,' she said.

'You're not under arrest,' he reassured her.

Her mouth dropped open in surprise. 'I haven't done a bloody thing wrong,' she said.

Sandys clicked the tape on. He noted their names, the time.

Wilde did not sit down, but stood by the window and looked at her. 'How are you?' he asked.

The question surprised her. 'I'm OK.'

'Sleep well?'

She frowned. 'Yes.'

'Lots of people don't. They say they can't. People who find a dead body.'

'Do they,' she murmured. Not a question.

'You didn't sleep the night before,' he said. 'Tuesday.'

She glanced up at him. She was still fuming over the tape, the presence of Sandys, the feeling that she had been set up. Worse still that she was under some sort of suspicion. 'I'm sorry?'

'When we looked in the house,' he said. 'I couldn't help noticing that you hadn't been to sleep.'

There was a silence. Anna looked down at her hands.

'The furniture was disturbed,' he said.

She did not move. Then, quietly, she murmured, 'I don't always sleep.'

He nodded, as if this were a quite normal reply to his observation. He walked round to his side of the desk and drew a piece of paper from the file lying there. He read it through. 'What did you think,' he asked, 'when you heard that car coming down the track?'

'Think?' she asked.

'Well . . . it's one o'clock in the morning. There's a storm outside. You're not expecting anyone . . . not waiting for anyone.' He looked at her steadily. 'That's right, is it? You weren't expecting anyone?'

'No,' she said.

'You were pulling a mahogany chest across a door . . .'

'No,' she said.

He acted surprised. 'I'm sorry? *No?*'

'I . . .' Her voice trailed away.

'Right,' he said, slowly, without tone in his voice. 'So you weren't expecting anyone. You were in your bedroom, awake, dressed.'

'Yes,' she murmured.

'And then you hear a car. You hear a car's horn blowing, and it's coming nearer.'

'Yes.'

'And it's obvious it's on your track. You see the headlights.'

'Yes.'

'How fast was it travelling?' he asked.

'I don't know.'

'Do you drive yourself?'

'Yes, I . . .'

'Could you guess the speed, perhaps?'

'I suppose it was travelling fairly fast,' she said. 'It came over the hill soon after I heard the horn. The headlights . . . they bumped. Going over the ruts in the lane. They bumped and swayed, as they would if you hit them too fast.'

'Right. Thirty miles an hour? Forty? Fifty?'

'Thirty maybe.'

'OK. Quite a speed for a rainy night on an unsurfaced road.'

'Yes . . .'

'The sort of speed you would do yourself?'

'No. I'd be worried about the car. The axle. The exhaust.'

He smiled. 'Yes, so would I.' He sat down, and drummed his fingers lightly on the desk. 'So you and I would go slower. But this person didn't. This girl.' He paused. 'Which suggests . . . what?'

'I don't know.'

'She was in a hurry?'

'Well, obviously.'

'In a hurry, and knew the road.'

Anna frowned. 'It doesn't follow that she knew the road. You could just be anxious to get somewhere . . .'

'She was anxious to get to the house?'

Anna gave a half-shrug.

'Anxious to get to the wrong house?' Wilde persisted.

'I don't know,' Anna said. 'I'm guessing.'

'And yet . . .' Wilde picked up Anna's statement again, and read it. 'And yet, when she gets to this house, she doesn't get out of the car at first. And when she eventually does, she just stands in the rain. She even wanders off a little way.' He looked up again. 'Is that correct?'

'Yes.'

'So she wasn't *that* anxious to find you. Casually wandering off, calmly standing in the rain . . . those aren't the actions of someone who's anxious, is it?'

'No,' said Anna. 'But—'

'So she wasn't driving fast because she was desperate, frightened, panicked. She was driving fast to get to you.'

'No,' Anna objected.

'And you were up, waiting for her.'

'No.'

'Not frightened yourself?'

Anna put one hand to her forehead. 'Why should I be?'

'At an unknown intruder, late at night?'

She frowned. Her noticed her hands twisting in her lap.

'And this girl,' he continued, 'said nothing to you. She didn't react in any way. You sat her down on the chair and then rang us.'

'Yes.'

'Why?'

Anna looked completely baffled. 'Why what?'

'Why go out there and bring her in?'

'It was raining . . .'

'Granted. But she's a complete stranger, she's standing out there in the pouring rain . . . it's odd, isn't it? Peculiar?'

'Yes, of course it was.'

'And you were in the house on your own.'

'Yes.'

'Couldn't sleep, restless . . . and a car horn starts blowing in the middle of the night, and this total stranger turns up in the drive . . .'

'I couldn't see where she'd gone once she got out of the car. She left the engine running, the lights on . . .'

'So you went out.'

'I said in my statement. I hesitated. Eventually I went out to the car.'

'And found a body.'

'Yes.'

'And then you brought the girl into the house.'

'Yes.'

'A complete stranger, who'd arrived in this high drama in the middle of the night. She might have murdered this woman. You bring her into your house.'

'I . . . I can't really explain it,' Anna said. She realized herself now that she was wringing her hands, and made a deliberate, concentrated effort to stop. Without revealing the truth, how could she tell him why the sight of the girl had been a relief? 'She looked helpless,' she said.

'With a dead body in her car?'

'Yes. I know it sounds strange. I just thought it must be her grandmother, her aunt, a relation . . . it never occurred to me that she might have killed this woman.' Anna stared directly at Wilde. 'Is that what she's done? Is that what you're saying? She killed her?'

Wilde didn't answer the question.

Anna looked away from him. 'I wasn't thinking very clearly,' she whispered. 'I probably did the wrong thing, I don't know. I've just been . . . I'm tired.' Her voice broke a little. She swallowed hard. 'It's been difficult lately.'

There was a silence.

Sandys stretched his legs out, crossed his arms, looked at the floor. Anna stared at him, then back at Wilde.

'Matthew Aubrete,' Wilde said evenly. 'You do know him?'

Anna frowned. 'Matthew? Of course I know him.'

'But not very well.'

Wilde noticed a flush, a telltale wash of colour, on her throat.

'No, not very well,' she said.

'So you wouldn't know that Alisha Graham was coming to see him.'

'No.'

'You don't know anything about his plans?'

'His plans?' she echoed.

'Plans for the gardens. Why Miss Graham was brought here.'

'Not really . . . look . . .'

'Not really?'

'Well, everyone knows there's some problem with the water.'

Wilde paused. He held out his own hands, steepled the fingers. 'And do you know Dominic Aubrete?' he asked, not looking up at her.

She stole a sideways glance at Sandys. 'No,' she said. 'Just to recognize, that's all.'

'Just to say good morning to?'

'Yes, that's right.'

He nodded slowly. 'So you wouldn't ever have been a guest at the house?'

She said nothing, but, holding his gaze, she shook her head.

'A private guest sometimes, as a friend of the family?'

'No . . .'

'Perhaps when Mr Aubrete senior and junior were there, over the last year or so?'

'No . . .'

'When Mrs Aubrete was away?'

There was a prolonged silence. Both men watched her. She looked down at the floor. The flush of colour had spread to her face.

'Miss Miles?' Wilde prompted. 'Did you hear my question?'

She closed her eyes for several seconds. The knuckles on her clasped hands turned white. She opened her eyes, and bit on her lip before replying.

'Look,' she said. 'I just didn't think it was relevant. I didn't see how it could be.'

'Didn't think *what* was relevant?' Wilde asked.

'My friendship with Matthew,' she told him softly.

'Friendship? Do you mean an affair?'

She shook her head. 'It doesn't matter now,' she murmured. 'It's all finished with.'

Wilde considered her for some moments. 'And why is that?' he asked, at last.

'It's very complicated.'

'Is that why you were barricading the door on Tuesday night?'

'No. Not because of Matthew.'

She realized what she had said too late; raising her head, she gazed at the ceiling in exasperation.

'Who, then?' Wilde asked. 'Who was coming?'

'I don't know. No one.'

'No one? Come on, Miss Miles.'

She lowered her head.

Glancing over at Sandys, Wilde saw his colleague's raised eyebrows.

'What had happened?' Wilde asked Anna. 'Was it something to do with Matthew Aubrete?'

'It was just . . .' She seemed to cast about her for a reason.

'You had argued?'

'No, not exactly.' She leaned forward, her elbows on her knees, and put her head in her hands. 'He wanted something I couldn't give,' she said. 'He wanted to get married.'

'Is that so unbearable?' Wilde asked.

'No—' she said. She stopped herself.

'What, then?' Wilde asked.

A sound of frustration, a high-pitched note, escaped her. 'I just don't see what the hell this is to do with you!'

Wilde was regarding her with acute interest, as if he had heard something that he recognized in her voice. 'Where do you come from?' he asked.

'Oh Christ,' Anna muttered. Just for a second, she looked down at the floor, trying to summon a reserve of patience. It failed her. She got to her feet, snatching her handbag back into its defensive position across her chest. 'I've done all I can to help you,' she said. 'I don't know the girl, I don't know the Graham woman, Matthew didn't tell me why she was coming, I don't know why they turned up at my house or why I was damned stupid enough to go out to her when I should have just rung the police.' She paused to catch her breath after the torrent of words. 'I don't believe that you can keep me here,' she said.

Wilde walked quickly around the desk.

'I'm leaving,' she said, and turned for the door.

He managed to catch her arm, as gently as he could, as she opened the door to the corridor.

'Miss Miles,' he murmured, his voice so low that she could barely hear him. 'Who were you expecting, if it wasn't Matthew Aubrete?'

Sixteen

It had begun, like all good fairy tales, with a handsome prince.

It might also, like good fairy tales, have been in another century. It certainly felt like several hundred years had passed since Anna had met him. In fact, it was barely two years.

Two years last Christmas.

Anna Miles – or Anna Cray, as she had been then – had been a music teacher at a school in Manningham. She had been twenty-six and single. She had first seen him at the school, standing in the reception area, carrying a portfolio and a briefcase. He was tall and dark-haired, with a Latin look; she had smiled to herself as she saw him turn to shake the hand of the headmaster. Whoever he was, the man was handsome in the way of fifties movie stars, with a soft-featured, doe-eyed face on a severely worked-out body.

'My God, who is that?' the supply teacher had asked her, stopping at Anna's elbow as Anna took files from the stationery cupboard.

'No idea,' Anna said.

'Is he real?' the woman asked. 'He looks plastic.'

They had laughed, softly shushing each other, and turning away as the headmaster brought the man towards them down the corridor.

He was, she had found out that lunchtime, one of the architects working on the re-design of the school scheduled for that summer. She had learned his name, too. Ben McGovern.

He was too good to be true. Too handsome, too smooth, too clean. Unreal.

Every year, at Christmas, the music department organized a fund-raising concert. Its metamorphosis had been Anna's idea. Without dispensing entirely of the usual carol concert, she had arranged a community play, amalgamating the juniors' nativity play with a strolling band of fiddlers, dancers and jazz brass. And several changes of scene that brought the art department to its collective knees. That first year, the play had turned out to be half a walking cacophony and half – thankfully, the second half – a triumphant success, with parents standing on their mock Paris-café benches, English village green, Hawaiian beach and Bethlehem stable yard to cheer Anna's flushed curtain calls.

She had not known that Ben McGovern was there at all until he had materialized out of the crowd, holding out his hand by way of greeting.

She had taken it.

Anna thought of that hand, and of Robert Wilde's restraining grasp on her arm as she had left the police station, as she drove back to the cottage. Ben McGovern's hand, so smooth and soft and unlined. Robert Wilde's rougher fingers, that slightly caught the thread in her jacket, and made a tiny, abrasive, sibilant noise as she tried to shrug away from him. Two very different hands. She had looked down at Wilde's, and seen the few first age spots on the back of his hand. Seen the broad hand, the square nails on short, practical fingers. Ben's fingers had been long and delicate.

'Like a pianist,' she had said, as a joke, that first night.

'Or a violinist, like you,' he had added, holding her hand slightly too long in his own.

She looked ahead, now, at the road.

The turning was coming up for the cottage. She saw other cars drawn up on the verge next to the gate. The occupants were out on the verge, apparently waiting for her in the bright afternoon sunlight.

'God, no,' she murmured to herself.

As she slowed down, she then saw the police car pulled up inside the gate. The officer standing alongside it waved her through. As she turned in at the gate, the car slowed down to first gear to get over the cattle grid, faces pressed up to her window.

'Who's the mystery girl?' one man shouted.

Worse still, 'How's Matthew?' yelled a second voice.

There was a flash of a camera. She put up her hand to shield her face.

Too late.

She accelerated away, giving the police officer the slightest of waves. It was tough going at speed down the track, the car bouncing from one side to the other; only when she had gone a hundred yards did she manage to take a breath. She looked in her mirror, and saw the knot of people still watching her at the gate. Gritting her teeth, she went down through the gears until the car slowed to fifteen miles an hour. Slowly . . . slowly. Think what it must look like to them. Slowly, slowly. Speed was guilt. *Speed was fear.*

Ben had told her that she drove too fast. She had never given much thought to it before he had remarked on it: she was always late, always in a hurry, but had never taken any serious chances with her driving and had never considered herself any sort of liability behind the wheel. Until Ben.

He had treated it as a joke at first. 'Whoa,' he would say, as if pulling on the reins of a horse. 'Red means stop.'

He had laughed, sitting there at the traffic lights on the night that she had given him a lift home. His own car had been in for a service; he had spoken of it, much to her private amusement, with great affection, as if the thing were alive. She had turned her head to him while they waited at the lights.

'It wasn't red,' she had objected ruefully, not quite minding the criticism. Not quite. Braking hard after his remark had forced her seatbelt to lock, and she had eased it away from her shoulder.

'You need one of those flying helmets,' he had said, returning the smile broadly. 'Like World War One. And a white scarf that sticks straight out at the side. And a pipe. And you can call me Biffo.'

It was only much later that his implication at recklessness wormed its way through to disturb her. To add to all the other things.

She drew up now outside the house.

She turned off the engine and stared at the view of the rolling hill, the line of the sea, the white horizon.

She was stuck, she thought. Stuck in a quicksand. Grimacing, she shut her eyes and tried to push that particular image away.

Impossible to move. Forwards. Backwards. Robert Wilde had made her promise that she wouldn't leave the area. He hadn't let her leave the station until she had given him her assurance. She sat for a few moments longer wondering what the odds were if she broke that promise and left tonight. Would the police officer on the gate ask her where she was going? When she didn't come back, would they trace the car? How long would it be before they found her again? Before she had to come back again, having neatly branded herself as some kind of guilty party by leaving . . .

She sighed. She looked at her watch. Three o'clock. She put both hands to her face, then rubbed her forehead. Getting out of the car, she searched for the door keys in her handbag without really looking up at the door itself.

When she did, she saw that it was already open.

She stopped. Put her hand, unconsciously, against the base of her throat, knuckles pressing against the windpipe.

She looked up at the rest of the house. Nothing else gave any kind of clue. The roses spread across the grey stone, the glimpse of curtain at each window. She looked around herself. No car. No one in the fields. She took a step forward, bending down a little to see along the hallway. It was empty. It looked the same as usual. She could see her jacket hanging on a peg. The hall table. The mirror. The end of the corridor hidden in shadow.

They called Robert Wilde down to the incident room at just gone three o'clock. When he got there, a small crowd was gathered around the TV monitor, looking again at the tape.

When they saw him come in, they moved aside to let him sit down. The DC rewound it.

'And where is this?' Wilde asked.

'Ballantyne Hill.'

'I know it,' Wilde said.

Ballantyne Hill, on the Somerset Levels, was a peculiar cone-shaped outcrop. From some angles, it looked perfectly regular, some two hundred feet high, an island on a flat green table. From the minor road that ran alongside it, however, it looked more like the bow of a ship, with a steep face and a smooth slope running off to the south. No longer an island, but a green ship breasting a shallow green sea. Trees fringed the path to the summit on this side: low-growing hawthorn that was a froth of white in the spring.

On the top stood what had once been a church. Everything but the tower had long since fallen down, and the tower itself was tiny, no more than twelve feet square inside. There were no legends attached to this tower as there were to Glastonbury, some twenty miles away. There was no holy well at the bottom of Ballantyne Hill, and no story of the Holy Grail being buried somewhere close. Few, if any, tourists stopped here. If they did, it was only to climb the slope to see the flat land spreading in all directions, to gain a breath of fresher air on hot summer afternoons. A forgotten little promontory, it guarded a minor road junction, a crossroads. A hundred yards down from it stood a farmhouse, and a small garage.

'Middle of nowhere,' Wilde mused.

'The garage has got two pumps, petrol and diesel,' the DC said. 'Two pumps, little shop. Only shop for ten miles. Yesterday's bread and papers.'

Wilde smiled. The most custom it could command was a breakdown service. Sure enough, to one side of the screen now, he could see the tow truck parked under a light.

'They put the camera in a couple of months ago. Some kids broke in and trashed a minibus they use for school runs.'

Wilde leaned forward intently. A car, Alisha Graham's car, was pulling into the forecourt.

The time was 1.56 a.m.

They watched without a word as the car came to a stop.

Alisha Graham got out of the driver's door.

A curious feeling went through Wilde as he watched her. For two days she had interested and preoccupied him. On first seeing her in that same car, still and cold to the touch, with a faint residue of condensation on her skin and clothes, he had pitied her. In death she had looked very old, her colour parchment.

But she had been a gifted and unusual person, that much was plain;

a vibrant and intelligent person with a circle of much younger friends. So vibrant, in fact, that it seemed she had maintained some sort of physical relationship when she was in her seventh decade. Everything about her spoke of a positive approach to life. This had been a busy woman, and yet, for all that he knew about her, he had never heard her speak, never seen her move. Until now.

She looked about her, one hand on her hip. Then she walked to the pump, and looked at the padlock. She seemed to shrug or sigh, probably with annoyance. Wilde watched her gait closely. She walked with ease, with a mannish stride.

'How much petrol was in the tank?' Wilde asked.

'Quarter full,' someone said at his back.

'So,' Wilde mused, 'she was running short, but it wasn't desperate. Why stop? Why not wait till morning?'

They watched.

Alisha walked away from the pump, straight down the forecourt, and out of sight.

In the moments that remained, they looked at the car, trying to see the passenger. That side was deep in shadow. There was no movement.

'Is the girl there?' asked Sandys.

They couldn't be sure. The car was parked almost under the camera.

'What's she doing?' Wilde asked. 'Where's she gone?'

On cue, Alisha Graham came back. She got into the car, started it up, reversed out of the petrol bay, and drove away.

'Did you see any other vehicles pass?' Wilde asked the men round him.

'No.'

Wilde sat back. He drummed one foot on the floor, a habit that he had when he was concentrating. 'See if we can get any enhancement on the passenger side,' he said, after a moment. 'Go down there and talk to the garage owner, the people in the farmhouse. They might have heard her or seen her.'

'In the middle of the night?'

Wilde sighed. 'You never know,' he said. 'Got to try.'

*

Another darkness.

Another hallway.

Anna Miles had been at a parents' evening at the school. It was January, seventeen months ago. Cold and pitch black. She had stopped for a drink with two other teachers, and then walked home. On the quiet and narrow street, the cars were parked either side. She had hurried up the step, her key in her hand, shivering. Still smiling from a joke that someone had made as they left the pub. She had carried her briefcase under her arm, a battered leather bag whose clasp had long broken. It was stuffed with papers, a bulky package. She had got in, closed the door, and pressed the light switch.

It didn't work. Cursing softly, she had made her way up the narrow hall, felt for the stairs, and put her bag down on the first step. The house was Victorian, an end terrace. It was her first home, and she had bought it cheaply because it was falling apart. Having spent all her money on a new roof and re-wiring, there was nothing left to decorate or furnish as she would have wanted. The rooms still had the florid, faded carpets of the previous elderly owner; the walls were still encrusted yellowish paper. The kitchen boasted a stone sink and an old gas heater and a series of Formica cupboards. In an effort to erase some of the gloom of the decor, Anna had painted a giant sun in a blinding blue sky on the far wall, using paint samples from the DIY store. Even now, in the darkness, she could see its comforting faint outline as she groped her way to the kitchen. Moonlight pooled on the floor.

She had opened the pantry and felt around for the fuse box. In here, on the back wall, was a fancy box that looked like Mission Control. She lifted the flap and carefully felt the switches.

One was up.

In the dark, she frowned. In an empty house, the circuit had tripped and turned off the lights. Slowly, she pulled the switch down. The lights came on. She walked back out into the kitchen, shaking her head, puzzled.

Perhaps the circuit was super-sensitive now.

There was a movement outside.

A face came up to the back window, a disembodied face cast into high relief by the light from the kitchen. She caught her breath. He stepped closer.

It was Ben McGovern.

'Oh, my God,' she said. 'You frightened me to death.'

He smiled, then made a gesture that he couldn't hear her. He pointed at the locked back door.

She had hesitated only a fraction of a second. He was grinning, shaking his head, saying something. And, after all, he wasn't a stranger. She knew him. She had opened the door.

'You caught me out,' he said.

'What on earth are you doing out there?'

He raised his eyebrow. 'Didn't I just say? You caught me red-handed.'

She stared at him, utterly bemused.

He had laughed softly, and looked at his feet. 'I thought I'd be very clever and deliver something to your back door while you were out.'

'Deliver something?' she had echoed. She caught sight of the kitchen clock out of the corner of her eye. It was twenty past eleven.

'This,' he said. He held out a parcel. It was small, rectangular. Wrapped in gold paper.

She had stared down at it. 'What is it?'

'A thank-you,' he said.

'For what?'

'Giving me a lift.'

She shook her head. That had been four weeks previously. Other than seeing him about the school, and passing the time of day, they had not spoken to each other since.

'I know this seems weird,' he had confessed. 'Lurking about in the shadows.' He gave a shamefaced shrug. 'Please take it. It isn't much.' He had turned to go.

She put a hand on his arm. 'Come in,' she had said. 'While I open it.'

She stood in her doorway now, looking down the darkened hall, thinking of Ben McGovern stepping into her house. Cold horror swept over her. She shuddered, an involuntary reflex, a sensation of disgust. Guilt. Anger. She even remembered the sound that his shoes made as he walked into the house. Little steel heel-savers. An old-fashioned noise. The noise of a careful, frugal man. He had stood wiping the first drops of sleet from his coat collar.

'It's not him,' she whispered to herself now. 'He's not here.'

She edged forward. Everything in the hall of the cottage looked the same. Under her breath, like a prayer, 'Not here. Not here.'

She looked around the door of the sitting room. It was just as she had left it. She edged towards the kitchen of the cottage, and pushed the door with the tip of her shoe. As it opened, it slowly revealed the fridge, the units, the bread still lying on the board. Her unwashed coffee cup. The rim of the memo board, with its pinned stack of bills. The corner of the table.

And on the table was a small, rectangular gold box.

Seventeen

When the police in Manningham arrived at the vicarage, they were shown into the Reverend York's study by a girl of twenty or so.

She smiled at the two men as they sat down, and closed the door softly as she left.

'Your daughter?' Wallis asked. He looked around himself, at the fine art prints. At the photographs of Venice, New York, St Petersburg. At the polished wood floor and the green linen sofa.

'No,' York replied. 'A theological student.'

Wallis fought down his instinctive response, *some student*. The girl had been neatly and expensively dressed. Wallis had not had many student days himself – he was limited to two years in sixth-form college – but, from what he could remember, no student could afford much more than jeans and an Oxfam jacket. *A theological student?* his brain continued to echo, trying to match up words and image, and failing.

York, too, contradicted all his ideas about men of the cloth. In the course of his work over the last dozen years, Wallis had met a dozen different varieties. He had met the elderly kind, who took life slowly and with tired eyes; he had met the young kind, the inner city appointees, who still had fire in their hearts. He had been given tea in comfortable rectories in the Cheshire countryside, and mugs of the stuff, thick and tarry, in sixties vicarages on no-go housing estates. He had seen gracious wives who entertained the local bishop to tea, and harassed wives who entertained notions of barricading up their kitchen windows to stop them being broken.

But he had never seen anything quite like Peter York.

The man was charmingly soft-spoken. He wore an open-necked shirt and chinos, and had an aura of money. Something in the set of the face; an assumption, not of superiority, but of security. The world would never fall down around Peter York's head. He was, Wallis realized, a high-flyer, the kind of man marked for high office – the Oxbridge graduate, the man with a private income. There were plenty of them in the police force, in the same way that there were plenty in every brand of business. Except that, until now, Wallis had not known that the church, too, could breed them.

This time, the thought in his head would not be suppressed.

'You don't look much like a vicar,' he commented.

Peter York smiled. 'Do I not?' he replied. 'Perhaps if I had my dog collar on.'

'Even then.'

'Well,' York said. 'Times change, even in the Church of England.'

How the old ladies must love you, Wallis thought.

Young ladies too.

'Are you married?' Wallis asked.

'No.'

'I thought all vicars needed wives.'

York laughed softly. 'Yes, I've been told that a wife would be an asset,' he admitted. 'But then, I don't want to marry an asset particularly. I'm a romantic in these things. I'm waiting for the right woman.'

The two men regarded each other.

Behind York was a computer and printer. York saw Wallis's eyes flicker in its direction.

'We do our magazines from here.' York took a small, stapled folder from a pile on the desk. 'Hot from the presses,' he said.

Wallis looked at it. There was a drawing of the local church on the front; the usual jumble-sale announcements and local advertisers inside.

'You do others?' he asked.

'Others?'

'You said magazines. The plural.'

York smiled. 'Oh, absolutely. We run *Wake the World* from here. And *Christ Almighty.*'

Wallis's colleague, Ebberley, let out a snort of laughter. He coughed to cover it.

'Have a copy,' York said, handing over a brochure.

This was a different enterprise entirely. The paper was glossy. A photograph on the front cover showed a woman and man facing each other. The head-and-shoulders shot suggested nakedness. Light poured around them.

'Classy,' Wallis commented.

York sat back and folded his hands in his lap. 'The church is losing clients all the time,' he said. 'I'm part of a group that aims to get them back.'

'Clients,' Wallis echoed. 'You sound like an NHS trust manager.'

'There's no reason why the church shouldn't chase buyers,' York said. 'We have an amazing product, after all.'

'Hardly a product.'

York shrugged infinitesimally. 'It doesn't matter what we call it,' he said. 'The fact is, we have something extraordinary on offer. Something that people are looking for.'

Wallis stole another look at the uncovered flesh of the female model. 'How well did you know Alisha Graham?' he asked.

'Not well. Hardly at all, in fact.'

'But she came to these services at the university?'

York smiled again. 'Ah, I see you've been talking to Beryl.'

Wallis did not react, other than by repeating the question.

'Yes,' York said. 'I noticed her.'

'Why?'

'I'm sorry?'

'Why would you notice one person at the services? I gather they're well attended.'

The phone rang. York reached swiftly across the desk and switched it to automatic answer. After two or three seconds, a fax rolled from the machine. He gave it the merest glance before considering Wallis's query. 'Alisha Graham wasn't the kind of woman to fade into the background,' he said. 'For one thing, she was fifty years older than most of the people present. For another, she was very popular.'

'And why was that?'

York's smile was ever-present. 'I can see you never met her,' he said. 'She had a rather loud voice, and she laughed a great deal. And questioned.'

'Questioned something in the services?'

'Oh, all the time,' York said.

'Didn't you find that distracting?'

'Not at all. I welcomed it. We bring all our conversations before God.'

Wallis was already lost. 'And how do you do that?' he asked.

'By affirmation.'

'Affirmation . . .'

'We bring our problems to the front of the room. Our questions. Hopes, whatever. Some like to prostrate themselves. Lie down. Some praise. It's whatever you feel you need to do.'

'And Alisha Graham did that?'

'No . . . she never did that. But she supported her friend.'

The door opened. The girl came back, with a tray of coffee. Wallis eyed the cafetière, the almond biscuits. Anything to prevent himself eyeing the girl, who leaned over him with a dazzling scent, and wafted away leaving the same heady aroma in her wake.

Wallis opened the folder in his lap, and took out the photograph found in Alisha Graham's house.

'Is this Miss Graham's friend?' he asked.

Peter York looked at the image for some seconds. 'Hard to say,' he commented, finally. 'She was certainly blonde.'

Wallis took out a second picture, one that had been taken at Melkham station on Robert Wilde's instructions. The girl from the car sat placidly in the forensic white overalls, her face calm and betraying no emotion whatsoever.

'Is this her?' he asked.

York straightened in his seat, held the image for a second towards the light and then, nodding, handed it back. 'Yes,' he said. 'That's her.'

'You're sure?'

'Absolutely.' He handed Wallis a cup of coffee. Just for a second,

Wallis sat slightly stunned, absorbing the fact that a name, perhaps an address, an identity could be put to the girl at last.

'Do you know her name?' he asked.

'Yes,' York said. 'Or rather, I know the name that she liked to be called. The name that Alisha called her.'

Wallis frowned. 'Do you think that it wasn't her actual name?'

'Yes, I do, rather.'

'Why is that?'

York smiled slowly. 'Because it was Omega.'

There was a fractional silence. 'Omega?' Ebberley said. 'Is that a name? I thought it was a dog food.'

Wallis shot him a withering glance.

York stood up. He walked over to a bookshelf, and took down a Bible, a handsome leather-bound edition. He turned its pages, found the place, and handed it to Wallis. 'Revelation, chapter 21,' he said. '"Behold, I make all things new ... I am Alpha and Omega, the beginning and the end."'

Wallis looked up at him after reading the text. 'This is what her name meant?' he asked. 'The end?'

York shrugged as he resumed his seat. 'It's certainly the literal translation.'

'But why would anyone call themselves that? Did she tell you?'

'No, never,' York said.

'You spoke to her?'

'Only two or three times. She was a very quiet girl. Intense. Alisha seemed devoted to her.'

The two policemen looked at each other.

'What is so surprising about that?' York asked.

'You spoke to her,' Wallis said. 'And she spoke to you.'

'Well, yes. Of course.'

'She speaks English?'

York laughed abruptly. 'Of course she speaks English. Why is that so remarkable?'

Wallis smiled. 'Because she hasn't said a word since she was taken into custody.'

York seemed indifferent. 'She certainly has no problem with speech,' he murmured. 'No impediment, that is.'

He stared at them for a moment or two, then at his hands in his lap.

'Yes?' Wallis asked. 'Is there something else?'

'I don't know how relevant it is,' York said.

'Let us be the judge of that.'

York looked up again. 'She's wearing forensic overalls in that picture,' he said. 'Why?'

'We're still investigating.'

'I see.'

'What else did you want to say about the girl?'

'Nothing,' York said.

'Where did she live?'

'I don't know that.'

'Did she live with Alisha Graham?' Wallis persisted.

'No, I don't think so.'

Wallis sat back, frustrated. 'So you don't know her real name, or where she lived,' he said.

'No. I'm sorry.'

'Was Alisha Graham interested in God, in Christianity?'

York gave another enigmatic smile. 'Well,' he said, laughing softly, 'no. Not really. She was interested in the afterlife. The progression of the spirit. Death itself.'

'Death?' Wallis echoed.

York again took his time to reply. When he did so, he leaned forward, carefully framing his words. 'My purpose as a priest is to lead forward to the light,' he said. 'Enlightenment itself. Clarity of perception. An opening of the spirit, a pathway to a greater reality. My own pathway is through Christ, but, as in these meetings, if I meet with those who can't see that pathway, but who stand hesitating at the gate, then I allow them to come through, to come with us, with whatever words, whatever guise of belief, they prefer. I see that as my absolute duty. To stand alongside them as they try to find the way.'

Wallis sat in silence, looking into York's face. 'That must get you into a lot of trouble,' he said, at last.

York sat back abruptly, patently surprised. Then a flush came to his face. 'Yes,' he said. 'The route hasn't always been easy.'

Wallis glanced back to the magazine that he had put back on the table between them. 'I bet you worry the powers that be,' he said.

York passed a hand over his hair, smoothing it. Smoothing ruffled feathers, Wallis thought, with a touch of minor triumph. He was aware of having pierced York's armour, found his exposed spot. The Church of England had come adrift in the recent past with charismatic worship, fending off accusations of abuse, paddling like mad to get back into line.

Wallis slowly put down his cup.

'What did Alisha Graham ask you about death?' he asked.

York shrugged. 'She seemed to have read a great deal on the subject of ancient ritual,' he said. 'She was interested in how mankind had changed its perceptions of God.'

'Did it surprise you to be asked about such things?'

'No. After all, she was a historian.'

'Ancient ritual . . .' Wallis repeated. 'What, specifically?'

'Gateways, sacrifices, passages. The pyramids. That kind of thing.'

'Sacrifices?' Wallis echoed.

'Yes. The Incas. She referred to them once or twice.'

'Human sacrifices?'

'She didn't say so. Our conversation was more about why man felt himself to be so much closer to God than in the past. Sacrifices were tokens, passports through to God's presence. She was intrigued as to why man didn't need such passports any longer.'

'I see,' Wallis said, only half seeing. 'And what did you say?'

'I felt . . .' York began. He paused. 'I remember saying to Miss Graham that man's relationship with God had indeed changed, changed its perceptions, and she turned to the girl – to Omega – and she said, 'You see? You see?'

Outside, in the large rectory garden, a blackbird flew across the lawn with a ripple of liquid song. Wallis watched the window as, gently and persistently, rain began to fall.

He remembered the shoebox that had been brought to him from Alisha Graham's room. He recalled telling Robert Wilde of its contents.

Wilde had suggested that he should come to Manningham the next day: the primacy of the investigation was to be discussed – which force was, in effect, in charge. And Wilde was as intrigued as he was to see Alisha Graham's house.

The shoebox had contained several neatly folded sheets of paper, measuring not more than three or four inches square. Each one was beautifully inscribed with what seemed to be prayers; pleas for God to intervene in some unspecified problem. One referred to a burden that had been carried for too long. But what the burden was, and who carried it, remained unanswered.

More puzzling were the tokens.

Feathers, stones. And four small vials of blood.

Wallis looked up at York.

'We think that Alisha Graham may have carried out sacrifices of some kind,' he said. 'There was animal blood kept in her house.' In fact, until this moment, he hadn't thought anything of the kind – it had come to him, suddenly, as he linked the contents of the box with the conversation about Alisha's interests.

York said nothing at all. But his face did pale.

'You look as if you knew,' Wallis said.

'No,' York said. 'I didn't know.' He got up abruptly, walked to the window, and looked out at the rain. Then he turned back to them. He seemed to collect himself. 'I wondered,' he admitted. 'Yes, I . . . wondered, because of the angels.'

Wallis, too, stood up. 'Angels?' he echoed.

York remained absolutely still. 'Religion is not all tea and biscuits and hospital visits,' he said. 'It taps into the deepest of human feelings . . . feelings that are not always controlled. People turn to faith in times of despair, for answers . . .'

'What angels?' Wallis persisted.

York walked to his desk, and unlocked the top drawer. From it, he took a rumpled piece of paper: as he handed it to the police, Wallis saw that it was a cheaply reproduced drawing by what looked like a very childish hand. Crudely drawn angels, with disturbing violent faces, reached down out of a lurid and thunder-threatening sky. In their hands were bolts of lightning. Below them on the ground, massed faceless crowds, their hands apparently over their heads, as though trying to avoid the beings hurtling towards them.

Under the drawing was an address, *3a Pennystone Road.*

'You will undoubtedly see this if you go up to the campus, and talk to any one of Alisha's students,' he said. 'There was quite some talk about it last year. But it was nothing – a flash in the pan. I was told they had disbanded,' York said. 'I'm sure they have.'

'Who are *they?*' Wallis asked.

York seemed not to have heard him: frowning, he had crossed his arms, and was staring at the floor.

'They are . . . they were some sort of cult,' he said.

Wallis walked up to him. 'With sacrifices,' he said.

'I couldn't speculate. A student thing. I wouldn't attach any significance to it.'

For the first time since they had met, Wallis felt a rush of fury. 'You knew all along that this girl came from this cult,' he said. 'You knew Alisha was involved with this cult.'

York shook his head violently. 'No,' he retaliated. 'I did not know. I knew very little.'

'Did you go to this house?' Wallis demanded.

'Of course not. Why should I?'

'Where did you get this pamphlet?'

'They were handed all over the university last spring.'

'And you consulted with the church?'

'Yes. Nothing needed to be done. There was no trace of them. The house was boarded up. That's what I was told. It was a rumour. Perhaps even a practical joke.'

'But when this girl talked about being an angel . . .'

York put a hand to his forehead, pinching the line between his eyes. 'It simply didn't cross my mind. I'm sure it's nothing.'

'But Miss Graham asked about sacrifices!'

'No, she didn't,' York said. 'She asked about rituals and never mentioned sacrifice at all. She talked about it . . . you had to meet her . . . she talked about it wryly, with a smile. Dryly, almost, as if it were the subject of historical research . . . She was very sceptical . . .' York's eyes dropped away from Wallis. 'I'm sure there was nothing untoward.'

Wallis snatched up the pamphlet from the table where York had let it fall.

'Thank you, Reverend York,' he said savagely, as he turned on his heel. 'Thank you so much for your help.'

Eighteen

The Egyptian went to the pit in the morning, on Sunday.

They never hauled coal on the Lord's day, even in those first days, and the buildings were empty, the mine deserted.

He walked along the lane, and cut across Ox Leys and into Great Ox. Just as he came through the fence into Great Ox, a shuddering caught hold of him. It shook him as if he were caught in a storm. He stopped, prayed. Walked on. Stopped again beneath the lip of the hill, the pulley building in front of him, set on a scar of red clay. He had seen his mother die of diphtheria, and it was like that, the shaking, the cold.

He prayed as he thought of his duty.

Aubrete met him. They stood in the pit house and the Egyptian looked at the empty horse gin, the empty harness, the circular walk that the exhausted horse made all day.

'This way,' Aubrete said.

A foul breeze blew out of the mouth of the mine. The rope hung loosely over it, descending into the shaft. Men and boys were lowered every day by this rope. There were no engines, no cages, only the rope knotted at intervals, and, at each interval, a plank of wood passed through the knot. Every day, a man would sit astride each knot of rope, each plank of wood, and they would each take a boy on their lap, and the rope would judder downwards and then stop, as the next man and boy above them climbed on. When one hundred and eighty men and something approaching one hundred and twenty boys were stacked, a human chain, on the rope, the horse would begin to turn the pulley in earnest, and they would pass down. Down, down . . . nine hundred feet into a dark lit only by candles.

On a good day, when the air tasted decently, the candles would burn

112

quickly, and a man could use twelve a day. On a bad day, when the air was bitter, the candles burned slow. Three a day, each man.

The Egyptian stood at the top of the shaft, knowing what was necessary, and afraid of what was necessary. Horror lapped at his feet with the foul air. A three-candle day, God's Sunday.

'I must go down,' he said.

Aubrete shook his head. 'You can't,' he said. 'There's no man to operate the pulley. And no man at the pit bottom.'

The Egyptian turned to him with a face full of sickness. He could feel the hands of the Gate clutching at him. He knew what was happening in the village. He knew why the typhus was going to come to the knot of cottages on the coast path, directly above the Peacock Vein that ran out under the sea. He knew why a boy called Thomas Rogers would fall forty fathoms in this very pit, this week. He knew why the priest's wife would contract consumption this summer, and lie, a yellow shadow of her former self, in an upstairs room, while her husband took the vestry minutes when the mine owners met.

'I must make a sacrifice at the bottom of the hole you have made,' he said. 'To appease the spirit you have wounded.'

Aubrete blanched at his blasphemy. 'Do it here, now, at the top,' he said.

'Sir, it won't work,' he replied. 'You will still have flood. You will still have bad air.'

Aubrete took out ten full shillings and put it on the ground.

'Do it here,' he told him.

Nineteen

Laura and Matthew Aubrete sat on opposite sides of the bed in intensive care.

Between them, Dominic lay like a stranger: bloated by drugs, he was almost unrecognizable even from the florid and overweight man who had been the centre of their lives for so long. His face was bloodless and round – very like, Matthew thought, with a touch of childhood memory, the kind of dolls that had inhabited so many nurseries. Wax-faced, swollen-cheeked, their mouths pushed into an impossible shape, their eyes bland under pencilled brows. Dominic had that same plastic appearance now. The old man's hair had been neatly combed to his scalp, but a little dark curl lay on the blue pillow.

They had been called to the hospital half-way through the afternoon. The monitors next to Dominic charted his inexorable progress into death.

Laura sat looking across at Matthew with a sour expression. At last, she leaned forward and spoke with a vicious whisper.

'You needn't think I don't know what you've been doing,' she said.

Matthew regarded her coldly. 'I don't know what you're talking about.'

'I've been to see the trust manager.'

'Do what you like.'

'Whatever you've got him to agree to, it can't work.'

Matthew sighed. He looked at his father, then at the machines.

'Aubrete's run by a bloody committee that even you can't bend,' Laura continued. 'And as for trying to get your woman in, and suggest that the land's lost value because of this water . . .'

'I haven't done anything of the sort.'

114

Laura's face reverted into the most dangerous expression of all. It closed down and became a mask, with the faintest suggestion of a smile. 'If he's changed his will, I'll take it to appeal, and you will regret it,' she said.

The girl in the cell sat up abruptly, looking at the patch of sky visible through the window.

The one who stood at the Gate had turned his head for a moment, gazing away into the middle distance. She felt him. She followed his train of thought, picked up his tremor of feeling. Death was coming like a cloud of changing light and colour. She felt it touch the hand of the man lying in his uneasy sleep, and turn the hand so the palm was uppermost. Conscious drops fell on the palm, and travelled like a drug into his blood.

Here came the darkness and the dawn.

Here was the weighing in the balance.

She stood up, looked away from the sunlight, and down at the floor. The man at the Gate was silent, looking towards the image of the bed, the exchange of light in a secondary soul. Dominic Aubrete's last fleeting thought in life concerned his estate and his will. He who was connected by that smallest of threads, a collection of written words that claimed his ownership of the physical.

The girl smiled at the old fantasy. No one owned anything in the world. It was the first illusion. It was Dominic Aubrete's illusion. It was the illusion favoured by every man in the building where she now stood, except perhaps one. It was the illusion of narrow-mindedness, avarice. Of every deadly sin. You put your hand on an object, and claimed it. You named it. You paid for it. But, in reality, you owned nothing. You had only put your mark on a piece of insubstantial property, that would eventually decay.

The beginning and the end.

She began to pray.

Here was Dominic Aubrete's end.

Poor little dreams and illusions, all that he had. All he cherished. Little things. Words on paper. Numbers and figures.

115

His life fell softly out of his grasp. It had been fruitless. In sixty-nine years, he had changed nothing, merely reinforced his immorality. He was empty. He had nothing to exchange for his immortal life. He had nothing to save his soul. Nothing to trade for his passage. The things he loved were only ghosts. He would not take his women with him. Most of them had long since forgotten him. He would not take his food and drink, or his photographs of a young man in a rowing team, or the thin badges sewn into a Sudanese cap, or the memory of himself astride a horse holding a piece of silver, or the sensation of luxury as he slid into the seat of his car, or the sensation of the pen sliding across chequebook pages, his entire hollow assumption of power. None of that would go with him.

He couldn't carry his room, his bed, his clothes, his books. He couldn't even take his seat in the very corner of the kitchen garden, the only place he enjoyed with any depth. He couldn't take the sun on his face as he lit a cigarette there. He couldn't take his newspaper. He couldn't take his soft doeskin gloves. He couldn't even take the taste of green tea, his one healthy vice brought back from times abroad as a young and ineffective Army officer. He couldn't take the smell of candles, a perplexing love of his, faintly linked to his mother lighting candles at Christmas. He could take no memories at all. He could only take himself, the very heart of himself, the burden he had carried for others, the sacrifices he had made, the love he had devoted through his life.

And because he had never carried any burdens, and because he had nothing in his heart but himself, and because he had made no selfless sacrifices, and because he had no love, he would move very quickly indeed. He would travel alone, with no guide, into a softly folding panorama of grey. He would be submerged in his loss of senses, feeling no boundaries, having nothing to hold, seeing no light. Disorientation would flood him.

Poor Dominic.

So far to go in that numb landscape.

Behold I shall raise up evil against thee out of thine own house . . .

Nothing to trade for his passage, when the angels were waiting.

And some of the angels were terrible to see. Creations of the abyss. Creatures of the dark. Vengeful messengers, with outspread wings, and faces composed of echo, of faint traces of life, of shadows of being, the last frontiers of creation, the guardians at the edge of nothing, of obliteration, of dark chaos. She had seen those angels summoned before. She knew that they roamed the very rim of creation, absorbing the currents, turning them inwards, condensing them to mere pulses of matter. To become nothing, to give up eternal life, to be cut off from the pattern of life, to be thrown out of the weave, to be discarded, to be a faint fold in the folding grey, the worst ending of all.

I remembered God and I was troubled . . . I complained and my spirit was overwhelmed . . . thou holdest mine eyes waking . . .

She closed her eyes tightly, trying to hold back the shadows that hurtled towards Aubrete.

Thou holdest mine eyes waking: I am so troubled I cannot speak . . .

Others moved at the Gate, watching him.

Thou holdest mine eyes waking . . .

Look at them.

Look at them, she prayed, and be saved.

She dug her nails into her palm.

She broke the skin.

Dominic's breathing hitched, and stopped.

The alarm tripped on the monitor.

'What is it?' Laura asked.

Matthew stayed alongside the bed, moving his chair back to let the nurses through. He watched his father's face, a face without any change in it from the last few days, yet still suffused and looking angry and denied, the lips open as if ready to speak.

Matthew had endured countless rages out of that mouth. It was all he could think of at that moment. He had taken a temperature reading of mood from that mouth's shape for thirty-four years. Dropped his eyes from those eyes not because he was especially afraid of them, but because it was shaming to see how furiously out of control his father could become. Agonizing to read vitriol in the glance. It was a look that could freeze anyone in their tracks, and Dominic was a master of the insult and humiliation of his only son.

Humiliation as a five-year-old trying to ride.

Humiliation as a teenager dialling a girl's number.

Humiliation alone. Alone with his father, receiving Dominic's godly decision on his son's incapabilities. Dominic slumped in a chair with a glass in his hand, thumping his knee to emphasize his point. Spilling his drink and cursing the child. Matthew at eight watching a school report torn in pieces, a report he had to return to the school in the following term.

A hundred excuses for a parent whose only relationship with him was one of contest and disgust. A hundred punishments for Dominic's sake. Or perhaps not. Perhaps for his own sake, to retain a father he wished he had, a picture he had drawn to show others.

Now the same man lay in front of him.

Matthew thought he heard something.

A girl weeping. The brush of wings.

The nurse turned towards him.

'I'm very sorry, Mr Aubrete,' she said.

He stood up.

He made no move towards Laura. In fact, in that moment, he forgot she existed. Instead, he turned away, and walked out of the ward.

Twenty

Robert Wilde sat in the temporary post-lunch silence of his office, head in his hands. Beside him on the desk lay the remains of a sandwich, its crust sweating in the polythene wrapper. He stared morosely at the Diet Coke in its cold can. He ran his finger down the side, making a trail in the condensation.

A sea of papers littered the desk. They had been tidy first thing that morning; now, they reflected his own growing sense of confusion. His fingertip traced a neat straight strip on the aluminium. No straight path through this case, he thought. Remembering Alice's old picture books, he wondered if he were the prince in the Sleeping Beauty story, lost in the blackthorn hedge, trying to find his way to the castle, and finding thorns growing around him even as he cut them down.

Wilde took his hand away from the can, forgetting his thirst.

Who was in the castle?

Was it Anna Miles, with her fierce defensiveness, her own thorn fence? Was it the unnamed girl in the cell below, who wept and put her arms around his neck? She was a storybook heroine if ever there was one, he thought. The imprisoned princess with her long fair hair and her innocent and wounded expression, and her patent terror. Struck dumb by a spell. A spell that had something to do with Alisha Graham, or Anna Miles, or both.

Wilde's eyes fell on the forensic report that he and the team had been discussing in depth before lunch. He lifted the page that had most mystified him, ran his eye over the neatly professional script, the cold facts, the unemotional language. The box of words that held Alisha's death and all its tortuous and winding wrong turns.

Alisha Graham had died around midnight on Monday evening.

She had not, as they had first guessed, been dead for longer. She was merely very cold because of the coldness of that stormy night.

She bore, the report noted, several bruises to her throat, not caused by the pressure of thumbs and fingers, as might be expected by strangulation. Nor were they the result of clawing at her face, if she had been suffocated. They were the marks, it suggested, of a soft cloth binding that seemed to have been tightened and then slackened in several places. While this had caused underskin bleeding typical in a woman of Alisha's age – the bruise looking so much worse than it might have done in a younger person – Alisha had not died from the pressure of such a ligature.

Other marks on the body were equally puzzling.

There were the marks on the heels, for a start.

Wilde himself had not seen them; Alisha's feet had been hidden in the footwell and by Alisha's own posture of sitting upright in the seat, her feet on the floor. But there were, the report noted, deep scuffed grazes on her heels, which had also been both muddy and greened with grass. Tests were being carried out on the pollen and grass seeds that had stuck in the mud and the skin of Alisha's feet. Similarly, the reddish mud – not typical of the chalk soil in the Melkham area – was being analyzed.

Alisha had been dragged across a muddy field or track, the report said. Dragged with her bare heels in the mud. Scratches on the legs, feet and the backs of the thighs bore testimony to the same journey. Yet more bruises under the arms showed where she had been pulled. Under the arms, feet trailing. Not roughly held, the report said. Carefully, possibly with the perpetrator's hands clasped gently over Alisha's chest and looped under her arms from the back. Yet more grass stains and mud and seeds on her clothes showed that she had been laid on the ground. Perhaps as whoever was dragging her paused, more than once, for breath.

Wilde put the sheet down and replaced his head in his hands, closing his eyes, trying to visualize the scene. He knew the rest of the report by heart.

Alisha's hands.

Yet another obstructed, labyrinthine path.

Alisha's palms had been stained by a dark substance. Her nails were ringed, too, with dirt, possibly more of the same. That, too, had gone for analysis, but the pathologist had been certain that it was ash. Not cigarette ash, either. It looked too much like charcoal.

What had she been doing? Wilde wondered.

The ash of burned wood. The ash of a fire . . .

But where?

And why?

But that was not all, by any means. And the fact that it was not all was the heart of Wilde's dilemma.

Because Alisha Graham had not died as the result of murder, the report concluded. She had died of a heart attack. One massive, first, and fatal attack. A natural cause. A cause entirely consistent with her age.

Wilde opened his eyes, and picked up the phone.

He was through to Chief Inspector Wallis in seconds, and, at the first note of the other man's voice, with its thick Manningham accent, Wilde relaxed visibly in his seat, and started to smile. There was something infinitely comforting to him in the sound of his old stamping ground – even if the abrasiveness of Manningham was different to the softer Cumbrian. It was still north of Watford. It was home.

'You got my faxes?' Wallis asked.

'Yes.'

'Are you still coming up here?'

'Tomorrow morning,' Wilde confirmed.

'We've got something else,' Wallis said. 'Something that might tie the girl in. We've talked to the local vicar. The girl and Alisha Graham went to a kind of weird church together. Alisha Graham was interested in cults, and it looks like the girl was part of one. And she has a name.'

Wilde was momentarily distracted from his own revelation.

'Name? What is it?'

There was a soft laugh on the other end of the line. 'A kind of name, anyway. Omega. The vicar reckons it's from Revelation.'

'Omega,' Wilde repeated.

'And a possible address.'

Wilde sighed heavily. 'Hold on.'

'What?'

'It's not a murder investigation, Mark.'

A pause. 'I thought it was strangulation.'

'Yes, it looked that way. But it was heart failure.'

Another moment of silent consideration. 'What else?'

'Dragged through a track or field. Charcoal on the palms.'

'Dragged after death?' Wallis asked.

'Yes.'

'She had this heart attack when the girl was with her, then?'

'Probably. Possibly.'

'That implicates her. What the hell is the charcoal about?'

'Pass.'

'Maybe she terrified the woman to death. Has she said anything?'

'Not a word. She seems terrified herself, though. She prays.'

'Prays?' the other man said. 'Yeah, that would be right.' Wilde could hear a door opening and closing. 'Hold on,' Wallis said. A hand muffled the receiver, then Wilde's voice came back on. 'Just have to bring this lot up to date, then,' he said. 'How much longer can you hold the girl?'

'Without a crime?' Wilde laughed softly. 'Not long.'

'Bloody funny business.'

'I know.'

'You're still coming up here?'

'Yes. I'll drive up early in the morning – be with you by ten or so. Collate this mess, if nothing else.'

'OK.'

'I've got a TV appeal tonight,' Wilde told him. 'I'll carry on with it. I still might come up with some answers.'

'Good luck. We'll check out this address.'

'Thanks,' Wilde said. He settled the final details of where to find the Manningham station, and then, in a mood of resignation, put the phone down.

It rang again immediately.

He almost didn't pick it up – he was already on his feet, ready to go down again to the Incident Room. Putting on his jacket, however, he snatched at the receiver.

'Wilde.'

'We've just got a 999 call, sir. Thought you'd want to know.'

'A 999?' Wilde echoed. 'Who from?'

'The cottage at Aubrete,' came the reply. 'From Anna Miles.'

Twenty-One

Robert Wilde arrived at Anna Miles' cottage at four-thirty.

After a word with the two officers who had preceded him, and passing the old red car that belonged to her – glancing at its rusty body, the patched wheel arch, the fraying rubber trim of the windscreen – he found Anna in the sitting room. She was alone, hunched in an armchair, staring out at the sea. Her eyes flickered towards him as he came in, then away again.

He sat down, noticing the open violin case in the corner of the room, and the music stacked all around it. 'Tell me from the beginning,' he said.

She took some seconds before she began to speak. 'There isn't anything that you can do.'

'What makes you say that?' he asked.

'Because nothing was done before.'

'By the police? You reported something to them? Something like this, is that right?'

'Yes,' she said. She rested her head on one hand.

She looked different to earlier that afternoon. Her defences had gone, he realized. The rigid tilt of the head – the fiercely private light in the eyes. She seemed to have shrunk, become suddenly fragile, the vulnerability somehow emphasized by the faint Celtic lilt in her voice.

'If you don't think we can help,' Wilde said, 'why did you ring 999?'

'I panicked,' she responded dully. 'I'm sorry.'

'Don't be sorry,' he told her. 'Just tell me.'

This time, she looked at him. She really looked hard at him. Her eyes filled with tears. She rubbed them away with the back of her hand.

'You're very tired,' he said.

She took a tissue from her pocket, blew her nose, and wiped her face with the grudging look of a small child. Wilde's instinct was to get up and try to comfort her – an instinct, he realized, that was a father's reaction. Anna Miles had something of Alice's look – the tightly scraped hair, the set of the mouth that belied her vulnerability.

'I was working as a teacher and he came to the school,' Anna said, at last. Her voice was so low that he could hardly hear it. 'I gave him a lift home. Four weeks later, he turned up at my house late at night saying that he had a present, to thank me for the lift. I let him in,' she continued, dropping her gaze into her lap. 'His name was Ben McGovern.'

In the silence, Wilde could hear the clock ticking in the kitchen.

She suddenly stood up, picking up a cup that was standing next to the chair. 'I'll make some tea,' she said.

'If you like,' he replied.

He followed her into the kitchen. While the kettle boiled, she stood in the corner of the room, her arms crossed over her chest.

'I suppose you think I'm crazy,' she murmured.

'I don't think anything of the sort.'

'He didn't rape me,' she said. 'He didn't even touch me that night.'

She made the drink. He took the cup from her, and they walked back to the living room, where Anna sat down again in the same chair. She drank her tea. Wilde waited for her to speak. Finally, she did.

'He just stood in the house,' she said. 'In my house. He gave me the present – a gold locket in the gold-wrapped box.' She frowned. 'I don't wear that kind of jewellery,' she said. 'Not hearts, not bracelets. Nothing like that. They're too fussy for me. I don't like things hanging around my neck or wrists.'

Wilde drank his tea, put his cup on the table next to him. 'You refused the present?' he asked.

'I tried to, but he wouldn't take no for an answer,' she said. 'Besides it was . . . inappropriate. A gold locket in exchange for a lift home. It felt all wrong.'

'I see,' Wilde said.

'Do you?' she snapped. 'How perceptive of you.' There was a silence, then she sighed.

'What else happened that night?' he asked.

She shrugged. 'It was getting late. Almost midnight. I had given him a cup of coffee, we had talked about the school . . . there was nothing left to say. I wanted him to go. He was just planted there in my kitchen with a little smile on his face. I was so stupid, so stupid to ask him in . . .'

Her gaze drifted away. Wilde thought of the way she had also brought in the girl from the rain. As if reading his thoughts, Anna looked up. 'I did the same thing the other night,' she said. 'When you questioned me, I realized I had done it all over again.'

'But you got him out of the house that night?'

'Yes, eventually. I'd become frightened,' she said. 'I'd realized he could attack me, hurt me . . . worse. Just as I thought he was never going to leave, he did. Just turned on his heel in the middle of a sentence and said something like, "I can't stay here all night," in the tone of voice as if I'd kept him there too long, and he had lost his patience with me. He just walked up my hall, opened the door himself and stepped out into the street almost without a backward glance. I don't even remember what I said to him on the doorstep. Thanked him for the present, maybe. Just gabbled something out because I was so glad that he was leaving.'

'And then?'

'I locked the door. Locked every door.' She huddled down in the chair. 'If it were just that,' she said quietly. 'But it was only the beginning.'

'Of what?'

Wilde caught a movement outside the window. One of the constables had passed by. He heard muted voices, then subdued laughter. Anna Miles looked in the direction of the sound. 'It's funny,' she said. 'They think so.'

'Not at all. No,' he told her. 'I'll tell them to move away, if you like.'

She put up her hand to stop him. 'Forget it.'

Wilde inwardly cursed the distraction. 'What happened?' he prompted.

She picked at a thread on the fabric of the chair. 'At first, he would come and sit outside the house,' she said. 'Not every day. Sometimes not even right outside. But somewhere in the street. I would come home from work, and he would be there. Or he might turn up halfway through the evening. He never got out of the car. He never spoke to me, or knocked on the door, but sooner or later I would notice him, and, of course, as soon as I did . . .'

'Your peace of mind was shattered.'

'Yes,' she said. 'It sounds innocuous, doesn't it? A man sitting in a car and then, sooner or later, driving away . . .'

'How long would he stay there?'

She put one hand to her forehead, traced a line across her brow. 'Sometimes only fifteen minutes. Sometimes hours. There was no pattern to it. Once he stayed there all night.'

'You reported him to the police?'

'Yes.'

'And what was done?'

'Nothing,' she said. 'Oh, they came out, they talked to him. He said he was waiting for a friend. Not me. Some other friend. What harm was he doing? He wasn't breaking the law.'

'He may be now.'

'Yes, I know. But there was no law to stop him then.' She flattened her palm to her forehead, as if the memory was an actual, physical pain. 'And he's very plausible, so plausible,' she said. 'So polite.' She sighed. 'After a month or two, he stopped doing that, and started something else.'

'Something else?' Wilde asked. 'What, exactly?'

'Phone calls,' she replied. 'Silent phone calls. Perhaps once or twice a day. Then odd little things.'

'Like what?'

'Well . . .' she sighed, almost a laugh. Almost. Not quite. 'This will sound crazy. But I would come out of the house, and there would be something lying in the path. Nothing unpleasant. Just odd. Peculiar. A coiled piece of string. A playing card. A bus timetable. A shell. Lying in the middle of the path. The bus timetable was weighted down with stones, very neatly, like a frame.'

Wilde leaned forward, frowning.

'I tried to convince myself that it was children,' Anna said. 'I taught ten-year-olds and I hoped that one of them imagined it was a joke.'

'How do you know it wasn't?'

'I don't,' she said. 'I mean, I can't prove that it wasn't. But I do *know* that it wasn't. It was him. I would still see him at school. He was an architect for the school extension, being done that year. If I caught sight of him, he would always smile. But it was the *way* he smiled . . .' She broke off, closing her eyes, taking a deep breath.

Wilde leaned forward, elbows on knees. 'How long did all this last?'

'Six months,' she said.

'And why did it stop?'

She opened her eyes. 'Don't you understand?' she asked. She looked both angry and amazed. 'It didn't stop. It didn't stop. And then one day . . .' She hesitated. He saw her tremble. 'I had to get out,' she whispered.

'Why?'

There was a long silence. She stared at a point on the carpet, her face blank. Then, she looked up at him. 'His mother died,' she said, her tone squeezed to a monotone. 'I saw the announcement in the paper. It was . . .' She searched for the word. 'Florid. An enormous boxed announcement. She had died of a stroke. The words . . .'

'What about the words?'

'They were . . .' She clasped her hands in exasperation. 'They were loving, of course, but . . . too much. So much, it made your flesh creep. It was a poem . . . mawkish. The kind of thing a husband might write about a wife. *My dearest darling you are gone, and I alone must carry on, no more your loving hand to hold . . .*'

Anna made a face, a grimace of disgust. She stood up, as if to wrench away from the thought. She walked across the room, and stared out at the track, and at the place where Alisha Graham's car had stood in the rain, and where her own was now parked.

'On the day of his mother's funeral, he came to my house,' she murmured. 'I hadn't suspected it was him. I opened the door, and then tried to close it quickly. He put his foot in the door. I started to scream. He brought his face close up to the crack of the door, and he grinned at me. He said, *"I'm going to take you home, Anna."*'

Wilde stood up, on the other side of the room.

'I got the door shut,' she said. 'He stood banging his fist on the door . . . then he stopped, and I could hear him whispering and laughing to himself. And then he went away.' She shuddered. 'An hour later, the phone began to ring. It rang every thirty seconds for five hours. At midnight, finally, I picked it up. But he said nothing.'

She turned and faced Wilde. Outlined against the window by the afternoon sun, it was hard to read her exact expression.

Wilde looked away from her.

'You don't believe me,' she said.

He glanced up. 'I do believe you,' he said. 'But let me get this straight. This man has never physically attacked you. In fact, he has never touched you?'

'Not with his hands, no.' She laughed shortly. 'You don't have the first idea what it's like being a woman in a situation like this, do you?'

'I sympathize,' he told her. 'Genuinely, I do.'

She gave a most peculiar smile. 'He's inside my head,' she said. Then, she whispered, 'Vulnerable. That's what I'm talking about. You don't understand that. What it feels like.'

'Did he ever write to you?'

'No.'

'Leave a message on an answerphone?'

'Just silence. I've had the same kind of silent message here, too, in the last month.'

'I see,' Wilde said.

She turned away, as if angry. 'The bastard's here,' she muttered.

'No letters, no recorded messages of any kind,' Wilde mused. 'I don't suppose you managed to video him waiting in the street?'

'No,' she said. 'Jesus Christ!'

'I'm trying to think of evidence,' he explained.

She said nothing.

'And this was the reason that you came here?' he asked, eventually.

'Yes,' she answered. Her voice was animated by anger, perhaps contempt. Although he couldn't tell if the contempt were for McGovern, or for himself, and the slow and shambling way in which she obviously considered that the police had reacted.

'I left that same night,' she said. Her words were fast, clipped. 'I packed my cases, and I left my house, and my job, and I told no one, no one at all, where I had gone. I didn't even know myself where I was going. I drove south, as far south as I could get.' She put a hand to her face, troubled by the torrent of words that she had kept to herself for so long. 'I don't think I was in my right mind when I met Matthew Aubrete the next morning,' she said. 'The car had broken down on the top road, I had no real idea where I was. I was exhausted. I was standing at the side of the road. I could hardly speak. Couldn't make a sentence. Matthew phoned a car breakdown service. He recommended a hotel, and when I left after a week, he paid the bill. He showed me nothing but kindness. He never asked a single question. And he offered me this house.'

She stopped.

Wilde walked over to her. 'Why did you tell me that you didn't know Matthew Aubrete?' he asked.

'Because it would just make more trouble,' she said.

'How so?'

'Well, in the obvious way. His wife.'

'Doesn't she already know?'

A pause. 'Perhaps.'

'Then how could telling me make things worse?'

'Because things are balanced on a knife-edge up there,' Anna said. 'Laura has a talent for making life hell if things don't go her way. It's one of the reasons I don't want to see Matthew any more. I can't stand all that and . . . this thing . . . these phone calls . . . it's too much.'

'Why the knife-edge?' Wilde asked.

'His father is dying. There is a history.'

'Of what?'

'Of battling over the house. The will.'

Wilde considered her. 'You got involved in this?' he asked.

'No,' she retorted, with a distinct edge of irritation. 'Look, I like Dominic – he's – well, he's eccentric. We struck up a kind of friendship. He used to come down to the café, to get away from Laura. He likes music . . .'

'He knew about you and his son?'

'Yes.'

'Encouraged it?'

'He didn't disapprove.' She twisted her hands in her lap. 'He and Laura started out all right – in fact . . .' She stopped.

'In fact what?'

'Just rumours,' she replied.

Wilde nodded slowly. 'I see.'

'A nest of vipers,' Anna murmured.

'The father favoured you to spite his daughter-in-law?'

Anna shrugged, a helpless gesture.

'What did Matthew do?'

She looked into the distance. 'Matthew doesn't know what to do about anything at any time,' she said, without bitterness. 'When it comes to the estate, Laura runs it and Matthew spends his time trying to spoil her plans. There's a problem with the gardens over the water supply at the moment, and Laura is convinced that Matthew's to blame. I think he called Alisha Graham in to prove that it wasn't his fault.'

Wilde raised his eyebrows in surprise. 'Mrs Aubrete thinks that her husband is trying to sabotage the estate?'

'God knows. Probably.'

'And he is trying to prove he isn't.'

She sighed. 'Look, Dominic is an old bastard and Matthew is lost and Laura is vindictive. They all despise each other. All this talk of Dominic altering his will is just Dominic's way of throwing lighter fuel on a fire. He would do that to amuse himself.'

'Using you as the lighter fuel?'

'Yes,' she said. 'You see now why I just want to steer clear of them. I thought that if I just denied that I knew any of them, you would go away. I got into the relationship with Matthew when I was in all kinds of trouble, and now I want . . .'

'Peace.'

'Yes,' she said fervently. 'Just that. Peace.'

Wilde picked up both cups and took them into the kitchen. He stopped for a while and looked out of the window. Anna Miles had a talent, it seemed, for attracting trouble to herself.

He went back into the room.

'Have you gone back to your house at all?' Wilde asked.

'No,' she said. 'I don't exist. I died.' She turned away from him.

'But he has,' she said. 'Ben McGovern has come back.'

The steely control that had so unnerved Wilde from the first moment that he had met her finally broke. Anna Miles slumped to the nearest seat, put her hands to her face, and cried. And the noise of her grief was awful to hear. It was as if the sounds were being dredged up from the depths, from a place he could hardly imagine. A place that no one should be.

He let her cry. The sobs were dry, agonized, guttural.

'He's found me. I told you. He's found me.'

'How can he have done that?'

'I don't know,' she said. 'Everything was through a post office box. All my letters. On the night I left, I pushed a note through my friend's letterbox, with the house keys. Asking her to check every week. I left no address. I haven't even phoned her.'

Wilde thought of Anna lying awake, listening for the slightest movement outside. Perhaps lying awake for many nights. Never quite sure that she had been successful in evading her pursuer. Feeling him reaching for her. Wilde walked into the kitchen, tore off a piece of kitchen roll, and returned with it, gently prising Anna's fingers apart and placing the tissue in them.

After a few more moments, Wilde asked, 'Were you Anna Miles?'

'No,' she answered. 'My name is Anna Cray.'

'Did you know Alisha Graham?'

'No. Never.'

'You came from the same city.'

'Yes, I know.'

'She was a teacher, too.'

'But I taught primary. She was at the university.'

'It's not possible that your paths ever crossed?' Wilde persisted. 'Perhaps a teaching conference?'

'I taught music.'

'Did you go to church?' Wilde asked.

The question astonished Anna. She looked up. 'What?'

'Church.'

'No, never.'

'And the girl . . .'

'I never knew the girl. Although . . .' Her voice trailed away.

'Although what?' he asked.

She frowned. 'I don't know her, I've wracked my brain, I have no idea of her name, but . . .' She paused. 'There is something familiar about her. Something. But I don't know what it is. I can't think what it is.'

He didn't press her to try to remember anything more about the girl. Instead, he gently put his hand on her arm.

'Show me this gold box,' he said.

Twenty-Two

The land below Ballantyne Hill had probably been farmed for three thousand years, give or take a thousand.

Not always for wheat crop or cattle or sheep. Until the fourteenth century, the whole landscape had flooded regularly, until sea defences had been built on the coast, twenty miles away. The crop then had been fish in abundance. Even now the fields tended to be marshy, cut through with irrigation ditches. Further south they called them, picturesquely, the water meadows. Here, it was just the Levels.

They *were* level, too. Mile after mile of gently rolling land, patchworked into alternate pasture and crop. Occasionally the green was broken by the surrealistic yellow of rape, or the blue of linseed, until the land began to rise, and Ballantyne Hill itself made its surprising appearance. But Mike Musterne's family hadn't farmed below Ballantyne for three thousand years – only a mere eight hundred.

A dour family man of very few words, he drove the Landrover along the land at the back of the hill. It was growing dusk – a red line marked the sky behind the hill all the way to the Bristol Channel. Even now, with the first dew settling, the chalk dust flew up in the Landrover's wake, obscuring the view in the driver's mirror. It had been a long, warm day. Musterne squinted through both the dust and the smoke from his own cigarette, leaning down to look at the summit of the hill through the windscreen.

They had sheep at Ballantyne farm. He kept half in the pasture close to the house, and the other half were on the hill. It was a common grazing right that Musterne guarded as fiercely as if it were his, and his alone. He put sheep and cattle on the hill out of a sort of obstinacy, to

134

spite its occasional visitors. He swung the Landrover over, and got out, opening the gate into the field.

The hill looked odd tonight. He stopped to consider it.

In some lights – early morning, late dusk – it looked like a series of rings or hoops straddling a vast green cone. Like something at a fair, on a hoopla stall. Over the centuries, the soil slippage had created a rippling effect on every side. In this light, tonight, it seemed that a giant hand had carefully ringed the hill over and over again with a grey pencil.

There were old beliefs, here. Much older even than the grazing right.

In Neolithic times, the hill had been used as a burial mound. A pit had been dug in the summit, lined with stone. As the soil eroded, the stones emerged – several blunt thumbs keeled over at angles. On old engravings they showed quite clearly. Then, sometime in the sixteenth century, a little chapel had been built over the stones, and, for perhaps another hundred years, services had been carried out here.

The chapel, too, however, fell into ruin, leaving only a ring of foundations where the church had been, and a curious flat rock to show where the Stone Age barrow had been re-used as a flooring for the chapel. Now, the stones had worn glassy and smooth and looked almost modern. A piece of fancy brickwork, like a driveway or path, or an odd piece of modern art, lying perfectly flat at the summit and only visible once you had climbed the long rise from the fields.

Musterne drove the Landrover forward, and closed the gate.

The jeep rolled forward across the land until it reached another entrance. Here, the fence post had split, the rusted chain lock had dropped. Musterne got out and looked at it, kicking it for good measure. The gate posts were made from two lumps of massive timber, eaten by worm, cracked by weather, bleached by heat, but sunk so far in the ground that he had supposed that they would stand until doomsday.

'Bloody thing,' he muttered to himself.

He shored up the post and, taking a bolt cutter and pliers from the back of the jeep, he cut the chain and reset the lock. As he finished, he put his hand on the post. 'Bloody thing,' he repeated to himself, puzzled.

It was then that he noticed the shoe.

It was stuck in the grass at the side of the post, deep in the bindweed and thistles. Reopening the gate, he leaned down and picked it up, scratching his hand for good measure in the process. He turned it over several times. It was a woman's shoe, a size four. A blue deck shoe with a white lace. An old shoe, well battered, with a hole wearing in the sole and the white rim fraying around the ankle.

He weighed it in his hand.

He had found a few odd items in his time, especially on the hill. Hippies had once left all kinds of stuff – quartz, flowers, threaded grass necklaces. Ribbons, too, on the gates. Someone in the village had told him that Buddhists used prayer flags, and that probably the ribbons were the same sort of thing. He knew there was such a thing as a wishing tree, too, because he had seen one once in Scotland, on the Black Isle; a huge tree hung with all sorts of rags, each one a wish, a desire. He looked at the shoe. Not so much a wish as a piece of fly-tipping. He threw the shoe over the fence, into the hedge. He walked through the gate and up on to the hill.

It was just getting dark as he reached the top. He had a fancy to look out at the view. As he came over the last rise, he was rewarded with a long panorama, twenty miles of green slipping smoothly into shadow. Down on the road, cars were switching their headlights on, and the long straight road was dotted with them. Directly overhead, however, the sky was amazingly blue, the violet-tinged blue of last light. He could hear a motorbike revving in the village three miles away. A dog barking. Closer at hand, the soft noise of the sheep tearing at the turf.

He looked at the old church floor, then looked again as he was turning away.

The other shoe, a blue deck shoe, was lying on the glass-like smoothness of the floor. Next to it was the remains of a fire, a circle of ash. And around the fire was a ring.

He stepped towards it, trying to make out what it was.

He squatted down, and touched it with the tip of his finger.

It was a ring of stars, made with blood.

Twenty-Three

Robert Wilde sat back from the television that evening. The police appeal had just been broadcast.

'You looked funny,' Alice told him.

'What do you mean, funny?'

'Not like you. Too smart.'

He smiled at her grimly.

'And she's really said nothing at all?' Alice asked.

Wilde began picking up the supper plates. 'Look, I never told you that, OK?'

'Has she got a tongue?'

'Of course she has.'

'Well, some people haven't.'

He made his way out to the kitchen. 'She has a tongue, but she doesn't use it.' He stacked the dishwasher. Alice came out carrying a single spoon. 'You're a real help, d'you know that?' he said.

She grinned. She made a pretence of watching him for a while, then started to wash the two saucepans at the sink. Standing up when his job was done, Wilde leaned against the worktop.

'Allie,' he said. 'Do you believe in God?'

She didn't look up. She washed the pan methodically, then laid it carefully on the draining board. 'Yes,' she said.

'The God I taught you about?'

She smiled. 'In a white frock, with a thunderbolt in his hand?'

'No. Maybe. A real God.'

'Yes.'

'You do?' he repeated, astonished.

'I don't know why you're so surprised,' she observed calmly. 'You were the one who gave me all that propaganda about it.'

'What propaganda?'

'Christmas and Easter.'

'That's what I was supposed to do,' he said.

'Are you saying you told me it, but you didn't go for it yourself?' she asked.

'I don't know,' he said.

'You don't know what, exactly?'

He fiddled with the worktop trim, self-conscious. 'Various things.'

She turned to look at him. 'You told me Mum was in heaven, remember? Well, where is she if she isn't there?'

'Alice, I don't know.'

'You don't? You were very definite about it once.'

'For you.'

'You told me that and didn't believe it?' she said.

'It's not that I don't believe it. I want it to be true. I wanted to reassure you.'

Now it was Alice that stared at him in amazement. 'You did it, but you had your fingers crossed behind your back, right?' Alice wiped her hands and faced him, the tea towel hitched in one hand on her hip. 'You don't think she's around?'

He considered. He thought of the dream. 'Yes, I do.'

'So do I,' she said. 'That's what religion is, isn't it? Believing what you can't prove.'

He paused, considering. 'You believe all I told you, everything they said in Sunday school . . .'

'Actually,' she interrupted. 'I don't.' She put the tea towel on the radiator, folding it neatly. 'Vengeance is mine and all that. But I think there's something else, and somewhere else. Like *Alice through the Looking-Glass*.'

'What, some kind of Victorian nightmare?'

She laughed. 'No, Dad. Just when Alice looks through the mirror, and sees another world. Then she steps through, and she looks back, and sees the room she just came from, the clock on the mantelpiece . . .'

'Mum is in the next room.'

'And they all watch us.'

He looked at her seriously, in a new light. 'You think God is watching?' he asked. A chill ran through him.

'Not the God in a frock. But a force, maybe. Whole load of souls. Higher beings. Evolved ones.'

'Angels,' Wilde said.

'Yeah, like that.'

Wilde turned and walked into the room they had just left. He sat down on the couch. Alice came to the door of the kitchen and looked at him. 'What?' she said.

'Come and sit with me.'

She did so. He put his arm around her shoulder. 'Alice,' he said. 'Don't ever get involved in a cult, will you?'

'What?' she said, laughing.

'I mean . . .' He searched around to find out just what he did mean. 'When you've got beliefs – and I'm glad you've got them, that's good – but when you're convinced about something, people can take advantage.'

'Dad,' she said. 'I'm not going to shave my head and sing on the street.'

'No, I know.'

They both looked at the empty TV screen ahead of them.

Robert thought of what Anna had said that afternoon, that men had no idea of what it felt like to be vulnerable. He thought he had experienced that – the sinking feeling, at least, of not knowing where to turn, of losing his grip on security. Reality, even. He had felt like that for a long time after Christine had died, and, even now, the same feeling could sometimes surprise him. He had done all the right things, all the so-called recommended things to combat his grief. He had joined clubs – his squash club, a night-school class – and he had maintained his friendships, and he had even taken out a few women, the last one for over eight months. But the feeling – that small hours, end-of-the-world feeling – would occasionally still creep up on him. It was a physical thing. It struck him, and left him winded, while he was doing the most routine and inconsequential jobs. He would suddenly realize he had lost a vital part of himself, and he would gasp, just for a few seconds.

Was that what Anna meant, he wondered. The ground falling away, the shortness of breath? He remembered going to a residential course several years ago, on equality in the workplace. There had been a discussion then about aggression, both overt and subliminal. The women there had maintained that they never lost the sensation of looking over their shoulder, especially alone at night. They had claimed that men were always looking for a way in, a moment of weakness. He had thought it paranoid at the time. Now, he thought of Anna, alive to the slightest sound, all the time. Losing sleep. Losing everything else.

He turned to his daughter. 'Have you ever been followed?' he asked.

'Who by?'

'Anyone.'

'Yeah,' she said, in the long-drawn-out tone that told him he was stating the obvious.

'A man?' His heart had quickened slightly.

'Couple of times round the shops. Just round a counter,' she said. 'You know.'

He swivelled in his seat to look at her. 'They follow you round shops?'

'Boys do. And the perve.'

'The . . .?'

'The perve in town. The man with his carrier bags.'

This was complete news to him. 'What man?' he asked.

Alice began to laugh. 'Everybody knows the perve. He looks at you, that's all. He sits next to us on the benches in front of Woollies.'

'He . . .'

'Oh Dad,' she said. 'He's harmless. He talks to the girls at the make-up counters. He's got a loud voice, a bit nasal. You *know*.'

'I don't know. I've never seen him in my life.'

'Well,' she shrugged. 'He's there. Maybe it's because when you go shopping you just whizz round and whizz out again and don't notice.'

He considered. Maybe he wouldn't notice if someone followed him, either. Is that what it was? Men had a blind spot. They had no reason to question their physical security. No woman was ever going to put an arm around their throat and rape them down a dark alley. No woman was ever going to . . . what? What was Anna afraid of? A man who rang her up and left no message. A man who sat outside her house.

He couldn't quite get his head around it. If a woman did that to him, it would make him furious. But not afraid. How could he be afraid of a woman who sat in her car, or sometimes left a playing card on his front doorstep? Why would that frighten him? Why would a woman frighten him by bringing him an inappropriate present?

Maybe it wouldn't frighten him because he had never had to deal with it, he thought. Because women didn't do that kind of thing.

Did they?

'Alice,' he said. 'Do you think that feeling unsafe is what every woman feels?'

'Unsafe?' she echoed. 'No.'

'No? Why?'

She snuggled into his shoulder. 'Because I've got you. I'm a woman, and I've got you.'

His heart contracted at her innocence. Innocence and maturity in one package. In two years she would be sixteen. My God, sixteen . . .

'What did she do?' Alice asked suddenly.

'Who?'

'The girl in the picture. On the TV.'

'Nothing,' he said. 'That we can prove.'

'Is that why you're going to Manningham tomorrow?'

'Yes.'

'Was *she* in a cult?'

'I don't know,' he said. 'Maybe.'

'Why did she come here?'

'I don't know.'

Alice leaned forward to switch the TV back on with a sigh. 'You don't know much about anything really, Dad, do you?' she said.

Twenty-Four

Anna Miles arrived at the police station at seven-thirty that evening.

'I want to speak to Chief Inspector Wilde,' she told the desk sergeant.

'I'm sorry,' the man said. 'Chief Inspector Wilde is off-duty. What is it in connection with?'

She drummed her fingers on the counter. 'There's the other man on the Alisha Graham case . . .'

'Inspector Sandys.'

'Yes. Is he here?'

She was told to wait, and did so with bad grace, pacing up and down. When Sandys finally appeared, he looked terminally weary. 'Can I help?' he asked.

'I want to talk to you,' she said. 'About the girl.'

Robert Wilde had told Sandys about his visit to Anna Miles that afternoon, and the younger man looked at Anna now with a mixed expression. He knew it was poor practice to jump to any conclusions – fatal, indeed, to do so sometimes – and yet he couldn't help a gut suspicion of the woman in front of him. She had a neurotic look, he thought. The look of an obsessive, her restlessness betrayed in a continually fidgeting hand. Even now she was pleating the edge of her coat. A *bag of nerves*, his mother would have said.

If what she said was true, of course, she had plenty to be nervous about. Pursued across the country by a frustrated lover whose speciality seemed to be stalking women. *If* what she said was true. He had his doubts. She was the archetypal example of an unreliable witness, the kind that shattered under close examination. In three days, he had seen her reduced from a monosyllabic, affronted woman whose only currency in conversation was to deny everything, to an aggressively voluble liar. She didn't know Matthew Aubrete. But she did. She had been his lover. Was still, probably. She didn't know Dominic Aubrete. But she did. She didn't know the girl . . .

He showed her through to an interview room. The moment that they were through the door, Anna Miles began to talk, without even seeming to see his gestured invitation for her to sit down.

'I suppose he's told you,' she began.

'What, exactly?'

'Chief Inspector Wilde. He's told you about . . .' She almost blushed. 'The box. The intruder in my house.'

'Ben McGovern.'

'Yes.'

'He has.'

More pleating of the coat. He glanced away. She was distracting him. He arranged a chair for her. She walked to it, but still did not sit down.

'He said I ought to move house, go somewhere else,' Anna said.

'It might be wise, if he has followed you.'

She nodded. 'I think . . .' But she lapsed into silence, looking at the floor.

'What about the girl?' Sandys asked.

'I'm sorry?'

'You said that you wanted to talk about the girl.'

She seemed to come back to him from a great distance. 'Yes,' she said. 'I remembered. I remembered where I've seen her.'

'Oh, really?'

It was out of his mouth before he could stop himself. The fact was that he wasn't in the least surprised that she could suddenly remember. In his opinion – and the last few moments had confirmed it – she had known who the girl was all the time. The alternative – that the girl had simply turned up at the wrong house by mistake, after negotiating a hellishly long track at night – was, in his estimation, too preposterous. And that disbelief now manifested itself in his voice – an inflection very like disdain.

143

Anna Miles reacted immediately. 'You don't believe me,' she said.

'No . . . no. Please carry on.'

'You don't believe me at all.'

She was perceptive, he would give her that. 'It doesn't matter what I believe,' he said. 'The facts are what matter.'

She had frozen where she stood. For quite a few seconds, she said nothing at all. Then, 'I want you to find me a safe house.'

'I'm sorry?' he said. 'A what?'

'A safe house,' she repeated. 'That's what they're called, aren't they? I know you can arrange them. I'm asking for somewhere safe where I can go. Somewhere that Ben McGovern can't find me.'

'We don't do such things,' he said.

A blush of anger. 'You do. You must do.'

He caught himself smiling, and made a real effort to stop. 'They might do them in the cities for – what? – maybe informants,' he said. 'But not here.'

He could see that she was really furious now. 'I'm in danger,' she said.

'So you've said.' He knew perfectly well that his lack of sympathy was against the book. Women in peril must always be taken seriously. That was the rule. Women tormented by men – the raped, the stalked. Special suites to discuss their fears in private. But he simply couldn't muster it for Anna Miles. She just smelled all wrong to him. She rattled his sixth sense. She was a liar. He knew it. She would drag trouble in her wake wherever she went, like a fishing boat drags gulls. Maybe she couldn't help it. Maybe she relished it, who knows?

'I'm in danger,' she insisted.

'Yes,' he replied. 'I've seen the box.' There was a profound silence. 'You have to admit,' he said quietly, 'that as threats go, it's unusual. A box.'

Her eyes ranged over his face. She was rigid, literally rigid with anger. Her chin was tilted. It was, he realized, with a small frisson of amusement, the way that small dogs looked at you before they took a bite out of your ankle.

'I want to see Chief Inspector Wilde,' she said.

'He won't be back until Friday.'

She continued to stare at him. Then, 'OK,' she said, in a voice of ice. She turned on her heel and opened the door.

'What about the girl?' Sandys called, rising to his feet.

She didn't look back. 'I made a mistake,' she said. 'Very sorry.'

Twenty-Five

The house in Pennystone Road was set back from the rest of the street. It had been built in the days when the cotton merchants in Manningham had tired of living in the filthy smoke of the city, and decided to convert a great green swathe of countryside into suburbia – and this was the result.

Once-handsome Victorian villas now stood, for the most part, in shadow behind shrubs that had grown into trees. The road thundered with traffic going into the city. The area bore a shroud of decay. Behind their red stone faces, the houses had been converted into flats – partitions slung across echoing hallways, kitchens rigged on landings, and attics changed to bedsits. Under each house, the enormous cellars lay empty.

3a Pennystone Road was worse than all the rest.

Occupying a corner plot, it had originally been the most desirable house in the road, closest to the new railway station. It had a handsome chestnut tree in the garden, and a sweeping drive behind iron gates. But its former grandeur had almost totally been lost. The gates, rusted beyond repair, were hidden in a dark forest of laurel and holly. The drive was green with damp. The chestnut tree, now eighty feet high – a glorious unchecked monster of a tree – crowded the front of the house, casting it in permanent gloom. The front door, too, was boarded, and the porch was full of leaves. The sound of the trains continuously echoed down the street and, where there had been a little patch of parkland on the opposite corner, the land had long ago been sold, and a row of shops had sprung up. A Chinese takeaway. A bookmaker's. A hardware shop with its daily apron of stacked plastic buckets, stepladders and ladders chained together, fastened to the iron grilles that covered the windows.

There had been complaints about number 3a since the owner had left. Rubbish was slung into the garden and left to rot. Vagrants slept in the porch and in the lean-to shed at the side, and regularly tried to break in. Only the rear wall, with its now-illegal topping of broken glass, kept the back garden free. It had become a minor jungle, choked with blackberry bushes, above which the walnut and plum trees grew wild. Now, in the early hours of the morning, they hung black against the yellow city sky.

Peter York arrived at one a.m. He parked his car far down the road, and walked quickly down the darkened pavements. Turning at number 3a, he walked through the rotting gates of the drive, past a *For Sale* board tilted to one side, and on through the shadows of the trees. Reaching the rear wall, he took a key from his pocket. He stopped and listened. Hearing nothing out of the ordinary, he opened the heavy wooden gate and passed through, locking it again behind him.

Almost immediately, a female voice filtered through the night.

'Peter . . . is it you?'

She materialized like a wraith, a lightly sketched pool of pale hair seemingly floating in the darkness. As she touched his arm, he saw that she wore a long dark coat. He couldn't see her face.

'It *is* you,' she said.

He put the key in his pocket. 'Oh ye of little faith,' he said.

She laughed quietly, and turned away. He followed her along the path, its uneven cobbles threatening to trip them both. The branches whispered overhead.

'There are foxes in here,' she murmured. 'I could hear them while I was waiting. There are baby ones. They cry like kittens.'

They had reached the fence. He felt along its length – the slippery moss-covered wood. The panels were still intact. After a foot or two, his fingers came in contact with the great curtain of ivy. He heard her lifting the stone away from the door, heard the scrape of metal as she pulled it back. She edged inside through the crack; her shoe grazed the step inside as she felt her way. Little by little, her body disappeared as she went down inside. Then, as he himself drew level with the door, he saw the faint acid flicker of a flame. He bent down and looked in, and saw her

147

putting the match to the candle in its metal cup on the wall. The light glowed green for a second. He turned sideways, went in almost on his hands and knees, and pulled the door shut on them both.

She was moving along the underground wall, lighting the rest. When she was finished, ten little stubs of wax guttered near the corrugated metal ceiling, casting a soft light on the bunks on either side of the door. Two stone slabs on each side had been covered with plastic sheeting, on top of which were two vinyl cases. She leaned down now and unzipped them, bringing out the blankets, spreading them on one bed. He watched her with only half an eye, his attention fixed on the wall behind her.

Here, directly opposite him, was an archway, framing total darkness. All around the arch were symbols, drawn in red, gold and green. At the top of the arch was the face of the green man, ivy-wreathed, with yet more tendrils escaping from his open mouth. On each tendril, dropping to either side of the arch, clung pictured relics of the world – human hands veined with sap, waterfalls full of writhing little fish, tongues of fire, streams of clouds, faces framed by snakes, animals crouched below birds.

It was cold. His breath was visible.

She had slung the holdall on the floor, and now took a laptop from it, together with a sheaf of papers. He sat down next to her, watching her careful separation of the various files. Maps of the skies gradually filled both beds.

'Listen to me for a minute,' he said. 'Something's happened.' She barely looked up. 'Something serious. Sara's been arrested.'

Now he had her full attention. She straightened, staring at him. But her voice was calm. 'For what?' she asked.

'They think she has murdered Alisha.'

The girl sank to the bed, the charts still gripped in her hands. 'But that's ridiculous,' she said.

'She's in Dorset.'

'Already?'

'She went down on Tuesday, in Alisha's car.'

'And Alisha is dead?' she asked. 'How?'

He shrugged. 'Continuing investigations,' he said. 'You know what the police are like.'

'Yes,' she murmured. She put the charts down. 'Has she spoken?'

'No. Nothing. Not a word.'

The girl nodded. 'At least she's keeping to that,' she said.

He looked at her.

Of all the students he had met, it was this girl that had always appealed to him most. She was not just a disciple. She had exceptional intelligence. She was much more than all the others – those who helped with the magazines, or at the services. She was a Guardian, and her absolute calm could be frightening.

'I gave the police the leaflet,' he said.

'You . . . what on earth for?' she demanded.

'Sooner or later, someone would, someone from the services, from the university, and then they'd come back,' he said. 'I told them that, as far as I knew, the group were disbanded, that no one lived here. I thought it would throw them off the scent. If they came to check, they'd find the house empty.'

'And that was all?'

'They wanted to know about Sara and Alisha.'

'And . . .?'

'I told them her name was Omega.'

'*Omega?*' She laughed.

'They wanted to know her name. If I'd told them, they'd have everything they want. Her background. Her father. Everything. *They'd know who it was.* They'd remember her. All these records are kept by name. Not photographs. They can't do anything with just her picture.' He shook his head. 'I simply said that they came to services. That Alisha was Sara's support.'

The flickering light played over her face. 'Poor Alisha,' she murmured.

He ran a hand through his hair. 'And they found one of the boxes.'

'Where? Where did they find a box?'

149

'In Alisha's house.'

'It should have been with them,' she said. 'What did the police make of it, anything?'

'I told them that because Alisha was a historian, she was interested in ancient ritual,' he said.

'I see,' she said. 'Good. That makes sense.'

He looked away from her, avoiding the pictures over the archway, and staring, instead, at the floor.

'Cold feet?' she asked.

'No . . . no.'

'Sara will be all right,' she said. 'She'll say nothing. Alisha must have died of natural causes – she wouldn't do anything to harm her. They can't hold her if she's done nothing.' She put her hand on his. 'And besides, she is protected,' she said.

He said nothing.

'You believe that, don't you?' she asked.

'I just hope she keeps quiet,' he said.

There was a silence for a moment. 'To cover your tracks?' she asked.

'No, that's not what I meant,' he said. 'I believe in your vision. I've proved that.'

She smiled. 'And made a little money along the way,' she said. 'And you wouldn't want them to know that.'

'I recruited with you!' he said, offended. 'Do you realize how that jeopardizes my career? *I'm* the one who has to walk the fine line. None of you has to do that. To protect you all.'

She gave him a contemptuous smile. 'Not to protect us,' she said. 'The Gates.'

'Yes . . . yes, all right,' he conceded.

'The Gates, Peter. You believe that, don't you?'

'Yes, of course.'

'You're sure?'

'Yes, yes,' he insisted.

'Not slipping back into your little Christian corner?'

He put a hand to his eyes. 'I'm a priest,' he said.

She regarded him coolly. Then she picked up the charts, and stood up. 'It's almost time,' she said. She finally put her hand in his. 'We can't fall at the last,' she said. 'There are no divisions beyond the Gate.'

He stood up with her, and they turned to the arch. Yet he still stopped on the threshold, under the green man's mouth.

'Has it ever occurred to you,' he murmured, 'that she might lose control of this thing?'

Amazement registered in the girl's face. 'Out of control?' she repeated. 'Sara? Out of *control*? What's given you that idea?'

He closed his eyes suddenly.

'Because she lived in her father's house,' he said. 'For too long.'

Twenty-Six

Robert Wilde reached Manningham at nine-thirty.

It was a fine, bright morning, and, following Wallis's directions, he found the District HQ without too much difficulty, although, as he pulled off on to the sliproad and filtered through the security gates, he realized with a jolt exactly where he was. Ten years ago, when he had last seen this place, it was an open field.

Wallis met him in the foyer.

They shook hands as Wilde looked around himself. 'Some set up,' he commented. A glass sculpture rose up through the stairwell. He thought of his own building, and the tiled corridors that bore every resemblance to a vast Victorian lavatory.

'It's all changed round here.'

'You know this area?'

'My grandmother used to live five miles down the road.'

Wallis led him up a flight of stairs and into an office that overlooked a landscaped garden. 'Look, my boss wanted to see you, but we've got this conference on today downstairs,' he said. 'So you're stuck with me.'

Wilde nodded. 'There's no priority now,' he said.

'Something like that. It's your primacy anyway, as Miss Graham must have died near Melkham.'

Wilde was opening his briefcase.

'Girl said anything yet?' Wallis asked. Now that he was with him, Wilde could hear the faint Liverpudlian inflection in Wallis's voice. He wondered what part of the city Wallis came from. He had his own – rather blurred now – teenage memories of turning up at Lime Street station to meet a girlfriend, and of waiting an hour in the windy street

152

outside before it had dawned on him that he had been stood up. He had gone down to the Mersey, just to say that he had seen it, and the verdigris birds on the top of the Liver Building, before taking the train back to Windermere the same evening, feeling like a country hick who had been humiliated by a city girl. He didn't even remember her face now, just her short skirt and round, white-lipped mouth. Sixties-style lipstick with a brown pencil lip liner. Such sophistication.

His mind flitted briefly to Alice, then to the girl at the station. Girls, the foreign country.

'No,' he said. 'Not a word.'

'No forensic on her?'

'Nothing,' Wilde replied.

'It's hard to believe.'

Wilde looked up. 'Yes,' he said. 'It is. And we have to release her today. Find her some sort of secure accommodation.'

Wallis nodded. 'We've got two girls,' he said.

'Sorry?'

'It's as if there are two girls in this,' the other man commented. 'The girl the vicar told us about, who leans on the shoulder of an older woman, seems besotted by her. Besotted enough to take her clothes off in front of her and have her picture taken. Then there's *your* girl, calm, with a dead woman in the car. The same woman she's been involved with, one way or another.'

'She's not that calm,' Wilde said. He told him about the incidents of weeping and praying.

Wallis leaned forward on the desk. 'You a religious man, Robert?'

'Not really.'

Wallis opened a file in front of him. 'My mother was Catholic,' he said. 'She came from Donegal. She was afraid of hell to her dying day. And she died afraid,' he added tonelessly, without looking up. 'And when I hear all this we found in Graham's house, about the gates of hell . . .' He looked up, impatience and contempt portrayed in equal quantities in his face. 'I've got no time for it.'

He opened an envelope lying next to the file, and handed Wilde a piece of paper. 'Miss Graham's sister's been on to us to release the house,' he said. 'Everything we found is bagged. We took disc copies of what was on the computer. The essays should go back to the university, and most of the books, from what I can tell.' He looked in the envelope, then handed it to Wilde. 'Took another set of discs in case you wanted to refer to what's on her computer,' he said. 'We haven't time to go through it. Orders from on high.'

'Thanks,' Wilde said, signing the paper and returning it. He put the envelope in his case.

'You know what interests me more,' Wallis said, 'is this vicar. This Peter York.'

'Oh?'

'Yeah, he . . .' Wallis turned his seat, and stretched out his legs. He picked up a cigarette packet from his desk, but merely studied it without opening it. 'He's got this high-tech operation. He runs magazines. Looks like he makes money from it. Smooth as you like. And he's been up the university, running services there.' He paused. Opened the packet, looked at the half dozen cigarettes inside. 'There are a lot of young girls interested in it.'

'And you think . . . what?'

Wallis shrugged. 'I don't know,' he admitted. 'Not without being given time to investigate it, which isn't likely to happen.' He closed the packet, grinned at Wilde. 'I gave up these things four weeks ago.'

'Keeping them by for emergencies?'

'No,' Wallis said. 'Just seeing if the misery can get any worse.'

Wilde laughed. He had never smoked, but he had thought that he smelt smoke on Alice a couple of weeks ago, and it had been bothering him, wondering how he could broach it without seeming to mistrust her.

'What's your gut feeling about the vicar?' he asked.

'My gut feeling is that the Church of England wouldn't like what he's doing. He's got an explanation for everything.' Wallis paused. 'He gave us an address of this cult. We went to the house, and it's shuttered up, going for auction at the end of the month. We talked to the estate agents and they said the owner was a Mr Acland, but he hasn't paid his mortgage for nearly a year. He isn't there, and can't be traced. He hasn't cashed his Income Support and Invalidity Benefit. To all intents and purposes, he's vanished. We asked the neighbours about the cult, the leaflet, and they didn't know. Not that I would expect them to, necessarily. They're all flats. No one seems to talk to anyone else.'

'And the girl belonged to this cult?'

'We don't know that. All that we know is that she called herself by an angel's name and Peter York gave us this angel-cult lead. But it's gone nowhere.'

'This Mr Acland doesn't sound like a cult leader.'

'No,' Wallis admitted. 'He was in his early seventies. Disabled by a war injury.'

'Did he have a family?'

'Not that anyone knows.'

'Did you go in the house?'

'No,' Wallis said. 'We found out that by looking up the Social Security record. Yesterday afternoon, after you told us that it wasn't murder, we got the stand-down. No more man hours except for tying up the loose ends, releasing the house back to the sister. There's no crime to investigate here. Unless you know different.'

'No,' Wilde said. 'I don't know any different.'

The two men looked at each other.

'Do you want to know *my* gut feeling?' Wilde asked. 'I think we've missed something.'

Wallis's foot tapped, unconsciously, against the desk. His fingers started to stray to the cigarettes.

'I can't put my finger on it,' Wilde said.

'Well, what? The girl? The old woman?'

Wilde frowned. 'The girl brought Alisha Graham to Anna Miles,' he said. 'Yet Anna Miles says she doesn't know her. Anna Miles is, meanwhile, being chased by some crazed boyfriend. She thinks he's followed her. Anna Miles used to live in Manningham. Within the space of two days, a girl has turned up from where she used to live, and a man she is trying like hell to avoid. She claims she doesn't know the girl, but there is . . .' His voice drifted away.

He put his fingers to forehead, pinching the place between his eyes. 'Then, yesterday, Anna Miles told me that there's something familiar to

her about the girl . . . and, somewhere back in this girl's past is a . . .
disappearing man . . .'

'What man?'

'This man Acland.'

'But he's a pensioner. A war veteran.'

'And missing,' Wilde said.

'Yes, but how can that be connected?' Wallis said. 'The address he
owned was split into flats. The cult, probably run by students, could have
operated out of any of those flats. And it needn't have been for very
long. The leaflet was amateurish.' Wallis lifted the very same leaflet out
of the file, and passed it to Wilde. 'Looks like a kid's drawing,' he said.

Wilde looked at it for some time. His fingertip rested on the face of
the nearest angel, a face contorted with fury. He glanced up. 'What did
this priest say about angels?' he asked.

'Not much. Something about the millennium and disaster theories.
He quoted the Bible. Revelation.'

'Why?'

Wallis gave a tepid smile. 'There's the advantage of having a god-
fearing mother,' he said. 'There are angels all over Revelation. Seven
angels and seven plagues and seven vials full of the wrath of God.'

'Vials?' Wilde repeated.

'Containers. Glass tubes, something like that.'

'Like test tubes?' Wilde asked.

They stared for a moment at each other.

Then, Wallis turned back to the file. Wilde leaned over the desk to
read the sheet with him – the list of items found in the shoe box in
Alisha Graham's house.

. . . *five sheets of paper inscribed with prayers . . . two small white
feathers . . . four vials of blood . . .*

Wilde looked up at Wallis. 'Have you tested this blood?'

'Animal. Cat.'

'What do these angels do?' Wilde asked. He felt something eerie,
disquieting in the number. Four. Four vials left, out of seven.

Wallis scratched his head. 'I can't remember exactly.'

They went out of the office and searched for a Bible. It was found in the office of the Chief Constable's secretary – a woman recommended to them as the source of all human wisdom – and who handed it to them with the greatest reluctance. 'It's my own copy,' she said. 'Be careful with it.'

'Do you know it?' Wilde asked. 'Do you read it?'

'Of course not,' she said. 'The Chief Constable uses it for his crosswords.'

They found Revelation.

'Seven angels,' Wallis read. 'Carrying the plagues of the world. Grievous sores . . . the death of the seas . . . darkness, drought . . .'

'Plagues?' Wilde echoed. 'Jesus Christ, let's hope not.' He peered over Wallis's shoulder at the page. 'What are the last four plagues?' he asked.

'Er . . . heat . . . darkness. Drought. And the last . . .' He turned the pages. 'Thunder and hail and earthquake and the voice of God.' He looked at Wilde. 'You're not thinking there's something significant about there being four vials?' he asked. 'There's nothing in them but some poor moggy's last remains.'

'In all four?'

'Yes.'

Wilde took the book from Wallis thoughtfully. He leafed through until the very end of the Bible. '"A new heaven and a new earth."'

'That's what York quoted to us.'

'. . . and one of the seven angels shows John the new city of God with twelve gates . . . and at the gates, twelve angels . . . *I am Alpha and Omega, the beginning and the end, the first and the last* . . .' He shut the book softly. 'And she called herself Omega.'

'Yes.'

'And the gates again . . . you said there were articles, books about gates in Alisha Graham's house?'

'Yes.'

'And this . . . this promise to the world, God's promise . . . the beginning and the end of life.'

'It was a dream of St John the Divine, a vision,' Wallis said.

Wallis turned away from him, his hands deep in his pockets. He thought of how the girl had been in the interview room, how she had looked up at the light from the window. Fallen to her knees. Crumpled into tears. 'Is God watching you?' he had asked.

Make the leap, Christine had said.

He turned back and looked at Wallis.

'The end of the world,' he murmured. 'She's waiting for the end of the world.'

He had lunch with Wallis in a local pub after speaking to the incident team at the HQ. The atmosphere in the team was quiet; the investigation had gone off the boil. Some of them had already gone, taken over to more pressing crimes. Wilde asked Wallis if he would mind if he visited the house in Pennystone Road alone.

'Be my guest,' Wallis said.

Yet when Wilde phoned the estate agents, there was no one available to show him the house. Twenty-four hours notice was needed, they said, to get a carpenter to remove the boarding. Wilde found himself having to agree to meet them there at ten the following morning. No carpenter could be commandeered from the police themselves – after all, there was no crime. No crime, no funds.

Feeling frustrated, he booked himself into a bed-and-breakfast recommended by Wallis. He rang the house where Alice was sleeping over with a friend. There was no reply. Kicking his heels, and disliking the loose-end feeling, he picked through the copies of the files that Wallis had given him. Finally, exasperated by the case and his own restlessness, he got into his car.

He had no definite aim in sight until he saw the signs for the university. He turned off, along unfamiliar new roads. This part of the country had been sacrificed to the car, he thought; motorway intersections everywhere. The university grounds appeared suddenly, a little patch of green with a cluster of buildings.

He walked through the site, finding himself at a crossroads with a refectory on one side and a group of lecture theatres on the other. He looked at his watch; it was three-thirty, but the place seemed deserted.

To his left was a launderette, a newsagent, and a second-hand bookshop. He walked over, pushed open the door.

Books crowded the shelves and the floor. Stacked in heaps, they were loosely arranged by subject. A woman at a counter was struggling with an enormous card index, the glasses pushed back on her head.

'Good afternoon,' he said.

She glanced at him. 'Hello.'

'Where is everyone?' he asked.

She leaned on the counter, a large, red-faced woman in her fifties, with a friendly, open expression. She wore an astonishing floral blouse, and had flower slides stuck in her hair. The effect was almost comical – a flower child stuck in a Marks and Spencer cardigan. 'Let's see,' she said. 'First-year finals. Football tournament. And in bed.'

He laughed. 'First-year finals?'

She considered him. 'They have to take exams at the end of the first year to determine their next two years' courses,' she said. 'Football is over in Lancaster, big thrash. A kind of war. So they tell me.' She returned to the cards.

'And bed.'

'The other sport,' she commented, without looking up.

He wandered around, picking up one or two copies from the floor. Sixteenth-century poets and inorganic chemistry. 'You've quite a collection here,' he said.

She was humming quietly to herself. 'They sell them at the end of term and buy them back the next.'

He looked on the shelves. The section on religion was tiny – a few orthodox titles on world religions, with a marked emphasis on Buddhism. A single Good News Bible in its orange cover. And then, below it, a mass of self-help therapy. *Embrace the Blessed You. Recollections and Denial.* He ran his finger over them. *The Morning World. The Ley Spirits. Stones and Secrets.*

He picked out one. On its cover was a conventional Ordnance Survey map, through which green lines were drawn. He put it down and picked up another. On the front was a photograph of a child, dressed in a billowing swathe of cloth, standing on a hillside. He turned it over and looked at the reverse.

'Interesting stuff,' he said.

She glanced over. 'Oh, that.'

'You've got a lot of it.'

'Well,' she said, shrugging. 'They all go through it, don't they? The world is made of green cheese, all that. We're all going to die.'

He looked up. 'We're what?'

'Calamity and doom,' she said. 'You remember the oracle in that old comedy series? "Woe, woe and thrice woe". All that. They love it.'

'Do they?' he murmured.

'The world is going to be hit by an asteroid next week, or they've found Christ's shoes in a can of baked beans in Norwich, or pollution is turning us all into hermaphrodites,' she said. 'Oh, it's great fun. Tremendous money in it.'

Wilde turned the book over speculatively.

'That one's all about ley temples,' she said. 'You should read it. It'll give you a laugh.'

He smiled. 'Ley temples? What are they?'

'You know ley lines?'

'Vaguely.'

'And you know quartz stones?'

'No.'

She pushed back the sleeves of her cardigan and put the last card back in the index. 'Oh, you haven't lived,' she said. 'The ley lines stretch – in straight lines, of course – all over the country. All over the world, apparently. They're supposed to correspond to natural magnetic lines on the earth. The earth's a big magnet, you see?'

'Is it?' he said.

'Absolutely. That's why they reckon that tampering with electricity and satellite systems and microwave transmitters is frying our brains, because we just can't take all the crossed wires – but that's another book. Third one down on the shelf behind you, in fact.' She was really warming to her subject. 'Ley lines follow straight routes from one point to another. Along these routes you find quartz stones. Waymarkers. Find them all over the place if you look for them, propping up parts of people's houses half the time. Find them in graves and in places like Stonehenge and Avebury.'

She leaned behind her and switched on a kettle on a shelf on the back wall. 'Cup of tea?'

'I don't want to take up your time.'

'Take all you want,' she said. 'As long as I can watch *Countdown* at half four, I'm quite happy. Sugar?'

'No. Thanks.'

'Where was I?'

'Quartz.'

'Oh yes,' she said. 'Now at various points along ley lines are important sites. Places used as celebration points, or beacons, or churches. Places of magic.'

'Like Glastonbury?'

'Exactly. Spot on. Places where all sorts of legends have got mixed up together. Places where more than two lines cross are especially powerful.'

'And these are the ley temples?'

'Yes.'

'And how do you know where they are?'

'Well,' she said, handing him a cup of tea in a purple-and-white flowered cup. 'There's the fun part. You don't. Some people claim they're here, others there . . . that's how books get published,' she said. 'Bermuda triangles and sacred temples and pyramid paths, they change every year. You know the kind of stuff. The Holy Grail is definitely buried here. Unless of course, it's buried over there. Or in Iowa. Or under the Antarctic.'

He laughed. He opened the book and leafed through a couple of chapters.

'That one says that children are the only ones that can really detect lines of power,' she said. 'Hence the poor little sausage done up in sheets on the cover. Children and virgins.'

He paused, then slowly closed the book. 'Are there any groups on the campus that believe in all this?' he asked. 'Organized groups, I mean.'

'Not that I know of. Why?'

'Someone told me something about angels.'

'Oh,' she said. 'Are you a parent?'

'I am,' he said. 'But she's not at the university.'

Not yet, he thought. But how long would it be before she was in a community like this, where exploration was everything?

'There's a Christian worship group,' she said. 'It's called Good God.' She was biting her lip to prevent herself smiling.

'Yes,' he said. 'I know about that one.'

'And a Zen Buddhist group, and the Young Christians – more traditional, those. And I think there's a transcendental meditation meeting somewhere. I suppose they're all into angels one way or another.'

'Right,' he said. 'Thanks for your help. I'll take the book.'

'Did you want any others?'

He looked around the piles at his feet. 'Is there anything on Revelation?' he asked.

She stopped, in the act of wrapping the paperback. 'Revelation, like the book of the Bible?' she asked.

'Yes.'

'Now there's a coincidence.'

'A coincidence?' he echoed.

'There used to be something a year or two back. They brought out a lot of leaflets and were reported to the Chancellor's Office.'

'Leaflets with angels on the front?' he asked.

'Yes,' she said. 'Oh, I see! Is that what you meant by angels?'

'What happened to the people who wrote it?' he asked.

'I don't think anything happened,' she said. 'No one knew who'd done it. It frightened a few students, you know. A real hellfire and damnation message. You rang the telephone number on the leaflet, and you were asked for money, and if you didn't give your own name and pledge something, you were threatened with – well, all those things that I was joking about a minute ago. Disaster and flood and famine, all that.'

'Did you ring the number?' he asked.

She laughed, her serious expression suddenly breaking. 'Me? Heavens, no. But some did. I don't know what happened after that. It fizzled out, I expect. There was only ever one leaflet.'

He gave her the money. She handed him the book.

'And there were no names that you knew?' he asked.

'No,' she said. 'I mean, angels! Honestly. You see what I mean? This year it was quantum mechanics. Everybody was a potted expert on the mysteries of quantum. Last year angels, this year physics, next year . . . well, psychic ping-pong, probably. No tables, no bats, no balls.' She chuckled at her own joke, closing the till.

'Got to go,' he said, looking at his watch. 'Thanks again.'

'Train to catch?' she asked, as he opened the door.

'No,' he said. 'But it's twenty to five and you're missing *Countdown*.'

Twenty-Seven

When the men came to him, they were drunk.

It was a revel day, and there had been dancing. They had blessed the well and the trees on the top road into the town, without remembering why they were doing it. A tradition as old as the hill, and one now overtaken by the debauchery that came afterwards. The wives shrank home with mutterings of evil, and old ways, and they complained to the ineffectual priest, but the men – larded with meat and full of ale – made mischief by themselves into the night.

And it was now past midnight.

The Egyptian sat waiting for them.

They lurched into sight, full of the false courage of the alcohol, their fists raised. He glanced around them, counting nine.

'You put the devil in they pit,' yelled the first, staggering.

'You put the devil's mouth in there, dirty gypsy,' shouted an invisible second, from behind the rest.

'I done no such thing,' he said softly. 'I've no truck with demon.'

They muttered among themselves, and pushed the first man forward. The Egyptian looked at him, this pitiful coal-scarred apology for God's handiwork.

'We can hear him down at the face,' the man said. There was fury and fear in his voice. 'We hear him 'long the crease, 'long the standing. He rides in the tubs, on the rails, on the puttway.'

'I am sorry for you,' the Egyptian said. 'For your work.'

'You'll be fearful sorry,' the man retorted.

The Egyptian got up. He walked towards them. 'If you've come to kill me, you had better do it straight off,' he said.

But he knew they hadn't come for that.

The bravado peeled off them; they were revealed to him in the shadows, a

164

patch of poor boys, frightened out of their wits. They stared in his face, no longer judging him. Desperate, mute.

'The pit must shut,' he said. 'It must be closed – careful closed, gentle, and the tomb quartz put back.'

Knowing, all the time, that it would not happen that way.

Twenty-Eight

On Friday morning, Anna drove down to the Manor.

It was eleven o'clock, and visitors were already in the house and grounds. She parked in the public area and walked through the visitors' gate to the house. As she stepped in through the front door, one of the stewards caught her arm.

'Anna – what are you doing here?'

Anna smiled at her, bemused. 'I want to speak to Matthew,' she said. 'Do you know where he is?'

The woman, whom Anna only knew as a nodding acquaintance, lowered her voice and pulled Anna to one side. 'Don't go in,' she said.

'But why ever not?'

'Mrs Aubrete is in there, in the gallery.'

Anna raised her eyebrows. 'I'm not going in the gallery.'

'There's been all hell to pay this morning,' the woman said. 'Screaming and shouting all over the house. They've been ringing you. It was the first thing I was asked as I walked in this morning, if I had seen you.'

'I'm not answering my phone,' Anna said. 'What is it all about?'

'Too late,' the woman said. Her eyes strayed to the hall behind them.

Anna turned to see Laura Aubrete bearing down on her. She had only a moment to register Laura's altered appearance: her air of practised smoothness had vanished. Her expression was incensed, out of control. She looked torn up by her own outrage.

'You bloody jumped-up bitch,' Laura said, stopping within an inch of Anna.

Instinctively, Anna stepped back. 'What?'

'You heard me. You bloody jumped-up scheming bitch.'

Two visitors, who had just come in through the door, their entrance tickets and house guides in their hands, stopped dead.

Anna looked at the steward for help, for explanation. And, at the moment she turned her head, Laura Aubrete hit her, hard, in the face. Anna staggered backwards, against the heavy mahogany door to the drawing room.

'How dare you show your fucking face,' Laura said. 'How dare you come in here!'

Anna put her hand to her mouth.

Laura lifted her other hand. In it were the house keys, a large ring of clattering metal. 'You see these?' she demanded. 'Well, take a good look at them!' she said. 'This is as near as you're going to get to them. Do you hear me? As near as you'll ever bloody well get!'

Anna had backed further, into the drawing room. She tripped on the edge of the thick carpet, and put a hand out to catch the red rope barrier.

'How long have you been here?' Laura continued. 'Not a year. I've worked for eight in this place. I've brought it up, I've made it solvent, it's mine.' She thumped a fist against her own chest. '*I* did it. *I* created it,' she cried. 'It's not yours. I'll burn it to the ground before you set foot in it, do you understand? You fucking grasping . . .'

Anna finally came to a halt.

'Laura!' Matthew called, from the doorway.

Laura turned. 'Don't come in here defending her,' she shouted.

Matthew closed the door to the hall. 'I'll do what I like in my own house,' he said.

Laura gave a short, bitter laugh. 'Your own house?' she demanded. 'Oh, hardly, I think. Don't you? Hardly that any more.'

Matthew put his hand out to Anna. 'You're bleeding,' he said.

Laura threw down the keys on the table. She leaned on it, breathing heavily. 'How you've got the audacity to come here,' she muttered. 'And how you can stand there, Matthew, and show any concern for her.' She gestured wildly in Anna's direction. 'Don't you see what she's done? Even you didn't see this, did you? She's planned this all along,' she said. 'Can't you see it? Can't you see what's happened? She turns up here and you let her crawl in here and get around your father . . .'

'I did no such thing,' Anna protested.

'And you're such a spineless idiot, you can't see what she's doing, you've never seen the purpose. I warned you, and now it's happened.'

'Sit down,' Matthew said, to Anna. He lifted a chair from behind the barrier.

'You can't see it now,' Laura said. 'Even now your plan's backfired.'

'What plan?' Anna said. She had take a tissue from her pocket and was wiping her mouth. It felt raw. 'Oh Jesus,' she murmured.

'Your lip is cut,' Matthew said. He looked back to Laura. 'Is this going to help anything?' he asked. 'For Christ's sake have a bit of dignity. Making a fool of yourself all morning – causing a scene in front of visitors . . .'

'I'll do what I like,' Laura retorted. 'Dignity! Christ!'

'I don't understand,' Anna said.

'The innocent,' Laura snapped.

'You're totally out of control,' Matthew told her.

Laura began pacing the room. As she walked up and down by the windows, she was on the boards and not the carpet. Her footsteps echoed around the panelled walls. 'All this time, I thought you were plotting with her,' she said. 'Even I didn't think she would by-pass you. Get past you to get to Dominic. A sick man . . . my God, it's obscene.' She stopped, and stared at Anna venomously. 'What did you do to him?' she said. 'Something especially degrading? Some filthy little trick or other? What did he want? What did he ask for?'

'Laura,' Matthew said.

'Tell me,' Laura said. 'I know a few turns myself. But I must have missed out on your particular talent. What did he like?'

'Laura,' Matthew said. 'Shut up.'

'Some perversion of your own?' Laura demanded. Anna stood up. 'OK, so what are you going to do?' Laura said. 'Throw us out now? Or later? Are you going to let us take our clothes with us?'

'That's enough,' Matthew said.

'Why are you defending her?' Laura screamed. 'She's taken your whole life away from you! My whole life!'

'What?' Anna said. 'What do you mean? I've done nothing.'

Laura hardly registered her voice. She was still staring at Matthew, her face suffused with a violent red, her hands clenched, her body bent over at the waist. She was possessed by her own fury.

'I will not talk to you in this state,' Matthew said. 'Three hours of screaming like the devil is more than enough.'

Laura froze. 'You witless sod,' she breathed. 'You and your bloody empty superiority. You imbecile. She's led you by your dick. She's taken you for everything you've got, and all you can say is that I mustn't raise my bloody voice about it!' She turned away, with one hand to her head as if she was really about to pull her hair out. She leaned on the window, gazing out through the glass. 'She won't succeed,' she said. 'That's why we've got trustees. He can't bring her in over me, and I'm fucked to hell if I'm moving out.'

Anna stared at her.

She turned and put her hand on Matthew's arm.

'What is it? What is it?' she whispered.

He put a finger to his mouth, and nodded towards the door.

He took her upstairs, to his own study.

She sat down opposite him, in front of the desk that had so fascinated her the first time that he had shown it to her. 'This is my life,' he had said.

She had been flattered then. No one, the stewards told her, had ever been allowed in the study. It was a room that Matthew Aubrete kept locked, and he carried the key around with him wherever he went. Laura Aubrete often made a joke of it to the staff, but in such a way that still revealed her exclusion, and her sensibility to it.

It had been autumn. Outside, the frost had been thick on the ground. She had been at Aubrete for four months. They had been lovers since September, since the leaves on the chestnut trees down the drive had shown their first faint tinges of yellow. Now, their half-clothed outlines were ranked against the skyline, a long grey hill.

169

Had she been in love with him?

Hard to say. She was secure. She had needed him so much.

Yet *he* loved *her*.

'This is what Aubrete is all about,' he had said. 'This is what made it.'

He stood now by the large table, his hand resting on the maps. There were over thirty of them. Tithe maps, parish maps. Maps of Poor Heart Hill. Section maps of the tunnels and shafts of the mine that they called The 1800.

He had his back to the light now. She slumped down on the nearest chair.

'My father died yesterday,' he said.

She tried to make out his expression. 'Oh, Matthew. I'm so sorry.'

'Are you?' he said. 'I'm not.'

Anna kept silent.

'I've been waiting for this for years,' he said quietly. Then, he smiled. 'And it's all rather a joke, as it turns out, isn't it?' he asked her. Mildly. Conversationally. 'I've waited all these years to be free of him, and to have some authority on the estate, some real . . . some final . . . authority . . .' His voice trailed away. His index finger traced the line of the marcasite seam. In gothic script against the line of the tunnel was written, *Peacock Vein*. He stared at it for some time, then raised his head.

'Well, what are you planning to do?' he asked. 'I'm afraid that Laura, as you can see, will take this to court.'

'Take what to court?' Anna asked.

He came around the side of the table. 'Please Anna, not with me,' he said. 'With Laura perhaps, with others. But not with me.'

She looked hard at him, then back at the maps. Her fingers traced the swelling at the side of her mouth. 'Dominic has left me the estate,' she said. Her voice was barely above a whisper. She said the words hesitantly, with wonder. She looked back at him. 'Matthew, I didn't know,' she said.

He did a little mime of an English gentleman, straightening the sleeves of his jacket, pulling at his cuffs. 'Come now,' he said.

'Matthew, I really did not know.'

'I've seen the will,' he said.

She spread her hands. 'Well, I haven't.'

'The land and house are in trust, of course. You can't sell it. But at least you may move in. You may take the income, alter the estate as you wish with the trustees' consent. You might want to turn it into a theme park. A caravan site.'

'Matthew, please.'

She had never actually seen him angry. It was a curious sight – a mood much deeper than Laura's. It was like looking into the still eye at the heart of a storm, and the sensation truly frightened her.

'You may wish us to move out, of course,' he said.

'Matthew . . .'

'A golf club. Golf clubs are very lucrative. A health farm, similarly.'

'I don't want to see Aubrete changed at all. You know that.'

'Ah . . . small mercies indeed,' he said bitterly.

She stood up. 'Matthew, I'm so sorry about your father,' she said. 'But I never had any kind of influence over him, and whatever Laura believes, or would have you believe, I've never had a physical relationship with him. For heaven's sake . . . you *know* that!' She tried to gauge his reaction. He had half turned away from her. On the wall was a large watercolour of the estate in 1810, the year that the house was built. It stood in the centre of bare parkland, looking outrageously new and ugly, unsoftened by time. There were no trees on the long slope to the top road. The hillside was still scarred.

'Matthew,' she prompted. 'Please say something.'

His hand tapped his hip, his pocket, as if searching for something. 'My father . . .' he began.

'Please . . .'

'My father called you his dearest friend,' he said. 'In his will. Rather a long document, in fact. Detailing his admiration for you, the beds you shared, the disaffection for his family, his son, his daughter-in-law . . . he lists, at some length, my failings . . .'

'Oh God,' she murmured. 'It's a lie.'

'He has left you his flat in London, to which, of course, he has absolute claim as the freeholder, and . . . the flat in Pollensa . . .'

171

'I don't want them,' she said.

'His personal effects . . .'

She strode up to him pulled on his elbow to turn him towards her. 'Can't you see what he's done?' she asked. 'With his last breath? It's a lie. I don't want the house, I don't want anything,' she insisted. 'It's yours. I never slept with him. You know that. In your heart, Matthew! You know what he was like. It's a sick joke, Matthew. The last in the line of his sick and terrible jokes. To cause suffering when he was dead, it's his style . . . I'm sorry,' she added hastily, 'to say that. But it's true. Look at how it's hurting you.'

He wouldn't look at her. She put her hand to his face, turned it.

'I came here today to say that I was leaving the cottage,' she said. 'And it certainly wasn't so that I could move in here.'

'Leave?' he said. 'Why?'

'Not because of you,' she said. 'And certainly not because of this. He never breathed a word to me. How could he? I've never seen him in private. Only with you.' She shook her head. 'Oh God,' she muttered. 'This is insane. My whole life is bloody insane.'

'It's not what he says,' Matthew told her. 'Not what father says in the will.' His smile was frozen, a rictus bearing only the faintest parallel to humour. 'It's quite a story. A romance. Very touching. I'm surprised the old man had it in him.'

'He didn't! I didn't. For God's sake!'

'I must be the fool he claims that I am,' he said. He flinched at his own remark. 'He is right. And perhaps the old stories are true. Perhaps every owner of this place is cursed.'

'Stop it,' she said. 'You're not a fool. You're not cursed. You're the kindest man in the world.'

'Am I?' he asked softly. 'Wouldn't that make me an ideal husband?'

'Look . . .'

'No, it doesn't,' he said. 'Apparently not husband material at all.'

'I don't want the house,' she repeated. 'I'll prove it to you. Give me something to sign. I'll sign something this morning. Now. A piece of paper. Laura can witness it. I'll give it back to you. And the flats. And all his things. What would I want with them?'

172

He looked at her. She saw the distrust still there, the deadly seed that Dominic had planted. 'I'll take any test,' she said. 'Go downstairs. Ring your solicitor. The trustees. Ring them up, bring them here. I'll sign it back to you.'

He took her hand gently away from him, disengaged her touch. Walked away, to the window. 'He's left you over three million pounds in assets,' he said. 'Perhaps more, who knows? You can't sign that away.'

'It isn't mine to keep,' she said.

His gaze never left the sea, the hazy blue line of the horizon.

'Matthew,' she said.

'The irony is,' he whispered, 'is that I wish you joy of it . . . I wish you joy.'

Twenty-Nine

The monthly gathering of the Parish, the Vestry Meeting, was held at the church. Only those on the Committee attended: and the priest, the two parish overseers and Aubrete were all that entered the long aisle that evening, flinging off their coats against the early summer rain, trailing the damp along the stone floor.

As the evening light grew dim, the conversation grew heated.

'Sink another shaft,' Joshua Maudham said. His face was suffused with angry colour.

'And bear the cost?' Aubrete retorted. 'And lose the seam in this one?'

'Steam coal,' Maudham said. 'Sink another shaft at Hammerton, up the coast, where the grade's likely to be better.'

'There's no need to sink another,' Aubrete insisted. 'Look on him as an engineer, an adviser.'

Maudham crashed a fist on the pew alongside him. 'He is no engineer!'

'He may as well be,' Aubrete said. 'We have had all the engineers in the district. We have had those from Bristol. And the only time that the water has sunk is after the Egyptian.'

'With his filthy worship, God help us,' Maudham replied.

Each man looked at the priest. The Reverend was fatter than Maudham, slumped in his corner seat, his face showing weakness, uncertainty, his hands hidden in his unseasonal and heavy coat.

'Even if you offer him shares in the pit, there is no certainty he'll do as you wish,' he said.

Maudham rose to his feet. 'Is that all you have to say, man?' he demanded. 'Drive him off the parish, or we shall be damned for all eternity!'

The priest shrugged. 'I can bring the village to Christ,' he said. 'I cannot make them believe.'

'Believe?' Maudham thundered. 'They are no more than cattle. They believe what they are told.'

The priest looked at him with shaded, cynical eyes. 'They believe in what their grandfathers have told them,' he said softly. 'Gods of the hill, wraiths in the dark, voices in the grass.'

Maudham advanced on him. He pointed into the priest's face. 'I'll see you run off this living, and take no other,' he said.

'I am a realist,' the priest replied.

'You are the devil!'

The priest said nothing at all.

Aubrete was already pulling on his coat. Above him, the rain beat on the stained glass, speckling the faces of the angels with tears.

'I shall offer him half my shares, if he can cure the water,' he said. 'Money may keep him, if nothing else.'

Maudham stared at the younger man. 'You shall be in hell with your idolatries,' he said.

'I do not doubt it,' Aubrete replied.

Thirty

They had given her back her clothes.

When they let her out of the cell, she followed quietly. A woman came forward to meet her, holding out her hand by way of greeting.

'I'm Carrie Phillips,' she said. 'I work for the Social Services.'

The girl looked at her. It was bright in the corridor, and the bodies of those around her fluctuated in her sight. The policeman who had opened the door of the cell, a small broad man of her own height, with flat eyes like a cat, reflective eyes, had struck her immediately with his patched energy – energy threaded together like blocks of colour, each block jostling the other for precedence. She had passed him sensing only the brittle touch of his interest, that bounced on to her, from her, back to her. He would soon forget her entirely. His attention never stuck in one place.

But Carrie Phillips had no light. The girl regarded her with interest. A curious phenomenon. Not even that deflecting contact. This woman who was holding out her hand to her, a tall woman, was entirely dimmed. Her aura was cool and bleak. Carrie Phillips was in a caring job, but she didn't care any longer. The girl looked into her eyes sympathetically and touched the fingers held out to her. Immediately, she saw another country – a busy street. A riot of colour. Carrie, who seemed to be looking at her so intently, actually had another picture in her head – colour in the picture, a street in some hot place, and a person in that street. And it was intimately connected with the letter that was in the black case slung on a long strap over her shoulder.

The girl looked at the case, and felt Carrie's disappointment. Carrie was trying to find a solution to a relationship that had gone terribly

176

wrong, but she would never get to the country, and the person who had written the letter would never come home.

The girl squeezed her hand.

'And we don't know your name,' Carrie said. 'Which makes things just a little difficult. Not impossible, though.'

She signed a form.

Another was put in front of the girl, but they wanted her name. She gazed at it apologetically, and put the pen down again.

'That's a nice dress,' Carrie said, as they waited for the girl's belongings. 'Is it new?'

It was. Alisha had made it for her. Alisha was very good at sewing, which, she had explained tartly one night, was not an easy, feminine task. It took a mathematical turn of mind to master the three dimensions of dressmaking. She had the fabric already in a drawer, and had held it against the girl's face.

'It's your colour,' she had said.

Gratitude had made the girl take up Alisha's hand. She had pressed it to her face.

'Come on now,' Alisha had said, a catch in her voice. 'All that is finished with. Forget what happened before. This is another life.'

The material was very pretty. Alisha's fingers were careful, deft. Alisha made many of her own clothes, a fact that the girl had not appreciated when she had brought the clothes from the shops. The reaction to them was still fresh in her mind.

'You stole these? All these?' Alisha had asked, plainly horrified. 'But why?'

For you.

'Didn't he teach you anything at all? Not a single common decency?' Alisha demanded. 'Did he teach you to steal, instead?'

She had thrown the clothes, still in their carriers, into cupboards in her bedroom, exasperated. 'How on earth am I going to get them back?' she had muttered. 'Didn't you listen the last time? Why do you persist in doing it?'

Alisha had turned. Her eyes had rested for some time on the girl's face. 'Write it down, then,' she had said.

177

She had.

For you.

'No, not for me,' Alisha had said. 'If that's what you mean, not for me. I don't like theft. Especially of something for which I have not the slightest use.' She had looked through the packages. 'Shoes!' she had exclaimed. And then begun to laugh. 'And look at them!' She had held up the polished black court pair and waved them in front of the girl's eyes. 'Can you see me in these?'

Humour had always got the better of Alisha. When she fell prey to one of her laughs, bright points of blue danced in her space. Alisha had a halo, an advanced aura of true perception and patience, a spirituality. It was the reason that the girl had gone to her in the first place. When she laughed, the blue shone out in fantastic wheels, that moved as Alisha spoke. The arc above her head radiated. She was an old woman, but she was full of energy, full of interest, of creativity. She would hold out her arms, and draw the girl into the light.

It was only on the last day, when she had tried to show Alisha that she must go, that Alisha had tried to pack, and it had taken a scene – a scene where she walked out without any other item of clothing, without any possession – before Alisha saw that she was fixed in her purpose, and, throwing a few jumbled items into a case, had run after her.

Remembering, the girl smiled to herself.

Oh, she had taken hold of life. She came with her. Wanted to be with her, despite her doubts. Would have held her hand right to the last, to the Gate itself, had her frail physical body not betrayed her.

Carrie Phillips looked at her. 'You look very well,' she said, thoughtfully.

The girl dipped her head. Of course she was well. She was the sixth chosen Guardian, and she had her task. She would be well until she had completed it. There was no more important task in the world. Any world. But, more than even that, which was astonishing in its significance, she had something more arresting still, which was the tender memory of Alisha's light. And now, going on alone, which was the task set before her – to go alone to the Gate – she could summon up Alisha's light, because Alisha was still there, an anxious spirit vainly trying to become physical, a task at which she was not accomplished.

But there was not long to go.

It would soon be done.

Carrie Phillips took her out into the street. They stopped on the steps of the police station, and the girl shrank back, for a moment, from the noise of the world. People hurried past; the traffic laboured along the road.

'Market day,' Carrie said.

It meant nothing at all.

Carrie linked her arm in the girl's. 'When I called to see you yesterday,' she said, 'I told you that the police wanted to support you, find you accommodation?'

The girl was not listening, which was probably just as well, because actually that was not quite true. The police wanted to keep the girl under observation but had no power to prevent her moving around the country-side. Carrie had come in as a go-between, sympathetic to the girl's plight, and intrigued enough to acquiesce to the wishes of the constabulary. Secure places were like gold dust, but she had found a room in a warden-controlled block. It was a place for young offenders. The girl was to be placed there, where an eye could be kept on her, but where she had some freedom.

'You remember that? That I'm taking you to a room, a place to stay?'

Carrie noticed the way that the girl's arm felt in hers. It was heavy, but not limp. Years of contact with the abused and threatened and deprived had taught Carrie that there were many ways to hold a hand, and to detect the personality behind the grip. This girl's hand was certainly accustomed to be placed; she complied easily, as if she had suppressed her own wishes. And yet the arm didn't drag. She had retained some sense of herself, Carrie thought. And a kind of dignity. Even grace.

'My car is along here,' Carrie said. She held the girl's small bundle of belongings still – the watch, and a mackintosh that had been in the car and was assumed to be hers, because it was a modern design. Carrie stopped and gave the bundle over to the girl. She inspected it only briefly.

'Have you got any toiletries?' Carrie asked. 'Cosmetics? Clothes?'

No.

All the clothes had been Alisha's.

'We'll have to get you some,' Carrie said. 'A few basics.' She unlocked the car. 'You don't have to worry about food, because the hostel will give you three meals a day.'

They got in. Carrie showed her the seat belt.

'I don't know how long we will be able to keep you in Brimmer House,' Carrie said. 'It's not that you don't need it, it's that there's such competition for room.' She started the engine. 'Still, don't worry about it. I'll sort something out. We'll go shopping for what you need. And when you feel better, you can talk to me. It's always a good thing to talk.'

The girl looked out of the window as the car pulled away from the kerb.

She wasn't worried in the least.

She didn't mind if she was fed or not.

She wouldn't keep the room for very long.

And where she was going, she wouldn't need clothes.

Thirty-One

Robert Wilde was just about to leave the hotel when the phone rang.

He picked the receiver up, and a woman spoke immediately.

'Chief Inspector . . . is that you?'

'This is Robert Wilde,' he confirmed, recognizing Anna Miles' voice.

'Thank God – I've been trying to get your number all morning.'

'I'm just about to leave. I've got an appointment at eleven. What's the problem?'

He heard her laugh, a rapid breath. 'I need to tell you,' she said. 'I remembered her.'

'Who?'

'The girl in the car. The girl with Alisha Graham.'

He stopped, staring blankly at the framed print on the wall ahead of him. 'You remembered her name.'

'No,' she replied. 'I don't remember that. Not yet. I'm trying to. But I think I know where I've met her.'

'And?'

'If it's the same girl, she was in a county orchestra. It met five or six times a year,' Anna said. 'One weekend I was invited to take seminars. Groups. She was in one of the groups. She played the violin.'

He paused for some moments. So, that was it. The fingertips. Damn it, he should have seen something so obvious. Years before, when Alice, as a six-year-old, had asked to play the violin, he had scraped together the money to buy her one, to give her lessons, only to have her roundly declare she hated it after three months. For a little while, her fingertips had been sore, and her teacher had shown her her own hands – hands where the fingertips were rounded and flattened by continually playing the instrument.

'I see,' he said.

'Well! You don't sound terribly interested.'

'No . . . I am, I am,' he said. 'Do you think she remembered you? Had she come to see you specifically?'

'I can't see why she would,' she replied. 'If it is the girl, I literally only ever had one conversation with her. But I'd have to see her again to make sure.'

'The tips of her fingers,' he said.

'I'm sorry?'

'From playing the violin.'

There was a silence.

'It must be her, then,' Anna murmured. 'Good God.'

'It does point that way.'

'Can I see her?' Anna asked.

'It's not quite that simple now,' he replied. 'Not in my jurisdiction any more. Have you spoken to the station?'

'I tried.'

'What do you mean?' he asked.

'I went there yesterday and tried to tell someone and got nowhere. And I asked for protection, and I got nowhere.' She sounded as if she had moved her head away from the phone. He could imagine her defensive, closed-up look.

'I'm sorry about that,' he said. 'It's difficult to find you accommodation. We just don't have those sort of resources. We have someone posted at the top of the lane, though – they're still there?'

'Yes,' she said, grudgingly. 'But you . . .' She paused. The remainder of the sentence was very low. 'I've got to get out of here,' she said. 'I know he's here somewhere. I've got to go.'

'Will you wait until I get back?' he said.

'Is there any reason why I should?'

Robert smiled. 'You must trust me, otherwise you wouldn't be ringing me,' he pointed out. 'Otherwise you'd have vanished already.'

There was a short silence. Then, 'Can I see the girl?' she repeated.

'Tell me I can, and then I can go back and tell *them* you said so. I don't want to get knocked back again.'

He stared at his own feet. 'She was released yesterday,' he said. 'If you wait until I get back, I'll take you to see her.'

'I can't wait,' Anna retorted. Her felt the crackle of her tension and impatience down the line. 'Look, if it is her, she once spoke to me about something very personal.' She sighed. 'But it's not fair to say what it was unless I'm sure it's her. Even then, I'm not sure I should break the confidence. She was thirteen then ... it was five or six years ago ...' She paused. 'Where is she?'

'OK.' He held the phone in the crook of his shoulder while he searched for the card in his wallet. 'Someone called Carrie Phillips.' He gave her the phone number. 'Good luck,' he said.

He heard her whisper the numbers as she wrote them down.

'Has there been anything else?' he asked. 'Anything to worry you?'

She gave a brief laugh. 'Chief Inspector,' she said. 'I am way, way down the rabbit hole. And out the other side in bloody Wonderland.'

He raised an eyebrow, looked at the receiver, then pressed it again to his ear. 'Do they serve drinks down there?' he asked.

'If you're buying,' she said.

He got to Pennystone Road a few minutes late.

The woman from the estate agent's was already pacing up and down outside with a mobile phone against her ear. As he approached, she glanced up at him, said, 'It's OK, he's here,' to the invisible caller, and switched it off.

She held out her hand. 'Sophie Tarrant.'

She was tall, blonde and fearsomely young. He returned her hand-shake. 'Robert Wilde.' Knowing the firm's carefulness over security, he showed her his warrant card. She handed him the details of the house, printed on four fulsome sheets of paper. The photograph had been taken from an oblique angle, he noticed, so that the boarding would not show too much.

He glanced up at the front door.

'The carpenter was here before me,' she said. 'He's just gone to the shop for *fags*.' She said it with a withering expression, looking over her shoulder at him as she took the keys out of her case, and unlocked the door. He looked at it as he passed: a vast oak panel, at least two inches thick, with signs of bubbled and scorched paint underneath the hardboard that had been nailed to it. The frame, too, showed signs of fire.

Sophie Tarrant walked into the hall.

It was gloomy, but light spilled down the staircase from a window that spanned most of the upper flight. Robert gazed up at the design, an Edwardian flourish of stained glass.

'I'm surprised no one's been in and filched that, for a start,' he said. 'It must be worth a fortune.'

She followed his gaze. 'The ground floor's boarded and the back garden is pretty inaccessible,' she said. 'So it would be hard. But yes . . . it's pretty.' She shuffled the papers. 'What did you want to see?'

'To tell you the truth, I don't know,' he said. 'The house was reported by the police here to the building society, following a fire?'

'I believe so,' she replied. 'The building society had written to the occupier many times. When the fire started, the door was broken down, and the fire people found all the accumulated mail. The electricity and phone had been disconnected. There were notices in amongst the mail. The police reported it back to the building society . . .'

'And it started the chain of events leading to this sale?'

'Quite.'

'What sort of damage was there?'

'Not much. The fire was in the porch. It damaged the door, cracked the glass in the windows.'

'And nothing's been heard of the owner?'

'Nothing, as far as I know.' She cocked her head on one side. 'But you're with the police, you know all that,' she said.

'This isn't my area,' he told her.

She gave him a somewhat frosty smile. 'Well, in that case, might I ask a favour?' she asked. Her fingers, he noticed, were tight on her file of papers. 'As you're not a buyer, would you mind if I sat in my car?'

The question surprised him. 'No . . . that's OK.'

184

'I have a few calls to make. I'll keep an eye out for you,' she said. 'And the carpenter will be at the door, waiting.'

He considered her. It sounded as if she were reassuring him of a quick getaway. 'Fine,' he told her.

And she left, leaving the door open.

He watched her walk down the drive and get into the small red coupé parked at the gate. Within seconds, the mobile was pressed again to her ear.

He stood in the hallway uncertainly for a moment, and then began to climb the stairs.

It was obvious that Ms Tarrant couldn't bear to be in the house a moment longer than was necessary, but its atmosphere made no difference to him at all. He ran his index finger along the heavy banister, picking up a thick grime of dust. He whistled a little tuneless phrase between his teeth, and wiped the dust on his handkerchief.

Robert Wilde was not overly imaginative, nor had he been as a child.

Even when very young, he had never been frightened of the dark, or worried by the kind of monsters-under-the-bed fantasy that keeps a child awake and jumping at shadows. He had experienced only one period of fear when he was seven or eight, and he had always, until now, looked back on that as a kind of misfiring in the circuitry, a brief and transitory phase that was hardly part of him.

It had happened when his father had been taken into hospital for a routine operation. His disappearance, one Sunday evening, armed with a small suitcase, hadn't, even then, unduly worried his son, for Robert's mother had soon returned, brisk and reassuring, an hour later, and the family – he had two brothers, both older – sat down to a regulation Sunday afternoon tea of corned beef salad on white plates on a white cloth starched to iron respectability.

The only hint at the world being awry was later on – when it came to lighting the fire. Without their father there, huffing over the reluctant kindling, and coaxing a flame by covering the chimney with a sheet of newspaper, the boys had been given the job themselves. They fell to it with a sense of enormous self-importance, and had promptly filled the room with smoke. Their mother had taken over with a flurry of impatience.

Just before bed, Robert had been given the job of bringing the dog, Rigger, in from the back garden. He had opened the door and shouted the terrier's name. The rain was coming over the mountain. Their garden abutted a field of sheep-cropped grass, a rapidly rising gradient, and a low stone wall before the body of the hill. He had strained his eyes, wondering if their dog had, as he did so often, jumped the wall and gone walkabout, worrying the sheep.

He had called once more into the encroaching darkness. Looking up, he had seen a rim of light on the hill under the raincloud. He could hear his brothers' voices as they went upstairs in the house behind him. Hear the opening and closing doors. Hear the low thud of music from the radio in their room.

And then, hands came down out of the hill.

It was no dream, no trick of the half-light. There were hands in the rain, in the breath of the rising wind. They came suddenly out of the light and swept down the slope, fingers extended, palms facing him. They were as big as the clouds, made from clouds – from swirling, dense vapour. Wreathed, swarming grey palms. And the palms were full of faces, and the faces were full of mouths. Thousands of open mouths in the outstretched, quick-falling hands.

He had slammed the door in panic, and put his seven-year-old shoulder against it.

'What's the matter with you?' his mother had asked. 'Where's Rigger?'

'He won't come,' Robert had lied.

'Don't be so daft,' she had retorted. 'Get that door open and get him in.'

He had felt, standing there in the little scullery with its thickly green-painted drop-latch door, that he was standing in the shadowy green safety of the house – the house with its now-red fire, the smell of toast, the faint odour of soap, of floor polish, of the red rug in front

of the fire whose dye, when hot, gave off a scent of thick-lying leaves –
and beyond the door, the door on which he had his hand, was another
world. A world full of the rain, and the hill, and the rain hands, great
shafts pressing down, carrying the voices of trees, of the bone-rock slope,
of the invisible, of the secret. He had felt sure that, if he opened the
door, the hands of the rain would reach inside and lift him out of his
safe green shade.

'Open the door to that dog,' his mother insisted, standing in
the sitting room, drying her hands on a tea-towel, half an eye on the
television.

He did.

Rigger came strolling in, unconcerned, wet through. Robert had
slammed the door and watched the dog shake itself.

'Bed!' his mother called.

And later, in the dark, with his brothers asleep beside him in the
small back bedroom, he had listened to the storm grumbling away across
the peaks, and watched the sky lighten a fraction. Yet, as soon as the
threat of the rain retreated, another fear came thundering in its place.

He had realized that his father was nowhere in the house. It had
kept him awake for a long time, hands clutching the sheet to his chest,
thinking that perhaps his father would never come home, and realizing
that, one day, his father would die, really die, and the thought hung over
him as heavily as the cloud, and with greater and more terrible hands, a
beast in the dark, a spectre of his father's fragility and fallibility. He had
prayed then for his father to come back. For him to get out of bed in the
hospital and come back. Robert had waited for the sound of his father's
key in the lock of the front door, the noise of his boots on the stone
flags, the shuffling of removed boots and the skimming hands looking for
his slippers in the dark. For his tread on the stairs.

But the key never came, and Robert finally went to sleep. And every
night afterwards, for a week, the horror of his father's absence lurched
over him. And, even when he did come home – just the same as ever,
bringing the scuffed leather suitcase back, and unwrapping boiled sweets
for the three of them, while all three tried to sit on his knee at the same

time and his mother shooed them away – even then, the doubt never quite left him again. The doubt that his father, and he, were only flesh in the hands of the storm.

He stood now at the bottom of the stairs, and looked up at the pretty stained-glass window.

There were no hands. There never had been any hands. His father had died, very peacefully, in his sleep, at the age of eighty-two, with a small smile on his face, the smile of a justly earned rest.

No hands.

No faces, no mouths, no hands.

He went upstairs, shrugging the memory away.

The house still had some furniture, though not very much. He went into a bedroom on the first floor, and saw a fifties-style dressing table, with a curved bow front and a central mirror. A double bed stood in one corner, with a plum-coloured eiderdown. An ottoman stood in front of the window. Wilde went over to it, and lifted the lid. There were blankets inside, and a small bag of lavender. He regarded it with a little frisson of affection. His mother had kept bags like that in every drawer, much to his teenage disgust. He had complained that his shirts smelled poncy, and thrown the bags out. *Poncy*, the word for the sixties. A little word to cut his mother to the quick.

He closed the lid of the box, interested that both his mother and father, both now long dead, should resurface in his mind in this cold and empty house that was so unlike their own. He walked out of the bedroom, and went up on to the second floor. Here, the landing had been partitioned off and a door with a separate Yale lock stood half-open. He went inside, and saw a completely empty room, with a sloping skylight. There was a sink, with an old-fashioned gas water heater. Lethal, probably. The room smelled both smoky and damp, the wallpaper patched with grey bloom.

As he was about to leave, he saw that something was written on the wall, just above the skirting board. He walked over to the place beneath the skylight, and squatted on his haunches.

It was written in pencil, with a faint, threadlike hand.

From tonight til a year from tonight

and this night
and forever
He stood up. He looked around the room, but could see nothing else. *From tonight . . .* What did that remind him of, he wondered? *And this night and forever.* It was like a prayer. *For ever and ever, amen.* He leaned down again, and peered at it. And, as he looked at it from a slightly different angle, he saw that there were three initials scraped into the plaster of the wall. Three letters, etched with something very sharp and fine, a needle or a pin.

B. M. M.

They formed a triangle over the words, a kind of umbrella. BMM . . . a name? If so, whose? The author of the prayer, or the person who wrote on the wall?

From tonight until a year from tonight

He straightened up. The house had been unoccupied for many months. Perhaps it was a year, he thought, since that had been written on the wall. He smiled a little to himself. Or it could be thirty years, or fifty.

He went back downstairs. There were two other bedrooms and a bathroom – archaically Victorian – on the floor. Funny, he thought, how these Victorian places look so big from the outside. He went down past the window, stopping for a second to look at the green sea of the garden, at the curling, pest-ridden leaves of the walnut trees.

He looked down at the windowsill.

He thought that he had seen something move there. A wriggling motion, as if the leaves in the window design had become animated.

But nothing.

No hands.

He frowned at himself, at the absurdity of the notion.

He found himself back in the hall, and walked along it, trying to determine what he was looking for. Even though he had now seen the angel poster, and talked to Wallis, they had nothing more concrete to go on other than that the girl who had been in custody may – or may not – have been involved in some kind of religious worship in this house. *And this night and forever.* Someone here – and it need not have been the

189

girl – had organized at least one meeting. It might have been a student. It need not have been anyone who lived permanently here. It need not have been the owner, the shadowy man called Acland who had vanished almost a year ago.

Standing at one of the downstairs doors, Robert Wilde fingered the heavy wood panel. Perhaps Acland had died. He had some sort of war injury for which he claimed benefit – that much they knew about him. He would, if he were alive, be sixty-eight. He could have died of the disability, or its complications. A dead trail to a dead man, and a litter of suppositions and half-truths in his wake, whose tenuous thread led back to the frightened, pale-faced girl who had flung her arms around Robert Wilde's neck without ever uttering a word.

Frightened . . .

Of what? Of *what?*

He pushed on the door, and it opened to reveal a small inner hallway. There was nothing in it but another, smaller door. He hesitated for a second, then opened it. He had half expected a cellar, but was surprised to see a wall facing him. The room was about six feet square, with a sloping ceiling, tucked, as it was, under the broad staircase. He fumbled about for a light, but there was none. He felt along the wall, but there was no other opening, no shelving, no panelling, no cupboards. The surface was very fine and smooth. Under his feet, the floorboards were bare. He frowned. An understairs cupboard with no sign of anything having been kept in it. He reached down, and touched the floorboards, in the shadows. They, too, were smooth.

Incredibly smooth. Polished and planed and waxed, they felt like silk. Silk or skin. Young skin, like Alice's.

And it was warm.

He pressed his palm to the wood, and was rewarded with the most curious sensation. It seemed to mould itself to his hand, not pressing back at all, but forming itself to his touch, as if it had a much softer quality that his own skin had triggered. Now, his fingertips could feel a fine down, exactly like skin, exactly like the fine down on a child's arm, the soft pliable texture of a baby's hand. It was very sweet and pleasant.

He thought at once of Christine.

The touch of her, the feeling of her body. He thought of waking next to her, the thousands of times he had woken next to her. He thought of her bringing Alice home as a baby, the first step over the threshold, a snowy February evening, the grey slush gritted hard to the door, the garden beyond a pristine white under the scattered squares of light from the house. He had made a fire – he had been anxious. Alice was crying. He thought of Christine settled in front of the fire, and Alice eventually sleeping, and Christine turning to look at him – and it was the first opportunity for them to look at each other in their own home with their own child – and he remembered the transmitted thought, unable to put into words, that sprang between them, in front of their own fire, with their daughter in their arms.

And Christine at other times. In her parents' orchard, opening the gate on to the lawn. Spring, and the double-fisted blossom of the cherry.

'Close the gate,' she whispered.

He suddenly saw it. The bleached larch gate that barely came up to his waist. The six cherry trees beyond it. The taller grass, the box hedge on either side. He saw the lock that had never quite caught tight. Christine's father would tie it with string. And after Christine died, Robert and Alice had gone up to Bowness to see her parents, and he had found Christine's father at the orchard gate, clumsily trying to tie the string on the gate lock, hunched over it. And Robert had walked up the garden and seen, to his horror, as he got closer, that Christine's father was crying silently as he fumbled with the fastening. And after Christine's father himself had died, Robert had gone to help her mother, and tidy the garden, and mow the grass – and he, too, had fumbled with that same gate fastening and felt the terrible weight of grief settle on him in the middle of such an ordinary task.

'Close the gate,' she whispered.

He looked up, where the wall should be.

And they were both there. Christine's father holding the length of frayed string in one hand. His arm around Christine's shoulder. They were standing in the sun. He could see the edge of the orchard. Robert started to get down, to scramble through the narrow space, under the low lintel of the door, to get to her. They were just through the wall, just a few feet from him, in a bright place. He saw the square concrete stones that her father had put down in the grass as a path. He had helped lay those stones. He had cut the grass around them dozens of times. The path led to the gate, swinging a little in a light wind.

'Close the gate,' Christine said.

But he had no interest in the gate. He only wanted to get to her.

'Robert, you must listen to me,' she said.

She had stepped forward. Her father was receding. The light that had played over their faces was changing. The trees warped and flattened. Paper trees in a two-dimensional landscape. The wind rose, suddenly flinging her hair back from her face. She stared at him with urgency, in the foreground of a shortening picture, of a collapsing image.

'Shut the gate!' she insisted.

He looked frantically around himself, at the grass, at the haphazard pattern of the stones. There was no string to tie the gate, which was now banging, the noise like a blow of a hand to his face, the sight of it a broken wing behind her. All he could see to tie the gate was the ragwort growing at the edge of the path. It had a fibrous stalk, hard to break. He wondered if he could pull it out of the ground, ground that was losing its depth, ground that was becoming grey, ground where the stones had become flat pieces of wet card on green tissue. Fear climbed over him, assaulting him, filling his head. He suddenly knew the terrible urgency of shutting the gate, and the consequences if he didn't succeed.

And, behind Christine, he sensed something coming down through the disintegrating trees. Mouths and hands. Mouths and hands . . .

He shouted a warning – a knot of garbled sound.

'Shut the gate!' Christine screamed. 'You must! You must help shut the gate!'

Her image was being torn to pieces, pulled into a grotesque shape.

He stared at her in agony for just a second more.

Then he stumbled back, out of the door, out of the space, down the little corridor, out of the mahogany door to the hall, down the hall, out of the house, down the steps.

Running.

He saw a figure coming towards him, and he stopped dead, his arms over his head to protect himself, his body bent at the waist.

A hand touched his shoulder, and he flinched from its gentle impact.

'Chief Inspector,' Sophie Tarrant said. 'Are you all right?'

Thirty-Two

Laura Aubrete lay on her back and looked at the ceiling.

The drawn curtains in the hotel room afforded very little light – certainly none of the afternoon sunlight which, when she had first arrived, had been pouring into the room. The fact that she could see very little, however, meant nothing to her. She was seeing far more in her mind's eye, its pictures projected on to the greyish surface above her. Most of all, she saw Anna Miles's face, and that assumed expression of innocence.

She got herself up on to one elbow, and took a drink from the glass on the bedside table. 'A pound of flesh,' she muttered.

'What?' asked a male voice from the adjoining bathroom.

'A pound of bloody flesh,' she repeated, then laughed grimly at the pun. 'I wish I could rip it out now.'

He put his head around the door. 'Flesh, or heart?'

She emptied the glass. 'Heart. Guts. Everything.'

He looked at her, his eye running the length of her. 'I warned you.'

'Yes,' she said. 'And forewarned is . . . but I never thought she'd actually manage it.'

He came out of the bathroom, throwing the towel down on the floor.

'Husband and father-in-law in less than a year,' he said. 'You have to admit, it's a neat trick.'

She returned her attention to the ceiling. 'And she looks so bloody innocuous.'

'Trembling little woman,' he said. 'I told you.'

'All right,' she said.

He smiled to himself. None of her fury had abated. It had lent a certain pleasure to the afternoon, that uncontrolled temper. But, despite the long hour in bed, her mood hadn't altered. If anything, it was blacker than ever. But he liked that. Even encouraged it. After all, he had no use for her otherwise.

'Where are you going?' she demanded.

'I've things to do,' he said.

'No,' she told him.

He looked at her, half-dressed, his eyebrows raised. 'I beg your pardon?'

She swung her legs off the edge of the bed. 'I want you here.'

'That's very nice,' he said. 'But I have to go.'

She got up, and put her arms around him. 'I haven't finished,' she said.

'I have.'

She took a piece of his flesh, on his back, between finger and thumb, and twisted it. He barely reacted. He took his trousers from the chair and started to put them on.

'I want to know what to do,' she said.

'You've got your Board.'

'I've talked to them.'

'Well then.'

'It's going to take weeks. Months!' she exclaimed.

'You'll have to be patient, won't you?' he said.

She regarded him, hands on her hips. Almost dressed now, he considered her. She had put a little weight on in the last few months, since he had first known her. It looked good on her, rounding out the shoulders and hips. She would progress, of course, getting heavier as she approached middle age, becoming overweight as she hit fifty. Nothing to do with genes, nothing to do with gender. She would get heavier because, at heart, Laura Aubrete was a greedy girl, and the greed would outstrip the grinding mobility of her twenties and thirties. She was lovely now, in her prime. A flower in bloom. One of her own roses.

'Aren't you pretty,' he murmured.

'Oh, for Christ's sake,' she retorted.

He pulled the sweater over his head. 'You have to go through the channels,' he said. 'You have to be seen to be doing the right thing.'

'She's defrauded me!' she cried.

'I know that,' he said mildly.

'She brought pressure to bear on him,' she said. 'That's what I have to prove.'

'And can you?'

She turned away, crossing her arms.

'Well . . . can you?'

'I will.'

'How?'

She said nothing.

'Difficult thing to prove,' he said.

She whirled back to him. 'Don't you think I know that!' she shouted.

'Unless Matthew will back you up.'

Her hands clenched. He picked up his keys from the table.

'He won't do anything,' she said.

'He'll do something, eventually.'

'He's retreated into his own little world. He's locked himself in!'

'Perhaps he's shocked, too.'

She laughed. 'Yes, I should think he fucking well is,' she said.

'And when he isn't shocked, when he recovers from his father's death, and the betrayal from the woman he loves, he'll see that he has to retain the estate.'

'He'll give it to her.'

'No,' he said. 'His father's already done that.'

She slumped in the bed, kicking at the coverlet that lay in a pile next to it. 'I'll think of something, with or without your help,' she said.

He walked over to her. 'Did I say that I wouldn't help?'

Laura looked up at him.

'I didn't say that I wouldn't help,' he told her.

He reached down and ran a finger down her neck, until it rested on the point between her breasts.

'I don't know what to do,' she said.

'We'll do what I always planned to do,' he replied quietly. His finger ran on downwards, his eyes on hers. 'Lie down,' he said.

'What do you mean?' she asked.

'We're going to help her fall,' he said. 'Lie down.'

She fell back on the bed. Ben McGovern unfastened his belt. Her eyes flickered to it as he measured the length of the leather in his hands.

'Fall?' she repeated.

He wound the belt around his fist. 'You see Laura,' he murmured, gently, 'you do fall a very long way when you're thrown out of heaven.'

Thirty-Three

After lunch, the girl came down from her room at Brimmer House, and sat in the entrance hall. The house mother, seeing her standing by the door, called out from her desk.

'Do you want something?'

The girl didn't turn. The woman looked at her assistant and sighed with exasperation. She got up, wrestling her considerable bulk from the chair, and walked out. She touched the girl's arm.

'What do you want?' she asked.

The girl was regarding the street, watching each car that passed. Down the short drive, the white petals fell from the chestnut trees. Occasionally, she glanced up at them.

'Do you want me to ring Ms Phillips?'

The girl looked down at the hand on her arm, and the woman removed it. 'You can't stand there all afternoon, can you?' she asked.

Getting no reply, she shrugged. 'I'm just inside this door,' she said. 'You can see me, all right?'

The girl's eyes strayed over her face, and lingered for some seconds on her short red hair, but she said nothing. The woman went back to her desk. 'What can I do?' she asked her assistant. She sat down in her chair, and fiddled with her hair, pulling the long strands of her fringe between thumb and forefinger. The feather earrings she wore swung back and forth. 'I can't let her out.'

'It's like the dog in Edinburgh,' he replied.

'What dog?'

'That one that waited by his master's grave for years.'

'Don't be daft.'

They both looked at her.

The young man leaned forward to whisper. 'She's weird,' he said. 'Never seen anyone so still. Look at her.'

They did. The girl was like a statue. The face of Artemis, profiled, on the Parthenon frieze. Cool marble.

'It's psychological. A psychological symptom.'

'Of what?'

Neither of them knew. Upstairs, the landings reverberated to the passing of feet and the raised voices of an argument. Downstairs, the girl's sublime expression hardly flickered.

They heard a car turn into the drive.

The girl walked forward.

The assistant went back out to the hall, and saw that the girl had almost flattened herself to the glass, both palms pressed hard against it. Outside, Anna Miles stood opposite her, her hand on the intercom. In response to the assistant's question, she gave her name and Robert Wilde's number. The door lock was released.

As soon as she was over the doorstep, the girl clasped Anna's hand. She looked earnestly into her face.

'Does she know you?' the assistant asked.

They went into a small sitting room, deserted because there was no TV. In the cramped space, two battered sofas faced each other, a table in the middle. Posters on the wall gave numbers for helplines: drugs, AIDS, abuse. The girl sat down, still holding Anna's hand, under a picture of a child, with its head on its knees, crouched on a dark stairwell. Anna, unable to extricate herself, sat down next to her, their knees almost touching.

It was difficult not to return the intensity of the girl's look. The attention of the blue eyes was almost unblinking. Anna glanced down at the grip in which her own fingers were caught: both the girl's hands, now, folded tightly over hers.

'I remembered,' Anna said. 'At least, I think I do.'

The girl smiled.

'Did I remember right? A concert weekend.'

199

Tighter pressure in the hands.

'It was at Marr Breck House. The house with the lake.' Anna nodded. 'I went to three summer schools at that house,' she said. 'You were at the last one.' Her eyes ranged over the girl. 'Was it really you?' she considered aloud. 'The girl with the Chinese violin . . .'

Most of the children who had gone to those summer schools were firmly middle class. Torn T-shirts, but expensive trainers and even more expensive – wildly expensive – instruments. If this was the girl, she had been the only one with a cheap violin. Anna thought she recalled it – its bright orange, too-shiny finish.

'You weren't at my school,' Anna said. 'And I don't know where you lived.' It was hard having a conversation with someone who could not, or would not, speak. As far as she could remember, the girl had had an unremarkable voice, very low, a little strained. Some of the lisped tones of childhood.

Whispered confidences.

'Do you remember speaking to me?' Anna asked.

The girl smiled again.

'You do? You *can* speak. You remember what you said . . . did you carry on playing the violin?'

The girl released her hands, and turned them over so that the palms were uppermost. Anna looked down at her fingers.

'You did,' she said. 'And you play still.'

The girl didn't move.

'I didn't play my violin for several months,' Anna said. She gave a ragged hitch of breath, not quite a sigh. 'And I left my piano behind completely. When I came here, I never even thought about it for a month. A whole month. It was as if I had been anaesthetized. It came back . . . slowly. Like getting warm again after being out in winter. Like hands getting feeling back. Pinched feelings. Realized that here I was. No piano. Nothing to play. Except the violin. Thank God I brought it with me,' she added, smiling slowly.

She got up, and walked to the window.

Behind her, the girl watched.

The chestnut trees dipped and swayed.

Anna turned back. 'Did you run away with Alisha Graham?' she asked. 'From something? Or to something?'

The girl leaned forward and, in a first attitude of weariness, put her head in her hands.

'Tell me,' Anna said. 'You can. I won't tell anyone else, I promise. I didn't tell anyone then.'

In the silence, Anna fought for direction.

'You told me that you lived with your father,' she continued. 'And that you had a stepbrother who came to visit you both. Your mother had died. You didn't remember her. You had no sisters. There was just you and he in the house. You told me that your father was in trouble, but you wouldn't say what. You said . . .' Anna sat down, looking at the fingers laced over the girl's forehead. 'You said that the police had come to the house.'

The girl took her hands away. There was an expression of defeat on her face.

'What happened?' Anna asked. 'What happened to him?'

Silence.

'They had been once, you said. And then brought him back. Did they come again?'

The girl glanced around herself eloquently.

'Were you taken to a place like this? And then . . . what? Did he come back? Did you go back home? Was there someone to look after you?'

Abruptly, the girl crossed her arms over herself.

'Someone looked after you . . .'

Anna recognized that look. She had felt it herself. Rock still, willing whatever frightened you to stay away. Powerlessness.

Five years ago, the girl had told her, in halting little sentences, out there by the lake at Marr Breck House, under a tree like the chestnuts outside, with the sunlight filtering over her face, over her hands folded neatly in her lap, that her father never slept. That he never let her sleep. That they spent the night walking through the house – some large and unkempt house in an unnamed street. Walking the dark down.

Anna had been confused at the time. She could see that it was a confession, that it was important, that her father's insomnia was far more significant than the girl could say. And she had stared at those same hands while recounting the visit of the police. But, when Anna had suggested that the girl talk to a teacher, or a family friend, or that they could go and see her father together, the girl had simply rebounded with shock. She had held Anna's arms and begged her not to breathe a word. Begged her to forget what she had said. Backtracked, denying that it was anything serious. Stumbled over her words. Her father was making her tired. He was often sad. He missed her mother. That was all. He had done nothing wrong. It was a mistake, she said. Yet there was horror in her eyes that belied her words. She had stared into Anna's face. *That was all. That was all.*

Much against her better judgement, Anna had promised not to tell anyone. The girl's face had immediately relaxed. She had walked away, out into the full sunlight, across the lawn, leaving Anna perplexed in her wake. And, when she had caught the girl's eye later on the same afternoon, the girl had smiled so broadly that Anna could almost have believed the whole conversation had been a dream.

And yet it had been no dream. More than that – it had been so curious, that she had remembered it for seven years.

And the girl.

'Who was it that looked after you? Was it someone close to you?'

She reached out to touch the girl. As she did so, she felt the girl trembling, shuddering. It was like passing her hand through an electric field.

'A friend of your father's?' she guessed. 'An aunt . . .?'

The girl shook her head violently.

'Not a woman. Another man? What man?'

The girl drained of what little colour she possessed, and looked ready to fall. She was totally closed off, inhabiting the memory.

'I wish you would give me a clue,' Anna pleaded. 'Why did you come to me? I don't understand. You brought Alisha Graham to me – for what? Why? What could I do?'

She saw that tears had escaped the tightly shut eyelids.

'Oh, don't cry,' she whispered, appalled that she had apparently caused such misery. 'Whatever it was, it's gone now. You're safe here. You got here, you're safe . . .'

The girl's eyes sprang open. She gripped Anna's arms just below the shoulder.

'What is it?' Anna asked.

Shaking, shaking. Eyes wide.

'You're safe,' Anna insisted. 'It's far away.'

The girl groaned, dropped her hands, and fell back on the sofa. She began to roll her head from side to side.

Realization dawning, Anna dropped to her knees beside her.

'You're not safe?' she asked.

The girl's head shook vehemently.

'You're *not* safe,' Anna said, slowly.

The girl placed her index finger on Anna's chest, weeping. The finger pointing, jabbing with insistent pressure. Returning to her own throat, where it pressed down hard. Swinging back to Anna. Back and forth. Back and forth.

You. Me.

You, me.

The world rolled with them.

'You're not safe,' Anna whispered. 'And neither am I.'

Robert Wilde was halfway home when he had to pull off the motorway.

He drove into the service area, and got out of the car in a hurry, slamming the door on a back seat piled high with paper, his case and briefcase, and a box of Alisha Graham's computer discs. He was gasping for air.

He walked away from the car, over to a grassy area, a windblown spot overlooking a vast field of wheat. He forced himself to take several deep breaths. A woman walking her dog looked at him, and looked away. He wondered if his fear was written on his face. He wondered if it showed. He felt that it must: he felt that it ought to be hanging over him, neon letters ten feet high. He felt that he radiated it – that it poured off him and stained the ground. Touched people's bodies as they passed. Communicated his cowardice like a disease.

203

He had hardly slept last night.

He had kept on seeing Christine's face. He had kept on hearing her pleas, kept remembering that he had run away from her. That she had asked him to do something, and he hadn't grasped what it was, hadn't done whatever it was, and he had been left with the dread that it was something important. Something shatteringly important.

To tell himself that it was just a dream, an image, a hallucination, whatever name you cared to put to it . . . well, it was no use. He could still see Christine's face. He could still hear her voice. He could still see himself falling out of the door of that house and running down the drive.

How he had got through the conversation with Sophie Tarrant outside the Pennystone Road house, he would never know. He had given her some sort of garbled explanation, claiming that a purely fictional asthma attack had driven him from the building. The woman had, unexpectedly, been all sympathy. She suffered from attacks herself, she said. Asthma and hayfever. It was the pollen and grass seed. It was the season. She had an inhaler in the car . . .

He had raised his face to her.

'It's the season,' she had repeated. 'Everyone's coming down with it. Haven't you noticed? People are getting it who've never had it before. It's the season . . .'

Poor girl. She really must have thought he was insane. He heard himself refusing the inhaler. He couldn't possibly touch it. He couldn't touch her. He was afraid there was something on him – something that would contaminate her. He could feel threads hanging from his hands. His face was crumpled in shock. He was not in his right body – it was not him. He was stranded in a jangle of skin and bone, a refugee – displaced. Disconnected. He had only wanted to run, and had done so, apologizing over his shoulder, pointing vaguely to his watch, thanking her in jumbled sentences. He could still see her standing, perplexed, in the drive, as he had got into his car, crashed it into gear, and driven away.

He ought to have had an accident, the state he was in. He had driven about for hours, and had only gone into the police station in mid-afternoon, without even accurately being able to remember where he had been since that morning. Now he knew what people meant when they said they were not themselves.

He hadn't quite lost that sensation of something foreign clinging to his hands, but no one at Wallis's station seemed to notice. Perhaps because they didn't know him well enough to see the difference. Perhaps because they were too busy. Whatever the reason, he had been glad not to have his discomfort commented upon.

He had collected the last photocopied papers from a sergeant at the headquarters building.

'Been to Pennystone Road?' the man had asked.

'Yes . . . yes, I have. Why?'

'Heard Inspector Wallis say so.' Wilde had signed with some difficulty, trying to feel the contours of the pen, feel its pressure against the page in front of him. He had leaned on his spare hand to steady himself.

The sergeant was lazily scratching his head. 'Been trying to remember that address,' he said.

'Sorry?' Wilde said.

'Pennystone. Rings a bell.'

'There was a fire,' he said.

The sergeant closed the book and returned it to the drawer. 'Yeah . . . it wasn't that though. Something else, way back.'

Wilde looked at him. 'What else?'

The sergeant had smiled broadly. 'It'll come to me,' he said. 'Sooner or later.' He had added, 'Probably not the same house. Just the same road.'

Wilde now stood on the patch of grass, staring at the field ahead of him. Behind him, the constant arrival and departure of cars, the raised voices of families, and the noise of the motorway itself, swiftly receded.

He looked at the wheat. Acres of it rolled away from him down a slight hill. The crop that was closest to him made a little noise as it moved, a sibilant patter like the turning of heavy pages. He looked at the dry trench next to the fence that still bore the imprint of the tractor wheels. He looked at the wheat itself, thick and green and straight, each stalk emerging out of a hard clay.

It's the season.

205

The words had echoed through him all night.

It was so unlike him not to sleep. He had never had a problem. He always fell asleep straight away, half hoping for the Christine dream. Eight hours. Like a clock. Asleep at eleven, awake at seven. He never woke in between. He never lay listening to the hours sounding on the alarm clock with a subdued single tone. It was not him. Not him . . .

He tore his eyes away from the ground and looked up at the sky.

Yesterday, he had run away from his wife. He had left her in that place.

It's the season.

Robert, Robert . . .

He was no longer himself.

No, no.

Not since yesterday.

'No,' Anna Miles said. 'No.'

She was standing by the front entrance of Brimmer House, by the plate-glass doors of the entrance hall. She tried to disengage the girl's hands from her arm.

'I have to go,' she said. 'I'll come back. Tomorrow, if you like.'

The girl's grip tightened.

The house mother emerged from her office. Anna turned to her.

'I have to go,' she repeated.

The woman stepped forward, and put her own hands on the girl's. 'Come on now,' she coaxed.

The girl tried to wrap her arms around Anna.

'I will come back,' Anna promised, shocked at the sudden grip. Her body was being squeezed so tightly that it was hard to breathe. The girl's breath was in her face, the odour of her body enveloping her. It was like being buried, wrapped in earth. She smelled of leaves.

'Please,' Anna said. 'I can't take you. I'm not allowed.'

The girl's arms suddenly swung upwards from Anna's body and wound around her neck.

'Oh no,' Anna said. 'You'll strangle me . . . please. I can't breathe.'

The assistant appeared on the stairs. 'What's going on?' he called.

'Give us a hand, Mike.'

He jogged down the steps. The two women were struggling with the girl. He tried to step in between them. Quite suddenly, the girl turned, releasing Anna, breaking free of the three of them. She flung herself on the door.

'Don't do that,' Anna said. 'Listen . . . I will come back. I promise you.'

Afterwards, Anna would find it hard to recall the sequence of events. The man at Anna's side reached forward to touch the girl, to take her wrist, her arm. Just for a second, Anna saw the girl's palm flattened against the glass, and that expression that she had first seen four days before, in the early hours of the morning – that serene, detached expression as the girl had stood in the pouring rain outside the cottage. But then, Anna felt the floor under her give a little ripple, as if someone had taken one end of the carpet, lifted it, and pulled. It was no more than that – just a ripple. A murmur. A contraction under her feet.

The house mother took the girl's hand in her own, and turned her away from the door. 'That's better,' she said. 'Come on inside and let your visitor get away.'

Anna looked from one to the other, and then back at the floor.

No one had felt it. The phone was ringing in the office.

'Come along,' said the house mother.

The girl smiled, reached up gently, and tapped her fingertip on the woman's earring. The feather curled around, against the back of her hand.

'That's right,' the woman said. 'That's better, isn't it?'

The girl inclined her head towards Anna.

'This isn't the place for her,' Anna said softly. 'It's not the right place.'

Thirty-Four

From the window of his study, Matthew Aubrete watched the visitors in the gardens.

It was late in the afternoon, two hours before closing. A family had sat down on one of the benches by the knot garden. Their daughter, no more than three, was pushing her own buggy up and down the path in the warm, slanting sunshine. Every now and then she stopped to scoop gravel into the seat. He watched the little blonde head, the striped dungarees, the surprisingly fat little legs on their purposeful journey. He was fond of children. He had not given up hope of having them, although Laura was adamant that she had no desire to give birth, and Anna . . .

Well, what future did he have with Anna? He couldn't say. He had never known. He knew even less now.

Laura was right when she said that he knew nothing about her. When he had first met Anna, he had been so struck with her – a feeling of having known her before, of resuming something left unfinished – that he had allowed himself fantasies. Loose and wayward threads of enthusiasm and desire. The fantasy of being with her, and not with Laura. The fantasy of a quiet divorce. The fantasy of a family. They were all things that he wanted, but he had never known – and he understood this now – he had never known if it was what *she* wanted.

He had supposed – well, such suppositions hardly bore the light of day. They seemed so naïve now. He had supposed, lying with her in his arms, having taken her to bed, having possessed her – oh God, all those afternoons, all those mornings – he had supposed that he had really been allowed to see her. To know her. Yet, in brutal fact, he had seen and shared only what she wanted him to see and share. He had travelled for months in what now turned out to be a totally foreign country, whose borders he had never really explored at all, whose secrets remained secrets, even though he had no secrets from her.

He had been open and honest with her, as he had never been with any other woman. And he had assumed . . . assumptions and suppositions. That was what it was all about. That was his downfall. They were all, truthfully, that his affair with Anna Miles was built upon. His assumptions. His suppositions. His nakedness, in every respect, in front of a woman who kept her secrets to herself.

And then there was another, less appealing fantasy. A more fragile hope. If he were honest, he supposed that he thought the lure of Aubrete would be enough. If she only loved him a little, she would surely love the house, the gardens. Which she had, of course. She had.

He turned away from the window, making a small grimace of despair. *You bloody fool, boy.*

His father's voice. An echo of Laura.

He sat down at the table and smoothed his hands over the maps. Yesterday, he had made a decision to clear the room, to box all the records he had so carefully compiled over the last twenty years, and seal them so that they would be ready for transport. He had started to fill the boxes with this overpowering feeling of shame. He had been set up by Anna Miles and never understood. He had been a target. He might as well have stood out in the fields with a bulls-eye over his heart. He had been so transparent, so innocent. And it was not as if he could plead youth, either. He was thirty-six – and he had fallen lock, stock and barrel for a woman with some sort of secondary agenda.

Even now, as he sorted through the records with a keenly aching heart, he could not get over how helpless she had seemed. Every now and then, the thought overwhelmed him . . . surely she *had* been helpless? Surely she had been. That first morning, her expression of desperation. Had that been manufactured, even then? She had never told him what she was running from, only that she *was* running, and had reached the end of her tether. Almost, literally, the end of the road. He had pitied her so very much. And felt this curious déjà vu.

He thought he knew her.

More fool him.

Mid-morning yesterday, Laura had come upstairs and knocked at the door.

'What are you doing?' she had demanded. 'Open this door.'

He had done so, dejected and heavily preoccupied. Laura had stood on the threshold, hands on hips, looking past him.

'I'm packing,' he had told her.

She didn't come into the room. 'Packing?' she repeated. 'Just like that?'

'It will take some time.'

She had slapped him. Her move had taken him so much by surprise that he didn't have a chance to put a hand up to protect himself. 'What is the matter with you!' she had cried. 'We're not going anywhere. Nowhere! What the hell is the matter with you?'

She had gone downstairs cursing him. At the bottom of the flight, he had heard her say, 'I'm married to an idiot, God help me.'

He picked up the nearest book, now, from a pile that he had sorted last night. Although he had read it many times, he opened it again, tracing his finger down the worn red leather spine. The pages inside were flimsy, fragile as threadbare silk, covered in an equally frail web of handwriting.

Vestry meeting 20 August 1799.

He folded his arms, and read carefully, slowly, with the old feeling of responsibility and guilt slowly settling on him with every sentence.

The lessees of Poor Heart are agreeable to the payment of £30 per annum in lieu of all parochial rates, read the first entry. *The Parish determined upon a catalogue to be taken of all goods in the houses of paupers receiving Parish relief . . . Upon setting the poor relief rate, the Parish lowers the weekly pay of the paupers in every instance where possible, and no pauper shall receive more than two shillings . . .*

Wearily, Matthew turned the page.

The notes of the meetings were economically worded. He imagined the vicar, sitting with his back to the cold wall of the church, the notebook held in his lap, listening to the church wardens, the two overseers, and the magistrate. Each vestry meeting rarely commanded more than half a dozen terse lines of script. In 1802, there was a scribbled note, almost like an afterthought, that children of those who received the Poor Rate – the Income Support of its day, but given with appalling grace and under a cloud of disgrace – should be apprenticed out. Just before Christmas, on 16 December 1802, a boy of nine and a girl of seven were apprenticed out of the parish, to a farm twelve miles away.

God knows what they had faced when they got there, Matthew thought. Two little beggars on a doorstep. Free labour. The depths of winter, a winter recorded with a heavy January snowfall that would not free the roads.

He turned another page.

It was the record of the pit workings and the amounts owed to the Parish by the mine. Every time he read them, Matthew's blood froze. He imagined dropping slowly through a thousand feet into the dark. A thousand-foot mine shaft lit with candles. *January, 1800.* The juddering and groaning of the rope as it shuddered around the wheel above ground. The thickening air.

Many times in the past, that image had woken him at night, with an overpowering sensation of claustrophobia. He would sit up, straining for air, as the nightmare fought the darkness, and he saw each guttering candle slowly snuffed out. He would be left in pitch blackness, where even the throaty and distant sound of the horse gin receded, and then eventually evaporated as neatly as the candles. And then he would know that there was no more air, no more air at all in the narrow thousand-foot drop – and his lungs, cramped, agonizing, tried to pinch oxygen and failed. He would stagger out of bed, and only then really wake, grasping the window sill, flinging open the window itself, breathing in the salt air of the coast with blissful gratitude.

He closed his eyes now and tried to banish the image.

They were still there, whispered an accusing little voice in his head.

Can't you hear those last gasps for air?

They drowned underneath you.

Right under this house . . .

He started gathering the papers together, his fingers labouring

211

clumsily over the task. Heaping them into a box, he walked to the door with the box in his arms, balanced it on one hip, and unlocked the door with his free hand.

A man stood in the doorway.

Matthew almost dropped the box.

'I'm so sorry,' the man said. 'I was about to knock.'

Matthew looked behind him on to the landing, for signs of Laura or one of the stewards. The man was tall, dark-haired, handsome. Immaculate in a dark suit, and carrying a briefcase.

The stranger held out his hand. 'Mrs Aubrete suggested I come up,' he said. 'My name is Ben McGovern.'

Matthew took him into his study. After shaking his hand, it seemed absurd to have him stand on the doorstep. Ben McGovern entered with an air of hesitation. He stood in the centre of the room looking, Matthew thought, like some sort of advertisement – for cologne, perhaps, or clothes. The kind of tailoring that carried a label and cost a fortune. He was incredibly neat. The suit was uncreased, the shirt and silk tie were pristine, the shoes highly polished. The man looked as if he had been scrubbed hard, like a wood cutting board that is scrubbed to a satin-white finish over the years. His face was so smooth that it was hard to believe he might shave. Even the parting of his hair was terribly clean, a white line in a blue-black palette.

Action Man, Matthew thought, amused and bemused at the same time. And he tried to immediately quash the childish comparison. The next thought came straight on its heels. *He's a lawyer. He looks like a London lawyer.*

'Has Laura employed you?' he asked.

Ben McGovern was looking slowly over the room. He returned his languid and friendly gaze to Matthew. 'Employed?' he repeated.

'Are you working on the will?'

McGovern smiled. 'No,' he said. 'Actually, I'm an architect.'

'An . . .?'

'I'm working just up the road, in town. On a suite of offices for Brindley and Machen.'

Matthew stared at him blankly. 'I'm sorry,' he said eventually. 'I don't understand why you're here.'

McGovern inclined his head towards the desk. 'Packing this is a lengthy task,' he observed.

'Yes, it is. Look . . .'

'Mrs Aubrete tells me that the estate was once a mine. A coal mine.'

'It was,' Matthew said. 'The mine closed in 1800. My great great-grandfather was a shareholder. He bought the land and built this house.'

'Fascinating,' McGovern said. 'It seems so unlikely now. In such a beautiful setting. I see that it's an interest of yours, history. Where was the pit head?'

'On top of the hill.'

'The hill I've just driven down, the avenue of trees? Quite amazing. One would never guess. And the house is built over the mine?'

'Over two of the seams. They went under the sea,' Matthew said. 'Two hundred years ago. Look, Mr . . .'

McGovern opened his briefcase. 'McGovern,' he repeated. 'Here's my card. Just to show you that I am who I say I am.'

Matthew read it. 'I don't doubt you,' he said.

'Good,' McGovern replied. 'I rather think that's important just now.'

Matthew frowned. He wasn't following this conversation. He felt absurdly at a disadvantage, while, conversely, Ben McGovern looked remarkably at ease.

'Mrs Aubrete and I met two weeks ago,' McGovern was saying. 'She's on the Museum Committee. I'm a freelance. I work all over the country. I was drafted in for an opinion. A professional opinion, on the stresses in the roof?'

Matthew was still staring at him. 'I don't know anything about it,' he said, at last. 'Laura doesn't tell me what she does on all her committees.'

McGovern nodded as if he knew this already. 'I saw her again the other day,' he said. 'Two days ago, in fact. And that is when we realized the extraordinary coincidence.'

'Coincidence?' Matthew said.

'Yes. Extraordinary,' McGovern repeated. 'Anna Miles.'

Matthew sat down. McGovern inclined his head towards a chair. 'May I?'

'Yes . . . please.'

McGovern put his briefcase on the floor next to him. 'I'm sorry,' he said. 'This is a bit awkward, isn't it? It does sound as if I've intruded on your affairs.'

'I don't know what you've done yet,' Matthew said.

Another smile. 'Other than to offer an opinion, nothing,' McGovern remarked.

'An opinion on what?'

'Anna.'

Matthew bit the inside of his lip, to force himself not to echo McGovern like a parrot. Anna's name, trapped inside his mouth, felt too large to contain. It was as if he could taste her, feel her smooth round shoulder under his tongue.

'I've known Anna for several years,' McGovern said. 'Until the day she disappeared, in fact.' He crossed his hands, one on top of the other, loosely in his lap. 'We were . . . well, it doesn't matter, any more, what our relationship was. I had supported her . . . I had supported her through several crises.' The smile was not quite so bright now. McGovern wore an expression of genuine regret. In fact, he turned away from Matthew and glanced at the maps and papers, taking a deep breath. 'I suppose I thought that we had an understanding,' he said quietly. 'But I was evidently wrong.'

It was such a perfect echo of Matthew's own thoughts not three or four minutes ago, that it was almost tempting to believe that this stranger had read his mind.

'You and Anna?' Matthew said. 'Where?'

'Where she came from. Manningham.'

There was a momentary silence while Matthew tried to assimilate this information. 'Manningham,' he said. 'I see.'

'She never told you where she was from?'

'No.'

'She didn't mention anything at all? About her house, her job?'

'No.'

McGovern gave a short, breathy laugh. 'But surely you asked her?'

'Yes, I did. She said she wanted to forget her past.'

McGovern said nothing. Then, he began to drum his fingers on the back of one hand. 'You see, this is what I find so very surprising,' he remarked. 'Mrs Aubrete has told me a little of what has happened with Anna, and . . . well, I find it so surprising.'

Matthew bridled. '*I* find it surprising that she should confide in *you*,' he said. 'My wife is not the confiding kind.'

McGovern shrugged. 'I don't think of myself as the sort of person that people do confide in, normally,' he admitted. 'But Mrs Aubrete was so obviously distressed the other day. We were both early for the meeting, and I bought her a coffee . . . she told me about this woman who had usurped her position. In . . . well, in every respect, it seems.'

Matthew felt himself colour. 'That's none of your business,' he said.

'No,' McGovern agreed readily. 'No, indeed it isn't,' he said. 'Yet when she mentioned the woman's name, when she described her, when she showed me her photograph . . .'

'Laura had a photograph of Anna?'

'A staff photograph. Taken here at Christmas.'

Matthew held up his hand. 'Just a minute,' he said. He was trying to get his bearings. 'Anna has a house in Manningham.'

'Oh yes. A very nice little terraced house.'

'And she had a job.'

'Year head, no less.'

'Year head? What is that?'

'She was a teacher.'

Matthew dropped his gaze from McGovern, and stared at the floor.

'And you knew nothing about it?' McGovern said. 'She was a music teacher.'

'I know she plays the violin,' Matthew murmured.

'Not just played. Taught,' McGovern said. 'And you really had no idea?'

'I didn't want to press her,' Matthew told him. 'When she arrived here, she was very upset. Very upset.' He was still staring at the floor, remembering Anna on that first morning. The terror in her face. The panic. 'I never wanted to pressurize her,' he murmured. 'I thought . . . I thought, in the weeks afterwards, that perhaps she had had some sort of breakdown.'

He looked up. McGovern did not seem surprised.

'Anna is a very confused person,' McGovern agreed. 'She has been in hospital. She was – what do the medics call it? – delusional. Depressed. She thought that people close to her were hell bent on cheating her, attacking her. Whatever. It was very sad. It happened twice. She recovered. The school put her on a kind of extended notice. She was given every kindness, every opportunity, to recover, to get back on her feet.' He leaned forward. 'But I wouldn't be here to interfere,' he said, 'if that were all.'

Matthew felt a prickle of unease. It ran down inside him like a draught of ice water. 'All?' he said. 'If that were all . . .? What do you mean?'

McGovern closed his eyes briefly, as if seeing something unpleasant in Matthew's face. When he opened them again, he gave a replica of the first bright smile. 'I can see myself in you,' he said. 'I do sympathize.'

Matthew gritted his teeth. 'Don't sympathize,' he said. 'Just tell me.'

McGovern returned his look calmly. 'Mr Aubrete,' he said. 'I loved Anna. I loved her very much. We were going to be married.' He paused. When he carried on, his voice broke slightly. 'But I have to tell you, that if you think that Anna is a proper beneficiary, an honest beneficiary, of your money – of this estate, in fact – then I'd ask you to reconsider the kind of person you're dealing with. The person,' he said, 'that, to be frank, you do not know.'

Matthew felt a deadly calm, a calm composed of rising horror, settle on him like a shroud. 'Tell me,' he repeated.

'Just over a year ago,' McGovern said, 'Anna Miles stole a great deal of money from me. And then, she disappeared.'

Thirty-Five

Beryl Graham was adamant.

She stood in Peter York's study, drawing herself up to her full five foot six, every inch bristling with indignation.

'Don't tell me what I can and cannot do,' she said.

Peter York had tried to offer her a seat, and failed. He stood opposite her, giving her a smile that only seemed to incense her further. 'I'm not trying to tell you,' he said quietly. 'But I would like to perform the service if you want Alisha buried here.'

York looked into her face, and saw that Beryl had altered, in some subtle way, since her sister's death. Her face was more florid; less pinched, but with a bright, hard, intense look that he didn't much like. She had lost that placid self-righteousness that she had borne in front of her like a shield. There was no shield now. She looked peeled and raw. He had seen faces like that in psychiatric units – the vivid preoccupation on some inner conviction, irritated by the knowledge that the rest of the world didn't share it. Beryl Graham had come loose, like a boat sheered away from its moorings. She was floundering.

'I want Alisha buried here, and I want Reverend Morton to do it,' she repeated.

John Morton was an elderly vicar, technically retired, but who conducted services occasionally and fulfilled speaking engagements. He was a kindly old man who had, once or twice in the past, stood in for Peter York while he was on holiday. Peter knew that he would have no objection to conducting the funeral, but that was not the point.

'Miss Graham,' York said now. 'It's really up to me, you know, who is buried here and who carries out the service.'

'Nonsense,' she said. She turned away from him and glared at the bookcase, her shoulders hunched.

'This is my parish and what happens in it comes under my jurisdiction,' he said. 'It's my decision. For instance, the churchyard is very full, and whoever is buried here has to have been resident here at some time . . .'

'Alisha was,' Beryl said. 'She stayed with me for a month when she came back from America.' She lifted her head. She was still talking to the opposite wall. 'I shall see the Bishop. I shall talk to the PCC,' she said.

'Of course you can speak to whoever you wish,' he said, trying to ignore what was an obvious lie about Alisha having lived with her sister, for however short a period. He couldn't imagine Alisha tolerating Beryl for more than two or three hours at a stretch. 'But it still comes down to this,' he continued. 'The decision is mine. Neither the PCC nor the Bishop will interfere.'

Beryl at last turned back to him. 'I want her buried here, where I'm going to be buried,' she said. 'I want us in the same grave.' Her hands knotted tightly over the handles of her bag. 'I've lived here for nearly thirty years and been to this church for nearly thirty years, week in and week out, and I want her with me. Not with you lot. Not with all your blasphemies. Not put in the ground under your hand. I want her buried where she'll be safe from you. Buried by John Morton. Buried where I can find her. We'll be here when you're long gone.'

York sat down at his desk. He waited until the initial rush of fury had subsided. 'Blasphemies,' he said, at last.

The word seemed to drive life into her. She advanced on him. 'I know what you do,' she said. 'I know what you believe.'

He waited again. Waited, this time, for a little electric charge of fear to drain away. 'And what is that?' he asked.

Her mouth worked as if she was trying to spit the words out. 'All this praising and falling down and being taken by spirit,' she said, finally. 'You take the ordinary services like a real priest, being an imposter, and then you do that. And that's what you really want. You want us all to fall about on the floor. Roll on the floor like animals.'

'No,' York said. His face twitched in a relieved half-smile. 'That's hardly blasphemous, even if it were true, Miss Graham.'

She shook in the effort to keep control. 'Oh no?' she demanded. 'When I speak to the Bishop, I'll tell him. We'll see then if you find it so funny. I'll tell him you're up at that university with those girls.'

'Which girls?'

'The ones that turned poor Alisha's head.'

'No one on earth could turn Alisha's head. She had a mind of her own.'

'Filthy girls,' Beryl said. She was deep in her private obsession now. He wondered if it was this that had been possessing her for the last week. If it was the reason why she had not come to church. He had missed her little catlike, pious face at communion. He suddenly felt very sorry for her.

'I'll speak to John Morton,' he said.

'And I'll tell the Bishop about these magazines,' she said. She was looking at the piles of fresh issues on the table in front of her.

'The Bishop is well aware of the magazines,' York told her. 'It brings a needed income to the parish.'

'Filth and rubbish,' Beryl muttered.

Peter York stood up. 'A parish must make money,' he said. 'It must repair its buildings. It must keep its churchyards. You know that, Miss Graham. You know how much income has been generated by what you call this filth and rubbish. There are three churches in this parish, large churches in city streets. Prey to vandals and theft. St Luke's on Chine Road, with its kitchen for the homeless . . .'

'That's not what God's about,' Beryl said.

'I'm sorry?'

'You're having people in the door who don't care about God,' she cried. 'Wouldn't put their hand in their pocket for their fellow man. Shirkers, alcoholics . . . they're not God's people. They're the devil's people. Do you think, if the tables were turned, that any one of them would be in here every Sunday, putting money in the collection? They would not. They've fallen by the wayside because they're too lazy to stand up and work. And you want us to be tainted by them . . .'

'This really isn't getting us anywhere,' York said.

'Tainted! You understand? These people are pollutants. It's pollution, you see? Like oil in water. They can't mix, they're not in society, they're not decent.'

'Miss Graham . . .'

'And you're just like them,' she said. 'You're tainted by them. That's what's the matter with you. You get so close to them, you start to think like them. You start to think they're all right. You start to behave like them. You start to ignore decent people and all you think about is them, and what they believe is nothing, it's worth nothing, it doesn't matter . . .'

Suddenly, she stopped. Still staring at him, she burst into tears. She stood in front of him in her rigid checked tweed coat, so old that the cuffs were pale and threadbare, and she shook from head to foot.

'Come and sit down,' he said.

She pulled her arm away from his hand. 'I shan't,' she said, choking over her grief. 'I shan't ever sit down in this house again.'

Not long after she left, Peter York went over to the church.

He trod the gritstone path between the graves. The morning was pale and clear, the sun high in a cloudless sky. It filtered down through leaves on deserted graves. He hoped for a fine summer. He hoped, more importantly, for two weeks at his brother's house in Fréjus, looking out on to a turquoise ocean. He hoped that, next week, he would be able to make the trip to London to his quiet little flat, and the discreet woman who came there.

Contrary to what Beryl believed, he had never touched any girls, not even the Guardians. Other than the vigils at the Gate beneath Pennystone Road, when the most he succumbed to was a gentle holding of hands and comforting, chaste kisses. He blessed God for his mercy. His family money allowed him to escape the insanity occasionally. And, if the worst came to the worst – and he did not like to think of the worst, the scenario that the Guardians had painted for him – well, if it came to that, his money might help him to disappear altogether.

If, of course, there was anywhere left to go.

He looked around himself at the graves – line after line of the godly sleeping under the beech trees. No one ever came here, except perhaps the teenagers in the evenings, after he had locked the gates. They sat down under the trees, he knew, on the flat-topped crypts, and smoked. One morning, he had found silver paper and a razor blade here. Left on the memorial to Josiah Adams, churchwarden of this parish, 1833.

He unlocked the oak door, and went inside.

The church was silent and cold. York stood at the bottom of the aisle and looked around at the pews. Last year he had suggested to the PCC that they be ripped out. The church furniture would make a lot of money at auction, and the resulting space could be used as a mother and toddler group, a youth club, an auditorium for music and plays. A *place to fall down*, he could hear Beryl Graham bitterly add. The sale of the pews had been roundly opposed by the PCC, and he had not pursued it. By then, of course, the angels were upon him.

He walked up the aisle and opened the Bible on the brass lectern. He had a small pact with God here every day. It was not unusual – one of his parishioners had once told him that they did exactly the same. He would open the Bible every morning at random, and see what message was waiting for him. He always tried very hard not to let his fingers select a particular place. Today, he found that the Bible fell open at Zechariah, almost at the very end of the Old Testament, just before the Apocrypha.

. . . *let none of you imagine evil in your hearts against his neighbour* . . .

He smiled thinly. Ah, that was for Beryl. Poor Beryl. She imagined her neighbour to be literally that – the woman next door who also lived alone just as she did, listening to the Morning Service on the radio.

He ran his finger down the page.

Woe to the idle shepherd that leaveth the flock . . .

The burden of the word of the Lord . . . *which stretcheth forth the heavens, and layeth the foundation of the earth, and formeth the spirit of man within him* . . .

He looked for a long time at the words.

Then, he turned towards the altar.

The idle shepherd leaving his flock.

That wasn't what he was doing, he thought, staring at the crucifix.

221

He had abandoned no one. As for the rest, he believed that. In his heart. In his soul.

He believed that God moved in the depths. He believed that His hand passed through the world. He believed in the power of prayer, that all the whispered prayers of the world altered and shaped it. He believed in Christ's intercession for man. He believed in the spirit of man, unconquerable and eternal, a part of a persistent and flawless power . . .

He knelt down at the altar rail.

Idle shepherd.

He pressed his hands to his eyes.

Acland didn't count. If Acland had been abandoned, that had been his choice, a choice made long before York had ever heard of Pennystone Road. Acland was on the road to hell for years before that. For the years when he had hidden the disappearance of his wife. For the years when the house fell dark and was filled with strangers. Acland was damned, and the place where he lay was only a logical extension of the life he had led.

He deserved his position, sacrificed to the Gate.

After all, it was his fault. If anyone deserved to lie out of God's grace, it was the bitter little man with the scar.

Idle shepherd.

'No,' he murmured, through his fingers.

He could see Acland now, in that shadowy room under the stairs. The hole in the floor. The straps hanging from the beam. The horror of that meeting, and the girl who stood between them, a wraith who seemed to belong nowhere – not alive, not dead. York had reached out his hand to her.

'You can't touch her,' Acland had said.

She radiated light as he spoke.

'God be with me lying down, God be with me sleeping,' York whispered. 'With me in my dreaming, with me in the light of waking . . .'

There was a crack somewhere ahead of him – the sound of stone contracting in the cold. Perhaps the wood of the vestry door. Perhaps in the lock that had not quite caught.

'Protection of the archangel all about me,' York continued.

Behind the altar, the window bellied as if it had turned to water.

'Oh son of man, the prince of grace, the heart of peace . . .'

Leaves pressed to the green stained glass. The saints pictured behind the cross glowed in their primary colours. Between the lead and the pane, a tendril forced its way into the church, inching, caressing. Exploring like a thin brown hand. High over the chancel, the beeches strained against the window. York could hear their breathing, their coursing determination. Feel the roots under the foundations. He kept his hands pressed to his face.

'If evil should bar my way, put thou between me and the night . . .' he continued, his pace increasing. Keeping his eyes closed, he crossed himself.

He could see Acland. He could feel Acland. He could feel him in the running brown tendril, in the sound of the trees, in the pressure building in the church. He could feel Acland pushing against the door. He could see him again now, with his head down, concentrating on his terrible task. He could hear his voice echoing in the space under Pennystone Road.

'There is no barrier! There is no barrier!'

Oh God.

Dear, sweet Father in heaven . . .

Put it back.

Put it all back.

'From tonight until a year from tonight . . .'

But the words of the prayer abruptly stuck in Peter York's throat. He pulled his hands from his face, and opened his eyes, and stared at the faces in the glass, all Acland, and yet not quite Acland, green men from the depths, brown hands cracking the doors and windows.

And then, in the darkest shade, just for a moment, he saw Acland himself.

Just as quickly, the church reverted to its lonely silence. The noise of the trees retreated, the glass cooled and shrank, the saints looked down again with their implacable calm. The altar was empty of everything but the cross, shining in its little patch of sunlight.

Except for Acland's thin, dull-accented voice, crawling in York's head.

'Idle shepherd,' he breathed. 'Get me out.'

Thirty-Six

It was eight o'clock in the evening when Anna Miles visited Robert Wilde.

Alice came to the door in answer to Anna's knock, rubbing her hair dry with a towel.

'Yes?' she asked.

'Hello,' Anna said. 'Is your father in?'

'I don't know. He's busy . . .' Alice looked warily at their visitor. She was protective of her father at the best of times, but, having seen his exhausted face when she had got home from school that afternoon, she was more than usually worried about him. 'You shouldn't work so hard,' she had told him. 'I'm OK,' he had replied. But she knew that he wasn't OK. He seemed preoccupied, and, as she had sat down next to him on the couch to watch the TV news, he had held her hand tightly, without saying a word.

'Who is it?' she heard him call now.

'Anna,' the woman on the doorstep said.

'Come through,' he replied.

Alice stepped to one side with an air of disapproval, and went upstairs. She paused for a moment at the top to listen to the exchange of conversation.

'I have a message here to say they can't find you,' her father said.

'Good,' Anna Miles replied. 'If you lot can't find me, neither can he.'

Alice frowned. She paused for a second, winding her hair absentmindedly around one wrist. Then, she shrugged, and went into her bedroom, and closed the door.

Downstairs, Anna had sat down opposite Robert. He was sitting at the corner table, with the computer turned on.

'We must know where you are,' he said.

'I've come here to prove I haven't deserted you,' she said.

'Nevertheless.'

She sighed. 'I'm staying at the Oaks in Connor Street. I've told them my name is Wood.'

He smiled slowly. 'As in *you can't see the* . . .'

She grinned. '. . . *wood for the trees*. You've got it.'

'So might he.'

'No,' she said. 'I doubt it.' She looked him up and down. 'How was Manningham?'

'It was . . .' He paused. 'It was interesting.'

'Did you find out the girl's name?'

'No.'

'You look tired.'

'Yes . . . I am.'

He looked away. Anna frowned at him, then left it, sensing his desire not to discuss the matter.

'Dominic Aubrete left his estate to me,' she said.

He stared at her for a moment. 'I'm sorry . . . what?'

'Dominic Aubrete died, and he has left me Aubrete.'

'The whole estate?'

'Yes.'

'Bloody hell! Did you know?'

'Before now?' she said. 'No, of course not.'

'Didn't he tell you?'

'Not a word.' She sighed, half-laughing at the absurdity of it all. 'I've told you, this isn't about me, but about annoying Laura and Matthew, causing trouble for them. Between them.'

He stared at her calmness. 'And what did they say about it?'

'They're contesting it, of course.' She drew an invisible circle on the table next to her, on which she was leaning. 'I went to see a solicitor today.'

'And?'

'I told him that I wanted to sign it all back to them, and he said that I ought to at least secure my future. He said I ought to think twice before signing away over three million pounds.'

'Jesus,' Wilde whispered.

She appeared not to have heard him. The traces of humour left her face. 'I already have a house,' she said, as if thinking aloud. 'I don't want Aubrete. I want to go home.'

'But three million . . . hell *fire* . . . It's a lottery win, Anna.'

She looked up at him. 'Don't you see?' she said. 'It's not a winning ticket at all. It's not real. It's not mine. It's nothing to do with me. I'm just something Dominic's used to hurt Matthew. A hammer to hit them with. I want to wake up from this nightmare and *go home*.' She stopped, took a breath. 'What is the matter with you?' she said. 'You look terrible.'

'I'm all right,' he replied. 'It's the driving.'

She inclined her head towards the computer screen. 'What are you doing?' She could see text on the screen, closely written, without paragraphs or headings.

'It's Alisha Graham's diaries,' he told her. 'From the computer in her house.'

'Oh,' she replied. There was a pause. 'Don't you feel a bit odd, looking through them?'

She had hit the nail on the head. It was exactly what he had been feeling before she had rung the doorbell. Odd, intrusive. The diaries were not a record of Alisha's work, but an intimate portrait of her life.

'It wasn't password protected,' he said, as if this excused him.

Anna gave him a doubtful look. 'Is it helping?'

'Not yet,' he admitted. 'This is last year . . . she mentions a girl called Rhiannon . . .'

'Our girl?'

'I don't think so. She says Rhiannon has passed her pure maths . . . is taking a research post in Edinburgh . . .' He pressed *Page Up* for a few seconds, to find the entry. 'She seems unsure. She says, "*I don't think she'll write.*"'

'Another girlfriend.'

'It would seem so. She mentions Rhiannon's sisters coming to see her. A meal out. No church, no Omega . . . I'm sure it's a different girl,' he murmured. 'As you say, a previous girlfriend.'

'What about the end of last year?'

'I'm just coming to it,' he said. He scrolled the page slowly. 'Faculty dinner . . . argument with a senior tutor . . .' He smiled, then laughed. 'Didn't like him much,' he said, to himself. 'Christmas, went to Ireland. First week of January, lecture at Birmingham . . . second week . . . hello,' he said.

'What is it?'

'Praise meeting. Nicholson Refectory. Seven p.m.'

'Praise? Like a church?'

'I think so.' He leaned forward intently. 'Nothing else but a list of names . . . Ballochroy, Callanish, Caithness. Just names, written in italic.'

'Scotland,' Anna said. 'Perhaps she was visiting her girlfriend.'

'Just a list,' he repeated, reading. 'Croft Moraig, Kintraw . . . Castle-rigg.' He paused. 'I know where that is,' he said. 'It's in Cumbria. It's a stone circle.'

'You mean like Stonehenge?'

'A little.' He frowned.

'Did she visit them?'

'It doesn't say.'

Anna got up, and walked over to him, and looked over his shoulder. The next entry was a long series of what appeared to be calculations.

'What is an orrery?' Robert asked.

'I don't know,' she said. 'Where does it say that?'

'Here.' He pointed to the screen. Anna shrugged.

He got up and went to the bookshelf, and took down a dictionary. After a moment, he looked up at her. '". . . devised to represent the motions of the planets about the sun by means of clockwork."'

'But things like Stonehenge aren't clockwork,' Anna said. She thought a moment. 'She must mean that they represent planets and stars in stone,' she said. 'They're supposed to be ancient observatories, aren't they?' she asked. 'Places like Stonehenge . . . Castlerigg and Ballochroy and Callanish too, presumably.'

Robert closed the book and moved back to the computer. 'And all this comes after the church meeting at the university. Nothing about stone circles before that.' He sat down in the chair. 'Do you know anything about prehistory?' he asked.

She sat down next to him. 'Not a thing.'

'Neither do I.' He reached down into the briefcase at the side of the desk, and brought out a slim book, which he handed to her. 'I got this in Manningham, at the university,' he said.

She looked at the cover. 'Ley lines,' she said.

'I went to the campus, trying to find some background to this girl.'

'And did you?'

'No,' he said. 'But there seems to have been a lot of interest in this kind of thing up there.' He nodded towards the book that she still held.

She leafed through the book. 'Hmm,' she commented.

'You don't believe it?'

'It's not that I don't believe or disbelieve it,' she said. 'It's just not relevant, is it?'

'You're Irish. You're meant to believe it. Relevant to what?'

'I am not Irish,' she retorted. 'I was born in this country.'

'Well, you sound it,' he said.

She considered him with the beginnings of a smile. 'I'm just an Irishwoman's daughter,' she said. 'And as for relevance, I mean to today. To modern life.'

'It might be relevant to Alisha Graham. To this girl.'

'You think so?'

He paused. 'I don't know what to think, to be honest.' He toyed with the book as she handed it back to him. 'Alisha Graham was intrigued by gates and gateways. They figure in her notes – the papers, as well as these discs. Gates, entrances . . . markers, temples.' He ran a hand through his hair. 'There was a note on the screensaver of her computer that was a quote from a psalm used at funerals. There have been references to the book of Revelation . . . which mentions twelve gates, incidentally.' He glanced at her. 'There's something else, too.'

'What?'

'I spoke to the station, and they tell me that a farmer phoned up after the news conference to say that he had found some kind of fairy ring on his land.'

Anna laughed. 'Oh, come on.'

'Well . . . not a fairy ring. I don't know how you'd describe it. A ring of blood. On Ballantyne Hill. It's about twenty miles from here.'

'Pretty disgusting,' she commented. 'Could it be a coincidence?'

'Close to it was a shoe that turned out to belong to Alisha Graham. One of her missing shoes.'

Anna stopped laughing and leaned forward. 'Blood, and a shoe? But I thought you said she had died of a heart attack.'

'She did. It was animal blood.'

'Oh,' Anna said, in a small voice. Then she frowned. 'I don't understand. What was she doing? Did they kill something up there? And why did she leave her shoes behind?'

Wilde put the book down at last. 'She didn't leave her shoes. They fell off. She was pulled . . . dragged.'

Anna stared at him. 'You mean that she died on this farm. She had the heart attack up there . . . on this farm.'

He raised his eyebrows, surprised at his own sudden inability to keep confidence. It was breaking the rules of a lifetime. 'It's under investigation,' he said.

'Is it black magic?' Anna asked.

'I don't know.'

'White magic, then.'

'I don't know, really.'

'You must have a theory of some kind.'

'I can't say.'

Anna smiled slowly. 'Ah . . . pursuing enquiries,' she said.

'Yes,' he told her. 'Sorry. All that was confidential.'

'All of it?'

'Yes . . . all of it. Sorry.'

She was right. He was tired. Too tired to work this out. Tired enough to let his guard slip.

Anna regarded him, weighing him up. Then, she sat back in her seat. She crossed her arms. 'Have you really got time for all this?' she asked.

'For what?'

'This messing about over Alisha Graham.'

'No,' he admitted.

'Is there any crime to investigate?'

'I can't say.' He looked away from her, remembering the house at Pennystone Road, the overwhelming feeling that it was wrong, wrong in the roots of the foundations, wrong in every brick. The little room under the stairs. The nightmare folded in its heart, a nameless shape with Christine's voice imprinted deep inside. Wrong . . . *wrong* . . .

Anna was looking down at her crossed legs. One foot tapped the air impatiently. 'Is being pursued by a madman a dangerous situation?' she asked, mildly.

He tore his concentration away from Christine, and back to the woman in front of him. 'Of course it is,' he said.

'Is stalking a crime?'

'Yes.'

She paused. 'Chief Inspector Wilde,' she said. 'Are you going to investigate the crime I've told you about? My problem?'

'Yes,' he told her.

'Good,' she said.

They sat in the living room later, where Alice joined them.

She had brought a little yellow card downstairs, which she gave to her father. 'Last payment,' she said.

Anna glanced up at her with a smile. 'What's this?'

Robert signed the card, and gave it back to his daughter. 'Alice is going to France in two days with the school.'

'We pay by instalments,' Alice said.

'What part are you going to?' Anna asked.

'Brittany.'

'That's pretty. You'll like it.'

Alice sat down in the chair next to Anna. 'You've been there?'

'Yes. Once. With another school.'

Alice looked to her father, and back to Anna. 'Are you a teacher?'

'I used to be.'

'Did you give it up?'

'Yes,' Anna said.

'Why?'

Robert raised a hand. 'Alice, don't pry.'

'I'm not prying. I'm asking.'

Anna smiled. 'It's all right,' she said. 'I left because . . . well, I was forced to.'

'What did you do?'

'Alice,' Robert warned.

'Nothing bad. Nothing criminal, anyway. I gave in to a kind of bullying, I suppose,' Anna murmured.

'And you left your job because of that?'

'Yes, I did. I left home and came down here.'

'To avoid being bullied?'

'Yes,' Anna said. 'Kind of.'

Alice drew her legs up under her, and crossed her arms. 'You should have told someone,' she said.

'Let's change this subject,' Robert said.

'I know about bullying,' Alice objected. 'You have to have strategies.'

'I just thought it was better to get out of range,' Anna told her.

'And then they bully someone else.'

'I don't know if they did or not.'

'They always do. You're supposed to stand your ground.'

'I couldn't do that,' Anna said. 'It was too dangerous.'

'But they'd just pick on someone else. Or follow you.'

This was so close to home, so unintentionally true, that a silence fell. Alice looked from one to the other. 'They followed you?' she asked.

'It's complicated,' Robert told her.

'Where are they now?' Alice asked.

'I don't know,' Anna replied.

'But they've come down here after you?'

'Yes . . . I think so.'

Alice stared at her. 'Is it a lady?'

'No.'

Alice looked at her father. 'A man's following her,' she said. 'Dad, a man's following her.'

'I know,' he said.

'You've got to catch him.'

Robert gave her a small apologetic smile. 'We're trying.'

'*Trying?*' Alice repeated, outraged.

Anna put her head in her hands. To her horror, Alice saw that she had begun to cry. She leapt up from her seat and hovered at Anna's side, not sure if she ought to touch her. 'I'm really sorry,' she said. 'Look, it wasn't my business . . . I'm sorry . . .'

Robert stood up.

Anna wiped her eyes with the back of one hand. 'It's not your fault,' she said.

Alice stared helplessly at her father.

'You see?' he said. 'When I say to leave a thing, leave it. When I say change a subject, change it.'

'Don't get stressed with me,' Alice retorted. 'I wasn't to know, was I?'

'All right, but . . .'

'It's just always my fault, isn't it?'

'Don't be ridiculous,' Robert said.

'I'm not six years old, Dad.'

'I ought to know that if anyone does,' he replied, deeply irritated.

'Then don't treat me like a baby!'

'I wish you were a bloody baby, you'd be far less trouble.'

They were suddenly distracted by a noise at their side. Robert looked down to see Anna, still with the marks of tears on her face, actually laughing.

'God, I'm so pleased the world's the same,' she said.

'Sorry?' Robert asked.

She looked at Alice, smiling. 'I'm glad adolescence is the same. My dad and I used to fight all the time when I was fourteen and fifteen.'

'I'm not fighting,' Alice said. 'I'm the only one living in this house that's anywhere near sane.'

Robert looked at Anna. Then shrugged. 'She's right,' he said. He smiled rather languidly, defeatedly, at his daughter, and sat down. 'She's always right,' he said.

Alice looked triumphant. She sat back down in her chair. She looked across at Anna. 'My mum isn't around,' she said, abruptly. 'She died.'

Anna paused. She had been wiping her nose with a tissue. 'Oh, I'm very sorry,' she said. 'I didn't know that.'

'Did yours?'

'My mother?' Anna asked. 'No. At least, not when I was at school.'

'She's dead now?'

Robert put his hand over his face, but said nothing.

'Yes, she's dead now,' Anna said.

'What about your dad?'

'Him too.'

'Haven't you got anyone you can tell about this man?'

'I did have friends up there, but I didn't want to get them involved with this person, because I felt he'd take it out on them, too. And . . .' Anna paused, thinking. Trying to arrange the sequence of words coherently. 'I was very frightened. Perhaps I had a kind of breakdown. I had no idea of where I was going, just that I *was* going.'

Alice frowned. 'And you got a house here somewhere, and lived by yourself?'

'Yes,' Anna said. 'That wasn't difficult. I'd lived by myself before.'

'But didn't you miss your job?'

'Yes, very much.'

'What did you teach?'

'Music.'

'Cool! What can you play?'

'Oh . . . piano, violin, cello . . .'

'Cool,' Alice repeated. 'What bands do you like?'

'All kinds.'

'Seen anybody lately?'

Anna smiled. 'I've been a bit of a hermit,' she said. 'Until this summer.'

233

Alice's eyes ranged over Anna's face. 'Men are such shit,' she said.
Robert's hand fell. 'Alice!'

His daughter turned to look at him. 'Except you, Dad,' she said.

He gave a great sigh. 'Isn't it time you were in bed?'

Alice stood up, grinning. 'Probably.' She leaned down and kissed
him. Then, she turned to Anna. 'Are you coming back to see us again?'
she asked.

'Well . . . maybe.'

'I hope you are,' Alice said. 'Good night.'

When she had left the room, and they had listened to her footsteps
on the stairs, Robert smiled at Anna. 'I have to apologize for my
daughter,' he said. 'She's a nosy kid.'

Anna smiled. 'She seems very bright to me,' she said. She sighed
briefly, and sat forward in the chair. 'I ought to be going.' As she stood
up, she asked, 'What is going to happen to this girl now, the girl in
Brimmer House?'

Robert shook his head. 'She'll be seen by a psychiatrist, probably.'

'What if she doesn't speak?'

'She'll get care,' he said.

'But she's not really ill, is she?' Anna asked. 'She's hardly raving.
She's not violent.'

'Maybe she will talk. Maybe it's just the shock of Miss Graham's
death.'

'And if she does . . . if she recovers . . . what then?'

'The Social Services look after her. Find her a council flat. I really
don't know.'

'She'll have to wait weeks. Maybe months.'

'Quite possibly.'

'In Brimmer House?'

'I don't know. Brimmer is for young offenders. It can get pretty
packed.'

'Do you think she should be in there with them?'

'Where else is there?'

'It's not right,' Anna said. She pulled her handbag on to her
shoulder, and plunged her hands into the pockets of her jacket.

'You asked me earlier why I was doing all this,' he said.

'Yes.'

'If there's a reason, it's that girl,' he told her. 'She seems . . .' He searched for the words. 'If I say that she seems too good to be involved in this . . . that sounds naïve . . .'

Anna said nothing. She went out into the hallway, and, just before the door, turned back to him. 'It's not naïve,' she said. 'I feel it too. I saw her today, and I felt . . .' She stopped. Well, what *had* she felt, when it came to it? A ripple under her feet. A change in the air . . . what was that? A proof of innocence? Hardly.

She thought of Ballantyne Hill, and of someone dragging Alisha Graham. Perhaps this very girl dragging Alisha Graham. Dragging an elderly woman, perhaps dying, perhaps dead . . . involuntarily, Anna shuddered. Robert Wilde was right. It was in all probability naiveté, and an unwillingness to believe that the girl could represent anything harmful, she thought, that had led Alisha Graham to her death.

Then, something else occurred to her.

'Do you think this girl was saving Alisha Graham from some threat?' she asked.

'Like what?'

'This ritual . . .'

'The same type of blood was also found in Alisha Graham's house,' Robert said.

They regarded each other in confusion.

Anna dropped her head, then gradually looked up again at him. He thought – very idly, almost offhandedly – that her hair was very dark, and her skin was very light. And that the crowded, wary, don't-touch-me expression in her eyes was nothing at all like Christine. 'Thank you for listening to me,' she murmured.

'We will get on this case with McGovern,' he promised. 'We'll do what we can for you.'

She smiled rather crookedly. He could tell that she didn't believe him, or, if she did, had no faith in his ability to protect her. It rankled with him. He made a mental note to chase the subject up in the morning.

'Take care,' he said, opening the door.

'You too,' she said. 'Go to bed. Get some sleep, you look weary.' She was half out of the door when she said, really as a throwaway remark, almost under her breath, 'God be with you sleeping, tonight until a year from tonight.'

He grabbed her arm. 'What?'

She looked at him in astonishment. 'Pardon me?'

'What did you say just then?' She looked, pointedly, at his hand. He rapidly dropped it. 'I'm sorry. But what did you just say?'

'It's a prayer,' she said. 'My mother used to say it when I went to bed, that's all.'

'A prayer?' he asked.

'Yes,' she said. 'It's a Celtic prayer. They call them loricas. It's a sort of spell, I suppose.'

'And you mother knew all about that?'

'About what?'

'Celtic religion?'

She frowned. 'I don't know. Probably. She was full of stories. You know, the endless knot, and Fintan the son of Bith, and Otherworldly trees, and Fionn mac Cumhail. All that stuff.'

He stared at her blankly. 'I don't know what any of that is,' he said.

She smiled. 'I'll tell you sometime when you've got a year or two to spare.'

'And the prayer . . . the . . .'

'Lorica. You say it before sleeping, for protection.'

'Against what?'

'The perils of the night,' she said. 'You know, like *When I lay me down to sleep, I pray the Lord my soul to keep* . . . It's like that.'

'*If I should die before I wake* . . .' he said.

'Yes, like that,' Anna told him. 'A spell to keep the dark things away.'

Thirty-Seven

Sergeant Harry Endersley sat by himself in the staff canteen in Manningham.

He had chosen a seat as far away as he could get from the rest of the men and women who used the room, and the move was quite deliberate. Because he hated them all.

He sat stirring his tea, watching it morosely. He was a heavy set man, with a florid face that was round like a child's. He had come to this area twenty-two years ago, and been on this particular patch for sixteen. When he had first come to the city, he had been a bright recruit of twenty-four: the kind of lad who was keen to get stuck in – probably too keen, wading into fights and being free enough with his own fists in some tight corners for him to have earned a couple of bad annual reports. The lads had all liked him. But authority didn't. He couldn't ever keep his mouth quite shut enough either, and so, as the years progressed, Harry Endersley graduated to sergeant but never beyond, and now the bright recruit who had weighed ten stone dead in his navy-issue socks was forty-seven, and sixteen stone, and facing a long, steady, comfortable slide into a quiet retirement.

Not that it had particularly bothered him until now. Harry had never been ambitious. He hadn't joined the force to climb through the ranks, but to serve on the streets. He was an old-fashioned policeman, a real policeman, a bobby on the beat. He liked his secret free packets of fags from the corner newsagent, and he liked riding about in the occasional car looking smug, and he liked playing footie for the station team, and he liked nicking thieves.

Psychology he could do without. Race relations seminars he could

237

do without. Equal opportunities and sexual harassment lectures he could do without. What he liked was slamming the door on little shites who had burgled old ladies, and he liked a pint, and he liked going home at the end of the day and having his wife bring his dinner. If he never saw the rank of Inspector . . . well, he wouldn't have cared for it anyway. He wouldn't have spent any time on the streets as Inspector, and, worse still, he would have had to go and stand at County Hall cocktail parties and shake hands with women in suits.

Harry Endersley, in short, had been a relatively happy man until today. Until the bombshell. A bombshell which had nothing to do with work and everything to do with being dropped from the football team.

Sixteen bloody years, he thought, putting the spoon in the saucer and staring into space. Sixteen years on that team. At the very beginning, he had been centre half. He had been their top goalscorer. And now they said that he could be coach. Harry bit the side of his cheek in an effort not to grimace. There was no glory in that. None of the lads listened to a coach. All they were interested in was getting out there on a Sunday morning and kicking a few shins. He was damned to hell if he was going to sit on the sidelines with a wet sponge and an empty holdall, freezing his bollocks off all winter, trying to look like he was still important. Watching the twenty-six-year-olds steaming up and down the wings.

He stared at the tea. It was stone cold, with a flecked brown skin forming on it.

Harry knew what the problem was, all right. They didn't think he had it in him any more. It was the same over work. He had seen them smiling behind their hands at him, or bending their heads so that they thought that he couldn't see the grins. Kids who thought that they knew it all. They thought he was behind the times, as if working a computer and fax machine were the be-all and end-all of the job. They thought that the world revolved around technology. They fought to get on the forensics courses, when they got as far as CID. They loved all that – thought they were scientists, probably. Talked in initials and reckoned that made them clever, when half of them couldn't fill out a form.

Harry, on the other hand, had been brought up on pen and paper. He trusted the old systems. He trusted his own memory, and the old card index files, and he trusted word of mouth, and the memories of old men in the bookies, who remembered the fathers and grandfathers of the criminals who now filled their cells. And he trusted his own hands and his own feet and his own bloody abilities, if no one else did.

He got up from the table and gave a deep sigh.

Past it at forty-seven. *Past* it.

He looked out at the motorway, cutting its blue-grey path through the fields. He watched the traffic and thought about speed, and being too busy to daydream. He always got his best ideas daydreaming. Like the way he'd fixed his brother's fence. He'd thought his way around it, letting his mind drift. Didn't need a computer to visualize what would work.

He watched an articulated truck pass. The great white block on wheels was on its way south. He thought of the Chief Inspector who had been here yesterday, and who would probably be back in his quiet little station by now. Harry had liked him. He had liked the sound of the sleepy country town that Chief Inspector Wilde came from. They had sat downstairs and talked for a while about football, while Harry was waiting for the fixtures list that had only come this morning. Chief Inspector Wilde was the kind of policeman that Harry respected – slow, thoughtful, careful. They had talked about how the city had changed, and about this girl who had turned up in the Chief Inspector's patch. Just a little. Not for long. And when the Inspector had gone – ever since, really, even this morning – Harry had thought about Pennystone Road, that the Inspector was so keen to find out about, and about which Harry Endersley did know something. Something that had been at the edge of his mind all yesterday, all today.

He picked up the cup of tea, and drank it.

Cold tea was still tea.

He went out of the canteen and downstairs in the lift. Glancing at his watch, he saw that his break was over and that he was due back on the desk. He had rarely been late for anything, but this morning Harry Endersley was a changed man. He was past it. Useless. Good for nothing but propping up the enquiries desk.

Right. He would show the buggers.

*

Even new buildings have dead zones.

The last offices – the enormous rambling, patched-together head-quarters in town – had been a monstrosity, five floors of what had once belonged to a cotton merchant, a man who, at the end of the 1880s, had made a small fortune from the sale of indigo cloth. The cotton merchant went out of business with the new century, and the place had been split into separate segments, until the government took it over for the Ministry of Transport. During the war, the building had been a communications centre, hiding a bunker two floors underground in the sub-basement.

That floor in the old building had been exactly what Harry Endersley meant by a dead zone – a long corridor of rarely-visited space, humming with ghosts. The sub-basement had acted like a drain, catching all the waste from the floors above – all the unwanted things. Each elaborate Victorian door was locked, and behind each door lay the detritus of years – old filing cabinets, chairs, screens, tables, paraffin heaters. As the accommodation officer for the old building, it had been Harry's job to squirrel away what no one wanted and no one knew how to dispose of, until the place was awash with old furniture and files.

When the District had eventually moved buildings, Harry's boss had told him, in no uncertain terms, that there would be no more useless stores. Everything in the sub-basement had been taken away and sold, with the idea that, in the new offices, there would be nothing but gleaming expanses of white walls and polished floors.

Harry smiled now as he got out of the lift in the basement.

They had been in this new building for three years, and it was growing its own beautiful little dead zone – like a living thing, slowly maturing in the dark, like mushrooms. He grinned as he put his key in the first door. Mushrooms. Human beings couldn't help it. Every office had a place like this, and it was the equivalent of the domestic loft, where everything is shoved away for the hazy time in the future when it might be needed again.

Except that it never is needed again. And, as Harry opened the door, he saw the equivalent of a whole street of house lofts – row upon row of gunmetal-grey filing cabinets. In another ten years, this room would look exactly like the one in the old building.

The dead zone.

He ran his hand over the nearest cabinet.

A lot of the people in here were dead, too, he thought. He opened the top drawer. Caseloads from 1958...'59...'71...'64. All mixed up. Handfuls that had been pressed into the cabinet, ready for the office junior who would one day come and sort it all out. The day, of course, that never came.

A lot of the stuff would be on computer, naturally. The more recent ones. But Harry wasn't looking for recent cases. He lifted the nearest paper folder out of its musty-smelling cocoon. It was dated 12 September, 1965. Shoplifting. Conditional discharge. A woman of fifty-eight.

He looked around himself, counting the cabinets. More than thirty of them. Thirty cabinets ... four drawers in each cabinet. Twenty files, maybe, to a drawer. That made ... he stopped, tongue unconsciously resting on his lower lip as he worked it out in his head. Two thousand four hundred files.

'Bloody hell,' he sighed.

He considered, for a moment, leaving the task.

After all, he had looked up the name *Acland* on the computer yesterday and found only the report of the house fire in Pennystone Road. Reporting the case to the building society. Ensuring the place was secured.

But that was not what he wanted.

Acland . . . Acland.

Harry knew that, somewhere in these cabinets, in these two thousand four hundred files, was another entry for the name Acland. Not recent. Maybe fifteen years ago. Maybe more.

He eased the collar of his shirt, wincing at its tightness.

Past it.

Useless.

'We'll bloody well see about that,' he muttered.

Thirty-Eight

Robert Wilde got in to work early that day.

On top of the papers on his desk was a note, saying that the car – the little snub-nosed Morris, once so much loved and cared for – now stood in the police pound waiting for the eventual sale at auction authorized by Beryl Graham.

He stopped in the act of taking off his jacket, and held the note up to the light. When he dropped his hand, he stood absolutely still, looking at the familiar landscape of the street underneath his window.

It was not yet nine o'clock. The shops were still locked, and the pedestrian walkways deserted. A postman's bike was propped against the old milestone guarding the pedestrian crossing. A few people hurried past on their way to work.

Poor Alisha, he thought. The wayward and brilliant Miss Graham, who had climbed a good many obstacles in this life, and who had probably considered that she would have no real difficulty in conquering the disturbance of the girl she had grown to love. Wilde sighed softly. And Alisha Graham *had* loved this girl. Tried to answer her questions. Tried to help her. And died, it seemed, on a hill, in the dark, hundreds of miles from home.

She had died for love, he thought.

His throat constricted with sudden pity.

Every time he thought of this case, he felt frustrated and depleted. And he was still tired, today, after a night's sleep. It had been a restless night, when he had got up three times, and found himself sitting on the edge of the bed with a sense of an unfinished dream. Words and faces evading him. Images muddled.

He looked down again at the note. The thirty-year-old Morris lay in the hastily typed words, a mute accusation. Alisha Graham stood behind the Morris – he could almost see her hand on its seat, as her hand had been lying that morning when they had found her. Upturned, as though frozen in the act of pointing something out.

I can't help you, he thought.

I don't know what it is that you want me to see.

The phone rang.

'Yes . . . Wilde.'

It was the WPC on the front desk.

'Chief Inspector, there's a man to see you. Will you come down?'

'Who is it?'

There was a pause as the woman read the name she had written down. 'It's a Mr McGovern,' she said. 'Benedict McGovern.'

He had formed a picture in his head, but the man standing before him in the interview room did not fit the picture.

He had thought that McGovern would certainly have a transparent weakness about him. He had imagined a very tall person – drawn, in his imagination, as large as Ben McGovern figured in Anna's fears. She had said that he was dark, and she had said that he was very smooth, very polished, but he had trusted himself to recognize fallibility. And it sincerely shocked him that there was no obvious fallibility about this man. McGovern was about six foot, quietly and unspectacularly dressed, and – and this was the thing that surprised him most – with a self-effacing manner.

'I'm sorry to bother you,' was his first remark.

'Please . . . sit down.'

They sat opposite each other, across a table.

'You must be very busy,' McGovern said.

'Not any more so than usual.'

Ben McGovern smiled. It reached his eyes, Wilde noted.

'I've come to speak to you about the woman you know as Anna Miles.'

Wilde waited, saying nothing.

243

'She's been to see you?'

'She has, yes.'

McGovern sighed. He looked down at the table, and gave a little shake of his head. 'Yes . . . I was afraid of that.'

'Can you tell me why?'

'Why I was afraid? Yes, certainly.' He paused. 'This is a little embarrassing.'

'I promise you I'm not easily shocked.'

As he said it, Robert Wilde felt the rapid lie. Such a statement might have been true two days ago. But if he hadn't been shocked in the house in Pennystone Road, what had he been? Running out of a house with his hands over his head. If he hadn't been shocked by that, shocked at his own lack of resistance, the seeming ease with which he had fallen into some sort of grey area, a place where he had never been before and never wanted to go again . . .

Yes, he had been shocked. And it had been very easy. Like staying awake last night had been easier than to sleep.

McGovern smiled again. 'I knew Anna a year ago,' he said. 'She disappeared one night, and I never knew where she had gone. I reported her missing. Her house is standing empty just as she left it. And now . . .' he stopped. 'I've found her here.'

'You came looking for her,' Wilde said.

'Looking? No. I had no idea she was here.'

'Then . . .'

'I'm working in this area,' McGovern said. 'I'm working with Laura Aubrete. I'm an architect. Mrs Aubrete told me about Anna. About Matthew. Her husband.'

'I see,' Wilde said.

'I spoke to Mr Aubrete yesterday.' McGovern stopped, evidently expecting a response. 'At the Manor. About the will.'

Robert Wilde hid his surprise. 'They've been very frank with you,' he said.

'Oh, it isn't a matter of them being very frank,' McGovern replied. 'It's a matter of all three of us being subjected to deceit.'

'Oh?' Wilde asked.

'Deceit and fraud.'

'You're alleging fraud?'

'I would if I could prove it,' McGovern said.

'Fraud on yourself, do you mean?'

'Absolutely. That's absolutely what I mean.'

'By Anna Miles?'

'Anna *Cray*. Yes.'

Wilde looked at him carefully. There was nothing but an earnest anxiety in the man's expression. 'Are you here to press charges?' he asked.

McGovern laughed softly. 'I can't,' he said. 'Anna took money from me, but I can't prove that I didn't give it to her willingly. In fact,' he added, 'in a manner of speaking, I did give it to her willingly. She asked me for a loan, a temporary loan, and I gave it to her, and she disappeared. I was a fool, and I admit it, and I realize that there is very little anyone can do about it.'

'How much?' Wilde asked.

'I'm sorry?'

'How much was the loan?'

'Ten thousand pounds,' McGovern said. 'She gave me a story about wanting a car, about a bank loan falling through . . . I'll spare you the details, Chief Inspector, since I can't prove it wasn't a gift, and it really isn't the issue here.'

'Is it not?'

'No,' McGovern said. 'The issue is, that I've seen Anna, and she . . .' he stopped again. This time, he lowered his head. Wilde watched the smooth dark hair, the neatly combed parting, for some seconds, and was taken aback to see tears in the other man's eyes as he straightened up again. 'She isn't any better,' he said.

'You'll have to explain that to me, Mr McGovern.'

'She was mentally ill. And I see she's no different.'

'You *see* that?'

'Yes. I've seen her.'

Robert Wilde took a deep breath. 'You've seen Anna Miles. When?'

'This morning. Just now.'

'Where?'

'At the Oaks Hotel.' Wilde said nothing. He could only imagine Anna's reaction. 'I saw her in the hotel lobby half an hour ago.'

'And she talked to you.'

'Yes, of course she talked to me.'

'She must have been shocked to see you.'

'No,' McGovern said. 'She knew I was in the area. Presumably she told you much the same thing.'

'Yes, she told me the same thing.'

'I've been ringing her,' McGovern said. 'Trying to get her to see me, but she wouldn't. I came down to the hotel this morning, and I caught her as she was going out.'

'And what did she say?'

McGovern gave another low, soft laugh. 'She was furious.'

'Furious?'

'She thinks I've tracked her down. She doesn't believe it's purely a coincidence. But you've heard all that.'

Wilde leaned on the table, crossing his arms, and leaning on them. 'And what conclusion did you reach, talking to Miss Miles? Between the two of you?'

'Nothing at all,' McGovern said. 'There's no reasoning with Anna. She's quite unstable. She was offered treatment, you know, at home, and refused to take it. Medical treatment for her paranoia, her sense of persecution. But she . . . well, as you know, she thinks she's perfectly all right and that the rest of the world is at fault.' McGovern sighed deeply. 'I mean, what kind of woman leaves her job, her house, her lover and partner, all those who have supported her and cared for her . . .'

'I can see why she might think that you had followed her. I might draw the same conclusion, if I were her. It's quite some coincidence.'

McGovern nodded slowly. 'Yes,' he said. 'It is. I'm as amazed at anyone else at that. But . . .' He shrugged his shoulders. 'That is the truth. And when I knew she was here, when I realized what havoc she has been causing, I felt I had to speak to her.'

'This morning. That's the first time you've spoken to her.'

'Yes. She never returned my calls or messages.' Now, McGovern too leaned forward. 'And because of what she has said to me, because of the way she's responded, because I see that, if anything, she is worse, far worse than she ever used to be, if that were possible . . . then I felt I ought to come and tell you that if Anna Cray makes any sort of accusation against me here, I will take legal advice. I will prove her to be a liar rather than let her tarnish my reputation here.'

Wilde listened to the even tone of the voice. No note of anger, even now. Just resolve. 'I thought you said there was nothing to prove,' he commented.

'So there isn't,' McGovern said. 'Over the money. But if Anna persists in this story that I understand she has told you, of my hounding her all over the country, I shall have no hesitation in proving how she hounded me.'

'She . . .?'

McGovern sat back in his chair. 'She sat outside my house and she telephoned me constantly, and she left . . .' He paused. 'This will sound ridiculous,' he said. 'But she left odd things on my path, on my doorstep. Strange things. Peculiar things. Playing cards, railway timetables, stones . . .'

Robert Wilde found himself staring at him. He thought of Anna's face, the haunted look in her eyes. He looked into Benedict McGovern's eyes and saw only equanimity and calm.

'But even that isn't the main reason I'm here,' McGovern said.

'It isn't the main reason,' Wilde heard himself echo.

'No,' McGovern replied firmly. 'The main reason, the thing that really infuriates me, Chief Inspector, is to hear from Mr and Mrs Aubrete that Anna is – well, the very idea astounds me, it just astounds me – but to hear that Anna has lied her way into millions of pounds. Millions! That makes my ten thousand look pretty poor, I must say. That she has somehow found a way to take everything that these people have . . . people who, I understand, have been kind to her, loved her . . .'

McGovern's voice tailed away.

Wilde sat back in his seat and looked at his own hands. 'Would you excuse me just a moment?' he asked.

'Of course.'

'Would you like a cup of tea while you wait?'

'Thank you,' McGovern said. 'That's very kind.'

'I'll be five minutes.'

Robert Wilde rang Wallis in Manningham.

'Sorry to bother you again,' he said. 'But could you check something for me?'

'Still to do with the girl?'

'No. Maybe. Can you check a couple of names?'

'Fire away.'

He asked if there was any record of two instances. The first, of Anna Cray reporting harassment by Benedict McGovern. And, secondly, if Benedict McGovern had reported Anna Cray missing.

He paced the reception, reading even the well-worn posters while he waited for the reply. He watched as one of the duty officers took the tea into McGovern. Wallis took only ten minutes to come back to him.

'We've got the last five years up to speed on computer,' Wallis told him. 'And we've got the missing person's report on Anna Cray. Reported missing in May last year by a Mr Benedict McGovern. Place of work confirmed her missing. Car was found in a dealer's in Bristol. She had taken cash for it. That's the last we know about her.'

Wilde felt his heart rapidly sinking. 'And the harassment?'

'Nothing,' Wallis said. 'We can't find any reports of this same Anna Cray being stalked – followed – whatever. It *is* the same woman as Anna Miles?'

'Yes,' Wilde said. 'It's the same.'

He put the phone down.

As he turned away, the WPC who had phoned him earlier called across to him. 'Chief Inspector, there's a message for you,' she said.

'Who from?'

'Someone called Carrie Phillips, from the Social Services.'

'Right,' he said. 'What was the message?'

The WPC walked over, handing him the written note of the phone conversation. 'She said it was about the silent girl,' she said. 'Does that make sense?'

He tried to fight down a rising tide of frustration. 'Yes,' he said.

The WPC read the note again over his shoulder. 'The silent girl has got out of Brimmer,' she said.

He folded the note slowly, and put it into his pocket.

Thirty-Nine

It was so much better alone.

If she stood in the depth of the trees, she could hear the Gate calling her here – even here, when its urgent messages were half-obscured by the town. She stood in the park gardens, under the oaks, listening not to the sounds of the small town waking, but to the distant music of the sky. In front of her was a children's playground, with a little boating lake, a shallow ring of water. She gazed at its surface intently.

The time was coming. She could hear it in the implacable circulation of the stars. She turned away, and pressed her body to the trunk of the tree.

Yet McGovern was somewhere between her and the Gate.

She had known it for days. Known it since first drawing up outside Anna's house. As soon as she had got out of the car, even in the driving rain, and especially in the dark, she could feel his presence. She knew he had been looking at this house. She knew that he had been inside this house. She knew that he wanted to touch the woman inside the house as badly as he had wanted to dominate *her* – as he had dominated her for so long.

The Guardians had helped her to get to Anna – and the sole purpose had been to take Anna from his grasp, to warn Anna that she must leave, run as she had done before. But, once here, once Alisha had died, she had lost the way – been torn by conflicting needs. Been deadened, plucked off course. Felt his loathsome touch.

She had stood at the field gate, hearing the sea roaring on the stone beach below, and asked again for help. And the reply had been so strong that it had almost smothered her – subdued her so much that, even when

Anna finally appeared, running through the rain towards her that night, she had hardly been able to respond. She had allowed herself to be taken into the very house, the wrong house – and it felt so badly, so *badly* wrong since it had been touched by him – she had allowed herself to be taken inside it, and she had sat down, and she had let the police come. Others whom she had fleetingly hoped might defend her, might help her.

Until, in the police station, she had known for certain that no one at all could help her, and no one at all could help Anna Miles.

She had to complete her task, if all else failed.

She would draw him to her, and away from Anna. He was a creature of trivial desires, weak in his soul. He would come when she called.

She felt the awful reflex in the Gate, where the others now waited for her.

Let him answer her.

She would be ready for him.

Forty

Aubrete stood at the pit head.

Behind him, the pulley in the horse gin groaned. They were bringing the men up as fast as they could – they could hear the voices crying to them from the shaft – but it was not fast enough. The pit head manager came though the building, pushing women aside who had gathered at the doors.

'We need a winding engine,' he said to Aubrete. 'They have a winding engine at Conygre.'

'I know it,' Aubrete said.

'A winding engine, winding by day and pumping by night.'

'Yes,' Aubrete said.

'Sir – 'tis common practice!'

'I know it,' Aubrete repeated. 'But we have no investment.'

'Then you have no pit, sir,' the man said.

They stared at each other as the first men came to the surface. Men and boys, faces blackened. Third in line came the Egyptian, tumbling from the rope. The colliers came running to the two men standing in the centre of the pit house, a crowd of dark shadows advancing on the light.

'The lowest seam is gone,' the Egyptian said.

Aubrete took him by the arm and pulled him to one side. 'You promised me,' he said.

'You have lit fires in the pit bottom,' the Egyptian said. His voice was cracked with fatigue and terror. His eyes held pictures Aubrete did not want to see.

'I have to have a furnace to burn away the bad air,' Aubrete said.

'It's no good.'

'I have given you money!'

The Egyptian put his hands to his face momentarily. 'I am only one,' he said. 'Take your money back. I don't have a need of it where I am going.'

Aubrete shook him, his grip tightening. 'You'll go nowhere,' he muttered. 'You are my bought man.'

The Egyptian said nothing at all. He looked for a long time into Aubrete's eyes. Then, he prised Aubrete's fingers from his arm. 'I am God's man alone,' he said softly.

The rope was up. Only eighty-four had come to the surface. The last boy was weeping, screaming.

The Egyptian caught hold of the rope. The men fell silent.

'Turn it!' the Egyptian called. 'Put me down, for God's sake – take me down!'

Forty-One

Matthew Aubrete sat on one side of the enormous drawing room, and looked at his wife and Benedict McGovern.

They were waiting for him to speak. Laura sat in one of the green brocade armchairs, her legs demurely crossed at the ankle, her hand resting on the arm of the chair. Her fingers drooped down. He found himself staring at the third finger of her left hand. Her wedding ring was twenty-four-carat gold set with five small diamonds, and it glittered now in the oblique light from the window. Behind her was the portrait of his great-grandfather, the man who had built Aubrete Manor.

Matthew's eyes strayed from his wife's hand to his ancestor's face. The man glared down at him, he thought. A strong, intransigent face. Much, Matthew thought, like Laura's. The same absolute assurance of being right. The same chilling superiority. The same icy dismissal of the rest of the world. One hand rested, too, on the arm of a chair. The other was inside the breast pocket of his waistcoat. A green brocade waistcoat. Laura had missed nothing when she had ordered this room to be redecorated. 'I have a feeling for the past,' she had reassured him then. *But not like my feeling,* he thought. *If you had my feeling, you would never sleep.*

'Matthew,' Laura said. 'We're waiting.'

He looked back at her. As he did so, he caught a glance pass between her and the man who now stood at her side. Matthew thought that McGovern was far too handsome. Exactly the sort of physical specimen that Laura liked, of course. One of her previous boyfriends had been just like him, although he had not had Ben McGovern's presence, his aura of calm. At least that previous man had had the grace to blush

254

when he met Matthew. At least he had turned his face away, not able to meet his eye. He had not stood like this, with his eyes ranging slowly over Matthew, as if taking stock of him, and deciding that the stock was, as Laura had evidently told him, very disappointing.

'Are we going to the police or not?' Laura repeated.

Matthew looked away from them both. 'I don't know,' he said.

Laura brought that same manicured, slim-fingered, ringed hand down firmly on the chair arm, clenched into a fist. 'Oh, for God's sake!' she cried. 'What more evidence do you need?'

'It's not evidence. What Mr McGovern has told us is hearsay.'

'I don't care,' Laura said. 'It fits. She's a thief.'

'I don't know that,' Matthew countered.

'He's just bloody well told you what she is!'

'I heard him.'

Laura's eyes narrowed. 'And you don't believe him, is that it?' she demanded. 'You believe that little slut. You believe her word over what a perfectly objective friend is trying to tell you, and over what your father said in his will.'

'My father was a tyrant,' Matthew told her, softly.

Laura paused. 'Mr McGovern is neither a tyrant nor a liar,' she said. 'He has nothing to gain out of this.'

Except to get his own back, Matthew thought.

And, perhaps, you.

'You want me to lie,' he said, finally. 'That's what it boils down to. You want me to say she forced my father.'

Laura got up, and advanced on him. 'Lying for a good cause,' she said. 'All you have to say is that Anna Miles, or Cray, or whoever she claims to be, has been pressurizing you. That you saw her pressurize your father. That she had a hold over him.'

'There's no point,' Matthew said. His voice was distant, despairing. 'My father made that will of his own free choice.'

Laura looked at Ben again, then back at the lowered head of her husband, at the hand he had passed over his face. 'William Templeton isn't above a little wheeling and dealing himself,' she said. 'And for a few thousand pounds, I'm sure that he would remember that Anna Cray came in with Dominic and practically forced him to change the will. That she had undue influence.'

Matthew dropped his hand, and stared at her. 'Lie?' he said. 'Him too?'

'Why not?'

'William Templeton wouldn't do such a thing.'

A satisfied smile came to Laura's face. 'I happen to know that William Templeton, pillar of society that he is, is not adverse to taking a small reward for services rendered.' She leaned down to Matthew, talking to him in slow, pointed tones, as if he were a backward child. 'William Templeton will take money,' she said, 'to attest that, much to his distress, he suspected that Dominic was perhaps drunk at the time of making the will. And that, in the light of these revelations . . .'

Matthew, at last, stood up. 'We only have *his* word for it,' he said, looking at McGovern.

'That's right,' Laura said. 'And it's all we've got to get this estate back from her.'

Matthew looked between the two of them. Ben McGovern's expression had not changed. He seemed utterly at ease. *You're not real*, Matthew suddenly thought. He turned away, walked to the window, and stared out at the sea.

'You ought to be damned grateful to Mr McGovern,' Laura said, at his back. 'He's given you a way out of this whole fiasco. You ought to get down on your knees and thank him, in fact.'

'As you do?' Matthew asked.

There was a knock at the door.

Richard Forbes, the estate manager, came in.

'Mr Aubrete,' he said.

'We're busy,' Laura said. 'Get out.'

Forbes glanced at her, but only once. 'Mr Aubrete,' he repeated.

Matthew turned to him. 'What is it, Richard?'

The man's face was ashen. 'I think you ought to come,' he said. 'There's a problem.'

'What kind of problem?'

'With the fish pools. And the weirs.'

Matthew glanced once at Laura and Ben McGovern.

'Don't you dare walk out on this discussion,' she warned.

He picked up his jacket, and followed Richard Forbes from the room.

It took them barely three minutes to get from the house to the top of the gardens. As they sped along the uphill road between the trees, Matthew looked at Forbes' face. 'Is it an accident?' he asked. 'Is anyone hurt?'

The other man swung the Landrover into the trees at the top of the hill. It crunched to a stop on the uneven gravel of the delivery bay at the back of the visitor centre.

'No one's hurt,' he said tersely. 'But I've roped it off. You'll see why.'

They ran down the path to the Victorian fish pools, the great circular stone bays built into the gradient. The trees overhead were reflected in the water. Matthew, following Forbes, at first could see nothing wrong in the pools. Nothing but sunlight bouncing from the water's surfaces. Could hear nothing but the sound of water filtering over the little gates and locks, the original water system put in when the house was built, when this area was feeding the great house, and the pools were the sole concern of a small army of gardeners.

It was only as he got closer that he realized that the sound of the water was actually much greater than usual. As he ran to the side of the first pool, he could hear it thundering through the small weir downhill, splashing from the retaining channel.

Forbes stopped at the side of the pond. Matthew saw his mouth turn down in sudden distaste. Two of the present gardening staff – a man in his fifties, and a lad who helped him – stood on the other side of the pond, thirty feet away, looking stricken.

'What is it?' Matthew called.

The older man merely pointed.

As he drew level with Richard, Matthew could see the surface clearly. And, between the lily pads, the light was not reflecting from the water at all, but from the bodies of fish. From the carp that inhabited the pond, some of them a great age, and over three feet in length.

They were dead.

Dozens of them. Perhaps forty.

Perhaps eighty thousand pounds lying dead in the water, the fish they bred from, that earned them so much revenue, that were so well guarded at night, surrounded by electrified fences built expertly between the trees, as camouflaged as they could be by day, and lit securely at night.

Then, Matthew smelled it. The stench.

He put his hand to his mouth. 'What the hell is it?' he demanded.

'We don't know,' Forbes said. 'We called the Water Authority. They're coming. But it's not the fish. They haven't been dead long enough to have decayed. And it's not the water itself. We took a sample out. It's clear. There's no smell to it.'

Matthew felt his gorge rising. Forbes already looked sick. 'Stand back,' Matthew said. 'Come away, down the path.'

They stood a few yards back. 'It must be something dissolved in the water. Some chemical in the soil?'

'I've never seen anything like it,' Forbes said. He picked up a handful of earth from the bed near their feet. 'Smell it. Nothing.'

Matthew did so. It simply smelled of itself. Richly so. Of a century of leaves. He shook his head in despair. 'And why is there so much bloody water?' he asked. 'Where's it coming from?'

'I don't know that either.'

'The lower levels will be flooded.'

'I've opened all the gates.'

'It'll break its banks.'

'I know that, Mr Aubrete,' said Forbes. 'I know that, but I don't know what to do about it. It's just coming faster and faster.'

Matthew turned away from the pond. He stared at the ground, trying to think, trying to find a solution. 'It hasn't rained for a week,' he said. He looked up at Forbes. 'Perhaps Jennings changed the water courses on the farm,' he said. Brake Farm was further along the road, privately owned.

'I phoned him,' Forbes said. 'He says he hasn't altered any water courses. In fact, he said he's drier than usual. The stream in his cattle field is hardly deep enough to water them. It's mostly mud.'

They stared at each other.

'It's somewhere in between,' Matthew said. 'Something's altered the course of the stream between here and the farm.'

'How can it do that?' Forbes said. 'The stream goes underground. It comes out as a spring and flows straight into the pond.'

The two men looked at each other.

'Something's changed its course underground, then,' Matthew said.

'And made it produce *more* water?' Forbes asked. 'How?'

They looked, perplexed, ahead of them.

'I don't know,' Matthew said.

Even as they watched, slowly, inexorably, the water level in the fish pools rose.

And the gates of the weirs all down the hill groaned under the pressure.

Forty-Two

Harry Endersley was out of breath by the time that he reached Inspector Wallis's office. He had walked all the way up the stairs, clutching the files to his chest in an attitude of defence.

When he got to the door, it was open.

Wallis was inside with three other detectives. The conversation was rapid, urgent.

'And don't ring up,' Wallis was saying. 'Nothing. Not the radio. No mobiles.'

Sergeant Endersley tapped on the open door. 'Inspector Wallis?'

Wallis glanced up. 'You're alive,' he said, sarcastically.

'You're in trouble,' said one of the younger men.

Endersley said nothing.

'What is it?' Wallis asked.

Endersley nodded down at the papers in his arms. 'I've got what I've been looking for,' he said.

'The sack,' one of the detectives said, and laughed.

'What are you talking about?' Wallis asked.

'I've got the files on Acland,' Endersley said.

Wallis gave a reflex grimace of impatience. 'Not this again.'

'Acland, Pennystone Road,' Endersley reiterated.

The three men ahead of Endersley glanced at each other. Then Wallis walked forward. He stopped too close to the sergeant. He kept his voice low. 'You've been chasing up Acland,' he said, without expression.

'I have sir, yes.'

'Chasing up Acland, for another Authority.'

'Yes, sir.'

260

'And that's where you've been whenever you've gone missing.'

'Yes, sir.'

Wallis looked at his own feet. 'Your boss will be fascinated to hear that,' he said. Then, he glanced up again into Endersley's face. 'Do you know what we're involved in here?' he asked conversationally.

Endersley had never particularly liked Wallis, and was not about to be intimidated by him now. 'You've got a burglary ring,' he said.

'That's right,' Wallis confirmed. 'That's absolutely right, Sergeant. We've got a shout, and we've got a chance to close down on this for good.'

'Yes, sir.'

'And that – ' he turned and indicated the other two men with a sweep of his hand ' – is what we're organizing just now.'

'Yes, sir.'

Wallis turned on his heel. 'Go away,' he said.

'Inspector Wallis . . .'

'Fuck off!'

Endersley implacably stood in the doorway. 'It's what Chief Inspector Wilde wanted,' he said calmly.

'Then fucking well tell *him*,' Wallis retorted.

He did.

He phoned Robert Wilde that same afternoon, getting through just as Wilde was leaving.

'It's about your girl,' Endersley said. 'And Miss Graham. And Pennystone Road.'

Wilde tried to ignore the short nervous flutter of response, somewhere deep down in his stomach. 'We've wrapped that one up,' he told Endersley, talking more loudly than he probably needed to. Endersley sounded so far away. 'Miss Graham's body is back in Manningham. It was a natural death.'

'I know,' Endersley said. 'But you've still got the girl?'

'Not any more. She's in care.'

'She lived there,' Endersley said.

'In Pennystone Road? Yes, we thought that was probably the case.'

'I know about it.'

'Know about what?'

'Your girl.'

Wilde sat down. He fiddled with a piece of paper at the edge of his desk. It was not his business any longer. He had told himself that ever since Benedict McGovern's visit. The girl and Miss Graham were no longer important. What mattered was Anna Miles. Anna *Cray*. He had been wondering all day who was right. Who was lying. Anna, or Benedict McGovern? He would have put his money on Anna, but, having met McGovern, the man whom she had painted as being such a threat, and who, to Wilde's surprise had seemed so very plausible . . .

'I can give you the address of the woman in Social Services who is dealing with her,' he told Endersley. 'It could well help her. The girl went missing earlier today from the secure unit she'd been put in.'

Endersley snorted contemptuously down the phone. 'Some security,' he said.

'Let me give you the number . . .'

'Acland,' Endersley said.

'No, this is . . .' Wilde began, mishearing.

'*Her name is Acland.*'

Wilde stopped rifling through the desk drawer for Carrie Phillips' number, and stared momentarily into space. 'The girl?' he asked slowly. 'The girl is called Acland?'

'Yes,' Endersley said. 'I've got the photo you faxed, and it's nearly identical to the one on file, even though there's five years difference. It's the same girl, no doubt about it. Sara Acland.'

Wilde paused, then drew a blank sheet of paper towards him. 'When was all this?' he asked.

'1995. That was the arrest date.'

'What arrest?'

'Of her father. Acland.'

Wilde closed his eyes, then opened them. 'On what grounds?' he asked.

'Abduction. A girl called Amy Richardson, aged fifteen.'

'What happened?' Wilde asked.

'Her parents withdrew the charges. The case never came to court.'
'Why?'

Wilde could hear Endersley shuffling through the file papers on the other end of the phone. The sergeant began reading at random from the notes. 'Girl regularly bunked off school. Tearaway kind of girl. Got done for shoplifting once. Parents hardly seemed to know where she was half the time ... interview with parents ...' There was more turning of distant pages.

'Here it is,' Endersley said, finally. 'The girl was taken from Acland's house – we thought at the time there was something bad, something wrong at that house ... there's a bench in the cellar, with two leather straps attached to it ... the girl is found living with Acland's daughter in an upstairs room, no bed, just a floor mattress ...' He sighed. 'She said at first that Acland had forced her home with him. Then said she'd gone of her own accord. Charges were dropped.'

'Bench in the cellar,' Wilde repeated.

'Yeah ... let's see ...'

'There is no cellar in that house,' Wilde said.

'There's a report here,' Endersley said.

'I went there this week,' Wilde said. 'There's no cellar.'

There was a puzzled pause. 'Well, I don't get that,' Endersley said. 'I remember this case – not everything, mind – but I do remember the lads talking about it, what a bloody awful house it was, what a flesh-crawler this Acland was. That's what was sticking at the back of my mind when you mentioned it. I just knew there was a case centred around a man called Acland. I remember the lads saying the house was freezing cold, it was damp, these two girls ...'

'And what happened to his daughter when he was arrested?'

'She was taken into foster care.'

'And when he was released?'

'She went back to Pennystone Road with him.'

'Oh, Jesus,' Wilde whispered. 'They put her back in there.'

'There's a Social Services report. Acland and his daughter were visited twice ... three times ... let's see, what's this? Another visit report. That makes four. It says ... girl well-nourished. House clean. Girl

263

talking about music . . .' Endersley's hand could be heard, slapping down on the table. 'They took her off the At-Risk Register.'

'God help her,' Wilde said. Then realized what he had said. Maybe that was exactly what had happened. She had turned to religion, found consolation in it. Poor little Sara Acland, so dislocated from life, so lonely. Fourteen years old by the time that she was put back in Pennystone Road with Acland. Alice's age . . .

'Where was her mother?' Wilde asked.

He could hear Endersley's sigh. 'Ah, now this is where it gets *really* interesting,' he said.

'Interesting?' There it went again, the cold, sick ripple of fear in his gut. 'Why?'

'Acland's history,' Endersley said. 'He married a woman in 1972. Mary Natalie McGovern. She already had a son – somebody else's son, I mean. He was five years old when they got married. Then, in 1978, Sara was born. But not to his wife. We interviewed Acland's first wife – she was still living in the area, about six miles away – and we interviewed her son, Acland's stepson. We wanted to know if Acland had ever done anything like this abduction before. Trying to get a case up on him, right?'

'Right,' Wilde confirmed.

'Well, it turns out that they had lived with Acland for six years, and left when he had an affair and Sara was born. The mother and son moved out, there was a divorce, and the new woman moved in with her and Acland's daughter.'

'Moved into Pennystone Road?'

'Yes.'

'What then? What happened with Sara's mother?'

'She went missing.'

'*Missing?*' Wilde echoed. 'When?'

'The year after Sara was born.'

'You mean that Acland brought up Sara on his own?'

'Yes.'

In a house that made the flesh crawl.

'Was it investigated?' Wilde asked. 'The disappearance?'

'Acland reported it himself. The wife told us so. She said that the police came round to *her* house, as if *she'd* done away with this girl.'

'Why would that supposition be made?'

'Because the first wife hated the new one, and made no secret of it. And because Acland had implied as much.'

'Had he,' said Wilde. He was disliking the invisible Acland more and more.

'It made a possible scenario,' Endersley said. 'Because the wife hated him.'

'Jealousy over the new wife?' Wilde asked.

'A bit more than that. Her son used to still go round and see Acland, apparently.'

'The stepson?'

'Acland's stepson, yes.'

'But he'd have been just a boy.'

'Went round there on his own, to see Sara, he said. Claimed he knew nothing at all about the first wife's disappearance, though.'

Wilde thought for some seconds. 'So, five years ago, Acland is arrested for having an underage girl in his house. The girl retracts her statement, the parents won't press charges, and the stepson is a regular visitor.'

'Yes . . .'

'How old would the stepson be at this time, in 1993?'

'Just a minute,' Endersley said. There was a renewed sound of pages being turned. 'Can't see that it says,' the sergeant said, at last. 'But he was five when they married in 1972 . . .'

'Twelve when Sara's mother disappeared,' Wilde said. 'And twenty-six when the abduction case came up.'

'Yes.'

'He must have been married by then.'

'It doesn't say so. He was still living at home with his mother.'

'And going round to see Acland.'

'Yes.'

'Acland, with young girls in the house.'

'Yes.'

Wilde paused for a moment. 'He'd be in his thirties now,' he murmured. 'Have you got a photo of him? Have you come across the mother and son since?'

'No, I don't think so,' Endersley said.

'What about when the house had the fire, and it was found that Acland was missing?'

Endersley sighed deeply. 'We'd had a lot of changes of staff by that time,' he said. 'Plus, we'd moved buildings. Lots of stuff got shifted . . .'

'So nobody asked where the daughter was? Nobody went back to see the stepson, who claimed he visited so often?'

'Nobody would've connected it.'

'Except you.'

'Yes,' Endersley said. 'And that's only because I'm past it.'

Wilde, while not understanding, didn't pursue the remark. He was still trying to disentangle the threads of the Aclands' lives in his head. 'She must have left home,' he said, thinking aloud. 'Maybe she lived for a while with this stepson and his mother.'

'Think so?' Endersley asked. 'Look at it from the mother's point of view. Would she want the second wife's daughter living with her?'

'Maybe not,' Wilde agreed. 'So, if she hasn't been living with her father, and there was no evidence of her living with Alisha Graham, and she didn't live with her half-brother, where did she live?'

'Dunno,' Endersley said. 'Maybe she *did* still live with her dad, and just left when he died, or moved, or whatever happened to him.'

'If he just moved, why didn't she go with him?'

'Dunno,' Endersley repeated.

Wilde drew circles on the piece of paper on which he had written. Inside every circle was a question mark.

'There's a couple of other things in these reports,' Endersley said. 'Might be nothing. Might be something.'

'What kind of things?'

'In this girl's statement – the girl who said she was abducted, and then didn't press charges.'

'Amy.'

'Yes . . . she said that Acland was religious.'

'Did she?'

'She said that was why she first went there. She thought he was some kind of priest. He said that he was going to protect her.'

'Against what?'

'The end of the world.'

'I see.'

'And he said . . . here's what you might think means something. He said that he was going to turn her into an angel.'

Wilde stopped drawing the circles and the question marks. '*Turn* her into an angel?'

'He said he needed angels,' Endersley said. 'That's all it says. Then the later statement says that she made it all up.'

'Do we know where this girl is now?' Wilde asked.

'She lived in Weatherby Flats,' Endersley said. 'They were pulled down last year.'

Wilde stared morosely at his own absent-minded designs on the sheet of paper, staring hard at the question marks. 'Thanks for all your time,' he said.

'It's OK.'

'Thank Chief Inspector Wallis for me.'

There was a slight pause. 'Will do,' came the response. 'Is it going to help?'

'I can't tell you,' Wilde said. 'I honestly don't know.'

He put down the phone a few seconds later.

He sat thinking of Acland.

A married man, who had an affair. A man whose second wife disappeared, and had never been found. A man whose wife had apparently abandoned her small daughter. Left her with Acland. A man with a penchant for young girls. A man who, some years later, was talking of changing young girls into angels. A man with a daughter who had been so traumatized that she couldn't speak. A man whose daughter prayed and wept, and seemed to be afraid of some sort of heavenly retribution.

A man whose daughter formed a relationship with a much older woman, whose work was her life, and yet who had interrupted that life to attend charismatic churches with this same girl, in an apparent effort to dissuade her from her religious convictions. A man whose daughter had fled home, or been thrown from it. A man with a cellar with a bench in it to which leather straps were attached . . .

And Sara's mother had never been found.

And Acland had never been found.

And there *was* no cellar . . .

Wilde got to his feet, pressing the palms of both hands against his eyes. He took a deep breath, dropped his hands, opened his eyes, and walked to the window.

A man whose house was damp and cheerless, and whose daughter and a girl of fifteen were found sharing a mattress in an upstairs room. A room with a prayer drawn on the wall, and the initials BMM.

BMM. What the hell was *that*, anyway? Wilde had looked through the ley lines book, and seen nothing of any significance to it. He ought to ask Anna Miles . . . Anna Cray. She might know. It was written around the prayer, after all.

The image of Acland rattled in his head, and wouldn't let go.

A man who had disappeared. Disappeared, taking no money, leaving no trace. Never cashing his benefit again. Leaving his house, which was probably worth a hundred thousand pounds, even in its current dilapidated state. A missing man . . .

Where had he gone, without money?

He must be dead, Wilde thought. It was the only logical explanation. He must be dead . . .

Wilde picked up his coat, walked to the door, glanced at his watch. It was now a quarter to six. Alice would be home – probably making supper by the time that he got there. He thought of her in her usual pose, standing with her hand on the handle of the kettle, waiting impatiently for it to boil, while she sang loudly to the music on the radio. He thought of her curled in a chair with a book in her lap. He thought of her talking to him, laughing. He thought of her asleep, with that small and secret smile on her face that he often noticed when he went in to make the last check on her at night. He thought of the slender hand in his.

They were all things that Sara Acland had been refused.

The security of home. Warmth. Conversation.

Oh poor kid, he thought sadly. *Poor kid.*

He walked down the stairs, and out of the building.

And it was only then, when he was standing at the roadside, waiting for a gap in the traffic, that the realization came to him with the force of a thunderclap. He banged his fist, hard, against his leg in a gesture of exasperation.

The first wife.

The stepson.

'You are too bloody slow by half, you fool,' he told himself out loud, ignoring the stares of passers-by.

The boy who repeatedly visited Acland, despite everything his mother must have wished.

A mother he lived with until well into his twenties.

'Too bloody slow,' Wilde repeated to himself.

Mary Natalie McGovern.

Forty-Three

He went round immediately to the Oaks Hotel.

He had to show his warrant at the desk before they would give him Anna's room number, and even then, at her door, he had a hard job trying to get her to open the door.

'It's Robert Wilde,' he insisted.

'I can't see you,' she said, from the other side. 'Put the warrant card under the door.'

He did so, not without some difficulty, and, at last, she opened it to him.

'Didn't you recognize my voice?' he asked, as he came in.

She shut the door quickly. 'I don't trust myself,' she told him. 'To distinguish properly.' She stood with her arms crossed, wrapped around herself as if for comfort.

'Are you cold?' he asked.

'Yes,' she admitted.

'Ask for the heating to be put on.'

She shrugged. 'I wrap the duvet around me,' she said.

He felt sorry for her. Doubly sorry when he thought what it was that he had to tell her.

'Sit down,' he said.

'Has something happened?'

'Several things.'

She sat on the bed, he on a chair. The room was comfortable enough, but too small. The TV remote lay on the bed, and the set itself was still on, with the sound turned down. Following his glance, Anna smiled self-consciously. 'Daytime television,' she murmured. 'Great fun.'

The afternoon news was just coming on. They watched for some seconds in silence as images of a ship, labouring on its side in a churning ocean, flashed on the screen. It was followed by the picture of a church, with what looked like rubble at the base of the spire.

'Bad weather,' Anna murmured. Then, she picked up the remote, and turned it off. She curled her legs beneath her.

'I think I have a name for the girl,' he said.

'You do? What is it?'

'Sara Acland.'

She looked at him, shook her head slowly. 'It doesn't ring any bells.'

'She's gone from Brimmer House.'

This took her aback. 'She has? How? When?'

'This morning. Just walked through a back door, they think, when a delivery was being made.'

Anna put one hand to her forehead. 'No sign of her?'

'Not yet.'

She pinched the bridge of her nose, then rubbed her forehead. 'Where would she go? She has nowhere to go.'

'Look,' he said. He gazed at the floor for a second. He was having trouble trying to find the right way to phrase this – to tell her without terrifying her. 'Look,' he repeated, 'you're safe here. The desk seems very good. Would it be better if I had a man posted downstairs, all the time?'

'Of course it would,' she said. Then she narrowed her eyes. 'Men posted twenty-four hours a day cost a lot of money,' she observed.

'He has been to see me,' he said.

There was not much colour in her face, but what there was drained completely away. 'Ben?' she asked.

'Yes.'

'Here, in town?'

'Yes.'

'I knew it,' she whispered. 'Oh God.'

'I don't want you to worry . . .'

'He's come all this way. He's found me. How did he find me?' she asked. She looked truly horrified, sick with the realization. Then she put both hands briefly to her face. 'All this way. Oh Christ, he's mad.' She finally raised her eyes to him.

'He said that he had been here to talk to you.'

'To me? No.'

'He said he'd been here this morning, first thing.'

'No. No one's been here. Ask the desk.'

Wilde nodded, holding her gaze. 'It's all right,' he said.

She frowned suddenly. 'But what did he come to see *you* for?' she asked. 'What did he say?'

'He came because he knows Laura Aubrete,' Wilde said.

She took this in slowly. Then she slumped back against the pillows. 'That's all I need,' she told him.

'He told me that you were swindling the Aubretes out of millions. And that you had taken money from him.'

'What!'

'Ten thousand pounds.'

'Christ Almighty!' She made a little, strangled noise. 'He's *insane*.' Her eyes widened. 'You don't believe him?'

'He's very plausible.'

'But – please – you don't believe him?'

'No, I don't.'

She sighed heavily. 'Thank God for that, at least.'

'I don't believe him because of something else I've heard this afternoon.'

She wasn't looking at him, and evidently not listening at that moment. 'He's met Matthew, then,' she said.

'Yes.'

She made a little face, as close to grief as he had seen in her. 'Well, that's the end,' she murmured. 'That must really be the end.'

'Anna,' Wilde said.

She looked up again. 'Yes?'

'When did you say that Ben McGovern's mother died?'

'A year . . . no, more. A little more.'

'And her name was McGovern.'

'Yes, of course.'

'Can you remember her other names? From the death announcement that you told me about?'

'Yes,' she said. 'It was a young name. Natalie. There was another, too. But I forget what that was. Why?'

'Had she been married to anyone besides Benedict's father?'

'I don't know. I never met her. He didn't tell me anything about her.'

'Did he talk of a sister?'

'A sister? No.'

Wilde tapped his finger on his knee thoughtfully. 'No matter,' he said.

'Why? Is there a sister?'

'I think there is.'

'Living in Manningham?'

'I think so,' Wilde said. 'I think the sister – stepsister, to be precise – is Sara Acland.'

She took a moment to absorb this. She sat perfectly still, her eyes fixed on his. Then, very quietly, she asked, 'Did she bring him to me? Was that why she came to the house? Was he there somewhere, that night?'

'I can't tell you that,' Wilde said. 'But I would doubt it. I think Sara Acland is a victim, and Benedict McGovern, like his stepfather, is the abuser. Perhaps she even came here to warn you.'

'But how did she know where I was?'

'Could Matthew have mentioned you when he talked to Alisha?'

She frowned. 'I suppose it's possible.' Then, his other statement seemed to register with her. 'Abused?' she repeated, in a small voice.

'Yes.'

'You have evidence of that?'

'Not directly.'

'But you think so.'

'Yes.'

'My God,' she whispered. 'Poor girl, poor girl.'

They sat in silence for a few moments.

'Anna,' he said, 'I haven't got any evidence against him.'

'Of the abuse?'

'Of anything. I can't prove that he's followed you, or what he did in Manningham. His stepfather – Sara's father – has vanished, but I can even less prove that a crime has occurred, much less that Benedict McGovern has anything whatsoever to do with it.'

'Vanished,' she repeated. 'You mean dead.'

'Probably.'

'Do you think he *killed* him? Is that what you're saying?'

'I really don't know.'

She thought, staring at the carpet for a second. 'Do you think Sara killed him?' she asked. 'Killed her own father?'

'That's possible too.'

Anna recoiled slightly, and took a long breath. 'You have two very sick people on the loose,' she said, at last.

'Yes,' he replied. 'I know. That's why I'd like you very much to do something.'

'Me? What?'

'I would like you to meet him,' he said.

'No. Oh, no. Never.'

'Hear me out,' he said. He leaned forward, elbows on knees. 'If you met Benedict McGovern – somewhere where we were close by – and you wore a tape—'

'No,' she said. 'No . . . no.'

'We would be close by. Very close. Hidden. Get him to admit to what he's done . . .'

'I couldn't speak to him. I couldn't have him near me,' she objected.

'Get him to talk about what he did . . .'

'No,' she echoed.

He looked at her carefully. 'Anna,' he said. 'Why did you tell me that you reported him to the police?'

'I did report him,' she said.

'No, you didn't. I've checked.'

'I . . .' She looked away from him.

'Tell me why,' he said.

'Because I knew how stupid it would sound,' she said.

'I don't understand.'

She gave a laboured sigh. 'I felt it was my fault,' she said. 'I hadn't dissuaded him. Maybe he had interpreted it as encouragement. I had my hand on the phone a dozen times to ring the police, but I never did. Because I didn't know how to tell them that I was frightened by him sitting outside in the car, or leaving playing cards on the path, or phoning me up. There was no law in place to stop him then. It was my word against his. And he's so very *believable*, and . . . I just . . . I just ran away,' she said. 'I can't even remember the night I went very clearly . . . he drove me out of my mind. That's all I can say. And that's the truth.'

She looked back up at him. 'I'm sorry that I lied to you,' she said. 'I thought that it made me sound more rational if I said that I had told the police. But I never really did have any confidence in the police's ability to stop him. Perhaps that was the bottom line. And until you've experienced this, a person like this . . . you just can't describe how threatened you feel. You just can't imagine it. I'm sorry.'

He watched her, then he got up, and walked to the window.

'But has he really come after me, or Sara?' she asked, behind him, after a while.

'I don't know that either.'

'Why did Sara come *here*?' she wondered again. 'Was it just to be with Alisha, or what?'

'All that we know about her is that her father brought her up in some kind of religious cult,' Wilde said. He was watching the heavy stream of traffic in the road outside. 'He talked about the end of the world and about turning her into an angel.'

'Angels again,' Anna said. 'My God. And this man you think was Ben's stepfather? No wonder he's crazy. Exposed to that.'

'Maybe she believes that she is an angel,' Wilde continued. 'A divine messenger, an instrument of God.'

'To do what? For what?' Anna asked.

He turned back to her. 'When she spoke to you at this music weekend, did she mention a gate?' he asked.

'A *gate*?' Anna said. 'No. What kind of gate?'

'I don't know. It just keeps coming up.'

'A gate where?'

He spread his hands wordlessly.

'To hold in something? Or to hold out something?'

'I've no idea,' he admitted. 'Alisha Graham talked about gates, too. But I don't know the relevance. And . . .' For a moment, he was going to tell her about Pennystone Road, but he thought better of it. She needed to believe in him as someone solid, reliable. 'It just keeps cropping up,' he repeated lamely.

Anna swung her legs off the bed, and ran her hands through her hair. 'Are you going to post this man downstairs?' she asked.

'Yes, I will,' he said. 'Will you think about what I've asked?'

'I can't.'

Wilde didn't like to press her any further. Yet, he had the unpleasant conviction that the only way he ever stood the slightest chance of arresting McGovern was if he actually caught him in a criminal act. And, if Anna wouldn't wear a tape and meet him, then perhaps the act that McGovern would be caught in might be an assault on Anna. No security was ever a hundred per cent. The idea made his skin crawl.

'I'll speak to him again,' he said.

She gave a small, tense smile.

He went to the door. But, just as he put his hand on the lock, she said, 'I almost forgot. I was thinking about those letters.'

'Which ones?' he asked.

'The ones you mentioned the other night, the ones by the prayer. The BMM.'

He raised his eyebrows. 'And?'

'It might be names,' she said. 'It might be Bride, Mary and Michael. Saints.'

'They are Irish saints?' he asked.

'Yes. Well, Celtic. Celts and Christianity sort of mingled. The Celts lived by spells and invocations. They asked for protection with the loricas, and they called . . .' She paused.

'What?' he asked.

He saw that she was frowning deeply, with a sudden concentration.

She glanced back at the television, and then briefly out of the window. He followed her eyes. 'What?' he repeated.

'They invoked nature,' she murmured. 'They believed . . . they still believe, I think, that God's power, the power of nature, allied together . . .' She looked at him. 'They believe in all kinds of things,' she said. 'The Otherworld, and magic, the power of the archangels, metamorphosis, reincarnation . . . they believe in the marriage of man and the earth, the balance of things . . .'

She stopped.

'Do you believe in them, too?' he asked.

'No,' she said. 'I always thought my mother was a bit barmy over it. I thought it was mumbo-jumbo. Like a fairy story.'

'And do you still?' he asked.

There was a fraction of hesitation, but, when Anna did reply, her voice was firm. 'Yes,' she said. 'It's just fairy stories.' She opened the door for him. 'These things don't really exist,' she said.

Forty-Four

The weather became worse overnight.

The storms returned with a vengeance. Beryl Graham woke on the day of Alisha's funeral to find rain battering against the window and her arthritis heralding the damp with the usual agonizing clutch of cramp. She got herself out of bed slowly, wincing at the pain. As she put her feet to the floor, her knees and hips burned with an internal fire. It felt like a hot iron was smouldering inside her hip joint, far down inside where it was not possible to ease it by massaging the joint.

She pulled on her dressing gown, tying it tightly about her waist. When she opened the curtains, she saw the laburnum tree opposite – which had been in full and glorious flower – robbed of its yellow blossom, thrashing as if an unseen hand had taken hold of it, and was shaking it to death.

She turned away.

It didn't matter, she told herself. It didn't matter one little bit.

It was entirely appropriate.

'Happy are the dead that the rain rains on,' she murmured, as she opened her bedroom door.

Beryl was destined, in fact, to recall nothing whatsoever about Alisha's funeral. Her memory of the event would be obscured, much as everything else about her would become a pale and discarded history, of interest to no one at all. But there was a little consolation, a consolation that Beryl would have liked, in that Beryl would be remembered on that one day, and even make a little paragraph in the local paper, a paragraph adorned with a small photograph of Beryl looking smart at a cousin's wedding in

1970, with a straw hat and white gloves and a prim dress with a lacy collar.

And, if Beryl herself would not have the luxury of being able to sit at home deliciously recalling every dramatic moment of her grief, and her moment in the limelight as chief mourner, then at least someone else would take a vivid memory of that day with them, wherever they went, for the rest of their lives.

Peter York sat in a side chapel and listened to Alisha Graham's service. No one knew that he was there, for he had come in a half hour before the cortège, and taken his place without even greeting the officiating priest. He sat like stone, staring into space, his hands locked in his lap. Occasionally the expression on his face flickered a little, as if light had played over it, and been rapidly replaced with shadow. He would glance, just once or twice, at the small brass cross on the side altar, and then look away.

They sang *Abide With Me*.

Beryl wept copiously. A woman alongside her, one of the faithful members of the Sunday congregation, who had taken it upon herself to support her fellow believer, gave her a handkerchief, and patted Beryl's arm.

As the storm rose outside the window, the priest went to the pulpit and opened the Bible at the passage that Beryl had specifically requested. Peter York leaned forward, elbows on knees.

'The reading is taken from Deuteronomy,' the priest intoned. 'Chapter thirty, verses fifteen to twenty.'

Peter York put his head in his hands.

'"I have set before thee this day life and good, and death and evil; in that I command thee this day to love the Lord thy God, to walk in his ways and keep his commandments . . . but if thine heart turn away, so that thou wilt not hear, but shalt be drawn away and worship other gods, and serve them; I denounce unto you this day, that ye shall surely perish . . ."'

'Oh, Beryl,' York whispered, behind his hands.

'"I call heaven and earth to record this day against you, that I have set before you life and death, blessing and cursing; therefore choose life . . . that thou mayest obey his voice . . ."'

As the reading ended, the congregation rose to sing the final hymn.

Peter York held his hymnbook tightly. *Number 296 in Ancient and Modern.* He knew it by heart. It had once been one of his favourite hymns, before he had met Sara Acland. Before he had met her father. Before he had ever seen Pennystone Road. He tried in vain to push Acland away again now; Acland, whose face had been hanging before him all yesterday, all last night.

The voices rose, thready and uncertain.

'Guide me O Thou great Redeemer, Pilgrim through this barren land . . .'

It was a wonderful hymn. As a young curate, Peter York had enjoyed its Welsh melody, so full of power. He looked up, and tried to raise his voice. The soaring tune was a good talisman against men like Acland, against the legacy of men like Acland.

'Open now the crystal fountain,' he sang. 'Let the fiery cloudy pillar Lead me all my journey through. Strong deliverer, strong deliverer . . .'

He fell to his knees in the shadow of the side chapel.

'Be thou still my strength and shield,' called the wavering band of voices. 'Be thou still my strength and shield . . .'

A quarter of an hour later, he followed the coffin to the graveside. He made sure that he stayed back where he would not get in Beryl's line of sight. The morning was darker than ever, the rain tearing at the wreaths of flowers. As the mourners reached the grave, the wind seemed to abruptly stop, and the rain came down in a sheet, turning the bottom of the grave to a small sea of mud.

York looked hard at Beryl. He saw her sway slightly. At her back stood four girls from the university, hand in hand, their faces ruddy rather than pale, as if they had come to a celebration rather than an interment. They said nothing, but they looked up instead of down, and they didn't cry. Instead, they looked, one by one, over at Peter York.

The pallbearers swung the coffin over the grave. It grated against the straps, swinging, and caught against the earth lip.

'In the midst of life we are in death . . .'

One of the girls began whispering. Holding their glance, York could not hear the words, but he knew what they were saying.

I am in the shape of the stag, I am in the shape of the hind
Not of mother nor of father was my creation . . .

Beryl turned round to look at them, registering their presence for the first time.

'Suffer us not at our last hour for any pains of death . . .'

I was made from water, I was made from earth . . .

'To take unto himself the soul of our dear sister Alisha . . .'

I was made from magic . . .

Peter York saw Beryl grasp the arm of the priest. He stopped, and looked back at the girls. York could hear Beryl's voice rising. The priest stepped back.

'Not here,' Beryl cried. The woman alongside her tried to hold her hand, but she brushed it savagely away. 'Not now!' she shouted.

The girls looked steadfastly at York.

I was made before the beginning of the world . . .

Beryl raised one shaking finger, and pointed at him. 'You!' she screamed. 'You!'

The rain ran into his eyes.

'I heard a voice from heaven saying . . .' he began.

'No!' Beryl screamed. 'No, no, no . . .!'

She came stumbling towards him, dropping her gloves and prayer-book as she slipped on the sodden grass.

'I heard a voice from heaven saying unto me, Write, from hence-forth . . .' York whispered.

And then, behind her, he saw Alisha. She was standing in the grave, her hands extended towards him, the palms thick with ash.

'Help me, Lord,' York prayed.

'I am made from earth,' one of the girls called.

She was only a foot from him when Beryl Graham suddenly stopped. Her eyes widened, her mouth dropped open, as if she had seen something astonishing. She put one hand to her chest, and wheeled around almost gracefully, a hesitant dancer caught out of step. She stared back to the grave through the teeming rain, towards the image of her sister.

And then she fell.

The woman who had been at her side rushed forward. The priest followed. Beryl crashed to the ground with an inhuman noise, a yell of blunt and animal surprise, a grunt of defeat. York stood transfixed. He saw the price label stuck on the bottom of Beryl's shoe, as her ankle turned with the weight of her crumpled body. He stood looking at the red sale tag, at its absurd and pathetic figures. Reduced, it said. He felt a terrible desire to laugh.

The woman squatted down at Beryl's side. 'Oh my goodness, oh my goodness,' she kept repeating.

Rain ran down his neck.

Alisha Graham shook her head. Once, twice. Slowly, slowly.

The nearest girl raised her hand. 'I am an indestructible stronghold,' she called.

York looked at Alisha's drawn, exhausted face.

'Help me, oh help me God this day,' York whispered.

Forty-Five

At the same time that the priest was kneeling beside Beryl Graham's body, Robert Wilde was knocking on the door of an office in the town centre.

It was a pleasant little place; a courtyard, where several old coach houses, now tastefully restored, faced each other across the original stone cobbles. Hanging baskets hung at intervals along the outside walls, a riot of luxurious pink. A tendril of ivy fluttered in Robert Wilde's face as he knocked again.

Finally, the intercom clicked. 'Yes?' asked a woman's voice.

'I'm looking for Mr McGovern,' Wilde said.

'Who is it?' she asked.

He gave his name.

'Just a moment, please,' she said.

He glanced up at the sky. It was streaked with livid yellow, brassy and bright.

The intercom clicked again. 'Come through,' the woman said.

He walked in and saw her behind a glass window. She smiled, and pointed to the left. At once, Wilde saw Benedict McGovern standing by a drawing board, arm resting along the top, a smile on his face.

'Well! This is a pleasure,' he said, and held out his hand.

Wilde took it. He wished, afterwards, that he had not. McGovern's touch was hot and dry. He felt a ridiculous need to scratch his palm when he let go.

'Coffee?' McGovern asked.

'No. Thanks,' Robert replied. He glanced at the huge model of a shopping centre that occupied the whole of one wall.

'Becklington Castle,' McGovern said, following his gaze. 'Do you know it?'

'I've heard of it.'

'I did some work on it,' McGovern said.

'It's very impressive.'

McGovern laughed softly as he walked over to it. 'Devil of a job,' he said. 'There was a medieval church under that. The archaeologists were there for fourteen months.' He grinned. 'Quite a nightmare.'

Wilde swallowed. He felt thirsty, suddenly, as he watched McGovern drink his own coffee. 'You travel around, then,' he said.

'Yes. Normally.'

'Where do you come from, originally?'

McGovern finished his drink, and set the cup down carefully. 'But you know that,' he said.

'Manningham.'

'That's right.'

'Were you born there?'

McGovern frowned. 'I don't understand your interest.'

Wilde looked away from him. He looked down at the model, and saw that it was split in half. On one side was a 'before' representation of the site – on the other, the 'after'. In the first, the town looked as if it had been hit with something, peeled back in its centre. As if it had been shot, a hole in its heart. The ruins of the church were marked out, the gardens and graveyard meticulously recorded.

'Was it hallowed ground?' he asked, his finger resting above it on the glass.

'Once,' McGovern replied evenly.

Wilde looked away from the model. He felt curiously slow this morning. After Christine's death, he had been given a sedative for a couple of weeks, and the effect had been just like this – a shuffling sensation, a reluctance to thrive, a desire to sleep. It was worse now that he was in the warm office, with the thundery ochre sky bearing down on the roof, and down through a row of skylights that threw the colour across the room between the two men.

'Is it about Anna?' McGovern asked. 'Is she all right?'

'It isn't about Anna,' Wilde said. 'Not entirely.'

He turned his back on McGovern and the aching sunlight. He sat down, without waiting for invitation, on a chair on the far side of the room.

'Sara Acland,' he said.

McGovern did not respond.

'Where is her father?' Wilde asked.

McGovern smiled. 'Who is Sara Acland?' he said.

'You knew her in Manningham.'

'No . . . I knew no one called Sara Acland.'

'You knew her father.'

McGovern smiled. 'No.'

'In fact,' Wilde said, 'Acland was your stepfather, and Sara is your stepsister.'

There was a silence. McGovern did not move. 'There's been some kind of mix-up,' he said, mildly. 'My mother and father are dead. I was an only child. I don't have a sister.'

'And you lived at number 3a Pennystone Road.'

'No.'

'And once you had moved from there, you came back, and visited it regularly.'

'No. How could I visit a place I didn't know?'

Wilde looked at him, waited. McGovern picked up a pencil and balanced it between the index and second finger of his hand, switching it from one to the other, the very picture of indifference.

I'm going to make a hole in that straight calm, Wilde thought. *I'm going to make a hole in it, like you made a hole in that town.*

'All I have to do is send a photograph of you to Manningham,' Wilde said. It was a gamble to say so, because he knew already that Manningham Police had no photographs of McGovern. But it was worth a try. He watched McGovern's closed expression. 'When did your mother die?' he asked.

McGovern put the pencil down. He sat at his desk and turned towards the drawing on the board. He ran his hand over it, as if soothing or stroking it. 'Eighteen months ago,' he said.

'Were you close?'

McGovern turned his head. 'Is it any of your business?'

'An only child,' Wilde said. 'You must have been close.'

McGovern said nothing.

'Was your father already dead?'

'Yes, he was dead.'

'Acland, do you mean?'

'I don't know any Acland. My father died soon after I was born.'

'He had a daughter, Sara. He lived in Pennystone Road . . .'

'Repeating a thing doesn't make it true,' McGovern retorted.

'But that is true. He had a daughter . . .'

'I don't know any daughter!'

'Your mother was married to him, and he had an affair, and you left the house. You and your mother . . .'

'We left no house . . .'

'Did he throw her out?'

'I don't know,' McGovern said.

'Didn't she tell you?'

'I don't know any bloody Acland!'

'Sara was only one when her mother went missing,' Wilde said.

McGovern bit his lip.

'Sara was one year old,' Wilde said. 'You were twelve. The police came round to see your mother.'

There was no response.

'She's here,' Wilde said. 'Sara. But then you know that.'

'I don't know anything at all,' McGovern said, at last. 'I come to you in all good faith—'

'Which one did you follow?' Wilde asked. 'Anna Cray, or Sara Acland?'

McGovern sprang to his feet. 'I've had enough of this,' he said.

'Have you?' Wilde asked. 'I've felt that way for days. I've been lied to. Had my time wasted. And I don't like that. Why did you follow Anna Cray?'

'I didn't.'

'Why did you follow Sara Acland?'

'I've followed no one.'

'Is Sara important?'

He saw a flicker. Just a flicker. Just a ghost. 'Why is she important?' he asked. 'Why do you want her? Are you trying to stop her doing something? Why did she come to Anna?'

'I've been perfectly honest with you,' McGovern said.

Wilde, too, got to his feet. 'You have not,' he said. 'Your mother was Mary Natalie McGovern and she was married to this girl's father, your stepfather, a man who has now gone missing. You've followed Sara Acland just as you followed Anna Cray and made her life a misery . . .'

McGovern advanced upon him. 'Prove it,' he said. 'Prove me a liar. Prove Anna Cray is telling the truth.' He stood in front of Wilde, and the older man saw, with some satisfaction, that at last the smooth veneer, if not broken, had at least been cracked. Fury glittered in McGovern's eye.

'You can't, can you?' McGovern demanded. 'Because Anna Cray never filed a complaint against me.' He rocked back on his heels, as if he had dealt a winning card. 'I know that,' he said. 'You see? I *know* that.'

Wilde looked straight into McGovern's eyes. 'What happened to your stepfather?' he asked.

'Fuck you,' McGovern said. He wheeled around and strode back to the drawing board, his back to Wilde. His shoulders heaved.

Wilde smiled. Finally. *Finally*. A hole in Benedict McGovern's polished armour, a flash of weakness and vulnerability.

'It must have been pretty terrible in that house,' Wilde commented.

McGovern said nothing. His head was lowered.

'The police said it made their flesh crawl,' Wilde continued. 'He had girls in the house. Was that the attraction for you? Young boy in your teens. Later, a young man in his twenties, still living at home with mother. Mother he couldn't confide in. Not about this, anyway. Claustrophobic. Couldn't tell her you were still going to see Acland. Acland, of all people. The one man she hated above all others. Couldn't tell her that.'

Wilde watched him, waiting as he spoke. McGovern's back was rigid, his fist clenched on the drawing board.

287

'You probably didn't want to go there at all,' Wilde said softly. 'Frightened to hell. You saw what Acland was doing to Sara. You didn't want to end up like that. But disgusting things draw boys, don't they? Secrets. I bet Acland had a whole army of secrets. Perhaps things he told you or showed you. Maybe he said that you shouldn't tell anyone. He'd show you, but you mustn't tell anyone.'

'No,' McGovern said. It was barely above a whisper.

'A boy of twelve can't be held responsible for things an adult does,' Wilde said. 'Even if that boy is involved in those things.'

Nothing. No reply.

'It wouldn't be his fault,' Wilde said. 'Even if that boy did something that he knew was wrong.'

He waited, watched for the moment.

'No,' McGovern repeated.

'It doesn't make Acland strong,' Wilde said.

McGovern lifted his head, but still didn't turn. He looked out of the window by his desk, out on to the cobbled courtyard and the patch of livid sunlight. 'You don't know anything,' he said. 'Otherwise you'd come here with someone else. You'd have someone with you taking notes. You'd arrest me.'

'What would I arrest you for?' Wilde asked. 'What have you done?'

At last, McGovern turned. His face was stripped of the charm that had previously characterized it. There was no smile, not the remotest glimmer of warmth. 'You don't understand anything,' he said.

'Don't I?' Wilde asked. 'Where is Acland?'

'Get out.'

'You can tell me,' Wilde said. 'I'll protect you.'

The reaction was astonishing.

McGovern stared at Wilde for a moment, and then began to laugh. He bent over with the force of it, and then raised himself, breathless. 'Protect me?' he asked. 'Protect *me*? You think you can do that? *You*?'

'Men like Acland are fundamentally weak,' Wilde said.

McGovern began laughing again. 'Where did you learn that?' he said. 'Some police manual?' He walked over to Wilde. 'You think a man like Acland is *weak*?' he insisted. 'Do you have any idea what the hell you're talking about?' He shook his head, the smile still clinging to his expression. 'Acland's alive,' McGovern said softly. 'He's dead. And he's alive. Dead and alive . . . and no one, not you, not Anna Cray, not any of your so-called Force, can find him, will ever find him, and you will never find *me*, understand? You can't get me. I'm not part of you, I'm not part of your laws. Do you understand? Understand?'

Exactly the same sensation that had struck Wilde in Pennystone Road now crawled over him. Instinctively, he took a step backwards.

McGovern reached out his hand. Slowly, he put it on Wilde's chest.

Wilde felt suddenly sick. Cold, sick.

Dry, dead, cold, sick . . .

'No,' McGovern murmured. 'You don't understand.' The sound of torn breath. 'How could you?' Cold dead dry sick breath. 'Don't meddle with what you don't understand,' he said.

With effort, Wilde tore himself away. He walked backwards, feeling his way at first, then turning for the door.

'Run away,' McGovern said, behind him. 'Like you did from Christine.'

Almost out, Wilde turned.

The light had faded from the room.

'What?' he gasped. '*What?*'

McGovern crossed his arms.

'You can't shut the Gate,' McGovern said softly. 'You couldn't do it, could you? Not even for Christine.' The smile was awful to see, as McGovern laid his hand over his heart. 'And that is a very good thing,' he continued, murmuring. 'Because a closed Gate is a closed world. *They can't get out if the Gate is shut.* And that is about to change, Chief Inspector. You can be sure of that.'

Forty-Six

It was almost five o'clock in the afternoon when the emergency number was dialled from Pennystone Road.

The call came from the row of shops opposite the house.

'You'd better send someone to 3a,' they said.

'What's the problem?'

'Come and hear for yourself,' the caller said.

By the time that the police arrived five minutes later, a small handful of people were on the pavement outside. Two uniformed constables got out of the car. A man immediately grabbed the nearest officer's arm. 'Been going on twenty minutes,' he said. 'Hear that? Hear it?'

They could.

From somewhere deep inside the house, came several voices. Two were plainly female. Another was male. And another . . . well, it was hard to tell what the other was.

'Bloody well murdering some animal,' one woman said.

The rain teemed on the small crowd, bouncing off the pavement. The man who had called them was hunched against the wind, his coat collar pulled up about his face.

'Have you been in?' the officer asked him.

'Have I hell as like,' he retorted.

'Has anyone come out?'

'No one.'

The officers ran up the drive, through the overhanging shadows of the trees. They found the front door barred, the boarding still in place. Each window was similarly obscured. But the side gate was open.

The blackberry trailers clung to the gate as they pushed on it, and, once inside, they slipped on the moss-grown path. Yet someone had plainly been through here. There was no boarding on the back door, and it hung open on a slant, wrenched from the top hinges.

They went in, following the noise through to the dark hall. There, in the thread of light from the back rooms, they could see that the floor was littered with rubble – plaster, brick, wood. The understairs cupboard door lay on the top. The noise was coming from inside.

The first officer leaned down. What had evidently been a partition had been pulled down, along with its plastered surface. The bricks that had been pulled away had been filling what had originally been the top of the stairs to the cellar. Now there was a gap, wide enough for a man to crawl through, and the first few treads of the steps leading down were visible. From below, the unearthly screaming rolled upwards and out of the torn-through entry. There was light down there, too. The small and wavering light of candles.

'Who's down there?' the first man called.

He was not heard. The screaming continued: wailing, begging. Then, quite suddenly, it stopped, and they could make out a man's voice, gasping and stumbling over swiftly spoken words. He was half crying, half whispering. Somewhere further back still, another dark voice stuttered over indistinguishable syllables. Both voices sounded like prayers. Or incantations. Or curses.

The officer tried to wriggle through the gap. 'Get on the radio and ask for back-up,' he told the other man. 'I'm going to see what we've got here.'

He edged through the hole between the remaining bricks, and put his foot uneasily on the stair. He could hear the women again now. He bent down and tried to see into the cellar. The stair ran steeply to the bottom, some fifteen or twenty feet down, where it met a wall. The light and the voices came from the left.

'Police,' the officer called. He felt a draft of air running up the stairs. The back of his neck tingled. He went down the stairs, feeling his way over rough concrete. There was soot in here – he could feel it on his fingertips. There was smoke.

'Police,' he repeated.

The woman's voice ricocheted around him. 'Don't!' she cried.

The man reached the bottom of the stairs. There, he saw that the cellar stretched away in front of him for perhaps thirty feet or more, descending into pitch black, so that the farthest walls could not be seen. In the centre of the earth floor was a hole deeper than a grave. All that the officer could make out was two women kneeling at the edge. Neither was looking down. They crouched at the edge of the pit, looking up as if they could see through the limewashed roof five or six feet over their heads.

The policeman stumbled forward.

'What's happening?' called the other man from the top of the stairs.

'Don't let him do it,' one woman said.

The first man couldn't understand, for the life of him, what the other noise was. It was like nothing he had ever heard before, a strange mixture. It was like a small child, little more than a baby, caught in a storm of frustration, gutturally choking over its own forced tears. It was like the succumbing slump of some kind of animal, hitting the floor in a slaughterhouse, the breath pushed out of its heavy body. The two notes alternated in terrible harmony.

'Peter . . .' the girl cried.

The candle flame guttered.

'What's going on?' the officer said.

The light went out.

Something came up from the floor. It didn't feel as if it were from the direction of the grave. Something came up from the very ground under his feet. He thought for a moment that he had somehow stepped into water, and lurched backwards. But the sensation remained with him in the dark, swarming rapidly up his body. A broad, heavy blast of pressure pushed his body against the wall and knocked his head against the stone.

'Peter!' the woman screamed.

An implosion sucked the room in, down. There was nothing at all for a moment: no sound, no air, no light – just a dropping vacancy, as if the entire house had hurtled downwards, as if the earth had given way and all of them – house, voices, grave, steps, *everything*, the dark hallway, the shattered doors and bricks, the tangled mass of the garden, the grimy dark glass windows, had plunged into a hole that had opened in space.

At the top of the stairs, the second police officer was also pushed back by the pressure from inside the cellar. He lost his footing, and fell against the wall. He pressed his radio almost by reflex.

'Fire Service,' he said, without any preamble.

'Tony – what is it?'

'Don't know,' he said. 'Explosion. Don't know.'

He realized that he was slumped on the floor. He couldn't remember falling. He looked at the ground around him, and saw with a kind of objective interest that it was littered with glass. He picked a piece up. It was green and gold. There was a piece of lead attached to one side.

'Is it still Pennystone Road, Tony?' the voice asked on his radio.

With a frustratingly slow effort, he depressed the switch for the second time. 'Pennystone Road,' he repeated.

He looked up.

Rain was coming in. Rain was falling hard on the thousands of pieces of glass that were scattered between him and the stairs. The enormous stained-glass window had gone, and the overgrown trees of the garden lashed against the empty frame. He stared at the living picture, which looked as if the window had come to life. Leaves flew in on the rain and fell among the glass, and he looked down at the steps and saw the little veins in the leaves pricking an iridescent pattern against the green. Each leaf moved. Each step moved. The colours in the glass heaved with life; they threaded together like a loosely woven carpet, until every inch of space on the dusty floor was obliterated, and replaced with a writhing mass.

'Tony!' someone shouted.

He tried to get up.

It was hard. Hard because the violent life under his feet clung to his hands as he tried to lever himself from the floor. The house was filling with a fast-forward three-dimensional portrait of life, plunged into overdrive – gestating, blooming, climbing, ripening, decaying and dying in the space of seconds. He walked a pace or two, steps clouded by the green tide at his feet.

'Tony!'

It was coming from the cellar.

He waded towards it, over the remains of the partition and door, dipping his head into the darkness. To his utter astonishment, he saw water. Water coming up the cellar steps. Water swirling closer to the mouth of the hallway door.

'Jesus,' he muttered. He kneeled down and saw the other officer half-way up the steps. In front of the man was a woman. Behind him, another had her arms around his neck. And, somehow between them, they were carrying a second man, whose unconscious head rolled back into the water. He was white, his lips beginning to turn blue.

'Catch hold of him,' the officer said. 'For God's sake!'

The first woman reached the top of the stairs. Here, she stopped, and, between them, they hauled the other woman forward. She thrashed in the water only once before circling the two men. Then, she held up the unconscious man's head.

'Pull,' muttered the officer in the water.

They did. The body shifted up and forward; they snatched at Peter York's arms and hauled, dragging him to the first step, and through the gap.

'Get out of there!' the policeman yelled.

The second woman crawled out; the officer followed. Water seethed behind them.

'Get out, get out, get out,' the first man said between gritted teeth. They went along the hall towards the garden, half dragging and half carrying York, slung between them like a dead weight. As they reached the back door and fell out into the rain, the officer who had been in the hall felt a tug from behind him.

He turned around.

It was nothing like horror. It was not even fear. It was something supple and clinging, there in the dark. An imperative, a demand. He felt a soft wet hand pass over his face, and settle on his mouth, prising his lips with narrow fingers.

He let out a cry, and sprang back, stumbling down into the knee-high grass of the old lawn, where the others were grouped. Peter York lay on the ground. The two girls held hands, wet to the skin, their clothes plastered to them. The rain hammered on them all. They heard, as if from a great distance, the sirens of the fire engines, howling along the road. They heard the screeching of brakes, the raised voices at the front of the house.

The second police officer wiped his face. Then wiped his hand on his coat, to take away the feel of his own wet skin.

'What happened?' he asked. 'What the bloody hell happened?'

Forty-Seven

Robert Wilde was at home with Alice that evening.

The trip to France was the next day, and at six o'clock they were standing in her bedroom, considering her case, packed to overflowing, negotiating as to what she could possibly leave behind without falling forever from the ranks of the super-cool in Year Nine.

'What's this?' Wilde asked.

'It's a body blusher.'

'What do you want that for?'

'Oh, Dad,' she sighed. 'You're just so hopeless.'

The ferry was due to leave at six the following morning. The plan was that Robert would drive Alice to the port, but if they couldn't negotiate a reduction in the luggage, Robert was afraid he'd need a trailer in addition to the car.

'You're only going for five days,' he observed, as the bag strained at the seams. 'You've got enough here for a month.'

'I *need* these things. I need it *all*.' Alice put both hands on her hips and regarded him critically. 'What's the matter with you? You've been in a bloody mood.'

'You can't even lift this, Alice.'

'It's my holiday.'

'OK, fine,' he told her. 'Take what you want.'

'What's up?' she demanded.

'Nothing.'

'You look wrecked.'

'It's nothing,' he lied.

The phone rang. He went to his own room, and picked it up.

'Wilde.'

'Chief Inspector, this is Wallis.' Robert glanced back at the door, where Alice was standing, watching him. 'We have some developments here. We have a body at Pennystone Road.'

Robert stared for a second at the floor, then slowly sat down. 'Whose?'

'We think it's Acland.'

'Acland,' Wilde repeated, slowly. 'Where was it?'

'In the cellar.'

Alice walked towards him. Wilde didn't ask how or when the cellar had been found – ever since talking to Endersley he had known that a cellar existed, and he knew exactly where the entrance was. It was behind the smooth-walled, smooth-floored space under the stairs that kept creeping back into his conscious thoughts.

Wallis continued to talk. 'We have a curious situation . . .'

'How, curious?'

'We have Peter York in intensive care and two women in custody. We have a broken water main flooding the bottom floors of the house . . . that's where we got the body from, the water.'

'What is this to do with York?'

'He was with the body. There was some kind of explosion.'

'*Explosion?*'

Alice put a hand on her father's shoulder. He glanced up at her, and put his own fingers gently on hers.

'It's an unnatural death.'

Nothing surprised him any more. 'Go on,' he said.

'The body was lacerated.'

'But he's been missing a year. How can you tell how he died?'

Wallis took a long pause. 'I don't think he's been dead that long,' he said, finally. 'I don't think he's been dead more than a day.'

Wilde took the phone from his ear for a second, took a long breath, then replaced it. 'Where has he been, then?' he asked. 'Not in the cellar.' In the ensuing silence, Wilde's blood really did run cold. *I never heard him*, was his first thought. 'I went to the house only a day or two ago,' he said.

'He couldn't have been there,' Wallis said. 'The wall was broken down from the hallway into the cellar stairs. We think Acland was taken down there. Whether he died in the house or in the cellar, we don't know.'

'What has York said?'

'Nothing. He's unconscious.'

'And the women?'

'Off the planet. We're about to interview them. Wish us luck.'

Wilde shook his head, baffled at the turn of events. 'Did you speak to your sergeant there?' he asked.

'Who would that be?'

'Harry Endersley,' Wilde said. 'Talk to him. Acland is the father of the girl we have down here.'

There was another pause at the end of the line, then Wallis's voice came back, with a slightly renewed, sharpened interest. 'You'll be coming in on this,' he said.

Wilde glanced up at Alice. 'I can't do that until tomorrow,' he said. 'I have something more important to do first. But I'll be with you about twelve.'

He put the phone down.

'What is it?' Alice asked. 'Who died?'

He stood up. 'Never mind.'

His daughter's face took on a belligerent expression. 'Who died?' she repeated.

'The girl's father. We think.'

'The girl who used to know Anna?'

'Yes,' he said.

'Her father's been murdered?'

'Maybe.'

'Did she do it?' Alice asked.

He stopped in his tracks, in the act of trying to usher her back to her own room. 'Did who do what?' he asked.

'Did this girl kill her father?'

'No, no . . .' They got out on to the landing before Wilde stopped again, putting his hand to his head.

'What is it?' Alice asked.

'I never could do crosswords,' he said.

'Crosswords?'

'Cryptic bloody crosswords,' he muttered, thinking aloud.

She smiled – a small, cryptic smile of her own. 'Give,' she said.

'Pack,' he responded.

He turned, and went downstairs.

He was thinking of McGovern. He had been thinking of nothing else all evening.

He had been thinking about Christine – how Benedict McGovern could possibly know about Christine. He had postulated all kinds of entirely rational explanations for this, among them the fact that McGovern's family came from within eighty miles of his own, and that feasibly – it *was* feasible, surely – McGovern had known the tiny Cumbrian village that Wilde came from. Either that – yes, and this was still just feasible – or McGovern knew that his wife had been called Christine because he had asked when he visited the station. Perhaps he had fallen into conversation with one of the officers, and been told . . .

But there, the line of his reasoning always slid to a halt. He imagined McGovern leaning on the enquiries counter and finding a way of asking the name of the wife of a man he had never met . . . how? How did one do that? Oh, it was feasible. Yes, it was possible. But not probable. Not at all. And the gate . . . how could McGovern ever know about that gate?

He tapped his fingers irritatedly against the kitchen work-top, against which he leaned. That was where he had found his line of practical problem-solving completely dissolve into all kinds of impossible theories. The theory, for instance, that McGovern could read his mind. The theory that McGovern and Acland had been involved in some kind of psychic cult. The theory that McGovern – and he felt this more acutely than he could admit in words to himself – the theory that McGovern was inhuman, impervious to human decency. And the conversation with Wallis had kept flashing back to him—

'What are the last four plagues?'

'Thunder and hail and earthquake . . .'

299

'*And the last?*'

He made tea, cut bread for toast, not wanting to think about the last.

'*I am the beginning and the end, the first and the last . . .*'

She believes in the end of the world, he had told Wallis.

That innocent-looking girl with the milkmaid's plait of hair lying loosely over her shoulder.

She's waiting for the end of the world.

'I don't believe it,' he said, aloud.

She had caught some sort of religious fever, Wilde thought. Some emotional infection from a plainly dangerous, even deranged, father. She had been brainwashed by Benedict McGovern himself, the older step-brother, pouring all kinds of poison in her ear. The world was not going to come to an end tonight or any other night, not for millennia, and nothing that an abused child believed, or what she had succeeded in making Alisha Graham believe, or possibly even what Peter York had been dragged into – *none* of that altered the fact that it was one vast decayed edifice of lies, playing upon people's fears. And what *did* they believe, anyway? Something to do with gates and angels. It was not even original, this continual obsession with Revelation. Every cult he had ever heard of pounced on those eerie chapters at the end of the Bible. It was not even anything new . . .

He found himself twisting the empty cups around on the tray in front of him. Even he had fallen prey to the same atmosphere, he thought. There was an atmosphere in that house in Pennystone Road, and he had let himself be swayed by it. As for Benedict McGovern . . .

His thoughts staggered to a halt.

As for Christine . . .

He turned on the television, trying to push this awful impenetrable crossword, this insane jumble of insoluble clues, to the back of his mind. The weather report was on, and he stopped what he was doing and looked at it.

'Storm force gales along the south coast . . .' the girl was saying, against a backdrop of an immense low pressure drawn against the map of the country.

The phone rang again. He swore softly to himself.

'I've got it,' Alice called from upstairs.

He watched the forecast.

'Severe weather warning issued by the Meteorological Office at eighteen hundred hours this evening indicates a deepening band of low pressure sweeping from west to east . . .'

They were showing pictures now, live, from the borders of Wales. Floods were pouring through riverside towns. The image flashed again, and changed location. In Exeter, the Exe was churning within six inches of the deep channels that contained it just below the city centre. People could be seen on the quayside, staring at the huge volume of water. The reporter leaned against the wind, the microphone sheltered in the lee of his shoulder. 'There is sleet here,' he was saying, his voice raised against the wind. 'The last sleet recorded at this time of year was . . .'

'Dad!' Alice shouted.

He tore his eyes from the screen.

'Dad!' He heard Alice come thundering down the stairs. She emerged in the doorway, out of breath. 'Dad, the phone,' she said. 'Quick, quick . . .'

'What is it?' he asked her.

She held out the cordless receiver to him.

'Quick,' she repeated. 'It's Anna . . .'

Forty-Eight

Wallis sat across from the girl in the interview room. It was half-past ten in the evening. Rain drummed against the windows. She sat impassively in front of him, her face devoid of expression. Wallis had an open pack of cigarettes in his hand, and, seeing her glance at it, he put it down on the table, and took one out.

'Do you?' he asked.

'No.'

'Does anyone in the world any more,' he muttered to himself. He didn't put the cigarette away but remained looking at it, not even raising his eyes to her.

'Tell me about Peter York,' he said.

'You've met him,' she said quietly. 'You know all about him.'

Wallis said nothing for a moment. Then, 'You were the girl in his office that day. The girl who brought the coffee.'

'Yes,' she said. 'I help with the network.'

'What network is that?' he asked.

'Just the magazines.'

He still didn't look at her. 'Did you know Alisha Graham?' he asked.

It was evidently not one of the questions she had been anticipating. She sat back in her seat, looking surprised. 'Yes, I knew her.'

'And you knew her friend, Sara.'

He had thought that she might deny it, but she seemed calm. Or resigned. 'Yes,' she said.

'Did you know that Alisha had died?' he asked.

'Of course. It was her funeral yesterday.'

'Did you go?'

'Yes.'

'As did Peter York.'

'Yes.'

'Tell me about Sara's father,' he said.

She was looking down at her hands now, closely inspecting her fingernails. 'How is Peter?' she asked.

Wallis bit back a grunt of frustration. He thought of the officer in the hospital, the man who had brought Peter York out of the cellar. He had refused treatment, but the second man had been admitted with concussion. He had seemed OK until he began wandering through the rain, resisting any offer of help, any shelter. He was now in a ward by himself, shivering and staring at the ceiling, while his colleague and Wallis had looked on from the corridor.

We cautioned them and they told us it was out of their hands, the man had said. He had given Wallis a perplexed, drifting look. *Have you ever heard anyone say that?* Wallis hadn't liked the look in the man's eyes, a look which gave credence to the doctor's verdict – shock. White-lipped mouth. Red-rimmed eyes. Dilated pupils.

'You've had quite a knock,' he'd told the officer, patting his shoulder. 'Let the doctors look at you.'

'I just want to get home, Inspector,' he'd said. And he had shrugged away Wallis's hand, almost apologetically.

Wallis had also gone to see Peter York in intensive care. He was tethered to a bank of machines. A monitor next to him gave a constant read-out of his blood pressure, pulse, temperature – but there was no flicker of response from York himself, who lay unconscious, like stone.

'What's the matter with him?' Wallis had asked the consultant.

'It's not a heart attack,' the man had said. 'No apparent blow to the head, no other sign of injury . . .'

'What then?' Wallis had demanded.

'Give us time.'

Wallis had looked at York's face – that smooth, bland face he had so disliked on first meeting him. He had thought it looked different now – fractured, somehow. As if it had been taken apart and put back together wrong. Crushed, displaced. Perhaps it was the effect of the overhead lights, mercilessly bright. It was odd. Just very odd.

He looked now at the girl before him.

'I can ask your friend instead,' he said.

She smiled. 'She doesn't know much.'

'And you do?'

She shrugged.

He lit the cigarette. As he did so, neither the two officers with them in the room, nor she, said anything. Although she put her head on one side and gave him, to his intense irritation, a smile closely amounting to sympathy.

'There's nothing you can do,' she murmured.

'About Acland? No. He's dead. Tell me why he is.'

She sighed. 'He killed himself with his own weakness.'

'Don't be ridiculous. He was cut to pieces.'

'Only today,' she said.

He leaned on the desk. 'What do you mean?'

'He died eleven months ago,' she said. 'He was buried in the house. We bricked up the entrance to the cellar.'

Wallis started to laugh. 'I've seen the body,' he said. 'That man has been dead for no more than a day or two.'

'I ought to know,' she said, mildly. 'I killed him.'

There was a sudden silence, in which Wallis heard his own breath. The rasping in his own throat. He put the cigarette down. He heard one of the men next to him sigh, as if with relief.

'You killed him,' Wallis repeated.

'Last year.'

'You . . .'

'I suffocated him. We all did.'

Another protracted silence.

'All?'

'The group.'

'You and . . .'

'The Guardians.'

Wallis glanced back at the man to his left, who wore an expression of bafflement that must have mirrored his own.

'Which guardians are those?'

She paused before telling him, 'It doesn't matter. There's nothing you can do now. There's nothing anyone can do. We tried to stop him, but he wouldn't be stopped. We're weren't powerful enough. Yet Sara . . .'

'Just a minute,' he said. 'Acland was murdered by a group of people you call the Guardians?'

'Yes.'

'Guardians of what?'

'The Gates.' She smiled briefly. 'There is one here, one at Ballantyne Hill, one at a place called . . .'

'Just a minute,' he said. He noticed the smoothness of her hands, and thought of them smothering an old man. 'What is this to do with Acland? Slowly. We've got all night.'

'Have we?' she asked. Then shrugged. 'He recruited us all,' she said. 'That's the irony of it. Sara brought us to him and he taught us all. Before.'

'Before what?'

'Before he changed,' she said. 'He believed in the right way, and then he changed. He darkened. He was dragged down.'

'Dragged. By who?'

'I mean spiritually,' she said. 'He was dragged to the dark. You must be vigilant. The line is so fine, so narrow. There's always darkness. There's a balance of light and darkness. He took such pressure.' She sighed. 'He was an amateur, and you can't afford to be that. He played with it, like a game. At first. And you can't afford to do *that*.'

'He changed?' Wallis asked. 'In what way?'

'He had fallen before,' she said evenly. 'And come back. We knew that. It was never discussed outright, but Sara knew it. He had struggled with it for years, and Sara had known, had witnessed it. But she was stronger. She had always been stronger. She was born with it.'

For the first time, he saw an unusual light in her eyes. He had seen that light before – the fixed light of wild conviction.

'It's what drove him down, in the end,' she said. 'Knowing his own daughter was so much stronger. Knowing that she knew his secret. Knowing what she was capable of.' She stretched her hands, flexed them, and laid them back, side by side, in her lap. 'He was afraid of her, you see,' she said. 'He thought that he had created her, but he had done nothing at all. He even tried to get Benedict to oppose her, but it was no use. Neither of them has any of Sara's power, though Benedict thinks he has.' She gave a short, breathy, dismissive laugh. 'Her power was greater than he understood. Greater than any of us.'

'Did Sara Acland kill her father?' Wallis asked.

'Of course not,' she said. 'She only instructed it. We carried out her wish.'

'Sara Acland told you to kill her father . . . and you did?'

'Yes.'

'Where?'

'In the cellar of the house in Pennystone Road.'

Wallis felt heat in his hands. It was the rush of triumph, the solution of the puzzle. The coursing of blood. 'You, and others,' he said.

'Yes.'

'How many?'

'Five. There are six Guardians. Sara is the sixth. The final one.'

'You and four other people killed Acland.'

'Didn't I just say so?' she asked.

'Do you know the names of these other people?'

'Of course.'

'Will you tell us the names?'

She shrugged again. 'I can tell you,' she said. 'But it isn't of the slightest relevance. Nothing will be, after tonight. He isn't dead. He won't be dead unless Sara overcomes him.'

Wallis took a long, deep breath. He glanced at both men alongside him. 'You have just told us that you and four others killed Acland,' he said.

'We disposed of his mortal body,' she said smoothly. 'But it wasn't enough. You saw today. It wasn't enough.'

'Not enough to kill a man?' he asked, astounded. 'What else can you do to him? He was beaten and cut. Did you cut him before he died?'

'No,' she responded. She looked offended at that, even shocked. 'We took the breath from him.'

'The man was slashed.'

'He was taken apart by the dark. He is still in there,' she said.

'He's in Blake Road mortuary,' Wallis retorted.

'You are blind,' she told him.

Strangely enough for him, he didn't feel in the least angry at this scathing rebuff. 'You said . . . he had fallen before,' he said quietly. 'That he had a secret.'

'Yes.'

'A secret that his daughter knew, and . . .' He smiled at her. momentarily distracted. She really was a very pretty girl, and amazingly calm despite all that had happened that day, and all she was telling him. It was not sane, of course. That calmness. The idea flashed into his head of the girl, Sara – of Wilde telling him how silent and expressionless *she* was.

He tried very hard to concentrate, to get himself back on track. 'What secret did Acland have?' he asked.

'He killed his wife some years ago,' she said. 'He killed Sara's mother when Sara was only a year old.'

One of the men at his side drew in his breath sharply. He leaned towards Wallis and whispered, 'Endersley.'

Wallis nodded. When he had spoken to Harry Endersley this afternoon, the sergeant had offered this same theory. An unprovable theory, they had thought at the time.

'He reported her missing,' Wallis said. 'He suggested that his first wife had something to do with it.'

'I know,' the girl said.

'And all the time, he knew where she was?' he asked.

The girl nodded. 'He burned her body, ground the bones down, and scattered her ashes in the cellar. We put him back with her – there, under the house.'

Wilde suppressed a shudder. 'Did he ever tell Sara why?' he asked.

'He told her when she was twelve. She knew.'

'Knew before he told her?'

She smiled. 'She is far more than her father. Far more than you understand.'

'Yet he . . .'

'He confessed. He had killed her mother in a drunken rage one night. He tried to atone for it. He brought up Sara as well as he was able, though after she knew . . .'

'He brought girls to the house.'

'Yes. He was a weak man.'

'And involved Sara.'

'No. Sara tried to protect them.'

'He brought *you* to the house, and the others.'

'Yes,' she said. 'He attended Peter York's church, and we held meetings occasionally at Pennystone Road. But Acland wanted more than charismatic worship. He wanted to break free of Christianity.' She shook her head, almost in pity, at the memory. 'He tried to make money from it,' she said. 'That was the kind of weak man he was. He told us two years ago that he was a pagan. He strayed into magic. He claimed it was white, but . . .' She sighed slowly. 'But he had broken down. He was not a pagan. Paganism isn't darkness, and he wanted darkness. He began to fall.'

'That must have shaken Peter York,' Wallis said.

She took some time to answer, then agreed, 'Yes.'

The hush in the room settled over them. It could almost be felt, like smooth hands covering the mouth. Wallis straightened his back, and flexed his shoulders, as though to take the weight of the silence from him. 'York must have tried to influence him,' he added. 'To . . . how would he think of it . . . to save him?'

'Yes,' she said, even more softly than before.

'Did he succeed?'

'No,' she whispered. 'Peter is a poor priest. He even went there today despite all our instructions.'

Wallis put his hands briefly to his head, then flattened them in front of him on the table. 'Let me get this right,' he said slowly. 'You all knew that Acland was a murderer, but none of you told anyone. You all knew that he abused young women, but none of you told anyone.'

She spread one hand eloquently. 'What could the police do?' she asked. 'Look for a body that wasn't there?' She leaned forward. 'And one of the girls did report him, but it came to nothing, because she was afraid of him.' She leaned back. 'The only one who could ever control him was Sara,' she said. 'She knew the law couldn't hold him. Only *she* could hold him. He would beg forgiveness. He would weep and pray. He would declaim at services. He would say that he had given himself to God.'

She shut her eyes momentarily. 'But he never gave himself,' she murmured. 'He was infected with his selfish needs. He was tainted. He began to invoke old powers. Powers he couldn't control. Powers older than the earth. Primal forces that ought to be in balance with us, that remain in balance if we give them true acknowledgement. If we don't defy them. If we don't try to overcome them. Powers that God gave to the world for good.' She stopped, breathing heavily. After a few seconds, she added softly, 'He tried to contain them, and dropped into the dark. Sara couldn't hold him.'

'And so she ordered him killed?' Wallis was having a hard time with all this. It showed in the sarcastic tone in his voice.

The girl opened her eyes.

'She tried to release him to his God,' she said. 'But we failed.'

'And this stepbrother of hers . . .'

She made a small grimace of dismissal. 'Him? He's nothing.'

'He saw you kill Acland?'

'He found out,' she said.

'Why didn't he report you?'

'He wanted Acland's place,' she said, in a tone of sour dismissal. 'He wanted women.'

'And you refused him.'

'There was never any question of admitting him to the circle,' she said. 'He was just Acland's petty little disciple. He thinks he has power, he thinks he can read minds, but he's nothing.'

'What happened when you refused him admittance to the . . .' he searched for the word.

'The Guardians,' she said. 'He took to chasing women. Hounding them. We let him alone. That's his sick life.'

Wallis regarded her thoughtfully. 'Do you know someone called Anna Cray? Or Anna Miles?'

'No. Why?'

He folded his arms, watching her. He glanced up at the clock. It was almost eleven o'clock. He had been on duty for just over fifteen hours.

'Here's a thought for you,' he said, finally. 'Maybe Sara isn't as powerful as you think. Maybe – let's just consider this a minute – maybe this is just a sad, bitter nineteen-year-old girl with religious delusions. Abused by her father and stepbrother. Maybe there's nothing else here. Sara just killed her tormentor. That's all there is . . . and now she's two hundred miles away, alone. Frightened. Abandoned by all of you.'

The girl began to laugh. 'Frightened?' she asked incredulously. 'It's *you* who should be frightened.'

'Me?' Wallis said. 'And why is that?'

'You – all of you,' she retorted. 'Have you any idea what rests on what you call a sad nineteen-year-old?'

'Tell me.'

She looked away from him. 'I can't.'

'Tell me this then. Tell me why she doesn't talk.'

She gave a prolonged sigh. 'Because she took an oath.'

'An oath? Not to speak?'

'Yes.'

'What the hell for?'

She raised her eyebrows, looking at him with tangible disapproval. 'To increase her power.'

'To . . .?'

Wallis stood up abruptly. He walked around the side of the table, hands in his pockets.

'You won't understand,' she said. 'I told you.'

'She took an oath not to speak,' he said. 'When?'

'Three months ago.'

'Why?'

'Because the conjunction was coming. Because Acland and McGovern were trying to release powers that should be contained. Because she *had* to close the Gates.' She flashed a look at him. She saw his brief smirk of disbelief. 'Because she is a force for good!' she said. 'God help you.'

'No, really, I believe you,' he said.

'You don't,' she replied. 'But it doesn't matter. She doesn't need your faith.'

'What conjunction is this?'

'It's not your concern.'

'And what are these gates?'

'Forget it,' she said. 'If you know, it will only confuse you.' She looked away from him. 'Go back to your missing dogs. Go back to your cups of tea.'

At last, Wallis's temper finally got the better of him. He pointed his finger at the girl. 'We're trying to protect you,' he said. 'That's our job, to protect the public from people like you, and to protect you from yourselves. To protect girls who can't defend themselves. To stop further abuses taking place.'

His anger didn't move her at all. 'What an awful lot of work for you,' she murmured.

'Yes, it is,' he said. 'Bloody hard work. So don't make it harder than it has to be. What are the gates?'

She regarded him for some moments.

He could hear a humming in the room, or perhaps in the corridor outside – a sound that he found distracting in the extreme. He glanced at the man next to him. 'Go and find out what that damned racket is. If it's the cleaner, tell her to go somewhere else.'

'OK.' The man went out.

'The cleaner,' the girl said, and laughed.

'Look—' Wallis began.

She held up her hand. 'You're bound by your cynicism.'

'That's my problem.'

'It *is* your problem,' she agreed. 'You're in prison.'

'So . . . enlighten me.'

She dropped her hand into her lap, turned it over. She sat perfectly still for a moment, then clasped her hands together.

'We are the products of many worlds,' she said slowly. 'Children of the air, the earth, the sea. We are alive in a living and changing earth.'

Wallis sighed. 'I want an answer, not a lecture,' he said.

She ignored him. 'We are subject to our own history and inheritance, we obey the laws of God and the physical laws of creation. We are creatures of choice.'

'I get the lecture anyway,' he said. He slumped back on his chair. 'Fine.'

'Everywhere you look, we exist on the boundaries of choices and other worlds,' she said. 'Balances between two opposing forces. Between the real and the imaginary. Between faith and deceit, partnership and war, science and art, darkness and light. We are creations of balance, whose very lives depend upon a fragile equation. Think of it. Have you ever thought of it?'

He merely returned her gaze.

'What would happen, do you think, if the world had five per cent more carbon dioxide, five per cent more heat?' she asked him. 'What would happen if the oceans rose by ten feet? What would happen if photosynthesis altered? What would happen to man if the balance changed? Where would the great technologies of man be, then?'

Wallis watched her, his head resting on one hand. The pressure in the room seemed heavy, the droning noise more piercing.

'We exist on a small thin line, held in God's hand like glass,' she said. 'We have no power at all other than the power to believe in the impossible. To acknowledge ourselves alive by the grace of God, by the finely attuned power of His creation.' She sat now straight-backed, fired by her conviction, staring at a point somewhere just over his head.

'But men like Acland can't accept that,' she said. 'They alter the balance. They put us all in danger, with their evil. We are in danger from our own sins, and from our insult to the life around us.'

Wallis dropped his eyes, to gaze at the scarred table-top and not at her. His head began to ache.

'We live in a living world,' she murmured. 'With its mouths and

312

hands and hearts all around us.' She was staring now, at Wallis's downturned head. 'There are Gates in this world,' she murmured softly. 'Bridges from reality to spirit. The Celts called it the Otherworld. They respected it. They invoked ancient spirits and allied themselves with Christ. They guarded the Gates.'

Wallis turned away from her, side on, hand defending himself against her stare.

'Acland thought he was greater than that fine balance,' she said. 'He thought he could move it at will. He thought he could let the rein of evil run through his hands, and still control it. Let the power loose, and still contain it. Go to the Gates and control what passed through. But he couldn't. He couldn't.'

She shook her head.

'The Gates are the pressure points, the safety valves of the world,' she said. 'They were markers before man. They were rings of light before life evolved. They were churches and graves when man was young. They are still. Every country has them. Every country has its Guardians. People whom *you* would dismiss as freaks, I suppose.' She gave a short, exasperated sigh. 'But be thankful for them,' she said softly. 'For when a Gate falls, so does that country – with wars, with floods, with famines. And only a great spiritual strength can close it again.'

Wallis shut his eyes tight. The light hurt him, and there was more light in the room than he could bear.

'Pray to whatever God you believe in, Inspector Wallis,' the girl whispered. She dropped back in her seat, looking at the man ahead of her.

'Sara is all we have, Inspector,' she said. 'And tonight, she goes to close the last Gate.'

Forty-Nine

He passed down the pit shaft quickly, fending himself from the pit sides with his free hand. With him alone on the rope, he fell like Icarus, wings burned. He could hear the rush of the water when he was still a hundred feet up. He looked up, then, to the pinprick of light above him that was the outside world. He fumbled in his pocket for the matches for the candle, whose flame had been drenched. He found them, and circled his fingers around them. God knew if he would ever light them. But they were a talisman against the pit bottom, a charm to ward off water.

In the dark, his body bumped hard on the rock of the shaft side. Stone at a hundred and thirty feet. Pennant stone for paving blocks. He thought, wildly, briefly, almost his last thought in life, of the feet that would tread on the stones in the city long after this haunted year.

There were a crowd of colliers at the bottom. They were standing among the wooden tubs. The boys still wore the leather straps – straps that went around the tubs as they pulled them on their hands and knees from the narrow seams.

The Egyptian grabbed the first boy to hand. 'Get on,' he said, shoving the lad. He pushed the nearest man. 'Get on any way you can.' The rope began to move. There was no panic. They moved forward smoothly, grabbing the slipping guides, pulling boys after them where they could, disappearing upwards.

One of the last caught hold of the Egyptian's sleeve. 'Get on yourself,' he said.

'I shall go down the twinway.'

'You'll not,' the man said. 'They are all drowned down there.'

He saw it was the same man who had struck him in the lane four months ago. 'Get on the rope,' the Egyptian said.

*

314

He sprinted down into the track, down the incline. Candles still guttered in their makeshift holders along the walls. He stopped himself with a prayer, forced himself to take out the matches, take off his cap. He tried to set the candle in the little half-moon metal holder. His fingers shook. The match scraped, gave a blue spark. Died. He tried another. There was nothing at all from the next – they were damp. Everything was damp. The wet ran down the pit sides, ran under his feet.

He gave up the light, and ran on, his feet now sloshing through water. To either side, a quarter of a mile along, puttways – the little roads on to the coal faces – sloped steeply away. On the left they were dry. On the right they were wet.

It was as he came to the last long drop to the last face that he ran straight into a river.

The Styx flowed here. Dark water rising.

He stopped. Got to his knees.

'God greater than the heavens,' he began. 'God greater than the stars, save us this day, break this stream, close Thou Thy hand against this force. Forgive us our sins against those who made this land sacred, who were buried here. Forgive us our sins of greed against creation that have brought us to this destruction . . .'

There was a grinding, muffled roar.

Down one of the side seams, the pit props gave way. The horses, tethered in the side entry, still chained to the tubs, began to scream.

'I stand in the Gate as Thy sentry and servant . . .'

For a moment, the water seemed to stop. It receded. There was no sound.

He opened his eyes to the pitch silence.

In time to see eternity, before he fell.

Fifty

It was dark along the lanes to Aubrete.

Robert Wilde drove at an enforced snail's pace, between trees whose branches lashed overhead, writhing in the light of the car's headlights. Leaves and parts of branches were continually hitting the car, and the noise of the wind was deafening.

Wilde could not believe Anna's stupidity. He clenched his fists on the steering wheel as he thought of it for the twentieth time since leaving the house. He liked the woman . . . no, it was more than that. So much more than that, he dare not think of it, put a name to it, give it a form of words, unless it vaporized, unless it crumbled as he tried to reach out and take hold of it. But whatever he felt for her, what she had done tonight *was* stupid – crass, stubborn idiocy.

And Matthew Aubrete was all that Anna had said he was – weak, ineffectual – for calling her out on a night like this, out of the safety of the hotel.

Her voice, from the hotel phone an hour ago, had been patched with static.

'She's . . . the Manor,' she had said. 'Robert . . . hear me?'

'I hear you,' he had said, wincing at the dislocation of her voice, the three words out of four. Alice had stood in the doorway, confusion painted on her face.

'Matthew rang,' Anna was saying. 'She's . . . they have . . .'

'I'll send someone for her,' he said.

'She won't . . .'

He lost her completely. 'Anna?' he demanded into the receiver. 'Listen.'

316

She came back. 'Danger. What else can I do?'

'Nothing. Do nothing,' he shouted.

She was gone.

He had stared back at Alice. She had immediately voiced his thoughts.

'She's gone out, and that man is looking for her,' she said.

He clicked off the phone, slammed it into the chair. 'Bloody Matthew Aubrete,' he muttered. 'He's called her out to see to this girl.'

'The girl from Brimmer House?'

'It must be.'

'But what's she doing all the way up there?'

'God knows.' He put a hand to his forehead.

Alice had walked up to him, took the hand down, and squeezed it. 'Go out to her,' she said.

He looked up into his daughter's face. 'I can't do that,' he said. 'You've got to get over to Poole by six tomorrow morning.'

She had shrugged. 'I'll cadge a lift from Mrs Cook and Melanie,' she said.

'Alice, I can't let you do that,' he objected.

'Why not?'

'Because I want to see you off at Poole.'

She had put both hands on her hips, a stance he knew very well.

'Dad,' she had said, 'if you don't go and help Anna . . .'

'I'll send someone else.'

'She rang *you*,' she had said, exasperated. 'What do you think she rang you for? Because she trusts you, and she doesn't trust other men.' She wagged a finger in his face. 'If you don't go and help her, I'll never speak to you again,' she said.

'Don't tempt me,' he told her.

She snatched up the phone.

'What are you doing?' he asked her.

'Ringing Melanie,' she said.

He reached a stretch of open road, a straight section of old Roman track that ran across the downland before the sea. He put his foot down hard on the accelerator. Aubrete was somewhere below, somewhere in the featureless darkness before the coast, somewhere down in the other ocean of dark trees. He glanced towards it, off to the right, the vast acreage that showed as a woven pattern of colour during the day. The roof of the house, and the lawns, and the stone terraces that hung above the steps to the beach, ought to be visible now, even at night. But there was nothing from the house. Not the merest distinguishing candle. Only down there in the trees – he saw it, then it was snatched away – he thought he saw an orange light. A flash, then nothing.

Exposed as the road was now, the car took the full force of the storm. 'Christ,' he exclaimed, as the heavy vehicle was wrenched sideways. He hauled on the steering wheel. Over the sea, he saw an extraordinary sight – clouds seeming to boil as they rushed across the Channel, huge midnight-blue cumulus against a star-strung sky, hurtling down on him.

The sudden, involuntary thought choked him as efficiently as if two thumbs had been pressed against his windpipe. He leaned forward, the car swerving. Like *hands*. Rushing down on him *like hands*. Wrenching on the wheel, changing down through the gears to third, he made an effort to slow, as the gale plucked at the car. He could feel it underneath the body, pushing upwards. That was not possible, was it? Not possible. Pushing upwards, tugging at the doors. *Like hands*.

'No,' he said, out loud. He steered the car around the last corner, where the fields were replaced by the first stray beeches of Aubrete's land. Dropping down through the incline, the wind, too, abruptly dropped, giving him a moment of clarity and release. Wilde hissed through his teeth, a sound of disparagement at his own foolishness.

He almost missed the car.

One moment it was there, hanging awkwardly on the high grass verge, its nose in the hedge. The next, as he passed it, it seemed to vanish, a neat trick of the light. Or lack of light. He crammed on the brakes, pulled over, looked into the driving mirror. Nothing. He turned around in the seat and looked through the back window. There was a faint glimmer of chrome at the edge of the road.

He got out, ducking his head against the wind, pulling his collar around his face. He ran back twenty yards, and found it at once, slewed into the long grass.

It was Anna's old red car. The front wing was crumpled, the light smashed. He ran to the driver's door, and saw Anna's bag, the small black leather bag that she always carried, on the passenger seat. He tried the door. It opened. He leaned in, picked up the bag, looked around the interior of the car confusedly. Nothing else. The keys were not in the ignition.

He got back out.

'Anna!' he called. 'Anna!'

The wind ripped his voice away. She was nowhere to be seen. There was no gap in the hedge here. He hadn't passed her on the road above. There was no sign of any other vehicle, and, as far as he could make out in the half-light under the rolling, heaving night sky, there were no tyre marks on the road, and no glass strewn on its surface.

He took Anna's handbag with him, and ran back to his own car. Getting in, he stuffed the handbag hurriedly into his glove compartment. He picked up his mobile, dialled the station. Putting the phone to his ear, he could hear no sound, and, looking at it again, he saw that the battery was dead. 'Shit,' he cursed. He had replaced that battery only two days ago. 'Shit,' he repeated, turning on the engine, and pulling back out into the road.

The lane narrowed, curving through a series of hairpin bends. Not more than five hundred yards down, he had to cram on the brakes, slewing to a stop with the back end of the car strung across the white line.

An enormous oak was down, completely blocking the road.

Behind it, he could see a tow truck, its orange light rotating behind the dense leaves. He got out. 'Hey!' he called.

A man's voice answered him, a muffled jumble of words.

He ran to the immense trunk, saw the roots forming a high barrier to his left. 'What?' he called.

'Get through . . .'

Wilde looked around for a gap, and found a space below the trunk halfway across the road. On his hands and knees, he crawled through the wet and the dancing, wind-torn branches. On the other side, he stood up, fingering a scratch on his face, a wet trace of blood. He saw that the trunk of the tree had hit the truck, collapsing its bonnet completely. The driver's door was open and a man sat in it, his legs trailing loosely. Wilde ran up to him.

'You all right?' Wilde yelled.

'No,' came the muttered reply.

Wilde felt carefully around the man's neck. As he touched the left shoulder, he could tell at once that it was dislocated. The arm hung loosely, broken.

'Have you rung an ambulance?' he asked, nodding at the radio set on the dashboard.

'Can't get through,' the man said.

Wilde tried it. More static. More violent hiss of disconnection. *What a night*, he thought. *What a hellish night.*

He thought for a couple of seconds. He put his hand gently on the man's knee. 'Stay here, I'll go down the hill for help,' he said.

The man's head rolled slightly.

'Can you hear me?' Wilde asked.

He could see the driver's consciousness flickering. He lifted the man's legs back into the cab. Then, he crawled back through the jumbled mess of the tree to his own car, flicking on its hazard lights, and taking the warning triangle from the boot. He crawled back, taking more lashing to the face and hands, and ran downhill with the triangle, putting it on the road to warn oncoming cars. Then, as he straightened up, he heard a sound that made his blood freeze.

Down the hill, in the heart of the trees, from somewhere close to the entrance where he knew the gold-on-green sign for Aubrete Manor stood at an angle to the road, he heard an unearthly roar, like some monstrous animal caught in a trap. Then, he felt the tremor. The ground under his feet rippled. He lost his balance for a second, staggering in the centre of the road. He heard a *crump*, as he had heard the sound of artillery described in the war – a heart-punching sound. He sensed some

320

reflex in the air, some inversion, as if the air had been sucked down and had then been heaved back.

'Christ,' he muttered.

He started to run.

The road was slippery with rain, and, as he rounded the last bend before the entrance to the Manor, he saw that, further down, the road itself seemed to alter. He jogged to a stop, frowning, trying to see through the dark. What *was* that down there, in the road? Something moving. Something big. His heart did a little stuttering dance, climbing towards his throat. He forced himself to stand still and calculate what it was that he was seeing, and then, with a flash of realization, it came to him. There was nothing on the road, because *the road was not there.* It was water, seething, writhing, thundering down from right to left, crashing down through the entrance to the Manor.

He started out again, running warily, his hands extended in front of him like a blind man feeling his way. He had a fear of suddenly finding there was no solid surface left, here where the shadows fought the eerie reflections of the flood. And then, through the trees, he could see the first lights. Flashing blue lights. Could hear the shouts of other people, their voices coming raggedly to him above the roar of the storm.

Another few yards, and he could see that the water was about twenty or thirty feet wide, gouging a great hole where the café car park had been, ploughing a new black furrow down through the trees. He glimpsed the twin red backs of two fire engines, and saw an ambulance pulled up, its white sides periodically illuminated by the flashing lights from the engines and from a police car alongside them. Higher up were two other vans, with a blue insignia. He recognized the logo of the local water company. On what had become the far side of the river, men ran about between lines of hoses. There was a drumming of a pump, but, as soon as he had identified what it was, its low-frequency humming stopped.

He hesitated. There was no way he could cross to the café buildings now, which had been his intention. He knew that there was a public call box in the outside seating area. But it would be a hopeless task trying to wade this torrent – he would be swept away in seconds. Besides, only the water trucks were on the opposite side. The police were closer to him. He shielded his eyes against the rain, and caught sight of movement on his side, down among the feet of the enormous chestnut trees and the handful of trophy redwoods. Planted two hundred years ago, a new species from the colonies. Shipped from Liverpool by special transport, 1834. He wondered if they would survive the night.

He looked to his left, and saw the low stone wall of the estate. He ran up to it and climbed its slippery, mossy surface. As he vaulted down on the other side, into a deep and yielding floor of leaf-mould, he could see the police, and those with them, looking back in his direction – not at him, but evidently discussing breaking through to the road another way. Half a dozen hands gestured up the hill. As he fought his way towards them, over clinging brambles, he could see that the officer closest to him – whom he knew by sight, but not by name – was shouting into his two-way radio.

Several people noticed him at once. Matthew Aubrete, looking like death – white-faced, gaunt, strung out with exhaustion. Richard Forbes, the estate manager. Other men he did not know, and, finally, the police constable himself.

'Inspector . . .'

'What happened?' he shouted, against the tearing rain.

'Road gave way. We've got subsidence of some kind . . .'

'You call this fucking *subsidence*?' It was Matthew Aubrete. He shouldered his way between them, and wrenched the radio out of the constable's hands. 'You call this emergency response!'

Wilde grasped his hand. 'Mr Aubrete. Robert Wilde.'

If he recognized him, Aubrete showed no signs of it.

'We called 999 an hour ago, we get – we get *nothing* . . .'

Aubrete was plainly deranged by his panic. His gaze shifted from one person to the other, hardly focusing. Wilde looked away from him, turned his back, pulled the police officer to his side. 'Get through to Emergency and tell them there's an accident on the road, half a mile back,' he said. 'Tree down, a man injured.'

'I can't,' the officer said. 'Radio's dead, sir.'

Wilde stared at him. 'Jesus Christ,' he said. 'Every bloody radio's dead. What the hell's going on?'

The other man shook his head. 'We don't know, sir. We answered the call, the ambulance beat us here by three minutes—'

'Who called the ambulance?'

'I did,' said Forbes.

Wilde turned back to look at him. The man was soaked to the skin. 'Who for?' Wilde asked.

'The woman – the Miles woman.'

Wilde gripped his arm. 'Where is she?'

Forbes gestured down the hill. 'We're looking . . . we're looking . . .'

Wilde followed the line of his arm. He was pointing down into the wall of dark water.

'Down *there?*'

Forbes wiped rain out of his eyes. Above them, one of the giant trees cracked ominously. They looked up, seeing only thrashing branches. Forbes looked back to him. 'She had a car accident—'

'I know that,' Wilde said. 'I found the car.'

'She's got . . .' Forbes was struggling for words. 'Cuts to the face, she's walking, she . . .'

'Why the hell isn't she with the ambulance?' Wilde demanded.

Forbes stared into his face. Wilde had never seen an expression like that – fear and disbelief mingled. The strain of keeping himself together was etched all over him. His arms were held in rigidly at his sides, his elbows digging into his own flesh, as if this stance alone could keep him upright and functioning.

'OK,' Wilde said, taking pity on him. There was another mighty crack from the trees that he tried not to hear. 'OK . . . slowly. Tell me.'

'She came down here. Mr Aubrete had called her . . . the girl, she . . .' Forbes clutched his arm. 'Who is she?' he said. 'That girl?'

'What happened?' Wilde demanded.

'She was standing in the trees,' Forbes said. 'Mr Aubrete called to her. She was standing above the pools. There was this light – this – I don't know what it was . . . she wouldn't come down. Miss Miles was here. She called to her. The girl was up on the pools. She was *in* the pools, in the water, it was waist high on her, she just *stood*, she . . .' He stopped, gasped for air, shook his head. 'Mr McGovern tried to get to her, then . . .'

'*McGovern?*' Wilde echoed. 'Oh Christ. Then what?'

Forbes was trembling. Shaking. 'She vanished. He vanished. Miss Miles went after her – McGovern followed—'

'Through the water?'

'It wasn't water . . .'

'You don't call that water? What the hell do you mean, not water?' Wilde demanded. He could hardly hear his own voice above the wind. Across the river, arc lights flickered on and off. There were shouts, cries.

The police constable stepped between them. 'The ground opened up,' he said. 'It just opened up.'

Wilde looked into his face for one second. Then past him, to Aubrete's stricken, deadly pallor. 'You knew about this,' Wilde said.

'No,' Aubrete objected.

'You must have known!'

'We knew there were workings below the estate,' Forbes said. 'But the mine was capped two hundred years ago. It was sealed.'

'What fucking mine!' Wilde cried.

It was a mistake. He knew it was a mistake. Aubrete's face closed. It was literally as if the last electrical current of life had been switched off. He stood, with the rain pouring down his face, like a dead man, arms hanging at his side, eyes vacant.

'There was a mine shaft here,' Forbes was shouting. 'Nine hundred feet deep. There was a mine accident. It was closed. Sealed by the owners on the day it happened. But it was years – 1800—'

'People were killed here?'

'Ninety men drowned.'

Wilde tried to make sense of what he was being told. 'Ninety men? They got ninety bodies up in one day?'

'No,' Forbes said. 'They left them down there. Sealed them up.'

'Oh Christ,' Wilde said. 'And that's it? You built over it – opened to the public—'

'We had everything checked. It was safe. Two hundred years ago! How could there be anything? There was no danger. There couldn't be.'

Wilde found himself grabbing the estate manager by the collar. 'No bloody danger!' he screamed. 'Look at it!'

He wheeled around to the constable. 'Where did she go?' he demanded. 'Where is she?'

'The fire people can't find her,' he said. 'They can't find any of them. They're down there – all the way down the hill, they secured lines . . .'

Wilde didn't stop to hear another word.

He left them, running forward into the black, finding himself, within yards, up to his knees in a secondary stream that was pouring down, out of the very hillside. He could hear Forbes shouting his name. He ploughed on, trying to get higher up, to scale the other bank of the swift, pitch stream at his feet. It felt as if it were full of grit, as if his legs were being pounded by tiny stones, and, as he slithered out the other side, he reached down, and felt just that on his clothes – thick, dark, abrasive grit all over him.

He tried to see down the hill. There was some stuttering light on the other side, and he could make out the fluorescent uniforms of the Fire Service – indeterminate orange patches appearing and disappearing behind the thick tangle of high rhododendrons. What had been a pretty, shaded woodland walk by the side of the small weirs and pools had become one seething channel of swirling dark. He could see no steps, no little bridges – only two sharply inclined banks, and a chasm between them. As he looked, he thought he glimpsed something else, too – wood churning in the water. Wood, and barrels. Barrels, or tubs of some kind. Open-topped wooden trucks. He stared, but the illusion was gone, and he saw a far worse image, an image that struck him like a fist. He saw three people, stranded in the centre of the surging, fermenting tide. Two women, holding each other. A man standing opposite them.

It was impossible, of course. Impossible.

Not possible to stand in that pressure of water.

Not possible to see them so clearly in the dark.

Except . . . it was not quite dark. Not dark any more, but what light there was, was unsteady, inconstant. It played over the figures in the water like phosphorescence. He tried to think what that was called . . . marsh gas? Ball lightning? Whatever it was, it was incredibly eerie, moving around them, wreathing first a face, a hand . . . they were speaking. Not shouting. Not crying. Not screaming. They were *speaking* . . .

His feet slithered, losing purchase on the wet soil. He tried to get his balance, clutching at stray fists of leaves. He slipped further, and his fingers brushed roots. They snapped under his touch like a whipped rope, alive under him, shearing out of the ground, twining themselves around his feet. He yelled at the grip on his legs, fumbled around his feet in the dark, tried to tear the greasy brown veins from him . . . he looked up.

They were standing on nothing.

They were standing . . . on *nothing*.

Nothing underneath them, under the feet of the people in the water. Nothing beneath them but empty space. A space that wasn't entirely dark, but which contorted with crude colour. Green reflections on their faces. The blue of summer. The red of dying stars. They hung suspended over the drop, seemingly oblivious to it. He saw the girl glance back at Anna, lift her hand, and gently release it, prising Anna's fingers loose. He tried to cry out, *Don't let her go*, as if it was the girl's touch that was keeping them both suspended, and, without it, Anna would drop into the gulf under their feet.

'Anna,' he said, but could not be sure if the word had come out. The syllables were smothered before they were out of his mouth, even out of his mind. She didn't look in his direction. He saw that she was bleeding, or had been bleeding. Her face was streaked with mud and blood, her hair matted to her head, her clothes soaked, her feet bare.

He looked from her to the girl, from the girl to her, and realized with a double shock what it was that was so desperately strange about them, if anything could be stranger than the sight of them in the centre of raging chaos. He realized that their clothes and hair were still. The storm was battering his senses – he felt it beating at some invisible division, where he occupied the farthest edge, caught between the women and the outside world, hearing them both. But the girl and Anna didn't hear the storm. They were untouched, unmoved by its fury. And, while

Anna was drenched, the girl was dry. Perfectly dry, her hair smooth and clean, her dress falling in soft folds below her knees.

Anna was saying something. Objecting, by her body language. He caught one word, *No*, and the girl's answering smile.

There was a crack of electricity. Not thunder. Not lightning. But electricity, a jolt of power. Then, next to McGovern, he saw another man.

It was momentary. The picture of the man trembled in and out of focus. Deep gashes scored his face, neck, arms. Wilde choked on a cry of alarm – the man wasn't looking in his direction, and did not seem to register his own injuries. Worse still, as Wilde looked at him, he seemed to turn inwards, coil in upon himself. It was an unfathomable sight – as if he were made of paper, and the paper were burning, its charred edges coiling around what little was left.

And then, between the girl and McGovern, light shot up from the refracting colours between them. It rushed upwards, vaulting into the sky. Wilde followed it, and saw the leaves of the trees caught up in it – a fantastic thundering stream of green and gold. And, woven into the green, were faces, and feathers and stones, and flowers, wings, and mouths, and hands. And hands. And *hands* . . .

He fell to the ground.

He tried to cover his head, while the roots around him crawled over his back, over his face, into his throat . . .

'No!' screamed Anna.

He dropped his fingers, and saw Anna thrown backwards, out of the stream of light. He saw the girl, illuminated by it, step into it, and take the other figures with her. The burning man was gone – he saw McGovern caught in the same green flame, clutching at his throat. And someone else . . . a thin, small man, with a flat grey face, like weathered grey chalk, holding the girl's hands in his own, facing her, while brilliant arcs of colour wheeled around them.

All three were caught for a second in the violent glow of upward movement – the girl, McGovern, and the man. And then, with a sudden booming contraction, the light was gone, the girl was gone, the green was gone, the men were gone, and Wilde saw, to his horror, the bottomless darkness into which they hurtled.

And there in the space where they had been, was Christine.

Christine, a faint warm impression against the dark, holding out her hands. Lifting one, pressing it to her lips, extending it back to him. A kiss sent into the stillness suddenly stretched between them.

Just for a second, he felt her lips on his.

Her arms around him. Her breath. Her blessing.

And then he was staring into vacancy, into the empty dark.

He looked down.

Ten feet from him lay Anna, curled on her side, like a child abandoned to a dreamless sleep.

Postscript

The autumn was, he thought, more beautiful than the spring.

Robert Wilde sat on Scarth Gap Pass, on the last stretch before the summit, looking at the lake far below.

It was October, and the Derwent Fells rolled before him. Dale Head dominating the land to his left, a smooth grey-green mountain. Fleetwith Pike falling dramatically to the water, its peaked ridge pointing straight down the length of Buttermere. The lake itself was very light this morning, almost white instead of the dark mass that he remembered.

He had been looking at this view for a long time. He had carried it in his head for years, taking it out in dreams to handle it. But he had forgotten how breathtaking it really was, and the sight of it, spreading away on all sides, brought him what he had been looking for all summer – a sense of peace, of homecoming.

On the way here, he had called in to see Anna.

She had sold her house and bought another – another terrace on the city edge, another high-ceilinged Victorian house. Her equanimity still surprised him – the way she had calmly taken up the scattered pieces, and put them back together. Released from Benedict McGovern's attention, what he supposed was the old Anna came back to life. She was not teaching, but she was playing, semi-professionally, and on the last night before he came to the Lakes, he had gone to see her in a concert in Manningham city centre.

She looked very vulnerable, there in the stage light. The irony was, of course, that she was not vulnerable any more, but, rather, it seemed, invulnerable. She had not said very much about that last night at the Manor. She had said nothing at all about Matthew Aubrete, who, after his prolonged illness, had retired to his father's apartment in Pollensa.

He had, as far as Robert knew, never returned to the Manor, which was run entirely now by Laura. After Anna had signed over the estate to them, Matthew's last task was to insist upon the cottage being given to Anna, who had sold it within six weeks.

Robert lay back, releasing his view of the mountains, and staring into the early morning sky.

They had found the body of Benedict McGovern near the house, washed there, they said, by the force of the flood. Robert had never mentioned the other men to anyone – the disjointed apparition of Acland, or the other man – the man he couldn't put a name to, the small grey-faced man who had stood at Sara Acland's side in the rush of light.

Her body had never been found.

He got up, feeling the damp of the ground on his clothes, and brushing it quickly away. They had called it the Third Hurricane on the TV news and in the newspapers. It had wrought terrible damage to the south coast, much the same as that in 1987. He recalled a case then, in Sussex, of trees being torn up and revealing an Anglo-Saxon burial mound, the bones coming to the surface as the trees were uprooted by the storm. Aubrete Manor had been the focus of very similar and intense attention this summer, with industrial archaeologists, investigating the old mine workings, calling in others – experts in Bronze Age burials. They had found quartz cairn stones in the hillside.

The storm had gone as quickly as it had come. Next morning, the whole hillside was still, and the emergency services did their job among the shattered ruins of the trees.

He had tried to get Anna to tell him about that night. But all she would say was that Matthew had thought the girl was trying to commit suicide. Knowing that Anna had known her, however briefly and however distantly, had been the straw he had grasped at when all efforts to reach her or talk to her had failed.

Anna was a pragmatist. She had dismissed Robert's hesitant references to anything extraordinary. 'It was the storm,' she had told him.

'But you saw him?' he had asked her. 'You saw McGovern?'

She had shaken her head slowly, as if this was something that confused or evaded her. 'He looked different,' was all she would ever say. In fact, she had not really been convinced that it *was* him until she saw the notice of his funeral in the newspaper – a funeral that only a priest and the undertakers had attended. Even the fact that Robert himself had identified the body did not seem to reassure her until McGovern was in his grave. And, since then, she had seemed to close the night away. Rush forward to reclaim her past. Wipe out the terrible intervening year, as if it had never happened.

Robert looked upwards, at the peak of Hay Stacks. It was blessed with the first sunlight high above him.

He understood, of course. Understood Anna's need to be herself again. To turn away from the horrors. To pretend that nothing inexplicable had happened that night. But he thought differently. He thought something *had* altered, something he didn't understand.

He had read the transcripts from Manningham from the girl who called herself a Guardian, and he recalled Sara Acland's utter tranquillity in the face of the light. He remembered the stillness, and the improbable picture of four figures suspended above an endless drop into the dark.

'Religious fanatics,' Wallis had called them.

'Misguided,' Anna had said. 'Tragic.' But she had not looked in Robert's face.

Perhaps she couldn't find an explanation yet. Perhaps, in time, she might allow him close enough for them to find an explanation together.

He turned, and looked back down the track.

The grass was cropped short under his feet, and there was a faint veil of dew on his face. It was just six o'clock. Far down the valley, three thousand feet below, the village was one or two small white rectangles. Somewhere down there was the house where he had lived as a boy.

There was a movement on the track.

She came up steadily, smiling at him. When she was within a few yards, she stopped, and they faced each other high over the empty air, at what might have been the top of the world.

'You're fitter than you look,' Alice said, grinning.

331

She walked up to him, and swung her arm around his shoulder, pressing her face to his.

'It's fantastic, isn't it?' she asked.

'Yes,' he agreed.

She moved back from him, still holding one of his hands, and appraised him with that sharp and perceptive gaze of hers.

'Will you bring Anna here one day?' she asked.

He turned for the track to the summit, gently pulling her after him with a smile.

'Maybe,' he said. 'One day.'